BITTER AMBROSIA

Lois M. Theuring

VANTAGE PRESS
New York

To my husband, Charles

Published by Vantage Press, Inc.
516 West 34th Street, New York, New York 10001

Manufactured in the United States of America
ISBN: 0-533-11961-8

Library of Congress Catalog Card No.: 96-90229

0 9 8 7 6 5 4 3 2 1

Chapter I

She hurried along the clothesline, plucking at the wooden pins that held the clothes to the wire line. The rumbling of thunder, though still in the distance, was rapidly moving closer. The wind lifted the top layer of sand from the newly plowed fields surrounding the house. The puffs of yellow grain twisted and turned, then drifted, according to the errant pursuit of the wind. Twelve-year-old Margie blinked rapidly as the stinging granules filled her eyes. Tears washed the intruding debris down her brown cheeks as she continued to wrestle with the clothes that seemed determined to become one with the wire. She had to get them into the house before the rain fell.

Long streaks of lightning etched the blackening sky. The storm was still far off, she knew, because it was some seconds before the accompanying thunderclap banged against her ears. But the low tumult of clouds was fast approaching Maylor from the west. The phenomena could be spectacular on these flat, coastal plains of North Carolina. One could watch a storm's birth on the distant horizon, follow it as it grew to maturity, then watch its demise on the opposite horizon. Margie was not in such an esthetic mood today, though, as she tried to rescue the family's clothing from the mounting wrath of the storm. Her mother's wrath would be far more sensational than any nature could generate if Margie allowed the now dry clothes to get wet.

It was the first day that her mother had worked since the end of last year's tobacco. That was last September and Mama's arthritic knees would surely be aching from the unaccustomed stooping and crawling about the plant beds. Yes, Margie knew, Mama would be real tired and even a minor mishap would most certainly rile her. And all the clothes they owned were either being worn or were on the line. Margie knew she must get the clothes off the line and into the house before the rains came.

Every so often she looked over her shoulder to check on Reggie, whom she had left on the porch. Reggie was her seventeen-year-old sister's little boy. He had been born when London was in her second year of high school. Though London had quit school to take care of her little boy, it seemed to Margie that it was she who was always minding him. Mama hadn't wanted

1

London to quit school, but London had said school was boring and besides, ever since the Pitt County schools had integrated in 1970, "You couldn't hardly do nothin' in school without being suspected of startin' a race riot." Margie's other two sisters, sixteen-year-old Teresa and fifteen-year-old Gayla, still attended school, except, like now, during the tobacco season, when they worked in the beds along with their mother.

Margie loved her little nephew but deeply resented missing school when her mother and her sisters had to work. It was hard to keep up with the class when she missed so many days. She had already gotten so far behind that she had been dropped back into the special education class. She hated being in that class. The kids were all so dumb. Margie's mother was illiterate and that had always been a source of embarrassment to her, and she did not want to be classified as dumb. And then, just recently, her guidance counselor had called her aside to warn her that if she fell back any further she would not be passed on to the seventh grade. She didn't know if she could stand such ignominy.

Theoretically, by state law, she was not eligible for promotion because she had missed too many days already. But the school tried to take an understanding attitude toward children in Margie's circumstances. If the child seemed to have gotten the required material in mind, then the excessive absence was overlooked. Else, in this predominantly rural community, there would have been a large segment of the student body that would never have been promoted.

Checking again over her shoulder, she saw that Reggie was sleeping. He sat on the porch step with his head resting on his chubby little arm on the porch. Margie shivered as the wind whipped the sand around her bare legs. The temperature was dropping rapidly and she worried that the baby would chill. Quickly she grabbed at the last of the clothes from the line. Hunching the heavy basket up into her arms, she stumbled, head down against the wind, toward the house. As she passed Reggie on the steps, a loud clap of thunder smacked imminently close overhead. The sudden bang startled the sleeping child. Jumping from his perch on the step, he clutched at Margie's dress as she passed him and let out a terrified squall.

"Come on, baby, get inside," Margie clucked. Reggie scrambled along behind, still clutching his aunt's dress.

It was dark inside the little two-room house. Most of the window panes had long ago been replaced with cardboard or else were so coated with many seasons of dust and grit that the inside of the house was a dingy gray even on the brightest of days. Now the little daylight that did escape the black curtain that was gathering across the tempestuous late afternoon sky just barely sifted beyond the open door. And the fire had almost gone out in the stove. Margie had been negligent and had forgotten to stoke it. The lightbulb hanging from the center of the kitchen ceiling was lifeless; Mama hadn't paid last month's light bill. Margie hoped that she would have the electricity turned back on with the first day's pay.

Even though the cold wind and sand of the rapidly mounting April storm swept much farther into the house than did the light, Margie left the door open. She was not afraid to be in the dark, but she knew that Reggie would be and considered that enough reason to leave the door open.

This house that Margie Braxton lived in with her mother and sisters was little more than a shelter against the most extreme weather. It was identical to almost all of the little tenant huts that dotted the sides of the back country roads of eastern North Carolina. Perhaps it had once been painted, years ago when it had first been built—no one remembered for sure—but now it stood humble in its naked weathered gray. The tin roof was brilliant orange with rust. One spot had rusted through, leaving a sieve of tiny holes that invited everything in except light. But it was home to Margie, the only home she could remember, and the rent was cheap, forty-five dollars a month.

Margie set the basket of laundry on the kitchen table, and with Reggie still dragging along by the hem of her dress, she took a couple of sticks out of the wood box by the stove and began to coax the dying embers of the fire. She wished she had some soft pine kindling or at least some paper; even the very thinnest of the oak sticks was reluctant to accept the fast-fading embers. They sputtered and spit in an effort to ignite, then sizzled out. Margie tried again. She blew hard into the belly of the stove in an effort to resuscitate the last of the dying coals. Still she got no flame. She sighed as she shut the stove's door. She would just have to wait till Mama came home; Mama could always get the fire started even without paper or kindling. But she would be angry with Margie for letting it go out in the first place. Margie shivered, partly from the cold and partly from the anticipation of Mama's anger.

Reggie shuddered as the chill that swept through the open door of the house increased. The rain had begun to fall in big spatters, making little dimples in the sand of the yard. The dry, porous soil sucked the drops up like a blotter. Margie hauled the rocking chair over near to the open door and pulled Reggie onto her lap, wrapping her arms around him to share her own body heat with him. His Pampers had absorbed as much as it possibly

3

could and was leaking through onto her dress. She didn't really mind, she was used to Reggie always leaking, but it did add to her discomfort now. She would have changed him, but she had used the last Pampers that morning when she had dressed him. She hoped Mama would remember to buy a box of Pampers at the store this evening.

Together they rocked and watched the road for Mr. Winston's blue pickup truck that would bring Mama and the girls home from the fields. The rain began to fall harder as the center of the storm swept nearer. The wind blew the descending curtain of water onto the narrow porch. She felt the drops spitting on her bare toes and scooted the chair back a little, just enough to avoid the rain but not so far as to lose sight of the road. Sucking his thumb, Reggie drifted back to sleep. He was hungry, but his thumb would hold him awhile yet. Even as little as he was, he already knew that he must wait till Mama got home with the groceries.

Margie was hungry, too. She had had nothing to eat all day since a bowl of grits and black coffee at breakfast. During tobacco, Mama and her sisters came home from the fields for lunch and they always had a good hot meal to sustain them through the long afternoon. But this was the first day of their seasonal employment, and the welfare check that supported them between seasons had run out a week ago. And they bought only the bare essentials "on account" from Pfeiffer's, the little country store that was just a half mile down the road from their house. Mr. Pfeiffer always let Mama have what she needed on account because she was faithful in her attempts to pay when she was working.

Margie was anxious now for her mama to return. The first day alone with Reggie always seemed so long. She squinted her eyes to penetrate the now pouring rain to see if Mr. Winston's blue truck was coming around the bend yet. It was always a little exciting to watch for the truck because of the bend that began just past their house. You couldn't see anything coming down the road until it emerged like a phantom, from out of the bend past the little thicket that edged the road and obscured the view.

Margie knew that they would be a little late tonight because Mama would want to stop at Pfeiffer's to pay some "on account," just enough to show Mr. Pfeiffer she did intend to pay; then she would probably buy something special for dinner to celebrate the beginning of the new tobacco season. Mr. Winston would grumble about having to stop at the little store, but he would do it. He always paid Mama at the end of each day; that's the way she insisted on doing it. She said she couldn't figure it all up when it came in one lump at the end of the week. And at her insistence, he also gave the three girls' wages to her. The girls fumed about this arrangement, but Mam knew what she was about. She knew the girls would not think of the long-standing "on account." They would spend their wages on frivolities, like lipstick and cheap cologne.

Margie still attempted to extend her vision to the road, some fifty feet away. Her stomach rumbled in anticipation of the expected feast. The tobacco season was running a little late this year. The farmers had put their seed in at the right time, but even though the beds were covered with huge sheets of protective plastic held in place by old auto tires, the heavy, unseasonable January rains had washed the seed out a little less than a week later. All the farmers had immediately reseeded, but a spell of freezing weather had followed the rain and had retarded the germination of the new seed. But now the seedling plants had finally caught up in their growth and were three or four inches high and pushing eagerly against their plastic blankets. It was high time that they be set into the big fields so they could be free to grow under the mothering warmth of the North Carolina sunshine. Margie's mother and sisters were out in the plant beds today pulling the tender infant plants from their nursery nests.

Mr. Winston would probably keep the women working in spite of the rain. There was much competition among the farmers to see who could get his fields planted first. Billy Winston knew that Jerry Jordan had already begun pulling his plants two days ago. But with today's storm Jerry would not be able to get a tractor into the fields tomorrow to begin transplanting. Billy could still catch up. It was important to him that he retain his status among the farmers; his was a bully nature, and because he owned nearly a third of the land in and around Maylor, he felt that it was his inherent right to be first in with his tobacco.

Some of Billy's land had been in the Winston family for over one hundred years, but Billy had greatly increased the estate during the depression years of the 'thirties by shrewdly taking advantage of the other less fortunate farmers who had gotten caught in the economic squeeze. Billy Winston was not liked by the other farmers, not because of the great size of his estate, but rather because of the way he had gotten that estate and the fact that he still, like a vulture, jumped in whenever he saw a man down and continued to add to his holdings.

Long before the blue truck rounded the bend, Margie could hear the rasp and whine of the motor coming down Gum Swamp Road. Billy's old truck could even out shout the pounding of the rain that pelted her tin roof like a thousand miniature drummers. The truck came suddenly into view,

omach jumped a little flutter in excited anticipation of hav-
and sisters home again. The lights from the truck cut a streak
gh the blackening night. In the red glow of the taillights, she
gures of her sisters climbing over the tailgate at the back of
the stopped truck. Billy had a special affection for Mama and always had
her ride up front with him. She never would have made it over the tailgate
anyway with her arthritic knees.

The courtesy light went on in the cab as Mama pushed open the door
and slid down from the high seat onto the roadway. Margie could see Mr.
Winston's round face in the light. He smiled and waved to her. She waved
back. She liked Mr. Winston. He was always friendly toward her and often
brought her dresses that his granddaughter had outgrown. But Margie
would never understand why Mama didn't like her to wave to him, and she
had always burned the dresses in the stove so that Margie couldn't wear
them. Once she had cried and screamed and pleaded with her mother to let
her wear one of the dresses to school, a pretty pink taffeta one with lace all
around the neck and a big sash that tied in the back. But Mama had been
adamant. She was a proud woman. She would accept help only grudgingly
when it was a matter of life or death. Pretty dresses for Margie were not considered to be a matter of life or death.

She didn't care. Margie still liked Billy Winston, no matter what her
mother and sisters said about him, and they said plenty, and not so nice
things either. Billy Winston looked just like the big white Southern
landowner one might see on the movie screen. He was tall, or so he seemed
to be with his big cream-colored Stetson always perched on his head. He
always wore a white Palm Beach suit coat that could just barely button over
his barrel-like stomach. The traditional black string tie hung loosely knotted
from under the collar of his white permanent-press shirt. And he wore
boots. All the farmers wore boots, but Billy Winston's boots just didn't look
like the other farmers' boots; somehow they seemed shinier, more aristocratic, not like ordinary farmers' boots.

One expects a man to be tanned after he has put fifty-odd years in the
fields. Billy was tanned, but his tan had a gray, pasty look like that of a man
who never exercised and who ate too much. And he always had tiny beads
of perspiration on his forehead no matter how cold it was outside; it took
much effort to haul that bloated body around. An unlit cigar was always
clamped tightly between his teeth and bobbled up and down as he wheezed
and huffed behind his workers, trying to keep them moving at, what he considered, a respectable pace. But because he never even lit his cigar, and since

6

the end was always protected with a plastic tip, his teeth were sparkling white; and when he flashed those pretty white teeth in a smile at Margie, as he did now, she just couldn't help but like him.

Mama and the girls were now sloshing through the muddy water that had already backed up from the road and filled the front yard. Each one carried a large brown grocery bag tucked partway under her sweater to protect it from the rain. Mr. Winston gave a farewell toot, and the old truck rattled on down the road. Margie waved, but Mama and her sisters did not turn a head. They proceeded toward the little house without seeming to even notice Margie. And she had waited so anxiously for them. In silence they clumped up onto the porch and through the open door into the dark interior. But Margie was happy that they were home.

The front door of the little house, the only door, led directly into the kitchen. Used also as a living room, the kitchen was a large room some twelve by fifteen feet in area. A big potbellied, wood-burning stove reigned in the center of the room. It served as the heating system for the entire house and as a cook stove. One winter, in a fit of generosity, Billy Winston had gotten them a small oven, which perched on top of the stove toward the back just in front of the flue pipe. (The oven was sort of in the life-or-death category so Mama had accepted the gift.)

There was a dry sink bolted to the corner of the long back wall. A window above it looked out over the flat North Carolina plains, the plains that were broken only ever so often by a row of pines that had been left standing to help break the wind, whose voracious appetite could sweep the fields clean of topsoil in a minute. The remainder of the sink wall was taken up by a "sideboard." This "sideboard" consisted of an eight-foot-long by ten-inch-wide length of pine board fastened to the wall with angle irons. There were no cupboards, as such, in the kitchen, but two wooden crates that were covered with faded, flowered contact paper were nested under the sideboard and served as a storage place for canned goods and staples. A similar crate stood on top of the sideboard in the corner next to the adjacent wall for china and eating utensils. There was also an ancient refrigerator in the room, but at the present, because of the lack of electricity, it was nothing more than a storage unit. A rocking chair, eating table, and four straight chairs completed the furnishings of the room.

One time London had made a set of curtains in her domestic ed class at school. When she had brought them home, Mama had proudly hung them at the windows by thumbtacking them to the window frames. That was three years ago and the curtains still were exactly as Mama had hung them.

7

They had become a part of the house just like the little square of linoleum in front of the sink whose painted pattern had long ago worn off, leaving just a tar-colored mat that had welded itself to the otherwise bare wood floor.

As soon as she came into the house, London deposited her bag of groceries onto the table and took Reggie from Margie's lap. Plopping the sleepy tot onto the table beside the bag, she fumbled in the dark to find the new box of Pampers. Deftly slipping the sopping diaper from under the baby and dropping it onto the floor beside her, she replaced it with a fresh one. Reggie lazily eyed his mother and grinned.

"Margie, get them clothes off the table an' them groc'ries too. Set them on the sideboard," Bertha Braxton commanded. "An', London, you ain't goin' to leave that piss diaper on the floor!" Margie could feel the tired angry edge in Mama's voice. She removed the basket and set it in the corner. She stacked the bags onto the sideboard. London picked up the wet Pampers and, opening the window over the sink, tossed it out into the backyard. It found a home on the pile of trash that had been accumulating for the past ten years.

Grumbling all the while about Margie's incompetence, Bertha set about relighting the fire in the stove.

"Gotta get some heat an' light in this house. Margie, shut that door!"

Margie obediently shut the door. Teresa and Gayla slipped quietly from the kitchen and, exhausted from their day's work, flopped onto the big bed in the next room.

The bedroom of the two-room house had even fewer furnishings than the kitchen. And had the electricity been on, there was no electrical outlet or fixture in this half of the house to capture it for use. There was one double bed in the center of the long, unbroken back wall and a single folding cot in the corner of the opposite wall. The braces having rusted in the open position, however, the cot no longer folded. An empty TV chassis with an elegant walnut-framed mirror bolted to the wall behind it completed the bedroom suite. The TV chassis served as a vanity and storage cabinet for hair rollers, combs, picks, and hair grease and sundry tattered small articles of clothing. A rope strung catacorner in the corner next to the vanity served as a wardrobe closet. There were no curtains on the windows of this room. In winter they were covered with brown paper, split grocery bags, to insulate against the cold winds. It was not so cold now in the middle of April, but no one had yet removed the paper from the windows.

Teresa and Gayla welcomed the relaxing gloom of the little room now.

But Mama would allow them no rest. Having gotten the fire going, she yelled, "Get offa that bed till you get dry clothes on, an' wash that plant juice off yourselves."

The girls sighed, got up, and complied with Mama's orders. A soft golden glow from the open door of the stove now bathed the kitchen in a friendly warmth. The girls lathered their hands and arms with Lava soap and scrubbed until their skin tingled then rinsed the stained lather off in the bucket of cold water that stood in the dry sink. London followed suit, while Reggie sat in the middle of the table babbling at the cookie that had come, like magic, from the same big bag that had produced the box of Pampers. When she had finished washing herself, London slopped the brown soapy water out the window. The water from the bucket quickly blended then disappeared in the muddy rain lake that had formed in the backyard.

"When's Mr. Winston goin' fix the roof?" Gayla called from the bedroom, as she shifted the bucket that was a permanent fixture of the room to more efficiently catch the rain that leaked through the hole in the roof.

"Don't know. When he gets ready, I reckon, or when the whole roof caves in," Mama answered dryly.

Margie guessed that Mr. Winston would never fix the roof. As long as she could remember it had leaked. She wondered that the leak never seemed to get any worse. She tried to remembered if it had leaked when they had first moved into the little house.

Ten years ago they had come to North Carolina from Mississippi. Then, Bertha Braxton, widowed, with four little girls to support, had been unable to find work in Mississippi.

One day a friend had told her of a white man who carried black folks to North Carolina where they could make "good money" in the tobacco fields. Bertha had protested that she had no money for the bus fare and lodging in North Carolina. The friend had assured her that the farmer who hired her would provide lodging for her and her family and that the bus ride was free. Bertha knew that it sounded too good to be true, but then what was she to do—there were the four little girls.

So against her own rational better judgement, on a warm April morning in 1965, she bundled her babies and a small packet of clothing into the big red and yellow bus along with sixty-two other blacks. They had barely been able to breathe, let alone move, in the crowded bus, and the driver hadn't stopped once for refreshments or comfort on the whole ten-hour trip to Maylor, North Carolina. Bertha's little girls were the only children on the bus, and when they had whimpered in discomfort the other passengers had grumbled and complained and told her to hush them. She did her best, but, by the time they had finally reached Maylor, the girl's faces were swollen from their constant crying and the heat inside the bus. They had been a pitiful sight that day as they stood lined up with the other passengers outside the bus parked in the Maylor school parking lot. The local farmers had all gathered at the parking lot and milled silently among the prospective workers, looking them over, occasionally probing the flesh of a man's back or upper arm with an examining finger. It had reminded Bertha of a horse auction she had once witnessed.

One by one the prospective workers had been drawn from the group by the farmers. In a short time all the workers were standing in separate little groups, each group having been hired by a different farmer. Bertha and her girls formed a little group of their own apart from the others. As each bus passenger had been hired, the employing farmer had handed the bus driver $10 to cover the cost of the transportation; then he had signed a contract stating that he would provide the newly hired hand with adequate housing throughout the season and pay him $1 an hour (after deducting the $10 transportation fee).

Within an hour all of the people that had arrived on the bus had been hired. Some had already been shuttled off in waiting farm trucks to their new homes and prospective places of employment. All except Bertha Braxton. No one wanted a hand who had four extra dependents to care for.

Ordinarily the bus driver would have taken any unhired hands on to another town in hopes of unloading them there. But since Bertha was the only one left of the group not hired, he had pleaded with the farmers to take this last one off his hands so he could return to Mississippi for another whole load. The farmers who had not yet left all shook their heads. Bertha had stood straight and tall, her little girls hugging close around her. She did not allow the tears of disappointment to escape her eyes. But then there had been a stirring at the back of the crowd. A cream-colored Stetson had bobbed up and down through the crowd until it emerged from the group and stopped in front of Bertha. Mopping his sweating brow with a white monogrammed handkerchief and clearing his voice to get the attention of the other farmers, the man under the Stetson wheezed in a most generous and aristocratic tone of voice, "Well, now, we can't let this little mama and her babies just wander about the country. I reckon I can find something for her to do somewhere. Yes, let me take them—for charity's sake." A sigh of relief and gratitude had escaped Bertha's firm set lips. The other farmers had snickered at the pronouncement; they all knew about Billy Winston's charity. *Sure*, he would find something for Bertha to do, for at that time Bertha had been a handsome and robust figure of health and strength. They wondered about the little girls though—but knowing Billy, they knew he had it all figured out.

And so the Braxton family had settled in North Carolina in the spring of 1965, intending to stay only for the summer tobacco season then return to Mississippi. But Bertha had fallen sick with a flu virus early in September. Mr. Winston had had to take her to the county clinic for treatment. But she did not respond quickly to the medicine the doctors had prescribed for her and the bus back to Mississippi left without her on it. Her flu symptoms lingered on most of that winter. Mr. Winston had been good to her in her time of need. He had brought groceries and firewood all winter—on credit. And though the contract for free housing was no longer binding on him now that the tobacco season was over and he could charge the family rent, he did not press Bertha for payment. When she had confided her financial worries to him, he had assured her that her account with him was good—and not to worry about the rent; she could pay it when she was well enough to work again. And yes, the roof had leaked even then.

For ten years now Bertha had been trying to pay up her account with Mr. Winston. But each year in order to pay up that account she accrued yet another account, and so it went year after year with her never getting any further out of her predicament. And in the meantime, Billy Winston's moment of charity had reaped him mightily. He eventually acquired himself three more excellent hands in Bertha's growing girls, and with these hands as regulars he no longer had to provide free housing for migrants so he was now collecting a regular income from the rental of the little shack.

Thus the Braxton family was unobtrusively absorbed into the community of Maylor. And though the house was located some five miles from the town limits, it was still in the Maylor postal zone so they became part of the town's schools, part of its churches, a consumer of its goods, and a regular member in its welfare and medical programs. They had become citizens of the town of Maylor, population 3,700.

The fire in the stove was now roaring hot. Margie shivered as the chill began to leave her bare arms and legs. The aroma of country sausage that Bertha had frying in a pan on top of the stove began to permeate the room and set Margie's stomach to growling again. It had been a week since they had had meat. Mama didn't like to buy anything but staples when the welfare check ran out; and it always did run out by the third week of the month. This month, however, it ran out much sooner because Mama had had to buy a gown and matching slippers for Teresa to sing in the spring choral concert at school. This was not considered a luxury by Mama, though Margie could never figure out just why it wasn't, when she herself had never been allowed to be in anything special at school. That was always considered a luxury. She reckoned it had something to do with being an older sister; she was the baby.

Bertha opened a can of collard greens and a can of Irish potatoes to lay in the fat that fried out of the sausage. Margie saw fresh collards and potatoes in one of the grocery bags and knew she'd be expected to prepare them for tomorrow evening's meal. She didn't mind cooking though; at least it was something to do to make the long, lonely day pass faster.

"Gayla, get your butt offa that bed and mix some biscuits," Bertha ordered.

"Yes, ma'am," Gayla grumbled, as she pulled her tired body off of the bed. Her sisters remained lying down and snickered as Gayla got up. She punched at Teresa who was closest to her. Teresa ignored the punch. Gayla went into the kitchen and poured self-rising flour into a bowl. She didn't need to measure. She knew just how far to fill the bowl; she'd done it so many times. She stirred in a heaping spoonful of lard, cutting and mixing until it was well blended. Then she slowly poured buttermilk into the dry mixture until it looked just about right. She set the remaining buttermilk aside and finished mixing the biscuit dough, intending to drink the milk right from the carton after she had put the biscuits in the little oven on top of the old stove. But Margie couldn't resist, even though she knew that Gayla would surely beat her if she did drink the milk. Gayla looked up just in time to catch Margie draining the last of the milk from the carton.

"What you go and do that for?" she screamed at Margie.

"Can't keep it anyways; don't have no ice," Margie excused herself.

"And who said you was Miss Big Shit? I the one what worked all day in the rain!" Gayla swung hard at Margie. Margie ducked but not quickly enough to avoid the smack of Gayla's hand across her cheek. Tears welled into her eyes as she braced herself for the next slap, but Bertha intervened and sent Gayla running from the kitchen with a smack from her own work-callused hand. Margie felt at the welt that had already risen along her jaw but nevertheless glowed inside at the cool sour taste of the buttermilk mixed with the rare sign of favoritism that Mama had just shown her. She sidled over close to her mother to watch the sausage fry and to get a better whiff of the spice-laden steam that rose from the skillet. She enjoyed the soft warmth that radiated from her mother's big fat-ladened body. It wasn't often that Margie could enjoy being so close to her mama; Bertha was not one to waste time on affection. Margie was aroused suddenly from her ecstasy as Mama bumped her aside with an unconcerned swing of her voluminous round hip and bellowed, "C'mon, eat 'fore it gets cold!"

The other three girls ran in from the bedroom and, together with Margie and Reggie, hassled each other for a seat at the table. Margie didn't hassle very much though, just enough to show that she was in the game, for she knew that none of her older sisters would ever give up their place at the table and since there were only four chairs, Margie always sat in the rocking chair away from the table with her plate on her lap. It wasn't because the other girls didn't want her at the table, it was just the natural pecking order; and Margie knew that when one of the girls left home she would inherit a place at the table. Besides, she kind of liked sitting in the rocker off by herself. From this position she could listen in on the conversation at the table without being conspicuous. She learned a lot of secrets that way as her sisters would get involved in their intimate tales of romance, forgetting all about her presence. One time Mama had said that she was going to try to get hold of another chair from someplace, just in case they ever had company, but that was a long time ago and she hadn't brought it up since. But then they had never had company either.

Reggie, however, never lacked for a seat at the table. He sat on London's lap at every meal. Margie reckoned, with just a tinge of envy, that he'd still be sitting on his mama's lap when he was big enough to go to school. Now he wiggled impatiently.

"Eat you supper," London demanded, squeezing her arm tighter around the baby's belly. "I ain't fixin' to get up in the middle of the night to fill you up again."

Reggie continued to struggle and finally pulled himself free from under London's arms. He scampered over to the brown bag that held the cookies.

"Oh, no you don't!" London jumped from her chair and confiscated the bag before Reggie could reach it. "No supper, no cookie."

"It ain't goin' hurt him none," Mama said, smiling a rare smile at her grandson.

"He's too rotten already and I ain't goin' raise up no bad baby," London said, stomping her foot for emphasis. But Margie knew that Reggie would always be bad because he was a boy. Mama had had only one boy and he had died in infancy. A boy was a very precious member in a family. Margie wondered why.

They had finished eating their sumptuous meal of celebration now, and Bertha sat leisurely at the table with a second cup of coffee. She tucked a pinch of snuff behind her lip and sighed as she leaned back in her chair to relax for a few minutes before settling in for the night. London tore open a new pack of cigarettes. Taking one out of the pack, she tapped it gently on the table to firm it; then, lighting it, she sucked long and hard to extract that first delicious acrid stream of smoke.

"Gawd! That tastes good! It's been a week since I had a cig'rette." (Bertha wouldn't allow the girls to buy such luxuries on account; even her own snuff was withheld on the lean "on account" days.)

"When I get rich I am goin' buy cigr'ettes by the carton so's I'll never run out them," sighed London, taking a second long drag from the cigarette.

"Shit, you ain't never goin' be rich," Teresa said, sniffing. "You ain't never goin' do nothin' but work tobacco 'cause you ain't got no diploma from high school."

Margie wanted to tell her sisters what Mr. Wilson, the principal of the middle school, had told them about the advantages of getting a high school diploma and how dropouts could still gain one by attending the community college to make up their lacking high school hours. But she knew they'd just laugh at her and her Mr. Wilson. It was hard to be the youngest.

"Don't do no good for no black to get a diploma nohow," grumbled Gayla.

"What you mean? Look at Alton Jones. He a successful doctor in Greensburg," argued Teresa.

"Successful, shit! Successful black doctor with all black patients," countered London.

"What's wrong with black patients? They needs doctors too," said Teresa.

"Just that no black doctor with all black patients ain't goin' get rich."

"He is, too, rich! He got a beautiful house outside Greensburg."

"Yeah, *outside* Greensburg," chided Gayla. "He is so successful and black he gotta live *outside* the city."

"Well, maybe he want to," Teresa said sniffling.

None of them had ever been to Greensburg, ten miles north of Maylor, to see Alton's office or his beautiful house; but Alton's mother had shown them pictures and told them often of her son's success, and Mrs. Jones was of impeccable character. She bragged a lot, but nonetheless, she was truthful.

The facts concerning Alton Jones's education and success as a physician obviously did not impress London. "Know what I don' understand?" she mused. "How come a black woman can go to a white doctor and that white doctor can thump her boobs and stick his finger up her ass and nobody says word one? But I bet if a black doctor did the same thing to a white woman, the whole country'd holler rape."

"Hush you filthy mouth," demanded Mama in a shocked voice. "You don' know what you talk about. And no respectable lady talk about privates and rape in front of her little sister."

The girls looked over at Margie, realizing for the first time since they had sat down that she was present. Margie stared down at the empty plate still on her lap and waited for the heat to creep up into her face like it always did when she was caught eavesdropping.

"For Chris' sake, why don't you make a noise or somethin' instead of just sittin' there wagglin' you ears so's a body'd know you was there!" accused London.

"Ain't no reason to talk that way nohow," warned Mama. "Ain't nice. Nice peoples just don't talk about privates and rape; no, they just don't."

"Yeah," teased Teresa, trying to lighten the mood, "*Mama* don't never talk about nothin' private; she don't even talk about nothin' public."

Gayla laughed at Teresa's joke. London said, "That's pure stupid."

Bertha responded with her usual, "Humpfh."

"Maybe she should of talked some about it, 'cause London claim she don't know how she got Reggie," Gayla jibed to add to the mirth.

London reached out across the table with a doubled fist and swung hard at Gayla. Gayla giggled and ducked the swing, and before London could swing her other fist around, Mama countered with a backhand and sent London flying off her chair and sprawling to the floor. Gayla continued to giggle but was cut short by Mama's other hand as it swung in an arc to finish the job of chastising her scandalous girls. The after-dinner conversation ended abruptly as Gayla and London went off to the next room to nurse their wounds. Teresa made herself busy with Reggie so she wouldn't be expected to help with the dishes. Margie didn't mind doing the dishes by herself though; it would give her a few moments alone to contemplate the worth of a black doctor, something she had never given any thought to before.

The rain still fell in a loud drumming rhythm on the tin roof overhead. Margie stacked the dishes in the sink to be washed in the morning when there would be more light in the room. Besides, she didn't want to go out in the rain to the pump for fresh water.

Bertha went into the bedroom and slipped her dress off over her head. Leaving her petticoat on for a nightgown, she fell, exhausted, onto the big bed. Pulling the shabby, thick quilt up until it nestled snug under her chin, she moaned for a few moments until her aching joints had readjusted to the new position, then drifted off into a snoring sleep.

London took Reggie from Teresa and changed his Pampers again; then she too slipped off her dress and got into the big bed, settling Reggie in between herself and Mama. Teresa and Gayla prepared to bed down together on the little cot.

Margie guessed it was only about eight o'clock. She wondered why Mama hadn't had the electricity turned on. It would have been nice to be able to turn on the light that hung over the table and look at the pictures in her social studies book; she just was not tired enough for sleep yet. Very little light came from the stove now that Mama had banked the fire for the night and shut the door. She sat for a moment staring at the soft glow that radiated from the belly of the stove. The rain pounding on the tin roof overhead made the room exude an eerie silence. She was suddenly overcome with a feeling of utter loneliness; perhaps it would be better to join the rest of her family in bed. She sighed in resignation and slipped off her dress and lay down at the foot of the big bed. She pulled the bottom end of the quilt up around her shoulders. Mama's and London's feet felt warm against her back. She lay listening to the sounds of breathing sump and snuffle about the room. It was comforting to have her family cuddled up all around her but, still, she hoped that one day she would have a bed, or even half a bed, all to herself. Maybe she would marry a doctor and live in a big, beautiful house in Greensburg. Maybe.

Margie snuggled closer to Mama's feet. She thought maybe she would begin applying herself to her studies in the morning, when it was daylight, so she would be intelligent enough to be worthy of her doctor husband. But it was always so hard to study alone; she could never understand what the books were trying to teach her. Drawing her knees up against her belly in an effort to better fit across the scant width of the bed, she sighed deeply. Maybe when she was thirteen she wouldn't be so *dumb*. But that was a long way off, almost a whole year.

Chapter II

The sound of Billy Winston's horn sent Bertha scrambling from her bed. "Lawd, we're late! Get up! Hurry up 'fore Mr. Winston gets mad!" she called in panic to the girls.

The three girls grumbled as they rolled sleepily from their beds. London let out a shriek as her feet touched the icy bare floor. The girls hurried into their dresses in an attempt to ward off the morning chill. After bundling a sweater around her shoulders, Teresa started to plait her hair.

"There ain't no time for that," Mama scolded insistently. Teresa sighed and wrapped a scarf around her straggling strands. But hurry as they did, Mr. Winston, impatient at their tardiness, had gotten out of his truck and was banging on the door.

"Ya'll up in theah? Come on, it's five o'clock. We got a day ahead!"

Mr. Winston should have known better. He should have known not to hurry Bertha when she was already hurrying. He should have known that she was not a woman who would be pushed beyond her self-made limits. Now his insistent intrusion got her anger up; and whereas, because they were late, she had not intended to have breakfast, she suddenly decided they'd have it after all.

"We ain't had breakfast yet, Mr. Winston, and you know we can't work good till we do," Bertha whined at the panting figure beyond her door.

Billy puffed a few more times trying to find the appropriate response, but he knew Bertha and realized too late that he'd made the wrong approach; it was of no use to maintain his stand because, true to her word, she would surely have a long leisurely breakfast.

"Well hurry up. I'll go on and get the other hands awhile and come back 'round for ya'll," he said, resignedly.

The girls giggled at Mama's victory. They loved it when she got the best of old putty-face. Margie was glad too because now Mama would refurbish the fire that had gone out during the night. The rain had stopped during the night; but even if the sun came out and warmed the sodden earth, the interior of the little house would remain damp and chilly for days yet.

Margie would be more careful today and not allow the fire to go out so she and Reggie would not have to shiver all day. She snuggled up to Reggie, who would sleep another few hours yet, and drifted back to sleep herself. Five o'clock in the morning was the only time Margie was glad that she had to mind Reggie and didn't have to get up for work or school.

Out in the kitchen, Mama and the girls had a good hot breakfast of grits and ham. They sipped their coffee leisurely and gloried in the extra time Mama had bought for them. Thirty minutes later, Billy blasted his horn again and Mama, satisfied that she had detained him long enough, hurried the girls away from the table. At the door she caught them up. Straightening herself, she said, "Now, girls, 'member, we are ladies. Walk pretty and *slow.*"

They all giggled as they paraded out onto the porch in beauty-pageant tempo. And though Billy's face grew redder at the indignity of his position, they sashayed demurely across the yard toward the truck. The other hands already in the back of the truck laughed heartily at the uncommon sight of the four women, their plaited heads wrapped turban-style in bright bandannas, their crudely shod feet slapping at the mud as they swayed gracefully with their arms akimbo to the phantom beat of an invisible drummer.

When they reached the waiting truck, the girls climbed into the back and Bertha, smiling sweetly at Mr. Winston, pulled her weight slowly up into the cab, spent some time adjusting her dress under her buttocks, then closed the door with a bang. As soon as the door was shut, Billy pounced his foot onto the gas pedal and, lurching the truck forward to emphasize his anger, almost dumped Gayla out onto the road. Clinging tightly to the gate, she gasped, "I do believe Mr. Winston is mad!"

"He sure is, but it does put some rosy in them fat cheeks of his," Teresa acknowledged, grabbing at Gayla's dress and pulling her down onto the truck bed beside her. Billy Winston sped down the road. Before the day was over he'd get even with these people. Nobody messed with Billy Winston—twice in the same day.

It was still dark when the crew arrived at the seed beds. There was just a hint of light streaked along the seam of the horizon. The flatness of the country allowed no time for a real dawn; the sun would just suddenly pop up and seep through the morning fog. The girls tumbled out of the truck onto the rain-soaked ground. Four elderly, shabbily clothed men climbed out after them. Bertha and the girls stood off to one side while Billy spoke to the men he had picked up while waiting for them to have their breakfast. The men were former primers of Billy's but were too old now to be efficient in that capacity. In recent years they had become the town bums and usually sat snoozing on the steps of the old Maylor bank building. Billy gave them a little work each season, just enough to keep them in snuff and wine money for a few weeks. Now he sent them a little yonder to begin pulling plants at the far end of the bed because he knew Bertha would not tolerate the smelly old men near her and her girls. Just then London pulled her foot out of the mud where it had sunk ankle deep. A sucking plop smacked the morning quiet. One of the old men laughed and said, "Who farted?"

"Dirty man, hush your mouth," warned Bertha. She waged a constant battle trying to keep the frustrated old winos away from her daughters. The chastised old man grunted and headed off with the others to the far end of the seed bed.

At the insistent honking outside her house, Margie scrambled from under the quilt. Bus 79 had stopped in front of the house and was now waiting for her to come out. Startled from a sound sleep, she stumbled to the door. Opening the door just a crack so the kids on the bus wouldn't see her in her slip, she waved the driver on.

"Ain't goin' to school today, I'm sick," she called.

Wade Linsey, the seventeen-year-old student bus driver, shook his head in disgust. This was the fifth stop he had made that morning in which he had received the sick complaint. It was the same every spring when tobacco started. He knew they weren't sick and mumbled, "How do they evah think they can bettah themselves if they don't evah go to school."

The children on the bus were silent at his rebuke. They wished they still had their old driver, Mark Little. He was black and knew about the economics that kept the kids home from school. He would have sympathized rather than criticized.

The tooting bus had also awakened Reggie. Margie sighed. She might as well stay up now. She pulled the wimpering sleepy head into her arms.

"Hush, baby, it's all right," she crooned in a motherly tone. Reggie sniveled and stuck his thumb into his mouth. Margie changed his Pampers and pulled a shirt on over his head. She didn't bother with pants because pants just made it harder for her to change his Pampers when it got soiled or wet. She slipped a pair of socks on his pudgy feet then gingerly picked away the blanket fuzz that stuck to his kinky hair. Impatient with this procedure, he wiggled and squirmed until Margie let him slide to the floor.

Sloshing a wash cloth in the pan of cold water that Mama had left on the sink drain board, she wrung it out and washed her face. Having warmed up the icy cloth with her own flesh, she swiped it across Reggie's face.

"Now, you set here whilst I empty this stinkin' pot," she ordered. Taking the chipped enamel chamber pot that occupied a place in a corner of the bedroom every night, she carried it out into the yard. Sometimes Mama called it the *throne;* more often it was simply called a piss pot. Margie knew that she should take it around to the back and empty it in the outhouse; but seeing that the backyard was still under water from yesterday's rain, she decided to empty it in the ditch next to the road. Mama would never know because the ditch was running a foot deep with run-off already. After emptying the pot into the rushing ditch water, she scooped some clearer water from one of the deeper puddles that dotted the front yard. Swishing it around the pot she emptied it again. She set the pot in the corner of the porch to dry and air out, reminding herself that she must bring it in before Mama came home for lunch. Mama wouldn't tolerate a piss bucket sitting on her front porch.

Inside the house Reggie had helped himself to a cookie. Margie scolded but didn't take it away from him. Reggie grinned at his little victory.

"You eat some grits, too," she ordered and stuck a spoonful of lukewarm, leftover grits in front of his mouth. Reggie shook his head violently and waved his arms in protest, which knocked the spoon from her hand. The grits spattered over the table. Still feeling the chagrin at having waved the bus on and having to miss school because of him, Margie was in no mood to play games. She took the leftover grits out onto the porch where she dumped them into a pan for the dogs. The family's two dogs had been awaiting just such action and raced each other, yelping and jostling, to the pan. Both were of questionable lineage, but Brownie, a German shepherd sort of dog, was the larger of the two and juggled Spot away from the pan to lap up the sweetened grits. Spot, a parody of a beagle, sat politely by and waited his turn. Brownie left just enough to give him a sample. When his turn came, Spot licked the pan down to its chipped and rusted bottom then continued licking it till he had scooted the pan right off the edge of the porch. Reggie had been observing the scene with evident amusement from the doorway; but when he saw the empty pan topple and clang onto the ground, he realized for the first time that the grits were all gone. He emitted a siren-like wail.

"Don't you cry now, boy. You're the one what wouldn't eat 'em in the first place," Margie said unsympathetically.

Reggie sat down in the middle of the kitchen floor and continued his wailing while Margie cleaned up the dishes from last night's meal and today's breakfast. She scrubbed the dishes diligently and meticulously cleaned the tops of everything in the kitchen. It would be another long day for her alone in the house and she was anxious to fill the hours with house-work in an attempt to shorten them.

Bertha heaved a tired sigh of relief when she saw Mr. Winston approach with the large box filled with bottles of soda and honey buns for the mid-morning break. He would deduct the cost of the treat from their wages at the end of the day. This was an accepted procedure among all of the farmers. However, the other farmers always gave each hand a choice of what he would like for his snack, or maybe he wouldn't want anything at all if he wished to save his money and increase his take-home pay. Billy Winston eschewed such democratic courtesy, however; he said it required too much bookkeep-ing. The way he did it, everyone had the same amount deducted each day, and it certainly was much less troublesome to just gather eight bottles of soda, all alike, and eight honey buns and tote them out to the field. He chided the other farmers, saying that they looked like waiters as they jotted down each hand's order on a scrap of paper. He wasn't going to be anybody's waiter!

Bertha took her snack and climbed wearily into the cab of the truck, a comfort that was her privilege alone. Today, however, Mr. Winston ordered her to get out of the cab; he was still stinging from her besting of the early morning. Bertha snickered and got out of the cab. She knew she had won and was not quite willing to get out of the truck. Sauntering back to the tailgate, she wiggled her bulk up onto it then sat cockily swinging her bare legs while she sipped her soda and munched her honey bun. From the corner of her eye she could see that her attitude was scoring another point for her as Billy strutted and pawed in frustration at the ground with his fancy boots.

The three girls had wandered off a little distance in order to get away from the obnoxious odor that reeked from the old men and the sickening noise that emanated from the smacking of their toothless gums as they sucked on their sodas and gummed their honey buns. They also wanted to be outside the range of Mama's censoring ear.

"Reckon Randy 'll come over tonight since it's Friday?" Teresa asked London.

"You know Mama'll kill London if he comes over. She hates the sight of that boy!" warned Gayla. London smiled slyly.

"Won't kill me if she don't know it."

"Well, I hope you don't intend to make a scene and cause Mama to rile up and keep us all in 'cause I got my own date and it's with a boy Mama respects," said Gayla.

21

"Shit, respects! Just 'cause he's the preacher's boy she thinks he don't mess 'round," snorted London.

"Well, he don't," defended Gayla. Her two sisters eyed each other knowingly.

"You mean he's a queer and can't mess 'round even if he wanted to," Teresa jibed. Gayla glared at Teresa.

"Anyways, I'm goin' off with Randy tonight and Mama ain't goin' know it and there ain't goin' be no scene 'cause I'm *smooth,*" informed London.

"How you figure you're so smooth?" asked Teresa.

"He ain't comin' and I ain't goin' till Mama's on the bed and snorin'," London said, laughing confidently.

"London, you're goin' to get it in the ass one of these days," warned Gayla.

"What you mean, 'goin' get it! She done already got it!" laughed Teresa. They all laughed at that, even London.

Mr. Winston cut their mirth short with a shout. "Come on, ladies, let's get back to work. Those plants won't jump out of the ground by themselves, ha ha." They all laughed politely and moved back to the seed beds.

Teresa squatted close to London. "Reckon you can get away with it?" she whispered excitedly.

"If some big mouth don't blab," London answered, with a nod toward Gayla.

"Oh, she won't, 'cause I know a few things 'bout Jimmy Jones that Mama don't know and Gayla don't want Mama to know neither," Teresa said encouragingly, then added wistfully, "Sure wish Sonny was home."

"When he gets his leave?" London asked sympathetically.

"One more month, and that's a long time away." Teresa moaned, rolling her eyes in frustrated agony.

Mama looked their way with that inquiring look that pried deep inside the girls. They worked the remainder of the morning in silence.

The early spring day was chilly in the soggy fields; but as the sun rose higher and higher in the cloudless blue sky, it warmed the wet earth into a muggy steam that engulfed the workers. As chilled as they were, they began to sweat under the plastic raincoats that Billy had provided for them. After returning to the fields from lunch, the girls removed their coats. Mama scolded and demanded they put them on again lest they take cold. The old men working at the other end of the bed were oblivious to the heat generating from the steamy soil. They were rarely ever warm anyway and relished the little warmth the raincoats provided. Billy would have let them take the coats home with them if he thought they'd keep them, but he knew that they'd sell them first chance they got and use the money for wine.

Billy Winston left shortly after returning the workers to the fields from their noon break. He usually conducted his business in town during the afternoon hours. Most of Maylor's business was conducted in Nathan's Grill, the town's one and only restaurant. The Chamber of Commerce held its meeting there on Thursday morning over coffee. The two men's organizations, the Rotary Club and the Kiwanis Club, held their meetings in the "meetin' room" in back of the main dining room. Sometimes even the receiver of a traffic ticket had to seek out the town magistrate in the restaurant in order to pay his fine. And, of course, all the farmers gathered there at least once every day.

When Billy arrived at the Grill it was nearly two o'clock and the long center table was already filled with overalled farmers and a few business men. Woody Reed, the town magistrate, was also there. Billy shoved another small table up to the end of the long table to extend it further. Junie Warren, who was sitting at the end of the table got up so Billy could butt the two tables together. Then Billy sat down at the newly created head of the table. Junie studied the situation for a moment; then, shrugging his shoulders, he pulled his chair around to the side of the table and sat down.

Billy banged for Nathan's attention. Nathan took his order for a barbecued pork sandwich and coffee while the other men continued their conversations in muted tones. Billy had that quality. Whenever he came into the Grill the normal raucous of male talk always suddenly calmed to a whisper.

While he ate, Billy canvassed the various conversations going on around the table with a discerning ear. When he had finished his sandwich he sat back in his chair with an air of satisfaction. Sucking on his toothpick after cleaning his teeth of any vestige of wayward pork he gulped a deep sigh, then let a low growling belch rumble up from his gratuitous belly. This was the cue for the others to become quiet—Billy was ready to hold court.

Not having removed his cream-colored Stetson when he sat down, Billy gave the appearance of towering over the other men at the table. By the laws of group dynamics his assumed seat at the head of the table easily led him in his role of intimidation. The others, by habit, assumed the lesser roles and waited politely for Billy to begin.

Addressing Woody Reed, Billy asked, "You evah heah anymore about the gov'ment subsidies?"

Without looking up Woody replied, "Too early to tell much, but I hear rumors that they're raising the rates some this year."

"Well . . . maybe—but you can bet they'll rob us blind even with a raise. I've never seen it to fail yet, but when we plant more we always seem to get less money. I can't figure what they take us for."

"Reckon you're going to beat Jerry Jordon this year?" one of the men suddenly asked Billy.

Billy eyed the man suspiciously, then asserted, "There's no way of beating him, but he's not going to get ahead of me."

"I hear he's planting tomorrow," the man informed.

"Tomorrow! Hell, tomorrow's Saturday!" Billy protested.

"That's what I hear."

"Those fields'll still be too wet to get into." Billy fumbled with the little packet of sugar that he had taken from the bowl in the middle of the table. He wondered if Jerry would break tradition and plant on a weekend. The only time it was considered legitimate to work Saturdays was late in August when the leaves were ripening faster than they could be removed from the stalks and there was a chance they might burn. And, of course, no one ever worked on Sundays, burnt tobacco or no. He let the sugar sift into his coffee and began to stir the mixture with a studied air.

The conversation had regenerated in low tones among the men at the table, but Billy didn't hear them now. He pondered the bait that had been dangled in front of him. He didn't for a minute believe that Jerry would attempt to put a tractor into those muddy fields, and he just couldn't believe he'd be able to get a crew to work a Saturday. Saturday around Maylor was the traditional shopping day, and if you didn't get your shopping done on Saturday you were out of luck because the county blue laws prohibited the opening of stores on Sunday at all. No, Jerry wouldn't plant tomorrow; someone had gotten their facts mixed up.

Nevertheless, Billy excused himself from the table saying, "I bettah be getting back to my beds. You know how those coloreds'll goof off when they're not bein' watched." He strutted in exaggerated casualness from the restaurant.

When he had left, the men remaining at the table laughed heartily. "Got him going now," Woody said, chuckling. "I can just see him speeding down the road to get back and try to hire up his hands for tomorrow. Reckon I ought to call over to the police station and recommend someone check for speeders on Route 3?"

"Nah, it wouldn't do no good anyways; they'd never catch him. He's probably already there by now," said Junie Warren. Even Nathan laughed at the thought of Billy's old blue truck streaking down windy old Gum Swamp Road.

"Anyway, we got him goin'. I didn't think old Jerry could keep his big mouth shut long enough. I thought sure he'd be in here bragging about getting his fields in first. But he sure enough pulled a fast one on Billy this time. Wait till Billy finds out Jerry's put his fields in today already!" The men slapped their thighs and guffawed at what they knew would be Billy's reaction when he found out he not only had lost the race but hadn't even tied!

"Hey, where the hell did Jerry get those mules anyway?" Woody asked.

"Well, you know he wasn't goin' to use them at first. Said his tractor had guts enough to get through the mud. Fact is, he did make it down the first row, but when he went to turn at the end of the row the ditch caved in and the tractor turned over. The crew really moved fast then! He just left the damned tractor lay in the ditch and ran back to the house and called Ossie Johnson to hurry and bring over his mules and planting sled," Junie Warren related. He continued, "And those coloreds of his weren't going to work on that sled behind those mules either! But Jerry promised them if he won and got his picture in the paper for being the first to get his tobacco in he'd have a pig-pick' for them all."

"And I know they went to work for that!" laughed Woody.

Billy Winston unstuffed himself from behind the wheel of his truck and, puffing and wheezing, trotted over to where his crew was pulling the young plants.

"I'm goin' to transplant tomorrow," he panted. "I'll need you, Mrs. Braxton, and all three of your girls."

"We don't work Saturdays," London said hastily.

"What you mean, 'we don't work Saturdays'?" Bertha asked. "We work when we can, Saturday, Sunday, Monday, whichever."

"Now that's what I call a smart woman," admired Mr. Winston, feeling more benevolent towards Bertha now. He knew it was a rare hand who'd put herself out for a farmer, though he knew inside himself Bertha's motives most probably stemmed from personal need rather than concern for his tobacco.

"Shit!" mumbled London. She knew she would never be able to get up at five in the morning if she was out with Randy all night. When Teresa was able to get London off away from Mama, she asked, "Now what you goin' do?"

"I know I ain't workin' no Saturday," asserted London, pouting.

"But Mama already said you was," Teresa reminded.

"That's all she know. I ain't workin' and that's that."

"Couldn't you just wait till tomorrow night for Randy?" advised Gayla. "I'm just goin' tell Jimmy to come 'round tomorrow 'stead of tonight."

"First off, Randy wouldn't stand for none of that shit. We got a date and he 'spects me to keep it. And I know if I don't keep him reigned up close he goin' find hisself 'nother woman," London affirmed.

"Well, Jimmy is a very understandin' boy and he won't mind at all," bragged Gayla.

"Sure, that queer would be understandin'; ain't nobody but you'd go out with him," chided London.

"He ain't no queer; he just careful."

"Careful 'bout what? He don't even know which end to work with."

"Least I ain't got no bastard."

"Well, least I go out with men who got somethin' to make a bastard with. Your queer Jimmy ain't even got one."

"Hush, you two. Mama's lookin' over this way!" warned Teresa.

Gayla whispered one more lick in the feud, "You don't even know who seed maked that baby."

Billy's shadow fell softly over the girls backs. All conversation stopped; their fingers methodically and gently pulled the baby tobacco plants in silence.

Margie had dinner all ready except for baking the biscuits when Mama and the girls returned home at seven. She quickly popped the pan of biscuits into the oven while the women washed the mud and plant stains from their feet and hands.

The girls ate their meal in silence. Margie waited excitedly for the dinner conversation to begin. Alone all day with only Reggie to talk with, she hungrily sought the evening fellowship of her family. Even though she had nothing to contribute to the conversation, or at least nothing her sisters wanted to hear, she enjoyed the banter and chatter that usually accompanied the meal.

Whether or not Bertha noticed the unusual reticence of her daughters, she didn't remark. Margie looked from one sister to the other, trying to elicit the cause for the strained atmosphere. Something was in the air, she could tell, but she was outside of it. Maybe when Mama went to bed she would find out, when the girls were alone.

Mama performed her usual ritual of having a second cup of coffee and

26

dip of snuff. Margie impatiently counted each sip she took. At last, stretching and yawning to indicate that the day was over, Mama said, "I'm goin' to bed. And y'all better, too, if you 'spect to get up and work tomorrow."

This was the first indication to Margie that they had to work tomorrow. She guessed that that was the cause for the pouting. She busied herself with clearing the table to hide her disappointment. London readied Reggie for bed, while the other two girls began carrying dishes from the table to the sink. Margie wondered why all the help all of a sudden, but decided not to comment.

The girls had just been stalling until London had gotten Reggie into bed.

"I'm goin' set here and wait for Jimmy to come by so I can tell him 'bout workin' in the morning' and ast him to come back tomorrow night," said Gayla.

London glared at her sister. The longer everyone stayed up, the longer it would be before Mama would get to sleep. Bewildered at the way her sisters sat around the table glaring at each other, Margie continued to straighten the kitchen. No one said another word; they just sat.

"Here he come now," said London, with a nod toward the sound of footsteps on the porch. "Go on and tell him, and hurry up so we can go to bed."

"I ain't in no hurry," Gayla reminded her as she strutted slowly to the door. Opening the door, she invited Jimmy to come in. The tall, gangly, pop-eyed youth entered and stood shyly beside the door.

"Come on and set down, Jimmy," Gayla invited.

"Go on and tell him what you have to and let him get his ass out of here so we can all get on to bed," hissed London through clenched teeth.

Jimmy's pop-eyes popped a little more; he was easily intimidated and London's attack had frightened him. He began backing out the door.

"I can't go out tonight, Jimmy, baby, 'cause we got to work for Mr. Winston tomorrow. Can you come over tomorrow night 'stead." Jimmy nodded quickly and turned and ran off the porch and across the yard to his car.

"I ought to whip your ass for bein' so damn rude," stormed Gayla as she closed the door on the vanishing figure.

"You ain't big enough to whip anyone's ass," snorted London as she turned and walked into the bedroom.

Gayla knew there was no point in pursuing the problem anymore tonight, because if they disturbed Mama they'd both get whipped. But she vowed to get even if it took her the rest of her life. In fact, Gayla had so many things to get even with with London that it probably would take her the rest of her life. Canning her wrath now, she and Teresa followed London quietly into the bedroom and prepared for bed.

Disappointment pulled in Margie's stomach. All day she had waited for the companionship of her family only to find herself alone again now in the darkened kitchen. Mama still had not had the electricity turned on. Too restless to retire yet, she pulled the rocking chair close to the stove to take advantage of the little light that seeped through the crack of the closed door. She sat staring at the glowing red belly of the stove; time ticked slowly in her brain. It would be hard in the faint light but maybe she could try to read one of her school books. Getting her social studies book from the sideboard, she returned to her rocker and opened the book on her lap. She sat staring at the pictures. The glossy, gay-colored prints shimmered in the soft red glow, but it just wasn't what she had waited for all day. Suddenly London appeared in the doorway between the rooms.

"You better come to bed, too," she advised Margie.

"I'm not tired yet. I'll set here and read a spell."

"The boogie man'll get you," warned London.

"I'm not 'fraid of the boogie man," Margie laughed nervously.

"Suit yourself," said London, knowing full well she had planted the seed and it would germinate shortly.

Margie moved the rocking chair closer to the stove. She strained her ears listening for a warning sound that might indicate the arrival of the boogie man. A pecan, a straggler that had not let loose in the autumn, now fell from the tree in the sideyard. It hit the tin roof of the house with a ping then rattled down its pitch off onto the ground with a soft thud. Margie was sure the sound was just a pecan, but just in case, she decided she had better crawl into bed with Mama, where such sounds did not seem so ominous.

She lay at the foot of the big bed, staring at the ceiling above. Some of the flickering stove light found its way into the bedroom to cast little dancing patches onto the ceiling. Ordinarily Margie would have pretended that these were fairy lights, but tonight they took on the ghoulish glow of goblin's eyes. Sleep was far away yet for a little girl who had done nothing more than rock a baby all day, but she squeezed her eyes shut anyway in an effort to erase the horrendous thoughts that were coming to fruit from London's mischievous seed.

The bed stirred a little. Margie turned her head anxiously. Peeping out of half-squinted eyes, she watched silently as London's shadow emerged from under the quilt. She watched as London slipped on her dress. She watched as London pulled the tight braids out of her hair, fluffing it and picking it with the big wire pick, making it stand high into a round smooth puff like a big black mushroom.

Silently, London tiptoed to the door. Looking back to check the sleeping figures of her family, she smiled in satisfaction that all was going well. Margie didn't budge. London opened the door and slipped out into the night. Margie listened as the soft footsteps padded off onto the road then disappeared. Her heart beat wildly in her breast. If Mama would find out— she hiccupped a frightened gasp at the thought. She knew she would never sleep tonight.

A black '65 Buick was parked off the side of the road about a quarter mile from the house. London trotted toward it, arriving out of breath but glowing at the sight of the grinning Randy sitting behind the wheel. She ran around to the other side of the car. Randy reached across the front seat and pushed the door open for her. Climbing in, she leaned over and kissed him on his whiskered cheek.

"When you goin' get rid of that brush?" she demanded, in disgust, while rubbing the sting from her lips.

"What you mean, woman! It's *cool;* gives me *prestige.*" That it did. The other boys all admired Randy's precocious beard. At nineteen he had a fuller beard than most men had acquired at maturity.

"Where we goin'?" London asked as Randy pulled onto the road and headed toward town.

"Paradise Inn."

"Whooey!" London whistled softly.

The Paradise Inn was the black nightclub located at the south edge of Maylor. (The white club was two miles across town at the north edge.) During the day the Paradise Inn was a benign little café where the older retired men and sometimes younger men who were out of work would congregate to exchange pleasantries, play checkers, or just sit. It was someplace to go. But at night the whitewashed, concrete block building became a jumping, jiving place of excitement. And, especially on weekends, the transformation was astounding. All the "cool cats" gathered there on the weekends. The sooty walls and grimy wood floor lost their repulsiveness and, under the glow of lavender lights, assumed an aura of mystique. The scarred tables and rickety chairs seemed soft and plush in the romantic atmosphere. The acrid smells of stale beer, cheap wine, and sweat were masked by cinnamon incense. London tingled. It was a good place to go.

At this early hour all was orderly yet in the club. A juke box blared a soul beat. Couples turned and swiveled in a hypnotic trance. The few older folks present watched in amused but envious reverie of a day gone by. London and Randy found a table in a corner of the dark room. In the dim light they could see the names of many of their friends carved into the top of the table. Some pairs of names were encircled in hearts. Some had been violently scratched out indicating a broken romance. London's name was cozily nestled beside a lopsided heart alongside Randy's.

Belinda, the barmaid and co-owner of the club, approached the couple. "Long time since I seen you in here," she greeted London. "How's your mama?"

"Oh, she fine." London smiled, confident that Belinda would never mention her presence at the club to Mama. And Belinda would not. Most of her trade was made up of these youth who were out on the town without parental approval.

"Give us a bottle of wine," ordered Randy cockily.

"A whole bottle! You musta striked it rich, man!" Belinda chided in mock surprise.

"Yeah, I got me a job at the Mill," Randy answered proudly (the "Mill" was really the fertilizer plant over near the Maylor depot, but for some unknown reason every one called it the Mill). Belinda grinned and returned to the bar to get the bottle of wine. Yes, Randy was rich for the moment, but Belinda knew he wouldn't last long at the Mill; the idea of working eight hours a day every day did not generally appeal to young bucks like Randy.

Mary Edwards, a former classmate of London's, spotted the couple snuggled in the corner. "London Braxton!" she called. "What you doin' in here? Your mama know you here?"

Mary started toward their table. London bit her lip as the girl swayed her round hips first to one side then in a large arc to the other. "Who that with you?" Mary demanded in mock ignorance. "Why, it's Randy Miller, the *man* hisself!"

London smiled sweetly at Mary. She hated Mary and wished she'd go away and stop giving Randy that come-on eye. But she dare not say a word lest Mary would spite her and let the knowledge of her presence sift back home to Mama. Randy grinned appreciatively at Mary. Mary was an all right girl, and all the boys knew it.

Sonny Summers called from the other side of the room, "Mary, you get your ass over here! You're with me tonight."

Mary winked at Randy and said, "Daddy's callin'. I'll see you 'round, sugar."

London made a mental vow to cut Mary the next time they crossed each other. Tonight, however, she only simpered a whiny, "Bye-bye, now honey."

She snuggled closer to Randy and sipped the cool sour wine from the glass they shared. Randy responded to her warmth and melted close to her. "Drink up, baby, and let's get out of here," he proposed.

"Not just yet, honey," London answered languidly. "The mood is warmin' me all over." Randy held her tighter against him, slipping his hand well under her arm around to her breast. London warmed more. She laid her head on his shoulder and nested in his wiry beard, not minding its abrasiveness now.

The beat emanating from the jukebox was interrupted by a scuffle in the center of the dance floor. Amid much shouting and swearing, two big youths were challenging the possession of the same girl. Suddenly one of the boys flipped a blade into the face of his opponent. All action stopped. The room became quiet and tense.

Howard, Belinda's co-owner, swiftly moved into the arena and got between the two boys. "Just get your ass out of here. Ain't goin' be no cuttin' in here tonight," he ordered.

The boys did not move. They stood rooted to their positions, the knife still separating them. The object of their feud stood at the edge of the crowd that had gathered in the center of the room. She glowed in obvious pride. That was her man with the blade.

Howard drew his hands into tight fists. He waited out the boys' steam. Slowly the hand holding the knife dropped; with a ping the blade disappeared within its handle sheath. A sigh of relief mingled with groans of disappointment sizzled around the room.

"Okay, now, boys, get on outside and don' come back in here again tonight."

The boys moved toward the door without taking their eyes off each other. Once they were outside, the action in the club returned to normal. Howard went back to his duties at the bar. He knew that the boys did not go outside to cool it; he knew they'd continue their difference but he didn't care as long as they were not in his place. The girl that had been the center of the controversy quickly paired off with another boy in the club, forgetting all about the first boy.

It didn't occur to anyone in the club to call the police to intervene in the difficulty. For one thing, the Maylor police were reluctant to investigate problems arising in the club. Such business could be hazardous for a white policeman. In his effort to abort or halt a fight between highly charged black youths, he might well get the knife himself. And if he did protect himself and one of the youths was hurt in the scuffle, he could lose his job. And right now the racial problem was in high gear, with the papers teeming with accounts of the black girl in Beaufort County Jail who had just murdered her warden in her cell. Some were saying it was self-defense—that the warden was attempting to rape her. Others said she had lured him into her cell in an attempt to escape. Whichever, it was quickly gathering into a racial issue instead of a murder issue.

Recently a black policeman had been added to the Maylor police force; but upon his own request, it immediately became policy that he would not be required to run a beat in his own neighborhood. It just wouldn't have been prudent tactics at the time. Thus the Paradise Inn mostly had to make and maintain its own laws. And Belinda's co-owner, a husky former New York longshoreman, was not one to be reckoned with, so there rarely was ever a disastrous event within the walls of the club. Howard always managed to delay any tragedy long enough to get it outside. Once outside it was out of his jurisdiction.

"This place stinks," Randy sniffed. "Come on, let's go over to Gene's house." He pulled a key from his pocket and dangled it invitingly in front of London.

"Where' you get that!" gasped London. "Gene's gone to D.C. for his cousin's fun'ral and won't be back till next week."

"I know."

"You sure is somethin' else again." London smiled and the couple prepared to leave.

"Where you goin', London?" Mary Edwards called. "I bet you ain't goin' home." The others in the club laughed.

"I got business and the night's young yet," Randy bragged, holding the key up for all to see.

"Whose key's that?" Mary asked.

"Wouldn't you like to know," teased Randy, kissing the key and dropping it into his pocket.

Outside London asked, "Gene give you that key or you steal it?"

"Gene give it to me out the goodness of his heart," Randy replied. London knew that Gene would never have done that. Gene and Randy, though not enemies, were competitors and Gene often had teased Randy for not being smart enough to have his own pad. But Gene wouldn't be back till next week and he'd never know. London felt secure and nestled close to

Randy as he drove toward their rendezvous.

It was nearly four in the morning when London tiptoed through the door of her house. Margie had drifted into a light sleep that immediately snapped when the latch on the door clicked. London slid into bed without the slightest movement or sound from the creaky springs. Margie sighed in relief and finally let herself fall into a sound sleep.

Bertha called out to her girls, "Get yourselves up!" Teresa and Gayla struggled out of their warm bed as soon as they heard Mama call. London didn't move. Mama went around to the side of the bed and, placing her big hand on London's shoulder, gave her a violent shake. "Get yourself out that bed! It's already five o'clock and we ain't got much time 'fore Mr. Winston be here bangin' on that door again."

Startled, London's eyes sprang open. She stared at Mama briefly, gathering her wits about her. Finally she whimpered, "I can't get up Mama; I'm sick."

"What's wrong with you?" Mama asked suspiciously.

"I got the cramps sooo bad," London moaned.

"That's what you tol' me last week!" informed Mama, her suspicion increasing. London had forgotten about having used that excuse just the weekend before. She moaned softly, this time in genuine agony at what Mama would do if she discovered she had been lying either time.

"Got 'em again," she replied, watching Mama's face for a hint of credulity.

"Lord, I hope you ain't got no tumor like Willy Mae had," Mama worried, frowning at London.

"Maybe the storm's what done it," London offered weakly.

"Maybe," Mama agreed hopefully. "I hope so." She pulled the quilt a little tighter around the shoulder she had just shaken and patted London gently. "That's all right, baby. You sleep now and them cramps will go right away." Her voice crooned in a gentle nurselike manner. Then reverting quickly back to Mama, she straightened up and added, "When you feel better, you get yourself out that bed and head on down to the field next to the store. That's where we be transplantin'. You hear me!" London nodded briefly, having already drifted back to sleep.

London finally got out of bed at ten o'clock. She would have liked to stay much longer but Reggie, tickled at the idea of having his mother home with him, jumped and squirmed all over the bed trying to get her attention.

"Margie, can't you keep this boy out of here!" she wailed.

"He's your baby. I can't do a thing with him," Margie simpered.

33

Defeated, London got up. Jerking Reggie by the arm, she hauled him into the kitchen and got a cookie to quiet him. Pouring herself a cup of coffee, she slumped into the chair and rested her head on her arms at the table.

"Whooey, does my head hurt," she moaned.

"Head hurt. Head hurt," chanted Reggie, kicking at a pot he had been playing with on the floor.

"Don't do that!" bellowed London. Oblivious to his mother's orders, Reggie continued his game of kick-the-pot. London held her hands over her ears.

Margie watched with curiosity. Soon Mama and the other two girls would be coming in for lunch. She wondered what London would do then. Finally getting up the courage, she asked, "Where you was last night, London?"

London looked at her little sister in surprise.

"What you mean, 'where I was'?"

"I saw you go out and you didn't get back till late in the mornin'."

"You smart ass! You just keep you goddamn mouth shut, you hear me!"

Margie had no intentions of telling Mama. She had a healthy respect for what London would do to her if she did tell. In fact, she wished now she hadn't said anything to London because if Mama did find out by accident London would surely blame her. But it was fun to be in on the secret of her older sister. Margie wondered if she would have such exciting secret to keep when she reached London's age. Margie flushed at the imagery in her head and made herself busy with the lunch preparations.

Already Margie felt ready for the glorious world in which her sisters lived. Oh yes, she was the baby and it was a common problem of "babies" to be thwarted from growing up. But she held the peculiar position of being the youngest in the family but still having a baby, Reggie, under her. In fact, she had cared for Reggie for so long now she already felt grown up. And hadn't she already had four "sick" periods!

She was so proud of her periods, the mark of womanhood, that she kept an intimate record of each one on a little calendar that hung on the wall by her end of the bed. Mama had worried a little when Margie had not begun her periods by her eleventh birthday, as had all her other girls. Mama worried about things like that. She had even consulted with one of the midwives who attended her church. The old woman no longer practiced her trade because of the laws governing midwifery, but she was most happy to advise Bertha concerning Margie's problem. She had given her a special herb tea guaranteed to ripen even the most stubborn of cases. It was also purported to have excellent abortive powers, in stronger brews.

And sure enough, the tea had worked. At eleven years and ten months, to Mama's great relief, Margie had bloomed. Now, just four months later, no one even noticed Margie's period anymore. She was the only one who kept the memory of her big day, proudly making a red circle on the calendar for each of her times.

London continued to languidly sip at her black coffee in silence. But for Margie the silence said so many wonderful things. She relived in her mind the events of the previous night that she had felt so fortunate to be a party to. Again she saw London slip from the bed. Again she watched as London primped her hair. Again she listened as the pat of London's footsteps faded down the road. She had heard the accounts of her sister's other adventures often enough that she could now almost see into London's night and imagine the thrills that went with it. One day, soon, Margie would join in her sisters' world, in fact, she was sure Mama would let her date when she was thirteen—well, she had let the other girls date at thirteen. . . .

The telltale ping of Mr. Winston's motor warned her to obliterate the romance for the moment. Indeed, she wouldn't want to take the chance that Mama might be able to read her thoughts. Giving the dough in the bowl one more punch, she began quickly to tear off the biscuits and place them on the pan. Just as the women came in the door, she slid the pan into the oven.

Mama glared long and hard at London, who still was not dressed. Margie would never tell.

Chapter III

When the Braxton women had finished pulling Billy's plants and setting them into his fields, he sent them over to the Troy farms. The Troy brothers were in no race to get their fields planted so they waited patiently for Billy's experienced help. Besides, it could be unprofitable to plant too early; some of the fields that had been planted that first week had to be replanted because the tornadolike winds that churned the fields had dumped tons of sand on the young plants and smothered them. Billy's were not victims of such disaster, however, because the fields he planted were largely protected by strips of dense pine groves that lined the perimeter of his fields.

Planting for Billy Winston and then the Troys gave Bertha two weeks of steady income in April. The Braxtons ate well, had their electricity turned on, and paid some of their account at Pfeiffer's. Through May and June, however, everyone just waited. Waited for the tobacco to grow. It didn't need any attention, at least of the kind a man could give. Once it was in the ground, until harvest, only God could control the growth. The rain, the sun, were all in His hands.

And Bertha would wait. Other than day work in town for the white ladies who were bred to eschew housecleaning, there would be no work until the middle or end of June.

Spring brought out the instinctive urge in all women to scrub and clean and get rid of and add to family possessions. Since Bertha's arthritis was acting up again, she did not go out this spring to clean the white ladies' homes but sent London in her place. London became "Miz Sarah's, and Miz Francis' and Miz Ginia's colored girl." Alone, this employment would not have been enough for the family of six, but along with the welfare check it seemed like a fortune. Ordinarily the welfare checks stopped when the recipient found work, but as long as the "welfare people" didn't know about the day work . . .

Teresa, Gayla, and Margie returned to school to finish out the year. This was the first time Mama had agreed to allow Margie to return to finish after the planting season. Other years she had said that it didn't matter and she liked Margie at home with her.

Even though Margie only lost two weeks this year, she had fallen far behind the other students in her class. She had fallen so far behind, especially in her reading skills, that her teacher, Mrs. Levine, recommended her for the new tutorial program at school. Every morning for forty-five minutes a volunteer, Mrs. Tierling, would sit with Margie and help her read.

At first Margie was suspicious of Mrs. Tierling. *What do a white lady want to teach a black kid for when she don't even get paid?* she thought.

At first her suspicion and antagonistic attitude toward the volunteer retarded her progress. But Mrs. Tierling did not rebuke her or shame her. She didn't make fun of her when she made a mistake. Sometimes Mrs. Tierling even hugged Margie. Though Margie longed for such attention, she found it difficult and uncomfortable to accept from the strange white teacher. And besides, white people smelled funny to her. She didn't even like to sit so close. And when Mrs. Tierling touched Margie, it gave her goose pimples. Her skin felt funny. It was all soft and squishy, not dry and rough like her mama's. It reminded Margie of a doll she had once gotten for Christmas from her church's Santa Claus. It had had rubber so soft that it was advertised to feel alive. That doll had also given Margie goose pimples.

But little by little Mrs. Tierling won Margie's confidence. Little by little Margie began to improve. Along with her improvement in reading came a significant improvement in her other subjects as well. She just might make it this year; she just might pass. She could almost taste the fruit of success, next year, junior high! The anticipation helped to sustain Margie in her heroic efforts to learn her lessons. Junior high! Thirteen years old! Somehow, to her it seemed that thirteen and junior high had to go together. She could not attain one without the other. She crammed her lessons without relenting day after day. She must pass!

The contemplation of all these marvelous circumstances would have been enough to keep Margie high all spring. When the letter from her mother's sister, Aunt Sissy, came, it was almost more excitement than she could handle. They never ever got a real letter in the mail. Sometimes weeks passed without getting even junk mail. Poor folk were not usually on mailing lists. When they did get something, something gay-colored, a brochure or a catalogue, Margie kept it for weeks, or at least till another came.

Aunt Sissy's letter arrived on a Tuesday, the third Tuesday in May. London was out cleaning windows for Mrs. Sarah. Margie and the other girls were at school. Mama couldn't read but recognized the writing on the envelope to be that of her youngest sister who still lived in Mississippi. Though Sissy had been the only one in her family to have learned to read and write, Bertha rarely ever heard from her. She was beside herself now with curiosity and excitement by the time bus 79 stopped in front of the house.

Mama was standing at the edge of the road with the letter in her hand when the bus pulled up. "Hurry, child, read me this letter from your Aunt Sissy."

Margie took the letter from her mother and scanned it with curiosity. She had been too little when they had left Mississippi to remember Aunt Sissy, but Mama had often spoken of her baby sister. It felt strange to be looking at the woman's handwriting now. It just didn't seem to be from a real person; it was detached, a message floating all the way from Mississippi.

"Hurry, child!" Mama said, impatiently poking at Margie to rouse her into action.

" 'Dear Bertha,' " Margie began, " 'How are you? Fine I hope. How are your children? Fine I hope. We have not been so good here. My heart ain't been so good. Lenny hurt his back and did not work since Christmas. I been doing the best I can but you know I never was strong and I can't do no heavy work. Lenny heard about a place in Greensburg what is hiring people. It is a potato chip plant. We thought we would come up and see about it. We will be there sometime on the 27 of May. We can't wait to see you. We miss you so much. Your Sister, Sissy Caldwell.' "

Bertha stood motionless, her hands clasped together over her heart. Several minutes went by while she digested the news contained in the letter. Then suddenly she shouted, "Hallelujah, my baby sister's comin' to see me!"

Margie was speechless with excitement and just stood there clutching the letter tightly in her hand. The high school bus arrived just then and Teresa and Gayla came upon the strange scene. Mama and Margie had been so absorbed in the letter that neither one had heard the bus rattle from around the bend and stop at the edge of the road next to where they stood. When the girls jumped off the bus, Margie struggled to find her voice. "Aunt Sissy's comin', Aunt Sissy's comin'," she finally shouted.

"When?" Gayla asked excitedly, clapping her hands, she caught the hysteria of the moment.

"Oh, when, let's see, when did it say, Mama?" Margie fretted as she tried to find the date written in the letter. "Here it is, 27 of May. Let's see, today is the 25th, that's the day after tomorrow!"

"Day after tomorrow! Lord, we have got to get ready!" Bertha cried, half running, half hopping toward the house.

"What we goin' to get ready, Mama?" Teresa called sarcastically.

"We're goin' to clean this place and 'range a place for them to sleep."

"Yeah, Mama, just where they goin' to sleep?" inquired Gayla.

But Mama would not let such a minor detail spoil the anticipation of seeing her baby sister again, and she continued running toward the house, huffing and puffing up onto the porch.

"They ain't gettin' *my* bed!" Teresa stated emphatically as the girls caught up with Mama and followed her into the house.

"We kin get 'nother bedstead," Mama said, with a finality that implied that she knew just where to lay her hands on one.

"Where from?" insisted Teresa.

"There's some beds 'round somewhere. Don't worry. We'll get one," Mama answered with confidence.

"Maybe Mr. Winston has one to loan us," Margie suggested. Mr. Winston had always been nice to them. And hadn't he brought the oven for them?

"Mr. Winston won't let no colored sleep on one of his beds, and 'sides, who wants to sleep on anything that sweaty ol' ball of fat might of laid on!" Teresa answered in disgust.

"Maybe we could make a bed on the floor," offered Gayla.

"We'll do somethin'; now let's start cleanin' this house," ordered Mama, putting an abrupt end to the problem of the bed.

"Ain't we even goin' to have dinner first!" Teresa wailed indignantly.

"Oh, Lord, I done forgot 'bout dinner. Hurry, Margie, run to the store and get some eggs. We'll have eggs and biscuits for dinner. Hurry!"

Margie took off and ran down the road to Pfeiffer's. The excitement seemed to charge her and lent momentum to her legs. She burst through the door into the dingy store, breathlessly proclaiming the news of Aunt Sissy's impending visit to anyone who might listen. Mr. Pfeiffer caught hold of her arm.

"We need some eggs!" cried Margie. "And charge 'em," she added. Mr. Pfeiffer sighed and got the eggs out of the refrigerated case behind the counter.

"That's ninety-five cents," he said, and pulled the Braxton card from the cigar box file he kept all his accounts in. All the while, he mumbled about how did people expect a poor fellow to make a living when everyone wanted to charge everything.

Margie didn't pay any attention to Mr. Pfeiffer's complaining. She had learned long ago that the mumbling went with the charging. At first it had embarrassed her and she'd truly felt that somehow she was depriving Mr. Pfeiffer of a proper living. But then she began to suspect that old Mr. Pfeiffer was living just as comfortably when she charged as when she paid cash. Now Mr. Pfeiffer shoved the eggs across the counter to Margie as he added their cost to the perpetually long column on the well-worn card in front of him.

While Margie was at the grocery, London had arrived home from Mrs. Sarah's and had learned of Sissy's expected visit. Margie heard her voice as she approached the porch.

"You think they're comin' for a visit? Don't kid yourself. I can 'member that ol' man of hers. That Lenny didn't never work more'n a few months at a time and you can 'spect he be just the same now. He's the laziest man I ever knowed. And Aunt Sissy's so sickly and whiny all the time; you know she ain't goin' do nothin'. They're just comin' to have a vacation with us'ens waitin' on them like this was a grand hotel or somethin'."

"Now, London, you hush that kind of talk. You don't even know what Lenny's been doin' since we left. And I know they ain't goin' stay here but a li'l while, just till they find a job for Lenny and a house of their own," Mama defended them. " 'Sides, it'll be such a proud pleasure to have 'em with us again."

"Humph," London grunted. "Still say they 'spects to freeload on us." She stomped into the bedroom.

Mama fried the eggs and laid them on top of hot biscuits. It was one of Margie's favorite dishes, but she was too excited to eat now and just stirred the yokes around on her plate.

"Quit messin," Mama rebuked.

"You better eat them eggs, honey, 'cause we ain't goin' get much to eat when that slob, Lenny, gets here," London advised. Margie couldn't understand her sisters' attitudes. No one seemed to want Aunt Sissy to come except her and Mama. It seemed so exciting to think of company. They had never before had company; why wasn't everyone excited?

The dust-covered, tan '68 Oldsmobile pulled into the yard at six o'clock on Thursday night. Bertha hurried out to meet it. Margie started to go out with her but saw that her sisters were going to remain in the house. Shyness suddenly overcame her and she stayed on the porch watching expectantly.

"He looks just like I 'member him," London said from the doorway. "A greasy, fat slob."

As Sissy stepped out of the car, Mama threw her arms around her and began weeping hysterically. Sissy joined in the tears and they rocked back and forth in the ecstasy of seeing each other again.

Lenny got out of the car and started walking slowly toward the house. He looked from left to right around the yard to acquaint himself with his new home. Passing Margie on the porch he flashed her a smile and, motioning toward the car, said, "Fetch them valises, child."

Margie nodded and ran off to the car. Pulling the heavy valises from the backseat, she began struggling, dragging and bumping them along the ground toward the house. Mama and Sissy followed her, oblivious to the almost impossible task she was performing. Inside the house Mama and Sissy continued babbling nonstop about all the things that had happened since they'd last seen each other. The girls began putting dinner on the table. Lenny was already making himself at home in London's chair at the table. Margie stood anchored to the valises for a moment; then when she saw no one was going to relieve her of them, she let them plop with a thud onto the floor in the middle of the room. She flexed her arms to loosen the strained muscles, then began to dash back and forth arranging the food, stirring the pots, and generally keeping herself in motion to prolong the electric excitement of the moment.

"Who's this baby?" asked Sissy, swooping Reggie into her arms.

"He's London's," answered Mama.

"He's beautiful!" Sissy admired. "We ain't never been blessed with children. Course, Lenny, he's got a boy what's growed, but we don't never see him 'cause he lives in Jersey." Reggie struggled to release himself from her awkward, viselike embrace.

"It's ready," announced Teresa.

Lenny began filling his plate as the others found their seats at the table. Though Mama did buy two new chairs at Dan's Used Furniture Store in Maylor, Margie was still to sit in the rocking chair. Besides, it was too crowded at the small table now for yet another person. Margie eyed the two new chairs with envy. Oh, she was proud to have Aunt Sissy and Uncle Lenny use them, but she could hardly wait till it would be her turn, when Aunt Sissy and Uncle Lenny found their own place to live.

Mama and Sissy continued to talk throughout the meal. Lenny just ate. The girls watched him with awe. He filled his plate three times.

"He sure do have an appetite," remarked Teresa in an undertone to Gayla.

Lenny heard but didn't bother to look up; he just kept right on eating. Margie watched in wonder as he rhythmically moved his fork from plate to mouth back to plate without ever interrupting the tempo.

One-two-three-four, one-two-three-four, she found herself counting.

After dinner Margie automatically began clearing the table. Lenny remained at the table and watched as she worked around him. Aunt Sissy began a tour of the two rooms.

"Oh, Bertha, honey, I hate to see your girls sleep on the floor 'cause of us." She said when she saw the neat pallet Mama had arranged on the floor in the bedroom. Unable to find a bed, she had finally settled for a soggy, stained mattress that Mrs. Virginia was most happy to have hauled from her attic.

"We knew you'd feel that way," London said demurely. "That's why we made up the bed on the floor for Uncle Lenny and you, Aunt Sissy."

On hearing this Lenny found such news stirring enough to push himself from the table. "I can't sleep on no floor. I got a bad back."

"Yes. Don't you 'member. I tol' you in my letter that Lenny hurt his back at work," Sissy reminded them.

"I'm sure we can work out somethin' for the li'l while you'll be here," assured Bertha. "Teresa and Gayla, they'll be happy to give you their bed," she continued, pointing to the little cot.

"Ain't very big," Lenny observed.

"Lenny, he's a big man and gots to have a big bed for him to get his back comfortable in," explained Sissy. Bertha saw Lenny eyeing her big double bed.

"I guess I could sleep on the cot with Margie," she sighed. "London and Reggie'll just have to make do sleepin' with Teresa and Gayla on the floor."

"Oh, you're so sweet and gen'rous, Bertha, honey, just like you always was," Sissy cooed.

Margie wondered just how she was going to sleep in that little cot beside her big Mama. The other girls said nothing; they had respect for the problem Mama was dealing with and would never have embarrassed her, but there were many rude and unkind thoughts flitting around inside their heads. Margie could feel them. Lenny may have felt them too because he looked at the girls, smiled, and shrugged his shoulders as if to say "That's life girls," then yawned.

"Fact, I think I'll go to bed now. I'm tired from that long drive," He slipped his pants off, folded them neatly, and hung them over the foot of the big bedstead. The girls all turned their backs politely. Taking off his coat and shirt, he held them out to Margie and bade her to hang them nicely over the back of a chair in the kitchen. Margie blushed and, without looking directly at her disrobing uncle, took the garments and did as she was told.

"You just get yourself to sleep now, sugar," Sissy said, then turning to Mama explained, "Lenny never complains just long as he gets his res'."

It was late when Mama and Aunt Sissy came to bed. London, Teresa, and Gayla had reluctantly cramped themselves together on the pallet, with Reggie between London and Gayla. Margie lay on the cot waiting for Mama. The older girls had all gone to bed without taking off their dresses. Margie had wondered just how they would arrange sleeping in the same room with their uncle, a man, the only man who had ever been inside their bedroom. She admired her sisters' intelligence and resourcefulness and, copying them, she also kept her dress on. Lenny snored softly in the big bed.

Margie hated to have to go to school in the morning. She wanted to stay home and listen to more of Sissy's and Mama's talk. But at dawn Mama had gotten all the girls up. She cautioned them to move quickly and quietly so as not to disturb their guests. When the buses came, she hustled them out the door, poking and prodding them to hurry them along.

London bawled, "What you doin', Mama? I don't go to school!"

"Well, go on, get over to Miz Francis 'while."

"Lord, I can't walk to her house! And 'sides, she won't even be up yet."

"Shush, now get."

"Mama! Miz Francis comes and gets *me* at ten o'clock!"

"Don't sass." Oblivious to London's protests, Mama pushed her out the door.

London shook her head in defeat. "Mama's pure crazy!" she mumbled and began walking the five miles into town, hoping someone would pick her up along the way and that Mrs. Francis would be up when she got there.

"I aches all over," complained Teresa as the bus pulled away from the house. "She thinks I'm goin' sleep on the floor 'gain tonight, she's crazy."

"Where you think you'll sleep?" Gayla asked sarcastically.

"Well, I ain't goin' sleep in the same room with that snorin' pig."

"Yeah, and I already asked you just where you *think* you're goin' sleep."

"Oh, shit, shit, shit," Teresa moaned.

"And I have that feelin' that London be right 'bout them stayin' forever," Gayla sighed to add to their misery.

"That's one good reason for goin' to school," Teresa laughed. This remark only served to irritate Gayla. It always irritated her when Teresa made light of serious matters.

Margie did not contemplate, as her sisters did, that Aunt Sissy's visit would be a permanent thing. The idea of having company still had control of her emotions. They had had a marvelous meal last night, a company meal; as long as they had company they would probably have company meals. She had been a little crowded on the cot with Mama, but Margie had had no trouble going to sleep once she allowed her mind to stray from the excitement of the whole past week.

But now in school she was having a hard time concentrating on the task at hand. She kept slipping back into the events of the day before. Once in a while Uncle Lenny's strange smile flitted across her conscience and made her a little uncomfortable, but it was barely noticeable mingled in among the laughter, fine food, and Mama's delight. Mrs. Tierling had to call her attention several times. Margie was embarrassed at her daydreaming, but she could not help it.

Visions of Aunt Sissy dominated. She was not at all as Margie had pictured. Mama had often spoken of her baby sister and how she had been frail and how she had never ever grown up to be a strong woman capable of taking care of a house and having children. Margie had envisioned a thin, but pretty and dainty, little lady. One who smiled in the face of imminent death. One who accepted pampering but did not want it. Aunt Sissy, according to Mama, was a special gift from God. Having arrived on the earth long after Gramma Edwards had expected any more children, Sissy was a "change baby," a real surprise. Her untimely arrival had spelled a sacred omen to the very religious Edward family, who was always on the lookout for such omens to assure themselves of God's favor.

But Aunt Sissy was not thin and dainty. She was large and bulky. Her flesh hung in languid brown folds from her arms and chin. She might have been pretty, but any beauty that was there was buried under soft blobs of fat. And she was not inhibited about her physical frailties; indeed, she panted heavily every time she moved and held her hand on her heaving breast and sighed and mourned her weak heart.

One thing that confused Margie, however, was that as sick as Aunt Sissy obviously was, and the whole family was instructed to be always aware of her needs and to anticipate her wants so she would not have to exert herself, she would jump to her feet at the slightest grunt from Uncle Lenny and begin fussing over him. Uncle Lenny? Margie had already decided she did not much like him.

Mama and Aunt Sissy were still reminiscing when Margie got home from school. They had much to remember for each other—ten years' worth. Uncle Lenny was sitting on the edge of the porch, his feet dangling just an inch from the ground. He smiled that funny smile as Margie jogged across the yard from the bus.

"Hey, baby, how you doin'?" he purred.

"I'm fine," Margie answered, her head down, her eyes on the ground at her feet. She found it uncomfortable to look Lenny in the eyes.

"Uncle Lenny's been waitin' for you. How 'bout runnin' to the store and gettin' me some beer?" Margie didn't answer; Mama didn't allow beer in her house. Should she tell Uncle Lenny? "And here's a quarter for your trouble." Lenny bribed at her hesitance.

Well, she thought. *Maybe if he drinks it out here on the porch, Mama won't mind.* Margie smiled and held her hand out for the money. Then, dropping her books on the porch, she took off running toward Pfeiffer's Grocery.

"I'll have a can of beer and a 'nilla ice cream cone—two dips," she ordered breathlessly. Mr. Pfeiffer looked up from his paper in surprise. The Braxtons had never bought beer before.

"Can't give you any beer, girly," he said. "You got to be eighteen to buy beer."

"But it's for my Uncle Lenny," Margie explained.

"Sorry, girly, can't give you any beer. Tell your uncle he has to buy his own beer." He handed her the double-dipped ice cream cone that he had scooped from the big buckets of frozen ice cream in the freezer behind the counter. Margie couldn't remember having seen such a large double-dip before, the great globs of satiny confection balanced precariously on the top of the fragile cake cone that Mr. Pfeiffer held forth. She hesitated only a moment. Uncle Lenny had given her the quarter as a reward in lieu of buying the beer for him. She really shouldn't spend the quarter now since she hadn't purchased the beer. A tempting drip slithered down the side of the cone and fell softly onto the counter.

"Well?" prodded Mr. Pfeiffer, pushing the cone closer to Margie. It loomed large and luscious before her. Slowly she slid the quarter across the counter.

Margie took her time walking home from the store. She had the feeling that she had better be finished eating the ice cream cone before she got back and informed Uncle Lenny about the beer. It had been a long time since she had had ice cream. Usually, in the summer months, when everyone was working steadily, they had ice cream on Saturday nights. But never in the long winter. She slowed her pace a little more so she could relish the sweet cream a little longer.

Lenny was waiting expectantly for his can of beer. Margie looked intently at her toes as she explained to him about Mr. Pfeiffer not being able to sell it to her. Lenny stared in disbelief.

"What the hell kind of store is that anyways what won't sell no drink for cash!" he exploded. "Where's the quarter I give you?" Margie didn't answer. She just stood very still in front of him. The ice cream rolled heavily around in her stomach. When Lenny realized what she had done, he sucked his breath in hard. He felt inadequate in the situation; no one had ever put him in such a position before. Margie waited.

"Son's a bitchin' li'l bastard!" he muttered. "Sissy, come here!" he bellowed. "That white bastard down the road won't give the young'in no beer."

Sissy hurried to the open door. "Maybe 'cause he don't know us, baby." she offered as explanation. Then without saying anymore she walked slowly out to the road, holding her hand over her heart as if to keep it in place. Margie wondered why Uncle Lenny didn't use his car to go get his own beer . . . Sissy disappeared around the bend in the road.

"I ain't seen nothin' so 'diculous in all my life!" Mama stomped her feet and slammed the door behind Lenny's back. Opening the door again, she yelled, "Child, get in this house this minute." Margie's feet moved like lead up the step past Uncle Lenny.

"What you mean buyin' beer?" Mama demanded of Margie when she had got inside.

"But, Mama, I didn't buy no beer. Mr. Pfeiffer wouldn't sell it to me."

"Humph, same thin'. You *was* goin' to if Mr. Pfeiffer would of give it to you." Mama felt a new respect for Mr. Pfeiffer. Unaware of the federal laws on alcohol, she thought that Mr. Pfeiffer must be a very religious man to refuse a sale in order to save an innocent child from the grasp of Satan.

When Sissy returned with Lenny's beer, she was panting and gasping. She clutched her breast in agony. Lenny ignored her gestures and, without even a thank you, ripped the pull tab off the top of the can and guzzled a long draught. Sissy struggled up the step and went into the house.

Bertha flung her arms around her baby sister and wept. "How you ever put up with that no good, lazy man?"

"Now, Bertha, Lenny a fine man," Sissy, still gasping, defended. "But he gots a bad back and can't do all the thin's he likes to do." Sissy flopped onto the big bed to recuperate. She lay there the rest of the afternoon until dinner.

"Take Reggie outside so he don't 'sturb your Aunt Sissy," Mama told Margie.

Margie picked up the baby and carried him outside. She took him way around to the back of the house so she would not be so near to Uncle Lenny. She worried that Aunt Sissy might die.

When her sisters came home Margie did not tell them of the events of the afternoon. Mama didn't either.

Aunt Sissy was fully recovered by dinnertime. She joined the family at the table. She was just as bubbling as ever and showed no adverse effects from her death march down the road. Margie was truly amazed by the miracle.

Margie shook a little salt on her corn bread. She didn't like corn bread; it was always biscuits in their house because that's what they liked. But Lenny liked corn bread. And since the oven was too small to bake both biscuits and corn bread and since both had to be served piping hot straight from the oven to be any good; well, they had corn bread now.

After dinner, when the table had been cleared of the dishes, Margie sat down to do her homework. She had twenty-five problems in multiplication to do. Lenny remained at the table sipping his coffee and sucking on a piece of broom straw that he had used to clean his teeth. It was a warm evening and the air inside had become oppressive from the hot stove, so the rest of the family had gone out onto the porch. Mama and Sissy sat on one side while the girls huddled on the far opposite side to giggle and discuss the habits of the boys Teresa and Gayla had encountered in the halls at school.

Margie felt uncomfortable alone in the kitchen with Uncle Lenny. She hoped he wasn't still mad about the quarter she had spent. Her stomach trembled a little at the thought. She guessed it was the ice cream that had never digested and that such phenomena was the sure work of the devil. She stared at the problems before her but was unable to separate the numbers in the blurred columns.

"Havin' trouble?" Lenny asked. Margie did not look up; she just nodded her head. She just knew Uncle Lenny was smiling that peculiar smile that she had come to hate so much. She wondered why his smile always made her scalp hot and tingly.

"Hell, I can help you," Lenny offered, pulling her paper toward him. " 'Rithmatic is my specialty. Let's see what we got here now," he mumbled, as he pulled his chair around the corner of the table so he could be on the same side with Margie. Margie stiffened as he leaned toward her. Still she did not look up.

"Now you see here, the way you do it easy like is just 'tend you're addin' 'stead of multiplyin'. Four times eight is easy; see, you take four plus four makes eight, then eight plus 'nother four makes twelve, then twelve plus 'nother four makes sixteen," he added diligently. Margie watched his left hand from the corner of her eye and saw the fingers bob up and down as he added. She had thought only children did it that way and was amazed that the experts also did it that way. Margie was also acutely aware of Lenny's right hand, which had crept around the back of her chair. It was now moving in from the chair and finally rested on her right arm. She sucked in her breath and held it. Suddenly Margie leapt from her chair as Lenny's hand slid deftly under her arm and around the front of her where it clamped gently, but tightly, on the spot where her bosom would be if she had had one. She ran from the house onto the porch where her Mama and Aunt Sissy were still babbling on and on.

"What's the matter with you, chile?" Mama asked in surprise.

"Hot in there and I can't study," Margie answered breathlessly.

"Lord, you ain't never goin' to mount to nothin' the way you shucks off your studies!" warned Mama.

Lenny was standing in the frame of the door now. He was still smiling at Margie. She felt sick in her stomach and raced around to the backyard where she vomited violently. She was sure her illness was caused from the ice cream—her sin. She vowed never to eat ice cream again as long as she lived. Now, the dogs lapped at the vomit. Margie returned to the front porch. No one had noticed that she had gone nor that she had now returned, except Lenny; he still smiled at her.

That night Margie lay awake long after everyone else was asleep. She listened to the flip-flap of Lenny's snoring. She felt the flush creep into her cheeks again as she remembered his fat hand on her breast. She wondered why she felt so ashamed. She had often listened to her sisters' accounts of romancing and dancing. They had often referred, giggling, to the warmth of a hand cupped around their breast. It had always sounded so good and snugly to Margie. Often she had dreamed of the day when she would be thirteen and Mama would let her go off with a boy and always in her dream he walked backwards in front of her with his hands cupped under her breasts. She had practiced strutting with her chest thrust out so her tiny budding breasts would be more accessible to her imaginary date. Now she was mortified by the sight of the fat black hand of her uncle that lay limp in repose across his heaving stomach.

All day Saturday Margie avoided Uncle Lenny. He followed her with his eyes though, always with that sweet smile crimped around his lips. Margie noticed that her sisters also avoided Uncle Lenny. She wondered if he had helped them with their homework, too. Mama didn't seem to notice any of this; she was so busy being happy with her baby sister.

After dinner on Saturday night London asked Mama if she could attend choir practice at church. Mama was delighted in this sudden church-oriented interest of London's and took it as an indication that she might be contemplating sanctity.

"My girls do sing good," Mama commented proudly to Sissy as London disappeared into the bedroom to dress for "church."

"Humph," Sissy responded suspiciously, as she leaned forward in her chair and peeked around the corner of the bedroom door as London sprayed herself heavily with cologne. Then the two women went back to their previous occupation.

Just as London slipped off her old dress, she looked up to see Lenny leaning against the frame of the bedroom door. He was smiling.

"What the hell you lookin' at, ol' man?" she gasped.

Lenny didn't answer, just smiled and continued to ogle London. London pulled the coverlet from the bed and held it in front of her. "Get you ass out of here!" she hissed, " 'fore I scream for you wife." Lenny turned, still smiling, and walked out to the porch. Mama and Sissy had been too preoccupied to notice.

"Son-of-a-bitch queer," mumbled London, as she quickly pulled on her dress.

"Have a good evenin'," Mama purred, as London left the house for "choir practice." "There is a nice lot of young'ins in the choir." Mama smiled at Sissy.

"Uh huh," acknowledged Sissy following London's departure with a still suspicious eye

Margie sat a long time on the step of the porch. Finally, sucking in her breath and pulling herself to her full height, she went inside. Standing in front of Mama she blurted, "Mama, do you think it proper Uncle Lenny should be sleepin' in with all us womens?"

At first Mama just stared at Margie in disbelief. Then, laughing, she said, "Lord, chile, you sure do come up with some funny notions. Lenny's your uncle, chile. That ain't same as a *man*." Sissy looked apologetically at her husband, who was leaning, hands in pockets, against the door jamb.

"Shows you what can happen when ain't never a man 'round the house. The child don't know how to act when one do come 'round," Sissy said. Lenny just shrugged his shoulders. Margie's whole body heated with shame as the three adults stared at her. Why was she so stupid? Lenny *was* her uncle!

Still he made her feel uncomfortable—still she didn't like him and intended to avoid him whenever possible but she would not be rude again— he *was* her uncle.

Chapter IV

School always seemed to drag the last two weeks. Everyone, students and teachers alike, found the sweltering May temperatures chip away at their dispositions. Margie had a hard time concentrating on her studies with Mrs. Tierling, and Mrs. Tierling found it equally difficult to remain patient with Margie. Margie was glad when it was finally all over. She had passed and she had known that she was going to pass some weeks before that last day. Knowing that she would be in junior high next year made it even harder for her to settle down into sixth-grade work. Next year, junior high, she could hardly believe it. It seemed to Margie that the years since she had been born had crept at such a slow pace, almost as if to tease her, and now, she found herself being propelled at a dizzying pace toward that magic age—thirteen.

Those early days of June continued in humid suffocating heat. Nathan's Grill became the daily scene of small groups of farmers who sat and sipped coffee in worried silence. The western part of the state fared well and that knowledge made it even harder for the farmers to reconcile the lack of rain for their crops. The searing heat seemed to suck all moisture from the few clouds that escaped the greedy Piedmont and mountain area, leaving only dry cotton puffs to tease the parched sandy coastal plains.

"Turn that radio up so we can hear it," Billy Winston shouted.

"It's as loud as it'll go; you deaf or somethin'?" Nathan replied from behind the counter. Billy strained to hear above the clank of dishes being washed. The exhaust fan pulled noisily at the hot stagnant air in the room. Looking at his watch, Billy began to fret and drum his fingers anxiously on the table top—11:58—the noon weather report was about to come on.

"Gawddamn it!" he boomed, jumping to his feet. "Can't that nigger stop all that clanking and banging for just a few minutes!"

Marie looked up from her task at the sink. Nathan nodded to her to comply with Billy's demand. She shrugged her shoulders and after drying her hands on the end of her apron she leaned languidly against the sink and lit up a cigarette to enjoy her unscheduled break.

"Gawddamn niggers haven't any sense at all," Billy grumbled. Marie stared blank-eyed at the suds in the sink. She was used to it and didn't let Billy's wrath at the weather disturb her tranquillity now. Billy really must have been beside himself because he rarely used that degrading term "nigger" anymore, complying with the newer term "blacks." After all, it was he who had initiated the extra smoking break for her. She could overlook a little relapse now and again.

Everyone sat forward on the edges of their chairs as Tom Woods, the meteorologist from station WZAG in Greenburg, began reading his weather statistics in a dry impersonal monotone.

"Damn Yankee! Doesn't give a damn about the farmer. Doesn't matter to him whether it rains or not," Billy muttered, as he listened to the drone of the forecaster's voice.

" . . . and so it looks like another several days before we can even look for rain. They're getting it in the Piedmont but it just doesn't seem to be able to get this far east, ha, ha," Tom Woods concluded his report.

Billy Winston banged his fist on the table and kicked his chair. It topped backwards with a shattering crash to the floor as he stormed from the restaurant.

"You'd think with all those fang-dangled rain dances Billy puts on we'd be having a deluge by now," chuckled Woody Reed.

"It isn't funny any more," Jerry said soberly. "If we don't get rain soon the tobacco will burn out before it's even grown. Some's already startin' to burn.

Sissy and Lenny sat on the front porch fanning themselves with homemade fans they had made by pleating a couple of brown grocery bags. Bertha pumped a rubber plumbers plunger up and down in a tubful of sudsy clothes. The action simulated the agitator of a washing machine. An ancient wringer-type washer sat unused on the front porch.

"Wisht I knew someone who could fix the plug on that washer 'chine," she said wistfully as she pumped the plunger up and down. No one answered. It was too hot to talk. Everyone had slipped into that oppressive depression that comes when there is no air to breathe and nothing to do but sit and watch the pale blue sky shimmer in its own heat.

London's day work had aborted as soon as school was out and all the white families in town had migrated to the beach for the summer. London hadn't had a cigarette since that last day's pay. She could do nothing to relieve the tension now but chew at her fingernails, which were already gnawed to the quick. She hadn't even been out an evening for the last few weeks. Randy had finally succumbed to Mary Edwards's wiggling hips. Reggie tugged at her dress with his free hand; the other hand was in his mouth in an attempt to stave off his hunger till their next meager meal. His cookies had been relegated to the luxury level, along with London's cigarettes. London shoved him away impatiently. He plopped to the floor and absently pulled at his bare toes.

"When's Uncle Lenny goin' over to that 'tater chip plant and get hisself a job!" Margie asked Mama.

He had been with them for several weeks now and had not as yet made such a gesture. Now that the weather was so hot, he rarely moved from his spot on the porch. He had rummaged through the dump pile in the backyard until he had found himself a fairly solid wooden crate. The crate became his personal throne on the porch. In her efforts to avoid the lecherous grin, Margie spent most of her time sitting under the pecan tree in the side yard. Years ago someone had tied an old rubber automobile tire onto one of the branches with a heavy rope. Margie liked to sit in the snug circle of the tire and swing back and forth in time with the jay birds' mocking chatter. But the yellow flies were already beginning to be a plague. They bit at her bare arms and legs, leaving angry itching welts. Already Margie had scratched her ankles raw. But it was either the fly bites or the oppressive heat of the shack, unless, of course, she wanted to sit on the porch with Uncle Lenny.

"I reckon your uncle don't 'tend to go into town to get no job 'longs he can sit out there and fan hisself," Mama answered to Margie's question.

"Aunt Sissy said she's goin' to 'ply for welfare," said Teresa.

"Uh huh," mumbled London. "When she takes up her wings and flies to Greensburg to the welfare office."

"Reckon the welfare lady'd come here, if we call?" Teresa asked.

"Why can't that lazy ass drive his car into Greensburg?" asked Gayla.

"It ain't got no gas," reminded Teresa.

"Oh yeah, shit, I forgot. I bet he drained it out so's he couldn't use it. He knowed if he got a car what run, he'd have to go to Greensburg. He's lazy but he ain't dumb."

"You better hush," ordered Mama from beside her tub of laundry.

She had long lost the delight of having guests in the crowded little house, but she didn't like her girls to malign a relative. And besides, she loved her sister dearly. It was only Lenny who had made it difficult for her to reconcile herself to their visit.

Reggie began to whimper. He had sucked on his thumb long enough and now wanted milk. London got him a cup of lukewarm coffee.

"Miz Levine says coffee ain't good for babies. She says babies gots to have milk every day. Reggie ain't had no milk for a long time," Margie remarked.

"You think I don't know Reggie 'posed to have milk?" said London. "What you think I should do 'bout it, Miss Smart Ass, find a cow tit hangin' on a tree somewheres?"

Margie flushed, she should have kept her mouth shut. "Maybe when I'm done here I can walk down to Pfeiffer's and call the welfare peoples." Mama reflected.

"Well somebody better," said Teresa, "or we all goin' to be out grubbin' with the hogs. Can't make the one welfare check what we got make do for that—you know what he looks like when he eats? He looks like a big ol' combine. He just run 'long the plates on the table and gobble up everything." Mama gave Teresa a long hard look but she didn't reprimand her.

Sissy and Lenny fanned themselves on the porch.

Bertha handed two soda bottles to Mr. Pfeiffer. He gave her a dime so she could use his telephone, which hung on the wall just inside the door of his store. All the while he grumbled about having to buy the bottles, which he knew she had picked up from somewhere in the ditch. They'd probably not even come from his store. (Usually he would not take bottles for cash, only for merchandise.) Bertha smiled graciously as he put the dime into the palm of her hand. She knew that he'd get his dime back from the drink salesmen when they came to get the empties, and she knew that he was not being especially generous now but still she was grateful.

Hesitating a moment, she handed the dime back to Mr. Pfeiffer.

"Will you make the call for me, Mr. Pfeiffer?" she asked. "I can't 'member how you tol' me to do it."

Mr. Pfeiffer sighed; he would never understand how these people got along at all in this modern mechanized world. "Okay," he answered reluctantly. "Who do you want to call?"

"The welfare peoples."

Mr. Pfeiffer sighed again; he'd have to look the number up in the phone book. Finding the number, he dialed the phone then he handed it to Bertha. Bertha backed away. "You talk," she said.

"It's not my call. Now come on, take the phone," he insisted.

"Pitt County Welfare Department, may I help you?" a voice on the other end said.

Mr. Pfeiffer looked from Bertha to the phone then finally he said into the phone, "Uh, just a minute." Then thrusting the phone at Bertha he hissed, "They're on the line, now tell them what you want."

Bertha backed farther away and said, "Tell them to send somebody out to sign up Lenny."

"Who the hell is Lenny?" Mr. Pfeiffer whispered hoarsely, holding his hand over the receiver.

"He's my brother-in-law," Bertha answered simply.

"Well, you tell them," he said again, thrusting the phone receiver her way.

Bertha shook her head adamantly. Mr. Pfeiffer rolled his eyes upwards and mumbled a brief prayer of frustration, then spoke into the receiver, "Hello, this is Ed Pfeiffer—of Pfeiffer's Grocery—out on Route 3—Gum Swamp Road. Well, this here Mrs. Braxton, Bertha Braxton, wants you to send someone around to sign up her brother-in-law."

"Is the family having problems?" the voice on the other end asked.

"How the hell should I know? Mrs. Braxton's here now—but she won't talk on the damn phone. Why don't you folks just send someone around to them and see what they want?"

"Just a moment, please," the voice said.

Mr. Pfeiffer began pacing back and forth as far as the telephone cord would allow him. After some moments another voice sounded on the line. "Hello, this is Miss Scott, your case worker. May I help you, Mr. Braxton?"

"I'm not Mr. Braxton! I'm Ed Pfeiffer and I'm placing this call for Mrs. Braxton!"

"I see. Is Mrs. Braxton indisposed?" Miss Scott asked.

"Damn it, she's right here, but she won't talk on the phone," Mr. Pfeiffer sputtered.

"I see. Well perhaps I can induce her to talk on the phone. Please ask her to come to the phone."

Mr. Pfeiffer rolled his eyes in anguish. What had he been saying? She won't talk on the phone? Holding the receiver limply toward Bertha, he shrugged and said, "They want to talk to you." To his surprise Bertha took the receiver immediately. Scratching his head in confusion, he backed away.

"You there?" Bertha shouted into the receiver. "You there, send me somebody 'round to sign up my brother-in-law."

"Is he ill—disabled?" Miss Scott asked.

"Yeah, he's disabled," Bertha replied.

"I see," Miss Scott said. "Well, if you bring him into the office, I'm sure we can help him."

"Can't," Bertha answered.

"Can't?"

"Can't," Bertha repeated.

Miss Scott sighed. She was familiar with the problems of the poor blacks who depended on tobacco for their living. It was probably also true that they could not make it into the office. Yes, she would come out to them.

"All right, Mrs. Braxton," Miss Scott agreed. "I'll come out to you. Now let me make sure we have your address correct. Box #421, Route 3. Is that correct?"

"No, ma'am," corrected Bertha. "I live on Gum Swamp Road."

Mr. Pfeiffer pulled the receiver away from Bertha and shouted, "She lives on Route 3, about half mile past my grocer—Pfeiffer's Grocery . . . Are you sending someone out?"

"Yes, sir. Thank you, sir. I'll be out there as soon as I can. Tell her I'll be out in a few days, as soon as I can."

"Jeez!" Mr. Pfeiffer sighed. "That's a relief. Thanks a lot. I'll tell her."

Mr. Pfeiffer hung up the receiver and, sinking onto an empty soft drink case, wiped his forehead. "Someone will be out in a couple of days, Mrs. Braxton."

"Oh, thank you, Mr. Pfeiffer. You're such a nice man, I always knowed you was nice. I sure do thank you," Bertha bubbled, as she hurried out the door and headed for home to tell the others. Ed Pfeiffer stayed for a long time on the empty soda case. It had been a long, hard morning.

"Mr. Caldwell," the woman from the welfare office said, "you're going to have to get a statement from your doctor describing the nature of your injury before I can process this claim."

Lenny viciously slapped at a fly that had settled on the stubble of his beard. "What the hell! You think I lyin'? You think I want anything from you white bastards?" he defended himself. "All I wants is what's right for my sick wife here." Though she was embarrassed by Lenny's denouncement of the white welfare workers Sissy played the role he had set for her and breathed a little deeper and held her hand to her bosom to emphasize her illness. The woman did not look up from her notes. She was used to such affronts; it was one of the hazards of being a social worker. Bertha fumed in embarrassed agony from the other side of the porch.

"I'm sorry, sir, but it's procedure," Miss Scott apologized.

"And how you 'spect me to get to a doctor when I ain't got one penny to buy gas for my automobile?" he questioned sarcastically.

56

The woman glanced at the battered car sitting alongside of the house. It wasn't only gasoline that it needed—both rear tires, bald of any tread, sat flat against the ground.

"I'm sure we can arrange to have someone carry you into town to your doctor," Miss Scott answered. "By the way, who is your doctor?"

"He goes to Dr. Ellison—Richard T. Ellison," Bertha answered before Lenny could find his foul tongue again.

"All right, we'll arrange for someone to carry you in to Dr. Ellison," said Miss Scott as she got up from the porch step to leave. Dusting at the back of her dress, she added, "I'll be getting back with you in a couple of days." Then addressing Bertha, she said, "Mrs. Braxton, are you receiving food stamps? You're eligible, you know." Bertha was only scantily familiar with the stamp program and had never applied for it because it was almost impossible for her to get to the distribution center to purchase them.

"No, ma'am. Ain't no way for me to get to town to get them," she informed Miss Scott.

"Oh, my," Miss Scott fretted. "But, Mrs. Braxton, you can have them mailed to you. You can have the money taken right out of your welfare check and the stamps will be sent right along with the remainder of your check." She paused, wondering if Bertha had understood her.

Bertha reflected for a moment. "Can't 'ford no money to be taken out of my welfare check," she said.

"But, Mrs. Braxton, you *have to* buy food anyway, and it would be a tremendous savings if you would use the stamps."

Bertha knew nothing about savings; she only knew that she did not want anyone to take anything out of her check. "I'll think 'bout it," she now stalled.

The welfare woman sighed; she knew that Bertha did not understand. Many of the poor eschewed government aid for just that reason. They just did not understand. Shaking her head in despair, she picked her way through the debris that had begun to spread around to the front of the house from the backyard dump heap. The family watched her disappear around the bend in her car.

It was only two days later when the Miss Scott returned. Lenny was still sitting on the porch fanning himself. Miss Scott envisioned him as having grown to the box, his arms and legs hanging like fat limbs of a tree.

"Good morning, Mr. Caldwell. I've arranged for Mrs. Lawry from Maylor to carry you in to Dr. Ellison. She's one of our volunteers. And I've made an appointment with the doctor for you for one-thirty on this coming Friday. Mrs. Lawry will pick you up at one. Do you know Mrs. Lawry?"

"Uh, uh," Lenny answered sullenly. He had developed a searing hatred for this woman that he thought was patronizing him and making him feel like a little kid. He was sure that she didn't believe he had a bad back. He *did* have a bad back.

"That the Miz Lawry what lives in the big two-story house by the park in town?" Bertha asked, as she came to the door.

"Yes, I believe that's the one," Miss Scott answered. "She's a lovely woman and I'm sure you'll get along just fine with her."

Bertha knew her and agreed that she was a lovely lady. Once she had washed the windows in the big two-story house and the woman had given her a little extra than the two-dollars-an-hour wage. But Lenny would not acknowledge that any white "welfare" person was lovely. In fact, he was sure that he would not like this Miz Lawry any more than Miss Scott.

"In the meantime, I do have some groceries that I was able to get to tide you over. I felt, since the baby and all, well, it seemed proper to put in a 'hardship claim' for you for the time being." Then nodding toward Margie, the woman said, "Honey, can you come out to my car and help me carry in the groceries?"

When they had put the boxes and bags on the table, Miss Scott said to Bertha, "I do wish you'd let me help you apply for food stamps. I'm sure once you adjusted to the program, you'd find that it was very beneficial for you." Bertha fingered the packages sticking out from the top of one of the boxes.

"Uh, huh. I'll thin' 'bout it." Miss Scott knew she was beating a dead dog. Bertha would never allow anyone to "take" money from her welfare check.

When Miss Scott had gone, Bertha gingerly pulled one of the packages from one of the boxes. She felt hot tears of humiliation well into her eyes. She had never minded the welfare checks because somehow she mistakenly had gotten the idea that the money was withheld from her wages when she worked. She felt entitled to it. But a "hardship case"! That sounded like pure charity. Bertha had never taken charity in her life! But then, Reggie needed milk. She began putting the things out onto the table. The girls watched in silence.

"What's that stuff?" Lenny asked as he came in from the porch to supervise the emptying of the boxes. "They don't 'spect me to eat that stuff, do they!" He poked a fat finger at a box of instant grits.

"It ain't just for you, you know. It's for ever'body," London reminded him sarcastically.

The boxes yielded mostly staples; flour, lard, sugar, cornmeal, instant grits, chocolate and powdered milk.

"There ain't no coffee," Teresa noted.

"There ain't nothin' fittin' to eat neither," pouted Lenny.

"I'm goin' make Reggie some milk," London said, grabbing up the box of powdered milk. Reggie danced and clapped excitedly as he watched his mother mix the powder with water, turning it magically into a cool glass of milk. London sipped a little from the glass before offering it to the baby. He stomped impatiently. Everyone watched with pleasure as Reggie drained the glass in one gulp and held it out for more—everyone except Lenny, who was still rummaging through the groceries.

"Hell, there ain't nothin' in here fit for peoples," he grumbled. "That's 'cause they think we ain't peoples." No one paid any attention to him. Bertha's pride had been abashed by the "hardship" boxes but she did have the good graces to be thankful, if only for the baby's needs.

When Mrs. Lawry arrived at noon on Friday for Lenny, he wasn't ready for her.

"Why the hell she here so early?" he asked Sissy suspiciously.

"Just hush, sugar, and get yourself dressed."

"They say one thing and mean somethin' else. They just plain-ass stupid," he grumbled as he put on the clean underwear that Sissy held out for him.

"You can't wear those," Sissy gasped when he had gotten them on. "They got a hole in the ass part."

"Ain't goin' hurt none. I'm wearing pants on top of 'em."

"No, no. You'll have to get undressed at the doctor's and they'll see the hole. Take 'em off so's I can sew 'em up."

"Oh, hell," grumbled Lenny as he struggled out of the underpants that were now sticking to him because the efforts of dressing had brought the sweat beading out of his body.

When he had gotten them off, Sissy took them and went looking for Bertha.

"Bertha, honey, you gots some cotton and a needle so I can sew up Lenny's underpants?"

"I think so," answered Bertha. She rummaged through a shoebox that was in one of the "sideboard" crates. Finding a spool of white cotton thread and a needle she handed them to Sissy.

"Can you, maybe, sew this here hole for me?" whined Sissy. "You know how bad my arthritis is. These fingers just don't work so good anymore."

Bertha sighed and took hold of the underwear and began stitching up the hole. Lenny fussed and fumed as he stomped naked about in the bedroom. Mrs. Lawry sat on Lenny's crate on the front porch, fanning the heat and flies away from her head. Reggie sat on the porch floor and stared at her. She smiled at him, but Reggie did not know this new white lady and had no smile in his repertoire for her. The two passed the time staring at each other.

Sissy handed Lenny the repaired underwear and stood silently by as he grumbled and struggled to get himself dressed. All this commotion was making him more impatient by the minute. He thought to himself, *One more thing and I ain't goin' nowhere.*

Lenny rode to Maylor in pouting silence. He didn't like riding while a woman drove. And he never ever thought that he would have to ride while a *white* woman drove. It was almost more humiliation than one red-blooded black man could handle in one day. Mrs. Lawry tried to make small talk, but Lenny only grunted in reply. Finally she gave up the effort and completed the trip in silence. Lenny took in the scenery as it unfolded before him. He'd not been to town before.

"I'll wait out here," Mrs. Lawry said, as she parked in front of the doctor's office. "Dr. Ellison probably isn't back from lunch yet, but you'll be the first patient when he does get back."

The reception room was empty when Lenny went in. Looking around at the empty seats, he chose one that had a magazine lying open on it. Picking up the magazine, he sat down and began to thumb through it.

"Excuse me, sir, but do you have an appointment?" a woman's voice asked. Lenny swung around looking for the source of the question. A young woman had suddenly materialized from behind the reception desk near the door.

"You talkin' to me?" he asked.

"Yes, sir. Do you have an appointment?"

" 'Course I do," he answered indignantly. He wasn't sure if he had one or not but decided to bluff it just in case he didn't have one.

"What is your name, sir?"

"Leonard Raymond Caldwell, Jr.," he answered proudly. The girl ran her finger down the list of names on the desk in front of her till she located

Leonard Caldwell then placed a check mark behind it.

"Have you ever seen Dr. Ellison before?" she asked.

" 'Course not. I just moved here from Mississippi," he replied.

The receptionist sighed. She would have to fill out a "new patient" form for him. She was sure that he'd not be able to do it alone.

"Mr. Caldwell, because you are a new patient, I'm going to have to get some information from you. I'll need to know your age, birthdate, social security number, address, and I'll also need to know about any health problems you've had till now, like operations, diseases, etc."

Lenny looked up in confusion. That seemed like an awful lot of questions. What did they need all that for? His suspicious nature began weaving a great web of government intrigue. He'd better think carefully before he answered anything.

The interrogation went smoothly until they had come to the "operations and diseases" phase. Lenny had had no operations that he could remember. As for diseases, what the hell was a disease? Chicken pox? He didn't know. Measles? He didn't know. Diabetes? What was that? Seizures? What was that. Hypertension? Now they were really getting crazy. The receptionist decided that this was the best that she could do, thanked Lenny for his cooperation, and left him to his magazine.

As Lenny continued to look at the pictures in the magazine, other patients began coming in and registering at the desk. They sat in the chairs along the walls of the room and chatted amiably around Lenny. Once in a while someone would stare at him with curiosity. He buried his nose deeper into his magazine. Dr. Ellison's patients were all from the town or from the rural area immediately surrounding the town. All knew each other and enjoyed the waiting time in the reception room with gossip and small talk. For many, especially the older patients, it was the only time they got out to visit with others. It was a social time for them. But Lenny was a stranger to them and they to him. He didn't feel like visiting anyway.

"Mr. Caldwell," the receptionist finally called and beckoned him into the doctor's office. After the preliminary of weighing in and temperature taking and checking of blood pressure by Dr. Ellison's nurse, Lenny was left alone in the examining room to wait for the doctor. He didn't have to wait long because he was the first patient of the afternoon.

Richard Ellison was a tall, lean man in his late thirties. His father before him and his grandfather before that had been the town physicians. Dick Ellison fell heir to the practice by virtue of being the only son of "Old Doc Ellison." As such, he was loved and respected by all of Maylor. He was the reincarnation of both "Old Doc Ellisons." Many of his elderly patients could remember expectantly awaiting his birth when they had been patients of his father. They loved to tease him about his boyhood years and what a skittish young'en he had been. And he loved it when they teased him.

To Lenny, sitting alone in a room filled with strange equipment and no windows, it seemed like hours before the doctor came in. Looking at Lenny's chart, he said, "You're Bertha Braxton's brother-in-law?"

"Uh, huh," Lenny agreed, becoming somewhat shy now in the face of the doctor.

"Hmmm. This says you've got some sort of back trouble. How long have you had it?"

"Since las' Chris'mas when I worked at the mills in Mississippi."

"Uh, huh. Well, let's see what we've got here." The doctor stood up and approached Lenny. "Stick out your tongue."

"What's that got to do with my back?" complained Lenny suspiciously as he thrust his tongue out to meet the tongue depressor that Dr. Ellison held forth.

"Just want to check you all over," mumbled the doctor as he peered down Lenny's throat. "Now say 'eeee'!" Lenny tried unsuccessfully to say it but it always came out "ah." His scalp tingled in embarrassment at failing to comply with the doctor's wishes. He didn't know that this was one of Dr. Ellison's pet jokes. The doctor enjoyed watching his patients attempt to say "eeeee" while their mouths were propped open with his wooden tongue depressor. Most of his patients laughed as they consistently failed the task. But they knew Dr. Ellison. Lenny did not and he felt foolish.

Lenny watched with suspicion as the doctor wrote something on the paper in the folder on the desk. After he had completely examined him from head to toe, Dr. Ellison leaned back in his chair and observed Lenny for a brief moment. Lenny squirmed in discomfort under the scrutiny.

"Mr. Caldwell, I really can't find a thing wrong with your back," Dr. Ellison finally said. "In fact, I think it would be good for you to get out and work and especially try to take some of that weight off. You know when you carry all that extra weight around it can really make your back feel tired and achy. Now, I don't know just what kind of injury you had back at Christmas, but whatever it was it doesn't seem to be limiting you now. You move around quite well for a man of your size and age." Lenny gaped at the doctor. Having gotten no response and thinking that Lenny didn't understand him, the doctor added, "Mr. Caldwell, I simply can't, at this time, recommend you for welfare. You're an able-bodied man and ought to be out working for your own bread."

Lenny slid down from the examining table and, without a word, dressed himself. Dr. Ellison watched in puzzled amusement. He was familiar with men like Lenny and wondered just what Lenny would do now that he was not eligible for welfare payments. Lenny walked brusquely out of the doctor's office.

"Good-bye, Mr. Caldwell," Dr. Ellison called after him. Lenny didn't acknowledge the farewell.

Mrs. Lawry was waiting for him when he left the building. She drove him home without intruding on his pouting withdrawal.

Sissy soothed Lenny, "What that ol' doctor know 'bout backs. He ain't no specialist. You needs a specialist, baby."

"Dr. Ellison's the finest doctor in the whole county," defended Bertha. "And if he say there ain't nothin' wrong with Lenny's back, then there ain't."

Lenny returned to his perch on the porch to reflect on his dilemma. Margie, who had been sitting on the porch in his absence, skittered off and ran around to the swing in the pecan tree. She hoped maybe Uncle Lenny would get a job now and not be around the house all the time. Ever since that first night when she had found herself alone with him she had made heroic efforts to avoid him. Sometimes, however, there was nothing she could do about it and was forced into situations where she was alone with him. At such times he always put his arm around her and smiled. Sometimes he nuzzled her ear. She always felt sick to her stomach. Her scalp would tingle and burn and she felt sure she would die before he would release her.

At Bertha's insistence, Lenny thumbed a ride into Greensburg on Monday. He went around to the potato chip plant and stood in the long line of applicants for nearly an hour. Mopping his forehead with his bare hand, he stepped up to the personnel desk. After having been told that the plant was taking no more applications for the present because of the rapid drop in the country's economy, he sighed a somewhat relieved "Thank you" and headed for the highway to begin thumbing back home. He wished he had a quarter for a soda; a soda would sure go good. Maybe Bertha would get off his back now, he reflected, as he waited in the sun alongside the highway for someone to pick him up. No one could blame him for the country's economy. No one could expect him to work if he couldn't even get an application to fill out.

Sissy joined Lenny in the long hot days on the porch. Together they fanned themselves. Bertha and her girls waited. Waited for the rain to come.

The rain that would turn the latent tobacco fields into an income for them. Miss Scott from the welfare office had been back twice in an attempt to encourage Bertha to purchase the food stamps. Bertha was adamant. Now that Lenny had failed in his endeavor to get a job (he hadn't tried again since that day at the potato chip factory), she was sure that she didn't want anyone taking anything away from her welfare check. She concluded that she needed every penny that was due to her. Mr. Pfeiffer still carried them "on account."

Chapter V

When the rains finally came in the third week of June it was as if the sky had split in two from its load. The downpour, with its accompanying cold front, brought relief from the dizzying heat wave. The clouds that had been teasing the horizon for two days spread over the countryside dumping their life-preserving cargo onto the parched fields. At first the thirsty sand sucked at the water as it fell, pulling it deep into the dry granules, then begged for more.

The farmers gathered in Nathan's Grill for celebration. Soaked from the downpour outside they just shook the raindrops from their hair and laughed in relieved merriment. Even Billy Winston allowed his cream-colored Stetson to become all spotted with the glistening drops—drops of gold.

"Reckon it's in time?" he asked of the joyful forum that had gathered.

"Too late for the table corn and maybe too late for the field corn," observed Jerry Jordon. "But I think the tobacco will green up just fine and be OK. If we just wait a couple of days before going into the fields, we should be in good shape."

The rains continued. The sandy soil absorbed all it could then let it run off into the ditches. Creeks and ponds ran out of their banks. Roadside ditches were raging torrents, pushing debris through their channels.

And the rains continued. The Tar River that flowed through Greensburg rose to eighteen feet, flooded the town commons, and turned the lowlands to the north of it into swampland. Families living in the lowlands scurried for high ground, where they watched as the angry river raped them of their modest properties.

Again the meeting in Nathan's Grill assumed an ominous tone.

"Gawddamn rain, it'll drown us all," Billy Winston fumed.

"We asked for it," Jerry said glumly.

"We did. But if it keeps up much longer the tobacco will drown," Junie Warren admitted. "I already got some washed out by the roots."

"Anybody in low spots is bound to lose," observed Jerry.

"I'm banking my end rows with sand bags," Billy said as he prepared to return to his endangered fields. "And anybody with any sense'll do the same." He left. No one noticed his departure.

Margie listened to the water drip through the hole in the roof and plink into the bucket. Everyone was sleeping yet. Margie had awakened as the first light of dawn had filtered through the grimy windows. She couldn't get back to sleep. The pot nearby smelled strong with the ammonia of urine that had accumulated during the night.

In the dim light of the dawn, Margie noticed Lenny stir in his bed. Presently he sat up on the edge of the big bed. Sissy mumbled softly at the disturbance. Lenny sat quietly for a moment till Sissy settled back into her deep slumber, snoring. Slowly he eased himself to his feet trying not to make a sound. A loose spring groaned when he relieved it of his weight.

Margie squeezed her eyes shut as Lenny approached the bucket. She listened with disgust to the rush of water splash into the pot. When all was quiet again, except for the plinking of rain water into the other bucket, she dared to open her eyes.

She gasped as she looked up into the bulging belly of Lenny standing over her. He smiled and held his finger to his lips. The dawn light flicked spasmodically in her brain; her heart skipped a beat then resumed at a maddening pace. Lenny's underwear draped open in the front but Margie couldn't focus her eyes. Everything was a blur. She was paralyzed. She neither gained enough mobility to cry out or to budge during the next few moments. She thought perhaps she had died. She felt her head float upwards as her arms and legs sank like lead into the mattress of the cot.

Her body began to tingle as the interrupted blood supply returned and consciousness resumed. She did not move as she listened to the springs of the big bed squeal out in resistance as Lenny lowered his weight back onto them. She lay on her back, staring at the ceiling, listening for the satisfied snoring that would emanate from Lenny's slack, fat mouth. She lay like that until the sun rose high enough to force itself through the dust-coated windows and shine into Mama's eyes, awakening her.

Margie did not tell Mama about Lenny. She knew that even if Mama would believe her, Lenny would deny it and Aunt Sissy would convince her that Margie was just a silly little girl. She recalled the last time she had said something about Lenny's presence in the otherwise all-female bedroom.

"He's your uncle, honey," they had said. No, they'd never believe her. Rather, they would only ridicule her for her stupidity. She would never tell.

The rain finally petered sporadically to a stop on the first of July. Spot checking their fields, the farmers found, to their surprise, that the tobacco had suffered little damage. However, the lower leaves that had just begun to turn yellow before the rain had started had now greened up again. And though the farmers were anxious to get on with harvesting, they waited patiently for the leaves to again attain their ripened yellow hue.

It looked like a good year ahead in spite of the long siege of rain. The pink-flowered tops of the tall plants waved in the baking southern sun. A familiar perfume drifted across the fields permeating the air even as far as the town. It was a beautiful aroma; it was tobacco perfume. Its heaviness smelled of success, a grand lady at court.

Billy Winston stopped by the Braxton house on the Fourth of July. The family was sitting in the shade of the porch sipping cans of soda when he pulled into the yard. Bertha had splurged and charged the soft drinks to their account at Pfeiffer's so they could celebrate the holiday.

"Ya'll ready to go to work?" he greeted gaily as he got out of his truck. Yes, they were ready. All were bored with just sitting and fanning; all except Lenny. And it had been awhile since a full hearty meal had appeared on their table.

"Reckon you can use Margie this year?" Mama asked. "My sister, Sissy here, she can mind Reggie if you can use Margie." Margie gasped. Work tobacco! She had never dreamed that Mama would let her work tobacco. She hadn't even thought about the possibility of Aunt Sissy minding Reggie. Her heart began pounding an anxious beat.

Please, say yes, Mr. Winston. Please say yes, she thought. Billy smiled at Margie in mock surprise. She ducked her chin into her dress collar and grinned back in embarrassment.

"You don't mean to tell me that this here sweet baby has growed up already," he chuckled. Poking a finger under her chin and lifting her head so he could see her eyes, he gave her a coy wink. Margie smiled but would not look at him. She liked Mr. Winston. He was always nice to her, but she could not look at him now.

"Of course I can use a growed up girl like Margie," Billy continued to flatter. "Fact, I can use all the help I can get. I especially need some good primers." Billy eyed Lenny, who was trying to make his bulk look small on the old box that he sat on.

"Ain't never worked 'bacco 'fore," apologized Lenny. "Don't reckon I be no help to ya'll."

"Don't take long to learn—for a growed man," answered Billy. Bertha gave Lenny a fixed stare that said, "I dare you not to accept." He sighed in resignation. He knew he had just been hired.

"Know anybody else who wants to prime?" Billy asked of the family in general.

"No, don't know nobody," Bertha answered quickly, in an attempt to cut short Mr. Winston's visit. His presence put a damper on their party even though he had just been the bearer of the good news that work would begin soon.

But Gayla did not catch the note in Mama's voice and said, "What 'bout those white boys what stopped by here the other day. Wasn't they lookin' for work, Margie?"

"What white boys you talkin' 'bout," Mama demanded.

"That was Andy Taylor and his brother," Margie replied.

"What they want with us?" Mama insisted.

"Mama, Andy's just a boy in my class what was ridin' his bike out here with his brother. He said they was goin' fishin' over in Griston."

"Well?" Mr. Winston asked anxiously. "Did they want to work?"

"Yes, sir, Mr. Winston, but I didn't know you was needin' anybody so I told them to try at Mr. Monroe's farm."

Billy stomped his foot on the ground. He was fast losing hope of getting a crew together by harvest time, unless, of course, he used coercion. But he really didn't want to have to do that. He turned and stomped off to his car, hollering back over his shoulder, "I'll pick you up on Monday. It'll be dry enough to top and sucker by then."

Topping and suckering only paid $1.50 an hour, but it had to be done and it was work. And the Braxtons wanted work. Even Lenny began to feel the tingle of excitement at the thought of going to work. Being cooped up in the little house with seven other people for the duration of the rain had had its effects on his normal languidness.

"Whooee!" London shouted, swooping Reggie into her arms and executing a dance across the porch. "We are goin' to eat soon, baby." Reggie chuckled with delight at his mother's sudden gaiety.

The weekend was a testimony to the glory of the Lord. Blue skies, gentle breezes, the sun at a warm therapeutic temperature. Churches in the area were filled to overflowing with thankful believers. Preachers pointed out the generosity of the Almighty to their followers. Parties were held in anticipation of the beginning of harvest. Everyone was happy.

Margie had a hard time getting to sleep on Sunday night. She lay awake long past the midnight hour thinking about her coming debut into tobacco. Restless beyond the capacity for deep sleep, she awakened little more than an hour after having fallen to sleep. An ominous sound met her ears. The tin roof of the house echoed with the plink of rain drops. Margie lay on her cot and let the splatter in the puddles around the yard lull her into a feeling of despondency. Fretting and turning, unable to shut the noise from her ears she finally got out of bed and went into the kitchen.

She guessed it was nearing the dawn hour. Surely the rain would stop by the time the sun came up. Surely there was not enough up there, after the previous two weeks of downpour, to last for long. Margie poked gently at the remnants of last evening's fire in the stove. Barely a spark remained. Gingerly laying a piece of kindling on top of a tiny flicker of light among the coals, she puffed ever so softly into the belly of the big black stove. The tiny spark leapt as if to avoid her breath, snagged onto the kindling, flickered then sent a thin flame up from its bed. Margie lay a few more pieces of kindling crisscross over the flame. Soon the belly of the stove growled in satisfaction with its morning repast.

Margie fished a drowned fly out of the bucket of drinking water that sat on the sink. She filled the tea kettle. Setting it on top of the stove, she sat down at the table to resume her vigil of listening for the rain to stop.

One by one the others began emerging from their beds like moths from their cocoons. After each had given due expression to the state of the weather they all sat around the kitchen staring into their coffee cups. Lenny crawled back into bed.

The rain continued for three more days. The farmers sat silently at the long table in Nathan's Grill.

"Wish to hell somebody would buy something besides just coffee," Nathan grumbled. "Gotta keep the air conditioner going and the lights lit— running up my light bill—and I'm not making one penny off that sorry bunch of people out there." He absently wiped at the counter for the fourth time that morning. A fly winged out of the way of the wet rag, hovered overhead for just a second then returned to its feeding ground near the sugar jar.

The rain continued for three more days. . . .
Though the fields were soggy and slimy with wet sand and weeds, when Thursday dawned forth in sunshine, everyone went to work. Margie hopped as gracefully as she could into the back of Mr. Winston's truck.

"Ye-ow!" yelped Lenny. "Watch where you plant them gawd-awful feet!" Margie picked her way over the outstretched legs of the others and

69

settled into the corner of the truck that was right behind Mr. Winston. She had never ridden in a truck before and felt safer to be near the driver.

"We ought to be able to get this whole forty acres topped and suckered in one day," Mr. Winston ordered optimistically.

"He be crazy or somethin'?" asked London. "We be lucky to get ten acres done in a day, an' that be if we works our ass off." Billy ignored her objections.

Each hand went off to the head of a row of tobacco. Bertha shook her head in bewilderment at Mr. Winston and began to show Margie how to snap the top clean from the plant without tearing any leaves off.

"You go on down this row an' I'll follow behind an' get the suckers. This ev'ning, when you're used to it, you can do both," she said as she tossed the pink and white bouquet of the tobacco plant into the mud between the rows. Margie looked at the flower where it lay in its muddy grave. It was such a pretty flower. She wondered why such a pretty thing had to come to such a desolate end.

"Go on now, you try it," Mama ordered. Margie reached up for the flower stalk of the next plant in the row. She had to stand on her tiptoes because the plants had grown so tall with the long heavy rains. Pulling the flower down to her, she tugged at it several times before it finally tore loose with a jerk, carrying several tip leaves along with it.

"Mr. Winston ain' goin' stan' for much of that," warned Mama. "You got to snap at it fast. Like this. Break it clean." And she demonstrated again.

All morning long Margie reached high, tugged, snapped, and discarded the beautiful flowers. Sometimes she had to actually jump to grasp the tall flower stalks. Her three sisters moved swiftly down their rows, working a row on either side of them as they went. The right hand reached out in rhythm with the left, and snap, toss, the flower disappeared into the mud. Almost at the same time and without breaking the rhythm, they also caught hold of any obvious suckers and disposed of them along with the flowers. Lenny lumbered down his row, puffing and panting. Each time he grabbed a stalk he winced as the rough outer casing bit into the pudgy flesh of his fingers.

"Break time!" Mr. Winston bellowed from the truck at the end of the field. The women quickly emerged from their rows and trotted toward the truck. Lenny shuffled after them and soon was left far behind to make his way through the tall weeds at the ditch bank. The others were already sipping at their sodas by the time Lenny, panting and mopping his forehead on the sleeve of his shirt, finally ambled up to the truck.

70

"You better hurry up," warned Mama. "We only get fifteen minutes an' most of that's gone already." Lenny slumped against the fender of the truck and took a long swig from his bottle of soda. Wiping his hands across his burning lips, he let out a loud belch.

"You ought not to drink that so fast. You'll get the heaves," Bertha warned. Ignoring her warning, Lenny finished his bottle of soda in a second long gulp.

Teresa shook her head in disgust, and said, "He ain' got no sense."

Margie barely sipped at her soda. Her honey bun lay unopened on her lap. She had always enjoyed the sweet-smelling tobacco perfume that wafted on the summer breezes across the open fields to mask the stink of the open latrines and seething trash dumps. But in between the towering rows of tobacco now she had found the concentration of the perfume to be suffocating and nauseating. The sick, sweet smell gagged in the back of her throat. The hot sun beating on her head all morning had sent rivulets of sweat streaming from between the rows of her tight braids down over her forehead and cheeks. Once she had attempted to wipe the sweat from her face but the plant juice from her hands had stung her flesh like a lye bath. She thereafter let the sweat run where it may, even into her eyes where its salt stung and bit. She learned to blink rapidly, which forced a flood of tears to dilute the briny sweat.

"You better drink your soda an' eat that honey bun," advised Mama. "You're goin' to need your strength."

"Reckon she don' feel too good," Gayla said sympathetically. "I 'member when I first started in 'bacco, I got pure sick."

"If she drinks that soda slow, it'll make her feel better," Mama answered. She knew about the nausea that accosted the uninitiated. Margie sipped a little at a time, but the soda burned her throat where the acrid tobacco vapors had etched it sore.

"Okay, okay. Let's get back to work," snapped Mr. Winston. "Break's over." They reluctantly tossed their empty soda bottles into the truck and walked back to their individual rows. The first day was always the hardest.

Lenny didn't eat lunch. Instead he plopped across his bed and moaned in agony. Margie felt a twang of sympathy for the man. She could feel the knot in her own swollen gullet. But her moment of sympathy was short lived. As much as she too would have liked to give in to the terrible nausea, she would not. She would never allow herself any semblance of the blubbering Lenny, who was by now retching in agony. Aunt Sissy fretted and worried over her stricken husband. She wrung her hands and lifted her head to heaven and prayed. "Oh, Lawd, have mercy. Lenny's a good man. Please don't let him die, please Lawd, please."

Lenny stopped his gagging long enough to bellow, "For Gawd's sake, hush up your fat mouth, woman!" He then returned to his retching.

The others didn't seem to notice the man's agony. They sat at the kitchen table and calmly ate the lunch of chicken and pastry that Sissy had prepared. The only acknowledgment came from London, who stopped eating only long enough to yell into the bedroom, "Keep your head back 'way from my bed when you're pukin!" Lenny let out a soul-searing wail.

Margie sat in the rocking chair and sipped at a cup of hot black coffee that Mama had given her, hoping that it would settle her stomach. She was determined to finish out this day, her first day, in tobacco.

"Truck's here," Teresa called from the porch as Mr. Winston pulled up to the front of the yard. Mama and the girls went out; Margie trailed a little reluctantly behind.

"Truck's here, Lenny, better hurry up," Bertha called back over her shoulder.

"I pure can't," Lenny moaned.

"Course'n he can't," Sissy agreed. "That's okay, sugar, you just lay here an' rest. Mama'll take care of you, poor baby."

Bertha shrugged in disgust and continued on out to the waiting truck. She was not surprised. She hadn't thought that Lenny could stand up to a field of tobacco. No, she reckoned, no one as fat as Lenny could possibly survive the heat generated in these flat North Carolina fields that, in spite of all the rain, now sizzled like fry pans under the noon sun. Mr. Winston wouldn't miss the little bit of work Lenny had done in the morning anyway.

After ten hours in the fields, the women had topped and suckered ten acres of tobacco. Mr. Winston hadn't really expected that they could do all forty acres; in fact, he was surprised that they had gotten ten finished, with it being the first day and all. But he was not satisfied. He was not the kind of man who would allow himself to be satisfied. It was just his nature to complain and berate his hands for their "poor" showing.

"Who the shit he thinks he is?" London said, after Billy gave his usual accounting of the day's work.

"Don't pay him no mind," Mama said. "We could have did sixty acres an' he still wouldn't been satisfied."

"Sixty acres!" Gayla laughed. "But, Mama, he don' have but forty."

"That's what I means," explained Mama.

Margie poured the icy water from the pump over her head. She gasped in shock as it ran down her back. But it felt so good that she continued pouring bucketful after bucketful over herself.

"Hurry up an' get done; there's other peoples who wants a bath," demanded London. Margie picked up the bar of Lava soap from the little wire tray and hung on the side of the pump and began scrubbing it up and down her arms and legs. After rinsing the lather off she ran into the house to change her dress.

"Don' drip all over in here!" scolded Teresa. "You're 'sposed to wring yourself out 'fore you come in." Margie hurriedly pulled the clinging wet dress over her head then, looking furtively behind her to see if Lenny was around, she slipped out of her sopping panties. Quickly donning fresh panties and dress over her still wet body she picked up the wet clothes from the floor and carried them outside, where she hung them on the wire clothes line.

After dinner Margie did not offer to help clean up the kitchen. No one asked her to. She had barely touched her food and even the little she had managed to get past the back of her mouth lay like a rock somewhere in the middle of her throat. She went outside and curled herself inside the old tire swing. She did not let it move though because the swaying motion only increased her discomfort. She wondered about this process of growing up and working and being strong and not getting sick. She wondered why she had gotten sick and her sisters or her Mama had not. Lenny getting sick did not make her feel any better. Lenny was the kind of person who could get sick just from the idea of working. She knew that some kids worked tobacco at a much younger age than she was now. In fact, her own sisters had all started when they were only ten. She couldn't remember if they had gotten sick when they had first started. Gayla had said that she had gotten sick, but Margie couldn't remember it. But Margie knew that she would go back to the field again tomorrow. She knew that from now on she would go back every day that her Mama did; she had been initiated. Some day she would be grown up and educated and married to a rich doctor and not have to work tobacco. She lay her head back in the crease of the tire and let herself dream of romance with her rich doctor husband.

Chapter VI

When Jerry Jordan's picture had appeared in the town paper for being the first in the county to get his fields in, Billy had been humiliated beyond consolation. He had never been reputed as being the most pleasant man to work for and now his snorting and stomping all around town had scared off anyone who might have been considering the idea of seeking employment with him. Of course, he had the Braxton family, but he still needed primers for the harvest and it was prudent to line up these "transient" hands well before the time they would be needed. Billy was not too worried about his situation because he had enough people beholden to him, either tenants or debtors, who he could hire. Even if they had no inclination to work, they would work. But he hated to resort to those tactics; he would if he had to, but he hated to.

Billy only planted forty acres of his vast estate; the rest of his land was planted by tenants. Many a young and ambitious farmer began as a tenant for one of the big landlords then, after saving for a few years, was able to buy a small allotment for himself. The tenant proceeded into the business just as if he owned the land himself. He had his own equipment; he hired his own hands; and if he wanted to use the new bulk curing method, he bought or rented his own aluminum sheds, otherwise he used the old flue barns already available on the farms. The only difference between tenant farming and owning your own allotment came at auction time. Thirty percent of the profit from the harvest went to the owner of the land.

Normally a tenant farmer would not see his "bossman" until market time. This year however, reacting to his humiliating experience during the spring planting, Billy was like a leech, refusing to let go of any of his holdings even if it was under cultivation by a tenant. He fumed about weeds, he fussed about equipment, he complained about procedure. In general he was a cantankerous pest.

Monroe Troy leaned against his new John Deere tractor and watched the blue truck as it bounced down the road toward him. He wondered why Billy Winston would be paying him a visit so early in the day. Billy usually checked on Monroe in the late afternoon, if he checked at all. Monroe could feel the nagging pain from his ulcer sharpen as the truck grew nearer. Billy Winston always activated Monroe's ulcer and an early morning visit was sure to have an ominous portent.

"Morning. How's it going?" Billy greeted, smiling his toothy smile accented by his bobbling cigar.

Monroe observed him quizzically. "Hey, Mr. Winston," he answered warily as Billy slid down from his truck cab, "I reckon it's going fair."

"Got all you tops off yet?" Billy inquired scanning the near field furtively. Monroe followed his gaze. The large pink and white blossoms waved gently in the breeze. It was obvious to anyone that Monroe had not yet finished topping.

"No-o-o, I don't reckon I'll be able to take 'em all off. I'm going to have to start priming my lugs tomorrow before they burn out on me." The "lugs" are the bottom most leaves on the stalks and are the first to ripen. If left too long they soon lose the golden yellow glow of ripeness and turn brown and brittle.

"Who have you got working for you?" Billy asked.

Monroe eyed him suspiciously. "I've got the Taylor kids, they just moved here from the North, and the Patterson boy, and a couple of girls the Taylors brought with 'em—besides my wife and her mother and my brother and his wife."

"Hell! What have you got all those people for? You don't need more than one crew to work this little bitty field. You're going to cut into your profit so much with labor costs that you're not going to have anything left for yourself." Monroe knew that it was not his profit Billy worried about but rather Billy's one-third.

"Me and my brother, we're working our fields together. That's fifty acres and we need two crews for that much," Monroe explained.

"Boy, I've been working tobacco since before you were a toad under a cabbage leaf and I can tell you that you've got too many hands here. There's no sense in working all year only to give it away to somebody else." Those were exactly the same sentiments that Monroe held except he was not worried about what went to his hands, after all they worked hard for it, but he resented every penny that went to Mr. Winston for the rent of the field. One day the field would be his and he would owe no one.

"Tell you what. I'll take a couple of them off your shoulders," Billy continued in tone of generosity.

Monroe sighed in resignation. He could see that Billy meant to have his hands and there was nothing he could do but concede to Mr. Winston's "offer." Billy Winston was bossman. Monroe knew that Billy was short handed and he knew that Billy would get his hands one way or the other. He wondered just how a man reached the coveted position that Billy Winston held. Billy owned the Tractor Company, the Seed Company, and the Fertilizer Plant, besides much of the land. Monroe polished the dust from the seat of his new green tractor. He hadn't made a payment on it for two months now. He could see from the corner of his eye that Billy was smiling at him. He could almost feel the possessiveness leap from Billy to reclaim his tractor. Monroe needed the tractor more than he needed the hands.

"OK," Monroe conceded.

"Now that's what I call a smart businessman. When it comes the end of the season, you'll thank me for taking this excess off of you."

Monroe doubted that he'd ever thank Billy for anything, but he sighed, "Yeah."

"Tell you what. Those Taylor kids, they can't be much help to you anyway, not being raised up around here . . . I'll take them."

Not realizing that Billy had already investigated the worth of the Taylors, Monroe attempted to defend them. "They've never worked tobacco before, but they're real strong kids and real anxious to please. I don't think it'll take much for them to learn."

"Well, go get them for me so I can see what I got myself in for."

Monroe got up onto his tractor and drove down the truck alley between the rows of tobacco. The Taylor kids were working Cecil's fields this morning. Monroe could see the pink flowers of the tall stalks flying here and there over the rows of tobacco. He smiled. The Taylor kids always seemed to have a good time while they worked; they threw the bouquets at each other and tossed them high into the air, but still they worked fast and efficiently.

He had first met the kids early in the spring when they had, at Margie's suggestion, come around to him looking for work. They ranged in age from nineteen to thirteen, five boys and one girl, sixteen-year-old Kathy. He had been impressed from the beginning with their eagerness and candor. He would miss them, not only for the work that they performed for him but for the spice they had added to this dreary business of tobacco. He was close enough to Kathy now for her to hear his tractor. She looked up from her topping job and waved as he approached her.

"Hey, Troy-bean," she called flirtatiously. Monroe laughed. He had no idea where the kids had gotten such a silly nickname for him, but he liked it.

"Hey, yourself," he greeted. "Go round up your brothers for me."

"Is it break time already?"

"No ma'am, it isn't break time. Now just go and do what I told you."

Kathy shrugged her shoulders then ran off across the end of the rows, peering down each as she passed until she saw one of the boys and called to him to come out to her. Having rounded up all five they trotted back to where Monroe waited on his tractor.

"Get on," he said.

"What's up," asked Rick as the crew scampered to various parts of the tractor, taking seats on the hood or hanging precariously from any projection that offered a foothold.

Monroe revved the tractor motor and stomped it into gear. "I'm firing you," he answered, without looking at them.

"Firing us!" they exclaimed in unison.

"What the hell for? We do something wrong?" Rick demanded. As the eldest of the brothers, Rick held the position as sort of a guardian of the group.

"Nope, just don't need you anymore."

"You ain't got nobody but us," reminded Andy.

"I got my own family and that's all I need," Monroe snapped in irritation.

The kids rode the rest of the way back to the barn in confused silence. As they came into view of Mr. Winston's truck, Monroe said, "You aren't going to be bad off. Mr. Winston's going to hire you."

"Mr. Winston!" Eddie groaned. None of the kids knew Mr. Winston personally, but they had heard of him from their friends.

"What if we don't want to work for him?" Russ asked.

"Haven't got any choice if you want to work; all the other farmers have already got all the hands they'll need," reminded Monroe.

"That's foul!" Kathy said in anger. She glared at the nape of Monroe's neck. He felt it and flushed in embarrassment. "Look, kids," he apologized, "it isn't my fault. Mr. Winston said I have to do it. He'll take my new tractor back if I don't. I have to have it. Now get off my back. It isn't going to be easy for me, you know. Cecil's wife is due to birth her baby in a couple of weeks and Sandy's mother isn't much more good than a nagging bitch. How do you think I feel about losing my help to a son-of-a-bitch like Mr. Winston!" They should have known that Monroe wouldn't have fired them of his own doing. He just wasn't that kind of a guy.

"Oh, Lawd, look what I have done. I have bought myself a pig in a poke! Isn't that the sorries-looking bunch of kids you have ever seen—city just dripping all over them!" Billy wailed in mock agony as Monroe pulled the tractor load of kids to a stop in front of him. Then he babbled on, "But I am an honorable man and I don't go back on my word. It'll take some doing but I reckon if I work hard enough I can make a respectable crew of the lot by the end of the season. Oh, Lawd! What have I done!"

The children stared at the ground with their hands in their pockets. Billy Winston smiled and chucked Kathy under the chin and said, "Isn't that right, girlie?"

She gasped and jumped back from his reach. Rick's hand formed into a tight fist inside his pocket. Monroe could see the kids tense up and intercepted. "This here is Mr. Billy Winston. He's going to be your new boss, and I reckon ya'll work as fine for him as you have for me." The kids caught the pleading message in Monroe's voice.

"Yes, sir," Rick answered. "We're pleased to meet you, Mr. Winston." He unclenched his hand and withdrew it from his pocket; he extended it politely toward Mr. Winston. Billy grasped it tightly and, grinning with victory, pumped up and down vigorously.

The Taylors obediently climbed onto the back of Mr. Winston's truck. Mr. Winston had invited Kathy to sit up front with him, but she had declined and had climbed in with her brothers. The truck lurched forward and bounced down the dirt road to the highway. They didn't look back at Monroe. Monroe had hurriedly chugged off through the field on his tractor to avoid any last-minute farewell.

It was only a short ride down the highway to the next dirt road that led back to Billy's barns. You could actually see Monroe's barns from Billy's place. Billy pulled to a stop next to the first barn in a row of four. The kids glanced around as they climbed out of the truck. Mr. Winston's barnyards were much cleaner than Monroe's had been. The barns were in better condition; the sticks were all stacked neatly in bundles of ten. Monroe had been rather haphazard in his operations. Fourteen-year-old John wondered if all the neatness meant anything.

"Ya'll can just sit here a minute while I go get my others for their break," Billy ordered as he drove his truck on down the road that circled his fields, leaving the kids standing alone to wonder.

"He reminds me of a pig," Kathy snickered.

"Yeah, squeal, squeal!" mocked Eddie.

"Boy, I'm sure gonna miss working with Tina," moaned Andy.

"I bet," Rick laughed. Tina had the delightful habit of removing her shirt as the day grew hot. She was only thirteen and developed just enough to satisfy the erotic needs of a thirteen-year-old boy. Yes, Andy would miss Tina.

It didn't take Billy Winston long to round up his crew from the fields and carry them back to the barns. The Taylor kids observed the Braxton family closely as Mama climbed down from the cab and the girls emerged from the back of the truck. The Braxtons held a similar inspection of them.

"They're all white!" observed London quietly to Teresa.

"You can tell they is city kids—they look like a bunch of ghostes," Teresa giggled. Mama gave the two girls her "you better hush up" look and they ducked their mirth behind cupped hands.

Billy passed out the soda and honey buns. "Ya'll get acquainted while I go round back and get those sticks straightened out for tomorrow."

"Hey, Mr. Winston," interrupted Rick. "I didn't order no honey bun." Mr. Winston turned and glared at Rick in amazement. But before he could answer, Mama explained, "We don' order, we just get, chile."

"But I don't like honey buns," Rick protested.

"Better learn to like them, you gots to pay for them," advised Gayla. Billy smiled at Gayla's wise philosophy and walked away. Rick thumbed his nose at Billy's departing back. Everyone giggled. A feeling of comradeship was developing between the two families.

"I'll eat your honey bun if you don't want it," Andy offered.

"You can pay for it too," said Rick as he held the roll out to Andy.

"Forget it," said Andy, backing away from the offer. Eddie reached out to grab the bun. Rick gave him a shove that made Ed spin backwards tripping over the numerous pairs of feet and spilling all of his soda.

"Now look what you did," Eddie flailed out at Rick. Rick held him at bay and, laughing, took a long drink from his own soda.

Bertha watched the brothers with amusement. She had had all girls and was finding the Taylor boys' antics an enjoyable respite. But she knew Billy would allow no such nonsense and cautioned, "Better behave 'for Mr. Winston gets back."

The boys separated. Eddie, grumbling a promise of retaliation, moved off to the side of the group.

"Ain't you the boy what stopped by our place a few weeks ago?" Gayla asked Andy.

"I guess so," Andy answered.

"He's the boy what in your class at school?" Mama asked Margie.

"No, ma'am, he ain't 'zactly in my class—he's in my *school.*"

"Well, whose class he in then?" Gayla asked.

"He's in the eighth grade."

"How come you know him so good then if he ain't in your grade?"

"He be on the football team." Margie felt the flush growing in her skull at the connotation in London's question.

"That don' answer me nothin'," demanded London. "I mean how come you know him so **good?**"

Andy's ears turned fire red. He dug his bare toe deep into the sand and twisted it around as if to wiggle right in after it. His brothers and sister waited, grinning, to see how he was going to handle the situation.

"He be a friend of Anthony," Margie said righteously. "He hangs 'round Anthony sometimes."

"Uh huh, I bet," teased Teresa. Tears of frustration welled into Margie's eyes. She hated it when her sisters collaborated in teasing her.

"Margie's in love with a honky," Teresa chanted, in a just barely audible voice.

Mama came to the rescue. "We are all brothers under Jesus," she said. "Now ya'll just hush up messin' with Margie. It's a nice thing to be pleasant to our white brothers."

Andy wished the hole he had dug with his toe would open up and swallow him.

The Taylors had never experienced any outright prejudice before. Before coming to North Carolina, they had lived in an integrated neighborhood—one-fourth blacks and three-fourths whites. Their schools had been integrated as long as they could ever remember. They had always gotten along well with their black classmates and neighbors. There was the line of separation, but it was not an obvious thing like they had been experiencing since coming to North Carolina. Here they had been introduced to segregated neighborhoods. Here they had experienced the still transitional unrest of the recent desegregation of the schools. They had known about bigotry but had never actually been in the midst of a confrontation before. Suddenly they felt the degrading effects of social prejudice. It was not a good feeling. They felt apologetic for being white. Everyone was glad when Mr. Winston returned to the group and announced the end of the break.

"You kids come on down yonder with me and I'll show you where to start," he said as he led off toward the north end of the field.

About fifty yards down the road, he set each child to working a row. "Now just work on back up this way." He started back toward where he had left the Braxtons then as an afterthought, a demanding one, "I expect ya'll will finish topping this field before dark." The kids watched as Billy led the

Braxtons off to the far end of the field.

"I guess he works a segregated field," Russ said in a snide tone.

"Knock it off," Rick snapped. "We gotta learn to do what the Romans do."

"What the hell does that mean?"

"Yeah, who are the Romans?" asked Andy.

"Don't be stupid," chided John.

"Well, who are they, then, if you're so smart."

"They live in Rome, dummy."

"I know *that,* but who are the Romans in this field?"

"Just shut up and work, before we get fired for not doing our job," ordered Rick.

"We got fired for *doing* our job for Monroe," reminded Kathy. Her brothers were already out of earshot as they moved expertly along their rows, snapping off the tall flowers. They didn't throw them at each other now or toss them into the air. It wasn't fun anymore. Kathy sighed and hurried along her row to catch up with them.

The day was long and slow. Billy Winston was bound to finish topping and suckering the remaining thirty acres. With two crews he reckoned it could be done in one day. He kept everyone working until they had finished. It was almost too dark to see by the time the last blossom was dropped in the dirt.

Monroe Troy, with his remaining hands, had continued to top his fields until six o'clock; then had retired for the day. He had no hope of completing the job now that Billy Winston had taken one crew away. He would just have to proceed with priming the sand lugs the next day. He knew that the heavy blossoms on his plants could be dangerous in a strong wind. They could act as sails and when caught in a gust would carry the top-heavy, shallow-rooted plants right out of the sandy soil. And the numerous suckers would take their toll in nutrients depriving the profitable leaves their due growth. But what else could he do? He was a tenant farmer and as such was subject to the whims of his bossman; and the bossman saw fit to rob him of a crew. He'd just have to do the best he could with what he had left.

Billy Winston still did all his priming by hand. Some of the farmers in and around Maylor had gone to automatic primers. They were much too expensive for Billy's kind of economy. He could see no profit in such an investment especially when his days in the field were numbered; he was already sixty-two years old and would consider retirement in just a few more years. Besides, to Billy, the big ungainly primers looked like voracious monsters chewing at the tobacco. They frightened him and he didn't trust them.

The Taylor boys had never primed tobacco before, but Billy was confident that they would work out just fine. They had done a good job of topping the day before. He had also hired a ten-year-old boy from the town to help with the trucking. Sonny, being black, had been "born on a tractor" and had been working tobacco for three years already and was now able to teach Andy the fine art of trucking. Andy was both amused and impressed with the seriousness in which Sonny attacked the instructions. And Sonny glowed with pride as the older boy became adept at the numerous gear-changing tactics involved in driving a tractor.

Billy really would have liked to have two priming crews but was grateful to at least have this one. He hooked the primer to the tractor. The primer was nothing more than a large cube framework of hollow iron pipes. A small metal seat projected from the frame at each corner. Beside each seat was a cagelike box about three feet high and one foot square. Billy lowered himself into one of the four seats. Deftly he reached out and with a quick flick of his wrist he had wrested four bottom leaves from the stalk next to him, then with another flick and a swing he flipped the packet of leaves over his shoulder into the cage beside him.

"Now that's all there is to it," he instructed the boys who watched him with reserved admiration. "Andy will drive your tractor—don't drive too fast at first till they get the hang of it."

The four boys took their positions on the primer seats. Each reached out to the plant nearest him and awkwardly tugged at the giant leaves. Two or three broke loose in their hands. They laid them on the rack next to them.

"That's the way." encouraged Billy. "Ya'll will get it after a few. Now Sonny, when their racks get filled, you take their leaves and throw 'em in your truck; then, when your truck's full, carry it on back to the girls at the barn. OK?" Sonny nodded. Satisfied that each knew what his job was Billy got into his pickup truck and headed for town to have a leisurely breakfast at Nathan's and to brag about having gotten a crew together.

Andy pulled forward a few feet then stopped till the boys could strip the sand lugs from the stalks. By the time they had proceeded halfway down the first row the boys had developed a rhythm and Andy could keep the tractor creeping slowly forward without stopping except when he heard an occasional "hoah," indicating that someone had gotten behind. Soon Sonny's truck was full to the top with the sandy lower leaves. He set his tractor to full speed and drove back between the rows to the barns. At the barns

Mama and the girls helped him unhitch the wagon from the tractor and hook up an empty one so he could return to the field to follow the primers.

The big flue barns had a low porchlike roof extending from one side. The loaded wagons were pulled under the roof and the "handers" and the "loopers," usually women, worked on either side of the truck in the shade, a looper and two handers on each side. Mama worked on one side of the truck that Sonny had brought in. London worked on the side. Teresa and Gayla handed for Mama to loop. Margie and Kathy handed for London to loop.

Kathy and Margie methodically gathered three to four of the oversized bottom leaves by their stem ends, gave them a gentle shake to loosen some of the sand, then "handed" them to London who, with the dexterity of a surgeon, quickly "looped" a length of twine around the stem end of the bundle then around the stick that lay cradled at each end in the notches of a "horse", then back around the stems again to secure the entire bundle to the stick. After London had looped thirty to thirty-five such bundles onto the stick, Margie hoisted the sixty-pound load and balanced it across her chest and carried it to the front side of the barn, where it was laid to form a neat stack for the boys to "hang" when they had finished priming.

"You like livin' in Maylor?" Margie asked Kathy as they worked.

"Yeah, I like it a lot."

"It's a lot different from the city, ain' it?"

"It's a lot different, but I like it better here."

"Do they have blacks an' whites goin' to school together up there?" asked London.

"Yeah." Kathy did not want to get into this race thing again. It made her feel very uncomfortable.

"Then you're used to bein' round black," said Margie. "You have many blacks in your class?"

"Look, I went to a private school last year we lived in Cincinnati, and it just so happened that there were no blacks in my school," Kathy explained testily. "But it was because the tuition was so high, not because blacks weren't allowed. Besides, before last year I went to the public school and there were blacks and whites all mixed up. And I wish you would quit comparing blacks with whites. You're black and I'm white and neither one of us can help it. I've always been taught that everyone is the same on the inside."

"You say that, but you don' really believe that. I bet you changed to a private school just to get away from the blacks. Lots of folks do that here," accused London.

"I did not! I went to a private school so I could get a better education. I haven't got anything against blacks!"

"You're talkin' white shit now, honky," sneered London.

"Andy always hangs 'round Anthony an' he don' act like he thinks Anthony less than him," Margie offered timidly.

"But they wouldn't have no black in their house to—to—eat," challenged London.

"We've had blacks to our house for supper a lot of times. Just because I didn't go to school with blacks last year doesn't mean that I didn't have black friends," Kathy asserted. "Now let's quit talking about it."

For a few moments the girls worked in silence.

Finally Margie asked, "Are you as smart as Andy?"

"Andy, Andy, Andy, that all she can think 'bout!" chided London. Kathy tried to ignore London.

"As smart as Andy!" she exclaimed. "Why he's the dumbest in our family!"

"He's in Level I at school an' he don' act dumb."

"Well he ain't smart."

"I wish I was smart," Margie said wistfully.

"Ain't you?" Kathy asked, then wished she'd stuck her fist in her own mouth.

Margie looked at her from under lowered eyelids. "I can't read too good," she admitted.

Kathy thought about this for a moment. Her mother had been a tutor in reading and Kathy sometimes had helped her. Feeling a bit of a kinship with the little girl because Margie had been the only one to have sided with her in the black-white thing, she now answered somewhat impulsively. "Maybe I could teach you. I used to help my mom teach. Would you like that?"

Margie looked at Kathy out of the corner of her eye. Her sisters stopped working and stared at her, waiting to see what her answer to Kathy's offer would be. "I would like that," Margie whispered shyly.

"Christ!" Teresa grumbled in annoyment.

"That sure be nice of you," said Mama, thus putting a damper on any other objecting remarks from the girls. They returned to working in silence again.

Billy Winston drove up to the barns with the morning break snack. "Here's your soda and buns." he offered. "When Sonny comes in with the next load, tell him to take these out to the boys in the fields; that way we can save some time going and coming." The girls were glad for the relief and stretched their arms and backs to relieve the strain on the muscles that were not used to being held in the same position for such lengths of time.

"Lawd, look at my hands!" complained London. "They just one pure blister from that twine. Your hands blistered, Mama?"

" 'Course they're blistered, but it don' do no good to cry 'bout it."

"Who's cryin'?"

"You are," noted Teresa.

"I'd like to see you loop once't," London said indignantly.

"I rather loop than have to carry them damn heavy sticks all the way 'round t'other side of the barn."

"Shit, you don' know what work is," London sniffed.

The tractor motor could be heard chugging through the field heading for the barns. They could see Sonny's head bobbing up and down between the rows of tobacco, then suddenly the old red tractor emerged onto the road that ran across the front of the barns. Sonny had another load of leaves for the women to put on the sticks. The girls moaned when they saw it then grudgingly helped him unhitch the wagon and replace it with an empty one.

"Don' work so fas' so you don' fill this one up for 'while," pleaded Gayla. Mama put the rest of the bottles of soft drink and the honey buns into the wagon and told Sonny to carry them out to the boys.

"Okay, but I bet that Eddie kid ain' goin' eat nothin'. He's pure sick."

"He the only one?" asked Mama.

"He the only one what's pukin'. The others just lookin' green-like."

"He ought to come in an' lay down 'while," Mama said. "Carry him back here for 'while."

"Mr. Winston be mad," warned Sonny.

"No he won'. Just carry him on in here."

Margie knew that Mr. Winston would be mad. She had heard Mama talk about it other years and he *always* got mad when someone got sick. He said that he never got sick from tobacco in his whole life so nobody should get sick. But she knew that Mama would stand up for the boy, Eddie, and she bet Mr. Winston would back down under Mama's authority. He was funny that way. He could be as mean and grumpy as all get out, but Mama could always subdue him. Margie wondered about that.

It was not an unusual thing for one to get sick the first few days of priming. Even veteran primers sometimes succumbed to nicotine poison. Usually people who smoked or chewed snuff were not affected, but most others suffered some kind of discomfort, in varying degrees, during the first

85

few days of each season. Some people were so allergic to the plant that they simply could not work with tobacco at all. Doctors in the area called the illness "nicotine poisoning"; farmers claimed that the stomach "turned upside down" when the workers were priming the ground level lugs. It probably was a combination of the two; the pungent smell mingled with the insecticides and herbicides being stirred up by the workers and the fact that when priming the lowest leaves on the stalk the primer is bent over double and the air between the rows of tobacco becomes hot and stagnant, while the sun beating on the upper canopy of leaves sets the moisture in them to steaming.

Eddie was lying in the bottom of the empty tobacco wagon. Beads of sweat rolled over his forehead running down into his eyes. He no longer seemed to even care that the sweat was stinging and blinding him. Every few minutes he hung his head over the side of the wagon and retched violently. The girls watched him helplessly. Mama wet a rag at the nearby water pump and wiped the sweat from his face. Eddie didn't respond.

"Isn't there anything you can do for him?" Kathy asked anxiously. She had never seen anyone so sick before and it frightened her to see her own brother lying there in a heap as if he were dead.

"Just let him lay till the poisons get out of him," Mama answered reassuringly. Kathy and Margie helped Eddie crawl out of the wagon. He kept his head hanging as low as possible, walked just a few feet from the wagon, then slumped to the ground. The girls were unable to brace him.

"Get him out of the sun," ordered Mama as she caught hold of him under his arms and began dragging him to a spot under the shed roof. Eddie lay where she dropped him.

"He look like he's dead," Gayla observed quietly.

"Hush, he ain' dead; he just passed out. He'll be OK in a little while; now get back to work 'fore Mr. Winston comes back an' catch us," Mama warned.

The girls went back to sorting and looping the wagonful of leaves. Kathy watched Eddie's limp body as she worked. If only he would move so she could be sure he wasn't dead. But she didn't dare go over to him or stop work. He just might be dead. She did not want to know.

When Billy Winston returned to carry the hands home for lunch break, he stared at the boy lying under the shed. "What the hell's wrong with him?"

"He be sick," Mama answered.

The girls waited for Mr. Winston's reaction.

"Oh, Gawd, don' tell me I hired a panty-waist Yankee to work my tobacco!"

Kathy flushed with anger, she didn't mind being called a Yankee by her friends, but she knew that Mr. Winston used the term in the most derogatory manner.

"There's no excuse for it, just no excuse for it." he yelled, pacing back and forth beside his truck. "These kids today have no guts. The teeniest bit of work makes 'em sick. Jesus, I'll never get a barn in today."

"He ain' worried 'bout nobody but hisself," grumbled Gayla. Teresa gave her sister a kick. If Mr. Winston heard her he would turn his wrath their way.

"Get up, boy," demanded Mr. Winston. Eddie stirred and lifted his head. When he did so he began to retch again.

"Keep your head down, son," Mama said. "You won' puke so much."

"Oh, Gawd, that's right. Just lay there—I'm paying you two dollars an hour to puke up my fields and barn. Where can a man get decent help today? Oh, Gawd!" Billy moaned, holding his hands over his face.

"Come on, son, we'll help you get over to the truck an' then you lay down on the floor. You stay home when you get there an' go to bed. You'll be okay tomorrow," Mama crooned as she began pulling Eddie to his feet. Eddie staggered toward the truck and fell prone over the dropped tailgate.

Usually Kathy had little love for her brother, who, just one year younger than she, was a constant source of annoyance to her, but she could not now bear to see the agony he was in. She took the wet cloth Mama had handed her and gently wiped his face, brushing his hair away from his eyes.

The pace slowed considerably in the fields as the sun rose higher in the afternoon sky. With one hand short, Rick tried to take up the slack on his side of the primer and worked a little faster but still there were frequent "ho's" for Andy to heed. Billy stayed around all afternoon and prodded them on.

"What's holding up the works?" he yelled, when he observed the tractor halted. Then inspecting the plants down the row that had just been primed he bellowed. "Hell, you're missing half of these lugs!"

"We're doing the best we can," answered Rick. "We're short one hand now and it isn't easy for one guy to keep up with two guys on the other side."

"Hell, I used to walk-prime a row faster than you kids are doing it."

"Well, why don't you do it then?" mumbled John.

"What did you say, boy?"

"Nothing."

Billy knew what the kid had said and it only made him angrier with the boys. "Rev that tractor up and get moving," Billy ordered. Andy pulled forward with a jerk almost spilling Russ from his seat. Russ grabbed hold of the crossbar to keep his balance. The bar raked at his blistered hands and he howled in pain.

"Now what's the matter!" growled Billy.

"My hands are all blistered," whimpered Russ. "They're bleeding and I'm going to get an infection."

"Oh, Gawd!" Billy moaned. "What have I gotten myself into? I hired me a bunch of babies who aren't even weaned yet." He stomped down the row in disgust, leaving the boys alone to their blisters and misery.

"Mrs. Braxton, where did you find those boys you recommended to me for work?" he asked accusingly when he had reached the barn. Bertha didn't remember any recommendations. She didn't honor him with an answer. He didn't expect one.

The women worked silently now while Billy watched. Whenever he was around all conversation halted. His anxiety quickened as the sun swung across the sky. Unable to remain still he stomped back out to the fields.

"That man is *sick!*" observed Kathy.

"Don' pay him no mind," said Mama. "He ain' nobody's god. After 'while you just learn to 'nor peoples like him."

"Yeah, he can just stick his ol' 'bacco up his ass," London advised. Mama gave her that look.

It was nearly six o'clock before they had primed and looped enough leaves to fill the barn. The boys came in from the field and prepared to hang the loaded sticks in the barn. Their hands were raw flesh and their backs ached as if broken but they had yet to put all that they had worked so hard to prime into the barn before going home. Billy was on hand to supervise. Expertly, Mama lined up her girls and Kathy in a single file row that extended from the mountain of loaded sticks to the door of the barn. Billy explained the procedure of hanging to Rick who, because he was the oldest, was chosen to climb the twenty-five feet to the top of the barn. Russ was stationed on a pair of rafters halfway up and John would be the "poker" who would remain on the floor. Andy and Sonny became an extension of Mama's line from the door to the inside of the barn. Slowly the women began passing the heavy sticks from one to the other until they had passed them through the door to Andy who then passed them to Sonny who handed them to John. With one mighty heave John hoisted the sixty pound load over his head and "poked" the end as high as he could reach. Russ reached down between his spread legs to cover the space which John couldn't span with his reach and grabbed hold of the end of the stick. Grunting from his grotesque posture, he hauled the stick up and, precariously wavering on his perch for just a second, continued the stick's journey upward to Rick, who likewise was perched in spread-eagle fashion on the next to last rafter under the roof. Rick grabbed hold of the stick, swung it into position so that each end would rest on the parallel rafters. Thus the stick was "hung" and he was ready to receive the next stick which Russ already was waving dizzily between his legs.

Once Rick lunged forward preventing himself from falling only by grabbing onto a rusted hook that someone long ago had nailed into the wall of the barn. It tore deep into the raw flesh of his hand. The juice from the bruised leaves mingled with sweat from his body searing the open wound.

"Lawd, don't you fall, boy!" Billy yelled. "I don't have insurance."

Billy didn't carry insurance to cover accidents because he seriously believed that by so doing he enhanced the attractiveness of injuries and his employees would take advantage of it. And no one ever even thought of suing Billy Winston. Billy Winston could not be sued; he owned the law. Besides he found it effective to just keep yelling as a way of reminding. Rick studied the dirt floor twenty-five feet below and decided he would not fall. His heart pounded in his chest as he dug his heels more firmly against the rafters.

By eight o'clock the boys finally finished hanging the last section, or "house" of the barn. Billy was feeling good.

"You boys did a right good job." It was a rare compliment.

No one thanked him for the compliment or acknowledged that they had even heard it. They were only relieved that the job was finished and that they could at last go home. Rick and Russ rubbed at their groin muscles which had been pulled to their maximum from the two hours of standing across the rafters. The others rubbed the backs of their necks.

"Now I know why they call this a ball-splitting job," groaned Rick, as he poked gingerly at his groin.

"Yeah, I think mine are going to fall off," Russ agreed, and he clutched his scrotum as if to hold it in place.

"You won't be missing nothin' if they do," quipped John. Andy laughed but Rick and Russ just glared at John. They didn't have the energy left to put him in his place. But Russ made a mental note that he owed John one. Billy smiled. He would make men out of these boys yet.

The two families, the Braxtons and the Taylors, rode to their homes in silence. They were too exhausted to talk. Billy sat behind the wheel of his truck and whistled a merry tune. He had gotten in a barn on the very first day. That was good. In a week that barn would be ready for market.

After dropping the hands off at their homes, Billy returned to his filled barn and began the task of lighting the stoves that were spaced on the floors under the rows of hanging tobacco. This was one job he liked to do alone. He didn't want any clumsy greenhorn around who might stumble over a lighted stove and send his whole barn up in smoke.

Carefully he turned the gas jet on in the first stove. Then striking a match he ignited the escaping propane gas. Then he did the same to the other three, expertly adjusting the flames to just the right height. The stoves would burn like this for about a week, the heat drying the leaves hanging above them. Billy inhaled the fumes and smiled. He liked the sweet smell of the tobacco mingled with the fumes from the stoves. It smelled of success. Walking outside, Billy sealed the door of the barn locking in the heat. Looking up towards the roof he determined that the vents were open just enough—just enough for the gas fumes and the moisture to escape but not so much that the heat would escape. Billy liked his flue barns. He felt that tobacco that was flue cured was far superior to the new bulk curing. He would never change. Flue curing had been the best for as long as he could remember. His father had used it, and his grandfather before that. He could remember listening to his father tell of the times when wood fires were used and how the Negro hands had to sleep on the floor of the barn and take turns feeding the fires so that they would not go out during the week it took to cure the tobacco. Yes, flue curing was the best and Billy would have nothing to do with the new bulk curing. His fellow farmers, who were trying the new shiny aluminum barns for the first time this year, would most certainly agree with him after a season of under-cured tobacco, which is what Billy predicted would be the result of such modern contraptions.

He gave the barn door one more shove to make sure it was tight, then climbed into his blue pickup truck and headed for home a contented man.

The Braxton girls lined up at the pump in the back yard. It was already dark now and Teresa slipped out of her tar-stiffened dress before she got under the chilling water of the pump. Mama had already bathed and had put her own sticky dress into a tub of Clorox and soap water to soak. Aunt Sissy had dinner ready when they had returned home and was now preparing the table while they bathed. Reggie crawled in and out between Sissy's legs.

"You'd think that lazy-ass Lenny sittin' out there on the porch fannin' hisself could at least watch Reggie for Aunt Sissy," grumbled Teresa as she lathered her hair to remove the sticky plant juice from its wirey tangles.

"Don' be silly," said Gayla. "He can't bend that fat belly of his down far 'nough to take reach of a baby." Margie giggled at the thought of Lenny's grotesque belly.

" 'Sides," added London. "I don' want his ugly black hand on my baby no-how." Margie shivered at the remembrance of Lenny's ugly black hands.

The girls sat on a rotting log that lay near the pump while waiting their turns to bathe. London rubbed at the small of her back. "My back sure do ache some today," She moaned.

"You sure you ain' pregnant?" asked Teresa.

"Why you ask that?" London snapped.

"Don' know. Just you say your back's hurtin' so bad, just wonderin'."

"Well, you just mind your own business. My back's hurtin' from workin'." But they knew.

"Who is it this time?" snickered Gayla.

"I-it ain't nobody," hissed London.

"A virgin birthin'?" laughed Teresa.

"You better hush for I whop you one," warned London.

Margie stared inquiringly at London's belly. She felt a twinge in her own back. She wondered. Suddenly she felt sick. Running toward the outhouse, she vomited before she could even reach it.

"What's wrong with her?" asked Gayla. "She should be used to 'bacco by now."

Margie sat on the floor of the outhouse with her head between her knees. The vision of Lenny standing by her bed loomed large in her mind. She squinted her eyes shut against the vision but it would not go away. Again she stared at the gaping flap of Lenny's underwear. Goose flesh crept up her arm where "it" had brushed against her. She scratched violently at the spot. Was she, could she be pregnant? With one hand on her belly, she squeezed diagnostically. She could feel nothing. Her flat little belly just rumbled in protest at the palpation. Somewhat relieved she got up and walked slowly back to the pump to wait her turn to bathe. Her sisters eyed her curiously.

As London stood dripping by the pump, her wet dress clinging tightly to her thin frame, Teresa prodded the telltale mound that was just beginning to show beneath her sister's navel.

"Ain' nobody, huh?" teased Teresa.

"Well, it ain' goin' be nobody," assured London. "I'm goin' get some of that 'bortion tea from Miz Higgins."

"You ain't!" gasped Gayla. "That's a sin, a terrible sin!"

"What you know 'bout sin," snapped London. "That queer preacher boy you goin' with tell you 'bout it?"

Margie pushed her hand into her stomach again to reassure herself that it was still flat.

"That tea ain' no good no-how," said Teresa. "You drank it when you was that way with Reggie an' it di'n' stop him."

"I took it too late then," said London. "This time it'll work."

"You better hope so 'cause Mama's goin' be real mad if you come up with another bastard to feed."

"You shou'n't call it that," said Gayla. "It's a innocent baby an' can't help it if his Mama's loose."

"Look who's talkin'," laughed London. "I 'member las' year how you jumped up an' down those steps tryin' to start your period after you went out with that Shelby boy."

"You hush!" screeched Gayla as she threw the bar of soap at London.

"You girls hurry up," Mama called from the porch. "Dinner's on the table." London ducked the bar of soap and, laughing, ran to the house. Gayla would store the retaliation till later.

Margie sat in the rocker staring at the plate on her lap. Supposing she *was* pregnant. She visualized a miniature Lenny monster within her womb. Again that twinge in her back. She jumped up and ran outside toward the outhouse.

As she stood braced against the wall inside the stinking little box, she flung her thoughts wildly about for a solution to her dilemma. Her heart was racing. She thought it might explode, which would solve everything. A tickling sensation on her leg disturbed her agony. Perhaps a spider, a black widow, another solution. She let her eyes lower to observe the expected attacker. A fine red trickle was winding toward her knees. She stared as a drop of blood fell onto the bare boards of the floor. Suddenly her body began to convulse in hysterical relief. She was not pregnant! She must remember to mark a red circle on her little calendar just as she had seen her sisters do.

Chapter VII

London waited until everyone had gone to bed. She listened for the deep, regular, breathing sounds that would tell that her world was safe, asleep. Slipping from her pallet on the floor she crept out to the kitchen. A frog belched its Morse bass pitch from somewhere in the ditch that ran beside the road. A mosquito hummed placidly overhead having already engorged itself on the sleeping bodies in the next room.

She had been careful to lay an extra piece of wood in the stove before going to bed so the fire would still be lit when she needed it. During the summer Mama always let the fire go out at night and rekindled it in the morning for breakfast. It was a nuisance, but the little cabin was sultry enough without adding to the heat with a stove fire.

Margie lay very still, squeezing her eyes shut tight and breathing evenly. When she was sure that London would not return to the bedroom, she peeked one eye open. She could just barely make out London's silhouette against the pale glow of the stove. She watched as London laid two more pieces of wood in the stove and gently stirred the coals until they ignited the new wood.

Mama grumbled in her sleep as the heat from the newly awakened fire pushed into the bedroom. London looked toward the sound. Margie squeezed her eyes shut again. She waited a few seconds then heard London stir about the kitchen. Opening her eyes just a tiny crack, she watched London dip a cupful of water into a pan. Quietly setting the pan on top of the stove, she reached into the front of her dress and pulled a small white packet from inside her bra. Carefully opening the packet, she shook the contents, a coarse brown powder, into the pan on the stove. Sitting down at the table she waited for the water to boil.

Hardly breathing at all, Margie watched. She knew what was in the packet, the tea from the Old Lady Higgins. She had heard the girls whispering about it after dinner. One of them had said that the Old Lady Higgins was a witch. Margie believed this to be true and feared that the potion that London now brewed would somehow transfer that witchery to London.

93

Margie was afraid. She knew the Old Lady Higgins, and she had always been afraid of her. The wizened little woman had to be at least one hundred years old. Only witches lived so long.

London poked at the fire. The sputter of flames brought Margie back to the business at hand. She had never witnessed an abortion before. She knew that London's baby would not be very big yet and visualized a miniature doll-like infant slipping from between London's thighs. She wondered what London would do with the little baby when it had aborted. Just what did you do with a baby that no one wanted? She didn't know.

The mixture in the pan began to boil. London watched it anxiously. She let it boil a few minutes to make sure the brew was strong enough to be effective. She did not want it to fail her as it had the last time. When she judged the brew to be strong enough she poured the tea into a cup. Blowing the steam from the surface she sipped slowly. Margie watched in wide-eyed anticipation from her cot.

After she had finished drinking the tea, London sat back to wait. The minutes pulsed by; after an hour of suffocating waiting Margie could no longer fight off sleep and slipped unwillingly into the dark of unconsciousness.

London began to rock her body back and forth in the chair. Why was nothing happening? She squeezed at her belly in frustration. Sweat was dribbling down her cheeks and running in a channel down the middle of her back. The fire in the stove crackled merrily, oblivious to the inferno already instilled by the July heat.

Sighing, she moved out onto the porch to continue her vigil. The cool outside air sent a shivering chill through her as it made contact with the rivulets of sweat on her body. Her sweat-dampened dress clung icily to her back.

Maybe it took awhile. She might as well sleep while she waited. Going back into the house she tiptoed into the bedroom. Stumbling against the TV dresser, she stifled a cry as she hopped forward on one foot while grasping the other throbbing foot in her hand. Margie jerked from her sleep at the thump. London held her finger to her lips and patted Margie. Margie slipped cozily back to sleep.

"Lawd, this fire's still red in this stove!" exclaimed Mama as she pattered into the kitchen at five a.m. "No wonder I was so hot las' night." Sissy waddled sleepily into the kitchen. Yawning, she observed the red coals through the open door of the stove.

"Won't take so much trouble to fire it up for breakfas'," she said in appreciation. "When Lenny gets to workin' steady again, he's goin' buy me a gas stove; then we won't have to put up with all this heat in the summer."

Mama let out a "humph." She could not visualize Lenny ever getting off of his box on the porch. She had given up hating him because it took too much of her energy. She just sort of ignored his presence.

"Ya'll get up!" she called into the bedroom. "Mr. Winston'll be here 'fore you know it."

London woke with a start. She lay for a moment in the confusion of the sudden awakening. Then she remembered. She probed her belly. It still carried the hard little lump below her navel. It was calm and unhurting. Disappointment reached deep within her and pulled forth a frustrated sob. She hated the Old Lady Higgins, the witch. Grumbling, she stumbled up from her pallet and dressed herself. Margie stared at her sister's belly. She could see no change, but then it was still quite dark in the room. She squinted into the vagueness. She had expected that London's belly would be concave this morning. She wondered what London had done with the little baby. A chill of sadness pricked her.

London sat at the table and absently stirred her grits.

"Better eat," advised Mama.

"Ain't hungry."

"You goin' be hungry."

"Shit," London mumbled. Teresa kicked Gayla under the table. Gayla looked up to observe Teresa making grotesque pantomime, wildly winking one eye, patting her belly and nodding exaggeratingly towards London.

"You havin' a fit or somethin'!" asked Mama startled by the contorted face of her daughter. Teresa ducked her head down and began shoveling grits into her mouth.

"Young'uns!" Mama said, shaking her head in bewilderment.

The morning had been unusually hot and muggy. The air hung still over the barns, like a huge wet feather bed weighing down on the workers' shoulders. At the morning break, after Mr. Winston had passed the sodas and honey buns around, the girls scurried off away from Mama and sat under a tree away from the barns. Kathy followed the Braxton girls. She had become one with them in their conspiracy against Mama. She delighted in the antics of the girls in their efforts to conceal from their mother all manner of secrets.

Bertha eyed the group suspiciously. She knew they were up to no good when they skittered off like that but she did not have the ambition to follow them. Leaning against the barn she strained her ears in an attempt to catch their conversation. It was useless; they were too far off. Sighing in resignation, she let her knees buckle under her weight; her back slid down the green tarpaper covering of the outer walls of the barn until she sat on the cool shaded sand.

"Did it work?" asked Teresa anxiously.

"Shit, no. Not yet anyways."

Kathy looked from one to the other wondering what it was that hadn't "worked." "Did what work?" she asked curiously.

Margie started to explain, but London reached a large hand over and clamped it across her mouth. Kathy flushed. It had been a long time since she had felt like an outsider. She had almost forgotten that they were different. But that fact was hammered home to her now as the three older girls glared at her. London still held her hand over Margie's mouth.

"Oh, she might's well know," Gayla said with a sigh after they had stood there a moment. "Ever'body's goin' know it anyways."

"Ain't nobody's business," London asserted.

"Well, you can't keep a thing like that a secret for ever!"

"London's pregnant," whispered Margie breathlessly as London conceded and removed her gag. Yes, everyone would know it soon anyway.

"She tried to 'bort it and it di'n't work," explained Margie further.

"Oh," Kathy answered awkwardly. She had known a girl once who had gotten "caught," but she had never known anyone who had had an abortion. She wondered why London would have wanted to get rid of the baby anyway. There was no stigma on illegitimate births in these parts, among the black, anyway. At least one-third of the black girls in the high school were either pregnant or already had had a child or even two. She had been told by her white friends that the blacks were attempting to overpopulate the world with their own kind in an effort to gain supremacy—black power. She didn't think she believed these tales. Yet sometimes she wondered about it.

Just now she felt genuinely sorry for London because in just the little while she had known the family she suspected that, notwithstanding the accepted norm of the community, London would have tough reckoning with her mother. But she also felt very uncomfortable to be a cohort in the knowledge of the attempted abortion. Her religion did not allow abortion; she was torn between two cultures.

Margie drew Kathy aside and explained all about the abortion tea Old Lady Higgins had sold to London and how it hadn't worked with Reggie and how it didn't work again.

"What's she gonna do?" Kathy stuttered weakly.

"Don't know," shrugged Margie. "Reckon she just goin' have to birth it."

The one girl who Kathy had known to have gotten "caught" had gone away to some home for unwed mothers and, after the birth of her baby, she had released it for adoption.

"Maybe she could set it up for adoption," she now offered as a solution.

"That's wrong!" exclaimed Gayla who had heard. "You just can't give a baby away, just like that!"

"There ain't nobody goin' 'dopt my kid. If I can't get no 'bortion then I'll raise it. That's the only decent thing to do," London asserted.

All this confused Kathy. London seemed to have no compunction against killing her child but neither would she consider allowing someone else to raise it for her. Kathy could not see the merit in subjecting another human life to the existence that the Braxtons had. She thought that maybe it would have been better had the tea worked; then, in a panic of shame and guilt for having thought such a thing, she said a silent prayer for forgiveness.

It looked like another record day for the heat. The temperature climbed steadily into the nineties. The boys in the field came in frequently for drinks of water. Ed, having somewhat conquered his earlier battle with tobacco sickness, looked pale under his glistening sweat. Billy Winston complained about their too frequent breaks. He had never let the heat bother him when he was a boy working in the fields. The boys doubted that he had ever worked in the fields. But today Billy kept a close watch on the proceedings. Mopping at his white brow, that was always shaded with the Stetson, he meandered up and down the rows, urging the boys to work a little faster.

"We aren't ever going to get that barn in today if ya'll are going to crawl along that way."

"Who cares?" John mumbled.

Billy heard him and snapped, "*I* care. And you better remember that when it comes round to pay day!"

The leaves were no longer wet with dew as they had been early in the day. When the girls handled them, the sticky tar balled up between their fingers. When the dew was still on the leaves, the tar did not have a chance to collect on their skin and the wet leaves felt cool against their arms. Now the leaves at the bottom of the pile in the wagon were hot from the sun steaming them through the heavy top layers. The sick sweet smell rose in noxious waves from the bruised and sun-limped mass. Suddenly, London doubled

97

over and yeowed loudly. Margie grasped Kathy's hand in fright. Kathy clutched at Margie and stared wide-eyed at the writhing London. She had fallen to the ground now and was squirming like an injured snake all the while clutching violently at her belly.

"Lawd, have mercy!" exclaimed Mama. "What ails you, chile?"

"I—I—I think I gots 'pendicitis," London gasped between shrieks of pain.

"For sure 'nough?" Mama hurried around the side of the wagon and caught hold of the groaning thrashing girl. "Hold still, 'fore you ruptures somethin'. Margie, run get Sonny to go find Mr. Winston. Hurry!" Mama soothed London the best she could but the girl still clutched at her belly and thrashed on the ground.

Margie ran as fast as she could down the rows of tobacco. The huge leaves slapped her face as she sped past them. When she could hear the chug of Sonny's tractor, she began screaming for him.

Sonny picked up the screeching over the clatter of his motor and turned to see what it was. When he saw Margie running toward him wildly waving her arms, he stomped his foot on the break. Standing up to get his full weight on the stiff pedal, he finally halted the machine.

"Where at's Mr. Winston?" Margie shrieked. Sonny pointed down the row. Margie ran past him without stopping. Still standing on the brake pedal he gaped in amazement at the raving girl.

Billy Winston now heard the commotion and bellowed, "What ails you, girl?"

"London's havin' a—I mean—she gots 'pendicitus. She gots to go to the hospital right away."

Billy moved his bulk quickly down the row till he could grab the panic stricken child. "Now hold on just a minute."

"Hurry, Mr. Winston, she's goin' die!"

"Gawd, what have I got this year!"

Billy was puffing spasmodically when he finally reached the barn. London still clutched her belly and moaned writhing on the ground. Mama stood aside wringing her hands in despair.

"She's dyin' for sure, Mr. Winston!"

"No, she isn't. Now everybody calm down." Then slapping his hand to his forehead Billy wailed again, "Gawd, what have I got?" For a moment he stood red-faced and panting over the stricken girl. "Come on, get her into the truck. I'll take her into the County Hospital."

"Oh, you're a gen'rous man!" Mama sobbed in appreciation as she half carried and half dragged the kicking girl to the truck.

She started to get in beside her when Billy yelled, "Christ, you can't go too, Mrs. Braxton. You're the only looper left. I need *somebody* to work. We aren't going to get this barn in today as it is. . . . Oh, Gawd, what have I got!"

"But she's my baby," pleaded Bertha.

"There isn't anything you can do anyhow. The doctors would rather not have a whole bunch of people around. Now just get out of the truck and start working. I'll take care of your young'un for you." On that note he reached across London, who sat doubled over on the seat beside him, and pulled the door shut with a bang and drove off, leaving Bertha standing sobbing and wringing her hands in the middle of the road.

Calling weakly after the truck she whimpered, "It'll be OK baby, it'll be OK." Then turning back to the barn she moaned, "I know she's goin' die for sure."

Dr. Ellison was still in the hospital after having made his morning rounds. Usually the resident took care of the cases admitted to the emergency room if there were no unusual complications. But Dr. Ellison had recognized London as Mr. Winston half dragged and half pushed her down the hall. He was curious as to what might be her problem, so he stayed on to attend her. Now, he gently palpated London's belly. She had calmed down considerably since having been admitted to the emergency room of the hospital.

London was grateful that Dr. Ellison was there. Doctors frightened her and doctors who were strangers to her completely panicked her. She felt a small comfort with her own Dr. Ellison. Just once, when a cramp tore through her belly, did she yelp like a stricken puppy. She apologized effusively.

"You've got *some* gas here, young lady," observed Dick Ellison. "Have you been eating green apples or something?" London stared at him blankly. He pushed gently on her tender belly again. She grimaced, but she did not cry out. "Sure is *some gas.*" The doctor nodded to himself.

In a very low voice London asked, "That's all?"

"Well, a little more than that, I think. But it's the gas that's causing all this pain. When was your last period, London?"

"Last week," she answered almost inaudibly.

"Come on now. When?" London did not answer again.

"Set me up for a *vag,*" he ordered as he began to write the details on the prepared medical form that was required for all emergency cases.

The nurse prepared a tray of sterile instruments and squeezed a glob of lubricating jelly onto a square of gauze. Dr. Ellison pulled on a pair of rubber gloves with a resounding snap. "OK, let's see what we've got here."

London winced as he probed deep within her pelvis. Dr. Ellison stared at a spot somewhere on the far wall as his sensitive fingers traced London's pelvic organs. "I'd say about four months," he mused as he stood back and pulled the gloves from his hands. "London, looks like you're going to have to see Dr. Peters again over at the gynecology clinic. You had some doozies of bowel contractions there, though." He patted her exposed brown belly and left the room.

There was a strained silence around the dinner table. Finally Lenny said, "How many extry mouths you 'spect to feed 'fore you get these girls raised up?"

London broke away from the table and ran outside. Lenny's eyes followed her accusingly. "It sure's a shame that a good woman like my Sissy can't get a kid, but the likes of that one can." He looked sympathetically toward Sissy, who flushed in embarrassment at her husband's crass accusations.

"Seems some peoples would pull their own nose," observed Teresa.

Mama stared at her plate full of food. She should ignore the worthless Lenny, but it was true what he said. How many? Yes, babies were a blessing—but how many? The welfare checks only went so far—the aid to dependent children was rapidly gobbled up by inflationary expenses. Yes, how many? She was getting old, too old to raise young'uns. How many? She looked over at Margie, her baby, already nearing a woman. Margie squirmed under Mama's scrutinizing gaze.

Now that London's pregnancy was common knowledge, everyone settled down into the pattern of expectancy. No one ever told Mama about Old Lady Higgins's tea. No one ever would. Sissy ripped out an old sweater of hers and began to reknit it into an infant sweater. Her frustrated maternal instinct was being placated by the anticipation of London's child. London went about her days as usual, looping as rapidly as her now callused fingers could fly. On weekends, she spent her evenings sipping cheap wine in a dark corner of Paradise Inn. Randy snuggled beside her.

"You wants to get married, baby?" he asked again and again.

But each time London answered, "Ain't ready for marriage yet. I love you but I don' know if I love you 'nough to live with you."

"OK, OK, take your time," he crooned patiently after each refusal.

Once the excitement of the abortion attempt was passed, Margie forgot all about the expected baby. The long, hot summer days were opening a new life for her. Kathy had begun to bring a reader along to work and at break times she sat with Margie helping her to sound out the words printed in the book. Under Kathy's patient tutelage Margie began to perform well with her new pleasure. She advanced rapidly through the readers that Kathy brought and on to more interesting books.

The happiest day of all was when Kathy brought along a paperback novel. Margie had always wanted to read a paperback. There was something very grown-up looking about the slick gaudy covers that beckoned from the book rack in Mr. Pfeiffer's store. She had never bought one of those books because, first of all she knew she would never be able to manage all those big hard words. Then, of course, there was the money. There was none for such luxuries as a paperback book. The book that Kathy now brought to her was one of Kathy's favorites, a novel of young romance, *The Yellow Rose*. It was written in simple but elegant prose.

At first Margie was content to sit and read aloud to Kathy. Kathy was proud of her pupil and had grown genuinely fond of the young girl. Margie's constant chatter on the subject of becoming a woman at the age of thirteen amused her. However, she did not tease Margie as did her sisters. Kathy respected Margie's dreams. If thirteen meant a great new grownup world for Margie, then Kathy would not burst her balloon.

Margie's contentment with reading her book only a half hour or so a day paled. Finally she asked, "Kathy, please let me take the book home tonight and read it. I'll be real careful and I know I can do it by myself now." Kathy, pleased that Margie should want to try it solo, happily consented.

Margie gobbled her dinner and could hardly wait till she was dismissed from the family group so she could begin her reading. Mama was very strict about everyone staying at the table until she had finished. Though she rarely joined in the mealtime conversations she felt that the time spent together was of some value in keeping a check on her brood.

The moment Mama emptied her plate Margie bustled over and swept it from the table with an air of finality. Startled, Mama scolded, "Set down, girl, an' let me drink my coffee in peace." Chagrined, Margie returned to her seat. She picked at her fingers, fussed with the hem of her dress, twisted her braids and, in general, was a nervous wreck as she watched Mama sip slowly at the hot coffee. And Lenny did not do much to ease her anxiety as he filled his plate for the third time.

Margie sighed in relief when Lenny finally pushed his plate away from him and wiped the sleeve of his shirt across his mouth emitting a satisfied burp. Now she could concentrate on Mama's sipping. And Mama sipped and she sipped.

"OK, chile, you can get now," Mama finally consented. Margie jumped from her chair and, clutching her book to her breast, she ran out to the old tire swing. It would be light enough for just about an hour yet. It was quiet under the pecan tree.

In a moment Margie was lost to the crude world surrounding her. She could neither smell the stench that simmered in the sun-heated trash heap nor feel the sting of the mosquitoes that feasted, unmolested, on her bare flesh.

Learning to read had emancipated Margie. As soon as she finished one paperback, she carried it back to Kathy who always had another one waiting. Nights she dreamed of lounging in the arms of handsome suitors. She no longer had to rely on the rich doctor image to satisfy her desires. She wore gossamer gowns that flowed transparently in the breeze. She dined from fine china and slept on silken sheets. Such was life for someone who knew the magic formula of the printed word.

Margie's sisters grew impatient with her reveries. Sometimes at work she would lapse dreamily into one of her "spells." Her hands would stop pulling at the tobacco leaves and she would stare longingly across the long rows of plants to somewhere on the other side of the sweet field of ambrosia. Her sisters followed her gaze but saw nothing but stinking tobacco weeds.

"Get off that cloud an' han' me some of them leaves," London would yell. Startled back to earth, Margie would hastily grab a handful of leaves and poke them into London's face.

"You ain't got the stems together," London would shriek. Margie would fumble with soggy leaves until she had the stems together then thrust them sheepishly toward London's impatient hands.

During these times Kathy worked a little faster to try to take up the slack that her little friend left. She felt personally responsible for Margie's euphoric inattention. The others also made accusing remarks toward Kathy. They said that if she had not messed, had minded her own business, the little girl would not be having "spells" now. But Kathy knew that she had liberated Margie and, though it was difficult to be the butt of their discontent, she was glad she had been instrumental in Margie's escape into freedom.

Mama never scolded. Sometimes she gently called Margie back to her work. But she was pleased with Kathy for giving her baby something she had always longed for, the key to unlock the mysteries that were imprisoned between the covers of those garish slick jackets that lined the revolving bookrack at Pfeiffer's Grocery. Sometimes Mama would slip out to the old tire swing and hover over Margie, staring incognizant at the pages of print. She wondered what wonders were trapped in those long strings of disjointed letters. Margie was never aware of her presence.

"She thinks she's Miss Shit since she can read so good; hell, I been readin' for a long time an' ain't nobody thinkin' that be so wonderful," complained Teresa jealously one day while she sorted through the hot sticky tobacco.

"Oh, she's just a chile; let her be," defended Gayla.

"Chile, my eye! You see the way she looks at that white boy, Andy! An' he ain't 'voidin' her none neither."

"They just school friends. Don' mean nothin'."

"You just watch that 'school friends' stuff. Ain't a white boy I knows what don't crave black ass."

Kathy gasped in indignation and shock at this accusation. "My brother doesn't think like that!"

"Don' fool yourself, sister, all men's do."

"But—but, he's not a man, he's only a little kid. He doesn't even know what it's all about yet."

"Men's borned knowin' what it's all 'bout," asserted Teresa. Mama finally rescued Kathy from the ignominy of the moment.

"Ya'll hush your dirty mouths an' get to work." Margie stared at the tobacco leaves through the tears of shame that welled into her eyes. Kathy felt a knot in her own throat.

How can anyone be so mean? she thought. *Especially your own sisters.* Kathy thought she would never trust blacks again, except, maybe Margie. But then, Margie was different. She was not like the others. She had innocently believed that she had been accepted by them. She wondered about the demeaning brand of bigotry that seared her now.

Margie hated her sisters even more, almost as much as she hated Lenny. But she expected that their dominance was to be short lived soon; well, in another half year, she would become their peer. Then she was sure she could cope with their ugliness, and even if she couldn't there would be other avenues of escape. One gained a lot of freedom on turning thirteen. She wondered how she came upon this most exhilarating truth. She was not certain if she had been told or if perhaps she had overheard, or perhaps, well . . . she knew, she just knew, that's all, else why was she so anxiously awaiting . . .

Chapter VIII

She didn't know just how long he had been standing there, his hands in his pockets, his breath coming in wispy grunts. When she did realize his presence, her entire autonomic system froze. Her heart stopped, her breathing stopped, she could neither see nor hear. When her heart began to beat again it sounded like a giant kettle drum in her ears. Slowly the blood seeped into her legs. When at last she was able to lunge forward from her tire swing she lurched backward against her forward motion and she stumbled headlong into Lenny's bulging belly. Once again her heart stopped as he clutched her under her arms to keep her from falling.

"Margie, you better get in this house an' go to bed, 'fore you won' be able to get out it tomorrow!" The sound of her Mama's voice sent the blood surging along its course again and she wrenched herself from the heaving mass of flesh that had engulfed her.

Running past her mother in the doorway, she darted into the bedroom and dived onto her cot. She buried her face into the limp feather pillow. For a moment the world spun around her then gradually slowed till it finally stopped.

"Chile, you could leas' take off your dress," Mama admonished as she snuggled her own bulk onto the cot beside Margie. "We goin' have to get 'nother bed," she sighed. "This is just too tight for the both of us."

Margie lay a long time, still clutching her book tightly to her breast. The others had been in bed for some time and were all sleeping. All except Lenny, who sat contentedly on his box on the porch, a rolled grocery bag in his hand for slapping at mosquitoes. Margie counted each slap sound that indicated another mosquito downed. She counted until she finally succumbed to sleep.

Billy Winston pulled a leaf from one of the bundles hanging above him in the barn. Rubbing the leaf gently between his thumb and fingers, he sniffed at the bitter sweet aroma of the cured tobacco. Snapping the large center vein of the leaf he judged from the crisp crack that followed that this barn was ready for market.

The boys began unhooking the sticks from the cross beams, beginning at the bottom of the barn and working their way up. The dried leaves crackled and snapped on the sticks as they were released from their positions on the beams. The sand that had clung stubbornly to the wet leaves when the girls had looped them to the sticks now sifted down onto the boys' heads as the leaves were disturbed. Squinting and blinking as the sand filled their eyes the boys let the tears flow generously in an attempt to keep the debris washed out. Sometimes minute tobacco dust also fell with the sand, stinging the tender membranes that lined their eyelids, which made the tears flow more copiously. The sand and dust also stuck to their sweaty flesh forming an itching layer of toxic brown that burned into every tiny scratch and blister of their skin.

The loaded sticks of cured tobacco were handed through the barn door to the girls waiting outside. Swiftly they ripped at the twine that held the bundles in place. At times the stubborn string would not turn loose its hold on the stick. The girls picked at the tangles with their tobacco-stained fingernails or sometimes, in desperation, bit through the knots with their teeth, spitting the bitter saliva hastily from their mouths.

The loosened leaves were laid in huge canvas sheets that were held in position by a large circular rack. When a sheet was filled to the brim of the rack the corners were gathered together in the middle of the bundle and tied together with a length of rope. When filled the sheet weighed about a hundred pounds and was hoisted onto a waiting truck by one of the bigger boys. When the barn was empty and all the cured tobacco had been sheeted and loaded onto the truck Billy Winston climbed into the cab alone. He did not much like driving the big truck; he was used to his little pickup. Besides, the big old '58 Chevy truck had seen better days. Billy never knew for sure if it was going to make the twenty mile trip into the market at Farmdale. As he started the truck bouncing down the dirt road toward the highway he yelled back to the crew.

"Just go on and take up where you left off yesterday. And be careful you don't grab off any green leaves. I'll be back in a couple hours."

Rick sighed as the truck disappeared in its own cloud of dust. Knowing that Mr. Winston for sure would be gone at least three hours was a comfort to the entire crew. They did not work any less hard or fast when he wasn't around because they knew they could not leave the farm until a barn was filled. But knowing that the puffing mound of sweating flesh would not pop up suddenly from behind a tobacco stalk in an attempt to catch a shirker relaxed the ever-present tension of the children.

The boys climbed into Sonny's empty cart and bounced merrily out to the field. Andy followed on his tractor to where the primer was parked. The boys helped him hitch the bulky mass of iron bars onto the tractor then climbed onto their chairs. Andy lurched forward sending the chairs to swinging in a wide arc.

"Hey, cut it out!" yelled Ed.

"Yeah, you'll make him seasick again," quipped John. Andy grinned as he backed the primer up a little then jerked it forward again. The boys clutched at the crossbars to keep from being thrown out of their seats.

"Enough's, enough," yelled Rick.

"Yeah, it ain't funny the second time," added John.

Driving the tractor up and down the long rows of tobacco day after day was about the most boring job a thirteen-year-old boy could do. Even Sonny's job was not as bad; he drove back to the barn at intervals with his loaded cart. It gave him a chance to climb down from his seat while they unhitched the cart and hitched up an empty one. He bantered with the women on these occasions. His day was broken into segments. Andy's, on the other hand, stretched forever down the rows of tobacco. He could not join in the chatter and joking that snapped among the crew on the priming rack because no one could hear him over the loud coughing chug of the tractor engine. He just rode his perch in the broiling sun and learned to sweat profusely—and to swear, which he practiced diligently hour after hour.

The relaxed atmosphere didn't last long. Less than two hours after he had left, Billy's big old truck bounced traumatically back down the road to the barn. The girls stopped handing and stared as he ejected himself from behind the wheel. His face was beet red, his fists clenched, their knuckles white with anger. His shoulders hunched forward and his neck jutted ahead of his body. He stomped toward the barn.

"Lawdy, he be mad!" Bertha whistled as she drew herself to her full height to brace herself for the expected onslaught. As he neared the barn one fist unclenched and raised, finger pointing menacingly at the crew.

"Damn niggers!" he sputtered. "Ya'll are no use to a decent man whatever!" No one acknowledged this, his first grenade. Kathy wondered if she was included as a "nigger."

"Sand, sand! That's all ya'll know how to sheet."

Bertha frowned at this unfamiliar weapon. What did he mean, *sand,*

sand? Was he going crazy? He surely looked like it. "Forty cents, forty cents! Ya'll aren't worth a nickel. Forty cents, forty cents?"

The girls were still confused as to just what Billy was mad about. Kathy began to tremble as he stepped closer, still waggling his pudgy finger at them. "Said it was because it had too much sand. Ya'll hear that? Too much sand!"

Mama was beginning to catch on now and steeled herself for defense.

"Forty cents, forty cents, ya'll hear that!" he repeated over and over. No one answered. "Just a little shake, just a little effort by you lazy bastards, that's all I ask for my two dollars an hour." He paused for a moment as if to refuel. His breath was coming in short little gasps now. "Forty cents, forty cents."

Gradually the volume of his voice petered off. Bertha did not relax her guard, however, not even when his raised hand with its daggerlike finger dropped limply to his side.

"Don't know how they expect a man to make a living. Forty cents, forty cents!" He was more moaning now then yelling. His breath was coming more evenly now and his remaining fist loosened. The blood rushed into the knuckles turning them ruddy pink. Taking out his handkerchief, he dabbed it across his brow and cheeks then patted the back of his neck. Slumping, exhausted, against the wheel of the tobacco cart he sighed a deep sigh of defeat.

Mama eyed the spent figure. She allowed herself to relax too, just a little.

"Cost me eighty-five cents to get the damn stuff to the market," he continued to complain. Bertha motioned for the girls to get on with their work and she too began to loop rapidly. She had no idea of how to comfort Mr. Winston, so she immersed herself in the business of looping to avoid revealing her inadequacy. Billy remained seated on the wheel of the wagon and continued to moan the injustice that had been done to him. "Forty cents, forty cents. Eighty-five to get it there. Fertilizer, equipment, seed, hands— forty cents!" he raved on and on to himself. Then suddenly he jumped to his feet and began shaking his finger at Mama again. "Forty cents. Do you hear that? Forty cents was all they wanted to give. Know what I did? Turned ticket, that's what I did! I'll let the stuff rot before I'll let it go for forty cents. Do you hear that? Turned ticket!" Mama felt an almost imperceptible flinch run through her as the fat finger continued to wave close to her nose. She did not back up. The girls continued to work keeping one eye on the raving Mr. Winston. Kathy wanted to run. She didn't understand the reason for his wrath and thought it had something to do with their work.

Billy seemed to have spent all his anger now and walked slowly away from the women. His chin dug deep into his chest. He muttered over and over, "Turned ticket—forty cents!" as he went to his truck. The girls continued to work but watched the slumped-shouldered man leave. When Billy had climbed back into the cab of his truck and turned it around, it was the first they noticed that the truck was still loaded with the sheeted tobacco. He hadn't sold it—forty cents. He would pack it in a shed somewhere on his farm and maybe try again another day in hopes that the prices would go up.

Bertha didn't understand the economics of the tobacco business. She didn't have a TV to watch the daily market reports. She couldn't read the reports in the papers. And had she had a TV or newspaper she still wouldn't have understood. She only knew that tobacco farmers were all rich like Billy Winston, and the workers, like she, were all poor. And she did understand that Billy Winston was not at all happy with the prices that had been offered to him at the market for his first barn of tobacco—forty cents per pound. And she did know that this was not her fault no matter how much Billy tried to make it seem that way. She had shaken those leaves good and the girls had shaken them good. There had been more sand than usual on the leaves because of the two weeks of rain just before harvesting. In fact, the boys had complained because some of the leaves were virtually buried in the sandy loam of the fields. But that was not their fault.

After Billy dumped his sheeted tobacco in a storage shed, he headed toward town. He was anxious to see what the other markets were offering. When he walked into Nathan's, he saw that the center table was already filled with farmers and merchants. He pulled a chair from another table and pushed himself into the center of the caucus. "What's Greensburg offering?" he plunged right into the business.

Nathan approached him with a menu. Billy waved him away. He had not come to eat. Nathan sighed; how could he run a restaurant business if no one ever ate anything? And no one at the long center table ate today. Only Woody Reed and Mike Oakes, the town news reporter, sipped silently at cups of coffee.

"Forty-two cents," Ossie Johnson replied solemnly. For a moment there was silence.

Then Billy banged his fist on the table and yelled, "What the hell are we going to do about it? I turned ticket this morning but I can't do that every day. Some day I'm going to have to let it go."

The men knew Billy was right. And they resented that he should infer

109

that he was the only one who recognized the problem.

"Doesn't the subsidy fill the gap?" asked Woody.

"Subsidy, hell!" mumbled Jerry. "No, and even if it did, it's only designed to bring us up to cost; who in the hell wants to work his ass off just to break even!"

"And the cost they're talking about is some damn figure they dreamed up, not what it really costs the farmer," added Junie Warren.

"They say there's too much sand in the lugs," explained Jerry.

"That's a lot of shit," Junie countered. "There isn't any more sand than any other year."

"Ya'll know what it is," Billy said with an air of wisdom. "They asked us to grow more this year. They increased everyone's allotment. Said they would make sure we got our price if we cooperated to fill the expanding market. But now they see a surplus and they can be choosy as hell about what they buy. And they think they can pay whatever price they want."

"Yeah, and some of us went to one hell of an expense to prepare for the extra allotment by getting automatic primers and bulk barns," reminded Ossie.

"Yeah, ya'll jumped in head first with all that new fangled jazz," chided Billy. "I didn't. I knew better—but I still can't sell at forty cents."

"I heard that a delegation was going to the secretary of agriculture, Butts, to try to get bigger subsidies," Woody said.

"Hell, they aren't going to do anything. You ever hear of the government giving the farmer a break? Big business—that's all they're worried about," said Jerry.

"Well, I'll tell ya'll, I'm not going to sell at forty cents. I'm not going to sell at eighty cents," Billy snapped, banging his fist on the table by way of confirmation. "We can't sell for less than one-twenty or we'll lose our asses." No one argued Billy's reasoning.

Ossie Johnson pushed his chair back from the table, saying, "Well, forty cents, eighty cents, or one-twenty, the damn stuff still has to be put in the barns now that it's grown." He left the restaurant to attend to his farm. The others followed suit.

"See ya'll at the food stamp office," yelled Mike, slapping the table and laughing at his own joke. Billy glared at him and shoved the table angrily as he too got up to leave. As a final rebuke, on leaving, he turned and began his finger waggling again.

"Ya'll just sit there and laugh but when the farmer doesn't sell his tobacco you watch and see just how much he spends in this here town." He stomped out the door, slamming it loudly behind him. Nathan winced as the big plate glass windows trembled under the assault.

"You know?" reflected Mike to Woody, "you know what I think? I think the tobacco companies have gotten together and made a pact to keep the prices down. They know there's plenty of tobacco this year and if they stick together they can force the farmers to sell at any price they feel like paying."

The two men were the only ones left in the grill now. Nathan called from the counter, "You fellows going to sit there all day with those empty cups in front of you or do you want to order some breakfast?"

"Nah, I'm not hungry," Mike answered.

"It's the poor quality," mused Woody.

"There's nothing wrong with my food," shouted Nathan. "You can't get a better meal anywhere in this county."

Mike and Woody looked up at Nathan. They stared at him for a moment. Then, when Woody realized that Nathan had misunderstood, he apologized, "No, Nathan, I'm not talking about your food. Of course you've got the best. I'm just not hungry today, that's all. I meant, the *lugs* are of poor quality this year."

"But I don't think that's exactly true," countered Mike. "Junie was telling me that, aside from the sand, this year's leaves are the best they've been in the past couple of years."

"But Ossie said that all the rain caused the stems to swell so bad that they won't cure out," answered Woody.

Nathan leaned over his counter, his chin propped in his cupped hands. Whatever the problem was, he sure hoped it would be solved soon. The whole town was in a depressed mood; all he sold was coffee. He still had meat left from the pig he had barbecued two days ago. Usually he just barely made it through each day when he barbecued a pig every morning. He poured himself a cup of coffee and joined the two men left at the table. The three sat sipping in silent reflection.

"I kind of feel sorry for Mr. Winston," Kathy said as she examined a leaf for sand.

"Sorry! Sorry 'bout what?" asked London in surprise.

"Well, he can't make it if they won't at least pay him enough to cover his cost." Margie observed Kathy; she had come to respect Kathy and thought that she was about the smartest person she knew. Now she wondered if maybe she, too, should feel sorry for Mr. Winston.

111

"Yeah, it's a shameful way to treat a farmer," she finally said in agreement.

"What you know 'bout it?" snapped Teresa.

"You ain' never seen a poor farmer," Mama observed. "They complains ever' year they bein' robbed but they all gots two, mebbe three automobiles an' a big fancy house an' even some, like Mr. Winston . . . he gots a boat!"

"Yeah, honey," London directed her explanation to Kathy. "They just complains so's they don' have to ever raise our pay none." Kathy thought about all this for a moment. True, all her friends who belonged to farming families got a brand new car for their sixteenth birthday. Her father was thought to have a good job but they had only one car.

"That isn't fair to blame us, then," she said indignantly, suddenly swinging her sentiments to the other side.

"Chile, you're goin' learn a lot this summer," said Mama. "A lot you never knowed. They always tryin' to brainwash us niggers 'cause they thinks we're ig'orant. Well, mebbe lots of us ain' so smart with book learnin' but we sure know 'nough to see what goes on. I works in those big two-story houses in the town; I knows what the 'poor' farmer gots."

"Well, now that I can read good I'm goin' keep on in school an' get a education an' mebbe even go to college," asserted Margie. "I ain' goin' grow up to be a ig'orant nigger."

"Shit!" London mocked. "Honey, you sure is ig'orant. You cain't never be nothin' but a nigger; you is borned a nigger."

"Alton Jones ain' no nigger," objected Gayla. "He gots just as much money an' class as Mr. Winston."

"I still say he's a nigger. They don' let him buy no house in the town, do they," London pointed out.

"Well, mebbe he don' want to live in the town," defended Gayla. "Mebbe he likes to live in the outside of the town."

"Miz Levine says everyone gots the same chance to be rich," said Margie. "She says it says so in the constitution. But you gots to stay in school an' study hard, then you get rich."

"Miz Levine, Miz Levine!" taunted London. "You ever seen where she lives? She lives in that little bitty shack on the end of Jackson St. in 'nigger town.' " Margie hadn't known this and was surprised, in fact she wasn't sure she could believe it.

"That ain' so!" she stomped. "Miz Levine, she's real smart an' she must be rich 'cause she wears such fine clothes to school, an' jewelry too."

112

"Yeah, it is, chile," Mama agreed with London. She hated to disillusion her baby but that was life and Margie must be taught to accept life for what it was. It was nice to be able to read and to be smart; it helped to soften the ugliness of the trash pile behind the house. But it didn't change the smell of it.

Margie looked hopefully to Kathy. Kathy would know, she was real smart. But Kathy didn't know. She could not refute Mama. All of the sudden she wasn't sure of anything. She felt the sticky tar ball up on her fingers and sting in the raw places where she had actually scrubbed the skin away in her efforts to remove the viscous stuff. She wasn't sure just what a nigger was or what the constitution had to say about niggers. She wondered just what she was doing, standing there in the sizzling heat of the North Carolina sun, handling tobacco with a bunch of niggers. Suddenly she flushed at her own bigoted thoughts. She hadn't been taught that way, but then she had never noticed before just how different they were. And that was before she had moved to the South. Life was very different here.

After work Billy Winston stopped his truck in front of Pfeiffer's so Mama could shop. He had cried and bellyached all the while he had been passing their wages among them.

"I'm not making any money myself, but I still have to hand it out to a bunch of lazy niggers." He had made no distinction between the Taylors and the Braxtons.

And now he yelled from his truck, "Ya'll hurry up there now; I'm not planning to sit here all night." It just galled him to death to see them spend their money the very same day he had given it to them. But they did it every day and, though he fussed about it to Bertha everyday, she still insisted on having him stop. And he stopped, because he knew Bertha Braxton. Besides his own mother she was the only woman who had ever been able to back him down. And this galled him too.

While Mama selected the groceries that they would need for the day, Margie examined the bookrack. Slowly turning it so she could view every one of the books, she let her fingers slip longingly across the slick, gay colored jackets. She promised herself that some day she would buy every one of those books.

The other girls looked at the combs and scarves that Mr. Pfeiffer kept hung on a pegboard above the soft drink cooler. London tried a green and yellow chiffon scarf on for effect. She was not pleased and returned it to its place on the board. All the while, Mr. Pfeiffer watched them nervously. He wished they'd get finished and leave, he was just sure something was going to be missing by the time they got out.

113

London moved over to the toy shelf. She picked up a yellow plastic duck. She squeezed it. It squeaked shrilly. The girls all laughed. She put the duck on the counter with the groceries, telling Mama to buy it for Reggie. Mama mumbled the usual something about luxuries but left the duck on the counter with the other prospective purchases.

"I reckon that'll be all," Bertha said, as she surveyed the mound of groceries she had collected.

Mr. Pfeiffer punched his ancient adding machine with nervous little pecks. Bertha watched suspiciously as the column of figures grew longer and longer.

"Twenty-two, ninety-three," he announced, as he gave the total button a resounding clack.

"Twenty-two, ninety-three?" Bertha bellowed. "Why I ain' got hardly 'nough here to put in one sack."

Mr. Pfeiffer sighed. One by one, he showed her what the price on each item was. He did it every day. Every day she doubted him. Everyday he attempted to prove that he was right. He knew what was coming next. She did it every day.

"Well, I can't 'ford all that." She fumbled around among the items on the counter, first picking up one, examining it, pondering its worth, evaluating its necessity, then putting it down again. Mr. Pfeiffer dabbed at the perspiration on his forehead. A horn tooted outside. Everyday the horn tooted outside.

"Let's see now, we don' need all this soda. Put it back." Mr. Pfeiffer removed the carton of soft drinks from the counter.

"But, Mama, it's so hot an' we're so dry," the girls whined at her decision. "We gots to have somethin' to drink."

"Well, mebbe we'll get some Kool-Aid," Mama said.

"Kool-Aid," they grumbled. "That don' help your thirst."

"Yeah, it do," Mama answered. "Give me some Kool-Aid, Mr. Pfeiffah."

"How many packs do you want?"

"Well, I don' know, how many I needs to make 'nough for these thirsty girls?" The horn tooted again. Mr. Pfeiffer sighed again.

"One package makes two quarts."

"Two quarts, that's all! That ain' very much." Mr. Pfeiffer tapped nervously on the counter waiting for her to make a decision. "You better give me two packs" she finally decided. Mr. Pfeiffer got the two packs of pre-sweetened cherry Kool-Aid. (Mama always got red.) He placed them on the counter.

"I thinks mebbe we'll get green this time, for a change." Mr. Pfeiffer replaced the two cherry Kool-Aid with two lime Kool-Aids.

"Now, add that all up 'gain an' let's see how much we're savin'."

Mr. Pfeiffer knew it would do no good to just adjust the prices between the soda and the Kool-Aid. Mama would never stand for that. He had to add up all the groceries from the very beginning. He began methodically pecking the keys of the adding machine again. Mama watched gleefully. She loved to see the numbers appear like magic on the long strip of white paper tape. The horn tooted outside again. Another customer came in the store and, seeing the Braxtons, knew immediately that Mr. Pfeiffer was very busy so he selected a soda and placed the correct change on the counter, nodding knowingly at Mr. Pfeiffer. Mr. Pfeiffer smiled and nodded a "thank-you."

"London, tell Mr. Winston we'll be there d'rectly," Mama said. London went to the door and relayed her mother's message to him. He swore into the end of his cigar.

"Twenty-two, ninety-two," Mr. Pfeiffer announced.

"Twenty-two, ninety-two!" Mama exclaimed. "Why, it ain' no diff'rent than when we had the sodas." Mr. Pfeiffer could have told her that it would not be any different. A carton of soda cost $1.19 and two packs of Kool-Aid cost $1.18, but she would never have believed him. And he knew what was coming next. He picked up the two packs of Kool-Aid and waited.

"Well the, if it don' make no diff'rence, then there're ain' no use in changin'," she reasoned. "We'll take the soda 'stead of the Kool-Aid." Mr. Pfeiffer was already making the exchange. The horn tooted again, this time with an insistent bleat.

Suddenly Bertha felt an urgency to get finished with her business in Pfeiffer's.

"We're in a hurry, so hurry up an' put this stuff in the sack. Here's your money." she ordered breathlessly. Mr. Pfeiffer hurried as fast as he could. He was just as anxious to terminate the sale.

Margie was reluctant to leave the bookrack when Mama called her to help carry the groceries. She gave the rack one more hefty spin for good luck. The rack wobbled and banged against a shelf that was too close. Margie winced and looked at Mr. Pfeiffer apologetically. He sighed and gave her a weak smile that said, "that's OK."

Yes, she thought. *Someday, Mr. Pfeiffer, I'm goin' buy every one of them books for myself.*

Chapter IX

Lenny sat on his box on the porch, eyes closed, head tipped back in reverie, tapping his foot in time to the music, his rubbery thigh jiggling with each tap.

Bertha stopped short when she climbed out of Mr. Winston's truck. She stared in disbelief at the black box Lenny cradled in his arms. The girls also stood staring at Lenny in amazement. Mr. Winston's truck left the scene, spewing dust on the awe-frozen group. They did not notice his departure.

"What's that?" Margie gasped as her eyes followed the shiny silver stem that jutted from the black box and lay gently against Lenny's shoulder.

"He gots a radio!" London answered, her voice barely above a whisper.

"I know *that,* but where at did he get it?" asked Margie.

"*I* sure don' know," Bertha sizzled, "But I reckon I'll know d'rectly." She stomped her matronly bulk across the sand toward the porch. The girls followed close behind. Lenny, oblivious to their approach, still tapped, his eyes closed, a gratuitous smile curving his bulbous lips.

"Where at did you get that?" Bertha demanded as she mounted the porch in one giant stride. Lenny jerked to the present. Confused for a moment at the sudden intrusion on his reverie, he quickly gathered his wits.

"What—oh, this? This is a radio," he explained, grinning.

"I *know* what it is," Bertha stomped again, her arms crossed menacingly under her heavy bosom, the sagging mounds thrusting up and outward in an air of authority. "I said, *where did you get it?*"

"Up to Pfeiffers," Lenny answered cautiously, watching Mama's now heaving breasts.

"Where at did you get the money?" she demanded.

"I—I—I put it on account," Lenny stuttered.

Bertha was rendered momentarily speechless. Lenny squirmed uncomfortably on his box, the radio still blaring its music. London began to sway to the beat. The other girls felt the rhythm thumping through their veins.

"A man—a man just can't set here an' stare into the sky all the day," Lenny offered as explanation.

Bertha gathered herself into a tall, threatening mass and, still holding her arms tightly under her breasts, she pounced through the door.

"Sissy!" she shrieked. Sissy did not look up from the pot of hot grease into which she was dropping hush puppy batter. "Sissy!" Bertha shrieked again, stomping her foot for emphasis.

Sissy turned her back square to her now frothing sister. Frustration clutching at her lungs, Bertha turned gasping back towards the porch. The girls were swaying and grinding to the soul-stirring moans and thumps emanating from the radio. The blissful smile reinstated on his lips, Lenny tapped his foot and slapped his hand rhythmically on his shimmering thigh. Bertha stared at the group in open-mouthed bewilderment.

"Dinner be on the table soon," Sissy called as casually as she could from her station at the stove. "Better go an' get your baths."

Completely incensed now, Bertha turned back towards Sissy. Not noticing Reggie clapping, bobbing, and gleefully sashaying about the room in time to the music. She stumbled over him as she attempted to gain her sister's attention for the second time. Reggie bounced with a thud to his bottom on the floor. Stunned for only a moment he let forth a bansheelike wail of pain and indignation. Sissy dropped the spoon into the bowl of batter and rushed to him. Swooping him into her arms, she smothered his shrieks with kisses.

"It's OK, baby, it's OK. Aunt Sissy gots the baby now, it's OK," she crooned.

Bertha was numb. What was happening? It was as if she were a ghost, no one paid any attention to her. The black box had them all hypnotized against her presence. It was the devil himself who held her family in his grasp. It was the devil himself who produced the pulsating rhythm that blared forth from that vile box. She watched in helpless frustration as her girls swayed and swung to the ecstasy of the satanic embrace.

Panic coursing through her bloodstream, Bertha rushed toward the now almost comatose figure of Lenny. Grabbing the radio from his hands, she hurled it across the yard. It hit the hard ground with a shattering explosion, plastic and wires and batteries flying in all directions. Lenny gaped at the bared teeth set in the contorted face before him. The girls froze in various positions of dance.

117

Lenny screamed, "Why the hell you go an' do that for?" Bertha did not move from in front of him. Her hands flexed in angered fists. She did not answer. "You bus' it, you bitch, you bus' it!" Lenny wailed, as he struggled to his feet. "That damn radio cos' seventeen dollars, an' you bus' it!" He began to flail his arms in a violent pattern about him.

Sissy stood in the doorway clutching Reggie to her bosom, her eyes closed, her head tipped up toward heaven in a praying attitude. Bertha and Lenny stood facing each other just inches apart. Lenny's arms had stopped flailing and hung stiffly at his sides. Beads of sweat were forming on Lenny's cheeks and forehead. Bertha was heaving heavily. They stared hard at each other.

Suddenly, the possibility of a physical clash occurred to Margie. She had forgotten all about the radio now and was concentrating only on the two figures on the porch. Her eyes strained to keep the two bodies from melting into each other. Panic rising up from her stomach, she lurched forward. Screaming, she thrust herself between Lenny and her mother. "Don' you hurt my mama!"

Margie's shrill cry brought Bertha to consciousness. Her hands relaxed and she began gasping for her breath. Clasping Margie to her breast she sobbed hysterically, "Baby, baby, baby."

Lenny backed off and dropped back down onto his box. He had a glazed and confused expression. His head swayed back and forth in bewilderment. London walked over to the shattered radio and began picking up the pieces. Her sisters watched.

"Leave it be!" screamed Mama.

London dropped the pieces back to the ground as if they were molten metal. Bertha straightened up and then, with total irrelevancy, she announced, "I'm goin' take my bath, an' you girls better get yours too." She descended the porch and walked unconcernedly around the corner of the house toward the pump. The girls followed in obedient fixation. Lenny stared heartbroken out at the radio pieces that were half buried in the powdery surface sand that covered the hard soil.

Billy Winston doggedly prodded the boys to work faster as Rick climbed a notch higher in the barn to unhook the next layer of sticks.

"Come on, get moving; I want to get started," he yelled. Turning to Margie, he shouted at her, "Hurry up, girl, get that stuff off of them sticks."

She was working as fast as she could. The string tangled and held tight. She bit at it with her teeth, grimacing at the bitter taste. She wondered how her Mama could suck on the bitter snuff that she always kept tucked behind her bottom lip. Tossing the loosened leaves into the sheet she grabbed for another stick.

When the barn was emptied, and the cured tobacco sheeted and loaded onto his truck, Billy drove off with the load to the warehouse in Farmdale. Every day was the same. The low prices angered him. Though now up to seventy-eight cents, it was still not enough. But he could no longer store it, there was only so much room. He had to sell at seventy-eight cents.

Bertha took advantage of his absence and ordered a break for everyone. It was against the rules, but everyone was happy to comply with the order. Kathy lit up a cigarette and lounged against the parked tractor. Margie, still feeling the sting of the tobacco on her tongue, sucked her cheeks in to activate her salivary glands in an attempt to dilute the bitterness.

"How can you stan' that stuff?" she asked Kathy.

"What stuff?"

"That 'bacco. Don' it tas' terr'ble?"

"I'm not eating it; I'm smoking it!"

"Miz Levine says smokin' gives you cancer," Margie warned. Kathy contemplated the little girl for a moment then tossed her half-smoked cigarette to the ground and crushed out its ash with the callused sole of her bare foot. Margie smiled in appreciation.

"OK, le's go!" Bertha broke the quiet of the illegal break. She had gotten her second wind after the rushing around to get the barn of tobacco sheeted and off to the market. If she was ready to work, everyone was.

Andy and Sonny mounted their tractors, and chugged them to a start. The other boys climbed on as passengers. Bertha watched a moment as they headed out toward the fields.

"OK, le's get them sticks counted." She began pulling sticks from the unruly pile on the ground where they had dropped them haphazardly in their haste to get the cured leaves off of them. There were seven hundred sticks. It took exactly seven hundred sticks to fill a barn. They sorted them all and stood them in bundles of twenty-five against the railing of the shelter. When they had finished sorting the sticks, Bertha sent London, Teresa and Gayla into the barn to sweep up the debris that had accumulated on the dirt floor: broken leaves and stems that had fallen when the sticks were dislodged from the racks. The accumulation presented a fire hazard and had to be cleaned away before the next barn was put in. Margie and Kathy swept and cleaned the area under the shelter. They had just about gotten it all cleaned up when Sonny arrived with his first cart load of leaves.

The leaves were dripping with the early morning dew. They were cool and sweet. Bertha put a plastic apron on over her dress to keep it from getting wet but the girls didn't mind the wet, it kept them cool. Though it was barely nine o'clock the sun had already attained a blistering temperature. They worked in silent rhythm. Usually the girls chattered while they worked; it made the time go faster. But today there was a pouting strain among the Braxton girls. Kathy was unaware of yesterday's episode with the radio and tried repeatedly to get a conversation started.

"How's your new book coming?" she prodded Margie.

"OK," Margie answered, without missing a beat of the rhythm that had been set for handing. She hadn't read any of her book last night. By the time she had finished eating dinner, it was too dark outside to read. She did not like to read in the house with everyone staring at her and teasing her. Besides, she hadn't felt much like reading, not after all the commotion that Lenny's radio had caused. Lenny always seemed to mess up everything.

"When's your baby due, London?" Kathy tried again.

"Round Christmas," London answered, without missing a loop.

Kathy sighed. It was so lonely to work with a crowd of people who wouldn't talk to you. And even though she could never really feel a part of the group, after what they'd said about Andy, neither could she work a whole day in lonely silence. In an effort to distract herself she began to hum. No one objected. No one seemed to notice, so she continued to hum to keep company with herself.

Lenny sat dejectedly on his throne on the porch. Reggie pushed a wheelless toy car across the rickety boards of the floor. "Brummm, brummmm," he hummed in imitation of a car motor. Lenny wiggled impatiently on his box.

"You gots to make so much noise?" he shouted at Reggie. Reggie continued his "Brummm, brummm."

"Woman, get out here an' hush this boy. He's bad. He's pure gettin' on my nerves."

Sissy obediently complied and came out.

Sweeping Reggie up into her arms, she carried him inside, cooing, "Le's' have some milk, baby."

Alone, now Lenny was even more disturbed. Off in the distance a chugging tractor could be heard. "Noise, noise, can't get no peace," he mumbled. A mocking bird trilled from the pecan tree. Lenny shuddered as the

120

shrill sound grated his nerves. He got up from his box. Standing on the edge of the porch, hands in pockets, he gazed out to where the radio lay in the sand. Slowly descending the step he walked out across the yard. Nudging a piece of black plastic with his toe he grunted and shook his head sadly then turned back to the porch. He sat back down on his box. His chin sagged against his chest. Life was getting to be too much for him to understand. A fly sat on his hand. He did not disturb it.

Margie's heart was beating double time as she stood next to her mother in the kitchen after dinner. No one, as long as she could remember, had ever questioned Mama's wisdom. One might disagree with her but one never admitted to that fact and most certainly no one ever asked her to explain.

"Mama?" Margie asked hesitantly.

"Uh huh," Bertha answered as she sipped her coffee.

"Mama?" Margie began again. Bertha looked up at her daughter with curiosity. Margie took a deep breath.

"Mama."

"Well, chile," Bertha exclaimed impatiently. "I knows my name. If you gots somethin' to say, say it." Margie stepped back a pace.

"Why did you bus' the radio?" she finally whispered in a rush.

Bertha stared unbelievingly at Margie for a moment, then shouted, "Why!" Banging her cup on the table, coffee splashing over the front of her dress. "Why! You as't me why?" Margie cringed but did not step back another pace. She really did want to know. She would stay to hear.

"The devil already gots to you!" Mama moaned. "He come out of that box just like I knowed he would an' he jumped right into my baby!"

"Shit!" hissed Lenny from the doorway of the bedroom.

"You hush! You're the devil! You're the devil hisself!" Mama screamed at him. Lenny shrugged his shoulders and sauntered out to the porch, ignoring Bertha's accusations.

"Chile, this whole worl's goin' to the jaws of the devil," groaned Mama. "Oh my, this whole worl's goin'."

Margie reflected a moment. She did not understand. Yes, she could believe that Lenny might be the devil, but what did the radio have to do with the devil, other than the fact that Lenny had put a luxury "on account," which Mama never allowed. Could the devil have been inside the radio? Mama had busted it. Was the devil shattered to pieces too?

"But, Mama, the music what come out of the radio—it was so purty."

"Oh yes, that's what the devil wants you to think. That's the work of the devil hisself, peoples a wigglin' an' simpin' their asses all 'round the place. You ain' never seen no angel dancin'."

Margie thought about it for a moment. She wasn't sure she had ever seen an angel, but she had heard all about them at Sunday school when she used to go.

"Angels play harps; that's music, so mebbe they dances, too," Margie observed softly.

Bertha was stopped short for a brief moment, she was not accustomed to having her theories tested. "Yes, they do play harps; sweet music too. But I knows they don' dance." She banged her cup again in a note of finality.

Margie winced at the crash. Then suddenly, in a flash of inspiration, she understood. It wasn't the music, but the things the music made you do, the way the music made you feel, all tingly and warm. It wasn't the radio Mama was mad about. It wasn't even that Lenny had put it "on account." Well, maybe a little of that, but mostly, it was because the music stirred deep in your soul, deep where it should not be disturbed, where only the devil would find comfort if you let him and she knew *she* would never let him.

Relieved at understanding this awesome mystery, Margie hugged her mother and skipped off to read her book. No dancing. Bertha sighed, she too was relieved to see that Margie understood. She herself had never fully understood the ways of the devil. But she was constantly aware of his presence. She was aware that he was always trying to tempt the really good people into his trap. She ought not to have let Lenny into her house. She knew he was no good. But then how could she have known he was that bad?

"Oh, Lawd, have mercy," she prayed fervently. "It's hard 'nough to raise young'uns without the devil messin' in."

Night fell fast over the flat plains of North Carolina. Without being aware that the final curtain of the day had fallen, Margie suddenly realized that she could no longer see the print on the page. She squinted but still could not make it out. She knew it was time she went in now but she remained lounging in her swing for a few more minutes, reveling in the sauce the words in the book had provided for her crude world.

Something rustled behind her. She turned her head and stared blindly at the black wall of corn that bordered their yard. Last year tobacco had been planted there but this year the rotation crop was planted. The land belonged to Mr. Winston but she did not know who farmed it. The rustling sounded again. Margie froze still in her swing. Maybe it was a varmint. Then she heard a giggle followed by a, "Shush." Someone was out there among the corn; who? Margie peered against the blackness.

"Ain' no one up no more," a voice whispered from the inky blackness. " 'Cept mebbe Lenny, an' he don' count." Margie tried to identify the voice. It giggled again.

"Who's that?" Margie shouted.

Silence followed her shout; even the crickets and frogs stopped singing. Margie sucked in her breath. She could feel the pulse pounding in her ears. "Who's that?" she demanded again. Still no answer. She waited, her eyes popping to penetrate the blackness.

Margie could not remember having seen such a dark night before, and the house looked so far away. She strained her ears to catch another sound from the corn field. There was none. Maybe it all had been just her imagination. But then, on the other hand, if it *was* a varmint, she had better get into the house now. She scuffed her feet casually through the sand that was still warm from the day's sun. Occasionally she looked back over her shoulder to make sure no one or no thing was following her. But she walked at a normal pace, she did not hurry. She did not want to attract attention; never run from a varmint, keep cool, or he might decide to chase you.

Arriving at the porch she stomped her feet to dislodge the grains of sand from between her bare toes. Mama did not like her to get sand in the bed. As she passed the nodding figure of Lenny who was still sitting on the porch she wondered how he could sleep sitting straight up without falling off his box. She wondered if she should warn him of the varmint. Better not, he might throw a fit at being awakened. Tiptoeing through the dark kitchen she went into the bedroom. The moon was halfway up in the night sky on that side of the house where the bedroom was. And though it had been pitch dark on the other side of the house where the swing was, the shadow of the house masking the moon's glow, a sliver of silver now cut across the bedroom through the grimy window. It fell directly across the pallet on the floor. Margie stared at the space on the end, the place where London slept. It was now empty except for the patch of yellow moonglow.

For a moment she stood staring and wondering. Then the familiar giggle echoed in her brain. She smiled to herself as she lay down on the cot next to her mother. Tucking her book under her pillow, she let herself slip immediately into her dream where she traded places with London in the corn patch.

In silver slippers and shimmering satin gown she danced between the rows of corn. Soft music wafted over the feathery tassels. She could not identify the instrument, something between a harp and a muted trumpet.

She knew he was behind her, her prince, suited in blue velvet. Demurely she glanced over her shoulder, yes, he was there. She turned in his direction and, without ever looking directly at him, she began to sway and grind in rhythm to the sweet music. He did not seem to be moving, and she had not moved from the spot where her feet twisted and turned in the sand to the ecstasy of the music, yet the distance between them grew shorter.

She did not remember just when she first noticed, his suit seemed to be taking on a—a lavender tint. Then suddenly the moonlight hit him like a giant spotlight. His suit glowed red, almost a dripping blood red. But she continued to dance unable to stop her hips from rotating, grinding. Her heart began to palpitate, but she was helpless in the gentle thrump of the sweet music. Then a stray streak of silver from the moon caught something on his head. A sparkle danced and rebounded from something shiny. It was a moment before she saw that the sparkle emanated from a glorious pair of diamond studded horns! Almost simultaneously, on seeing the horns, she saw the fluorescent eyes, vibrant green arrow-piercing the dark corn field and penetrating her heart.

She tried to run, her feet pounding heavily at the soil between the hills of corn. Her silver slippers sank deep into the sand holding her fast to the spot. The figure bore down on her. She pulled free of the slippers leaving them buried in the lecherous sand. She tore blindly past the tall stalks, their stiff dry leaves catching on her satin gown shredding it as she struggled down the row.

She didn't remember when she began to breathe again or when her screams had brought her mother dashing across the yard and plunging into the corn to rescue her. The walls tipped back and forth. Her bed rocked gently on an invisible sea. Mama lay on the cot beside her, dabbing at the beads of perspiration that had collected on her brow.

"Lawd, have mercy," Lenny called from the porch. "What possess that chile to holler like that?"

Margie tried to focus on Mama, but she continued to bounce slowly around the room. She could hear Reggie sobbing hysterically somewhere in the room; had he seen the red-suited figure too? She began to tremble, her flesh raised in myriads of tiny bumps.

"It's OK, baby," crooned her mother. "It's OK. You just had a nightmare, it's OK now." Margie heard her mother's voice trailing way off down the miles and miles of corn.

"Gawd, no one can sleep in this house!" complained Lenny, as he stumbled through the door of the bedroom and flopped onto his bed beside Sissy.

The room spun slowly to a stop, Mama's voice faded at the end of a row of corn. Margie snuggled close to her mother's soft warm body, a secure nest. The diamond-horned prince disappeared into the night mist. Mama held her tightly; she slept.

Mama was right. No good had come from the music released by Satan from the shiny plastic radio. As Margie walked across the yard toward Mr. Winston's waiting truck, she skirted the spot where the pieces of broken plastic still lay. She did not look at them but she could feel their presence like the electricity that snapped through the air after a lightning strike. She knew the vile black pieces would lay there forever, taunting her, never giving her a moment's peace of soul. She wondered that her sisters were so complacent in the presence of the black devil. London lounged against the wheel cover of the truck as it lumbered down Gum Swamp Road toward Mr. Winston's fields. Margie stared curiously at the relaxed countenance of the girl who had giggled with the devil in the corn patch just the night before.

After Mr. Winston passed around the soda and honey buns, Margie pulled Kathy away off to the other side of the barn.

"What's the matter with you today?" asked Kathy as she stumbled along behind Margie.

"I gots to talk to you."

"OK, OK. But let go of my shirt. You'll tear it."

Margie released her friend's shirt but clutched at her hand instead and grasped it tightly in hers to prevent Kathy from getting away. Kathy began to feel the urgency of Margie's clandestine actions. She put her free arm around Margie, her bottle of soda dangling over the child's thin shoulder.

"OK, now what's up?" Kathy asked the girl.

Margie hesitated a moment, looking quizzically at Kathy; could she trust her? Finally she whispered. "You ever seen the devil?"

Kathy reacted momentarily in surprise, then composing herself, she answered, "I'm not really sure; the devil takes on so many forms."

"I mean, did you ever see *the* devil."

"You mean, pitch fork and all that jazz?"

"Yeah."

"Not really, I guess," Kathy admitted. Margie bit her lower lip in contemplation. Should she tell her? She had to tell someone!

125

"I did!" she finally admitted in a voice hoarse with embarrassment.

"You did!" Kathy asked in surprise.

"Yeah, an' he's awful, an' I ain' never goin' sin again; I ain' never goin' dance in the corn again; I ain' never goin' listen to the radio again; I ain' never goin' . . . "

"Hold on!" interrupted Kathy. "I'm not following you. What's radios and corn and dancing got to do with the devil?"

The tears began to gush from Margie's eyes. She swiped frantically at her dribbling nose and began pouring out her shameful confession. When she had finished she let herself slump against Kathy's breast; it was such a relief to have shared her burden. She felt totally spent.

"Hey, honey," soothed Kathy, "everyone sees that kind of a devil, sometime or another. It's from your puberty." Kathy felt very grown up to be counseling the young girl on the facts of puberty. It had not been so long ago that she herself had been introduced to the phenomena of the teen years and raging hormones. In fact, hers seemed to rage more and more as the time went on.

"What's that?" Margie gasped, pulling away from Kathy, her eyes popping in wonder at what other strange thing might be wrong with her besides being possessed by the devil.

"It just means you're growing up," explained Kathy knowledgeably. "It happens to everyone. When you're around your age and really growing fast your imagination grows even faster than you do and you get all sorts of weird feelings and visions." Margie stared at Kathy. She wondered if she would ever be as smart as this white friend.

"It'll all go away when you grow up, in a little while, and then you probably won't even remember any of it," continued Kathy.

Margie reflected on this for a moment. "You reckon it might go 'way when I be thirteen? I be 'most thirteen, an' thirteen is growed up. I be all growed up then. Will it be gone then, huh?" Margie pleaded assurance from Kathy.

Kathy laughed and hugged the distraught little girl. "Yeah, thirteen is probably when it will stop. But don't worry about it none now, 'cause nothing is gonna hurt you. Remember, it's all part of puberty—just like getting pimples and stuff."

Oh, thank the Lord for an understanding and wise friend. Margie's anxious contorted face broke into a wide grin of relief. For the rest of the day she wore her puberty like a cloak, an insulation against the devil.

She had almost forgotten about the radio when she jumped out of Mr. Winston's truck at the end of the day. But, as she skipped across the yard, stirring the dry sand into little puffs of dust, her eye caught the glint of the dying sun on one of the silver knobs that lay in the sand. She veered spasmodically to the left to avoid direct contact. No sense in taking any chances. Without looking back she continued on around the side of the house where London was already pushing vigorously on the pump handle.

"Here, catch hol' of this pump whilst I get my bath," London ordered Margie.

Margie clutched the worn-smooth, iron handle and pumped, sending the water gushing over London's hot body. London reached her arms over her head to stretch the knotted muscles of her back. As the water soaked through her dress and pulled it tight to her skin Margie could see the ever-expanding mound that was beginning to thrust upward almost to London's navel. She remembered the giggles from the corn field; she observed the contented look spread over her now refreshed sister's face. Yes, it must go away when you grew up. London was grown up, she didn't act or look like she had seen the devil in that corn field last night. Margie sighed with relief, it wasn't so bad being a child if you knew you were growing up.

Chapter X

Monroe Troy stared up into the pale blue sky. He let his gaze sweep from horizon to horizon. Nothing broke the blue except the long thin vapor trail of a jet. The temperature at 10:00 A.M. was already 94°. He sucked in a long deep breath in an attempt to extract a comfortable amount of oxygen from the humid air. He wondered how the air could be so dense with moisture without actually raining. He kicked at the sand under his feet; a suffocating cloud of dust rose around him. The minute particles tickled the sensitive hair that lined the membranes of his nose; he sneezed violently to expel them.

The chug of the tractor was growing nearer. Another truck of leaves was coming in to be processed for the bulk barns. Turning, he walked back to where the women were working in the shade of a tree near the long aluminum barns. Cecil was priming in the fields along with another brother, Allen, whom they had been able to coax into helping them while he was on vacation from his job at the textile mills. After Billy Winston had taken the Taylor family over to his own fields, Monroe and Cecil were hard-pressed for hands. They had managed to pick up a few inexperienced hands here and there but none of them had stayed more than a week; they were drifters, winos who worked only long enough to collect one paycheck to pay for their habits. But that was the only kind of labor left this late in the season. All the good hands had secured jobs long before the season had even begun. Sometimes Monroe's mother-in-law, Milly, worked on the primer, but that was not a job for a woman of her age and she always complained so bitterly that Monroe would end up relieving her himself.

Monroe and his brother had invested in the rental of four bulk barns. The bulk barns were in some ways better than the old flue barns but now, under the circumstances of being short-handed, Monroe was finding them a drag. Whereas a stick of tobacco leaves prepared for the flue barn weighed about sixty pounds when full the metal-toothed racks that were used in the new aluminum bulk barns weighed one hundred pounds full. The women simply could not handle this weight, get the racks hooked up into the slots in the rails on the sides of the barns, and then push them along those racks to the end of the barn. Two women could handle them, but if two hands were used to perform the one job another job had to be sacrificed. To keep up, Monroe would prime awhile then go back to the barns and rack awhile. It was all very exhausting.

The truck had caught up to him now and he grabbed a handful of leaves to inspect them. They were not a golden yellow, but deep yellow with crisp brown edges. He shook his head and tossed the leaves back into the truck.

"If we don't get rain soon, we're going to burn out," he said to the stifling air around the barns.

"Wish we had some of that rain now that held us back in the beginning," said Sue.

"Would help," Monroe agreed, as he hoisted a loaded rack across his chest and maneuvered it into the slots of the metal rails. It clanged into position as metal met metal. Heaving his weight against the rack he forced it to ride the rail to the back end of the barn. Sweat poured from his pores as he emerged from the giant aluminum box. The sun beating on the shiny metal roof had raised the inside temperature to 120 degrees. The moisture-laden leaves steamed in the oppressive heat, drops of bitter water cascading down the packed racks dripping into slippery puddles on the metal floor of the barn.

"Don't know as how I like these damn tin-foil barns," Monroe remarked as he adjusted the band that was tied around his head across his forehead to prevent the salty sweat from running into his eyes.

"I do believe it takes a longer time to cure out the same amount of tobacco than a flue barn takes," observed Hilda, Cecil's wife. "And those stems are so swollen from the early rains that some don't ever cure out."

"There's an awful lot of weeds in these last couple of trucks," Milly grumbled.

"Yeah, I know. We just can't get through the weeds without getting some along with the tobacco," Monroe answered. "I don't know how the weeds grow so good as dry as it is."

"If you would have used a herbicide like I told you we wouldn't be having any trouble now," reminded Milly.

"We couldn't afford herbicides."

"And if you'd be a little more careful when you're priming, you wouldn't be getting so many weeds," Milly continued with an air of authority. "I don't get any weeds in my leaves when I'm priming." Monroe looked at his mother-in-law with disgust.

Yeah, he thought to himself, *and you don't prime hardly any tobacco either with your finicky worrying about the weeds.*

"And you ought to get it off the stalks before it burns," she prated on. "This stuff is pure sad."

"Go to hell!" Monroe mumbled.

"Yes, you ought to get it off sooner," she continued, oblivious to his curse. "This stuff isn't going to bring hardly anything."

"I'm not but one man!" Monroe shouted in anger and frustration. "I can't prime and rack and take it to market and everything!"

Milly ignored his outburst and added, "I bet you don't even get seventy cents for it. How much you get yesterday?"

"Seventy-two cents! Hell, that isn't even going to pay for the electricity in these barns!" He did not answer as he grabbed up another rack and hoisted it into place. He knew how much the electricity cost.

"A lot of the farmers are holding back to see if they can force the prices up," suggested Sue.

"We haven't got a place to store ours," Monroe reminded her sullenly. "Besides, I don't think it'll help anyway. The tobacco companies got us over a barrel. They know we have to sell eventually and they can just wait us out."

"It's all that damn Butt's fault. They ought to fire him," sputtered Hilda.

"Who's going to fire him?" asked Monroe. "The tobacco companies think he's pretty good—they're making money."

"I'm glad somebody is," sighed Sue. "Maybe we're on the wrong end of the business."

"Yeah," snickered Monroe. "The shit end."

Margie and Kathy danced up and down in the spray from the sprinklers. It felt cold on their hot skins and sent shivers through their bodies.

"Ya'll get back here an' han' this 'bacco," shouted Bertha.

The girls reluctantly returned to their jobs. Billy Winston had his giant irrigation system going. Whichever field wasn't being worked at the moment got a good soaking. The source of his water came from a large pond just on the other side of the trees that bordered one of his fields. He had a huge pump on the edge of the pond that pumped water through pipes that ran up and down the rows of tobacco. The water was forced out in a jet spray as the spigots jerked spasmodically round and round wetting every inch of the field. He had no burnt leaves; all his were a golden yellow, perfect even to their edges.

Nor did he have to contend with weeds in his bulk. Billy Winston was a firm believer in herbicides. He did not believe in allowing weeds to suck up his costly fertilizers or steal any precious water from his plants. Still, he was not getting much more for his tobacco than was Monroe Troy. Seventy-eight cents was the best so far.

London put her hands against the small of her back and pressed hard to relieve the muscle spasms. "This chile's goin' be the death of me," she moaned.

"It ain't even that big yet. Wait till it grows big at the end an' then you can bellyache," said Gayla.

"My mom used to wear a girdle to keep her back from hurting," Kathy advised.

Margie gasped at such a notion. "Don' that squeeze the baby?"

"It was special' made so it couldn't hurt the baby."

Margie eyed Kathy with a look of skepticism. Kathy was smart but this girdle business just didn't sound right to her. "Oh," she said. "Well, I don' think London'd wear somethin' like that."

"I smell rain," Bertha observed, not paying any attention to the prenatal discussion. She never talked about London's pregnancy. She firmly believed that it was best not to make mention of an unborn child. As long as the evil spirits that lurked about her world did not know of the child no harm could come to it. She worried about the young women of today who foolishly discussed their pregnancies to anyone and everyone. They were simply courting danger with such candor.

Margie sniffed at the stifling air. "You smell the sprinklers," she corrected her mother.

"No, I smell them too, but I smell rain 'sides."

Margie sniffed again. "It smells like ol' 'bacco to me."

"There are a few clouds in the sky that weren't there earlier," admitted Kathy.

"Them's cotton puffs, them's not real clouds," Margie corrected scornfully.

"Look yonder." Bertha nodded toward the southwestern horizon. The girls followed her nod. A dim bar of gray was slipping up from the tops of the distant trees.

"Well—mebbe," conceded Margie.

"Maybe the hurricane is coming," Kathy said excitedly. Having come from the north central area of the country she was familiar with severe storms like tornadoes but had never thought much about hurricanes. Now, here in this southeastern coastal plain town she listened excitedly to the weather bulletins that charted the paths and progress of the hurricanes that often battered the coastline. She listened to the talk of hurricane Hazel of a few years back and of the damage it had done even this far inland; roofs and carports had been torn off homes, trees uprooted, power lines downed. It all sounded very exciting from an outside observer's point of view.

Bertha also remembered hurricane Hazel and asked anxiously, "A hurricane's comin'?"

"Well, maybe not coming here, but one's starting out in the ocean, out by Bermuda."

"What's a B'muda?"

"You know, those islands under Florida," Kathy described vaguely. She was not sure of her geography.

"Oh, them," Bertha acknowledged just as vaguely, without having any idea of what the girl was talking about.

"We ain' goin' have no hurricane," asserted London. "The win' blows in a hurricane, an' ain' even a leaf stirrin'." They looked up at the tree next to the barn to affirm London's assessment. Not a leaf stirred.

"You hear that?" Margie whispered anxiously to interrupt their gaze.

"What?" everyone whispered in response.

Margie put her finger to her lips and rolled her eyes in concentration. The others strained to hear whatever it was she had heard. "That!" she finally said. A faint rumbling emanated from the direction of the row of trees along the distant horizon.

"Thunder," Mama whispered, catching the mood of the mystery. They all nodded in agreement.

Kathy finally broke the spell, saying, "I guess you're right, Mrs. Braxton. It does sound like we might get rain."

The afternoon wore on. The sun continued to beat down on the heads of the boys in the fields. The gray bar that had earlier bordered the horizon like a band on a man's straw hat had grown into a black churning mass that crept slowly toward Maylor. The rumbles were growing louder and more serious sounding now. The lightning flashes shattered the threatening mass, then sizzled out, which allowed the wounded sky to heal itself before another strike splintered through. As ominous as it all sounded and looked the sun continued to simmer the surrounding fields.

"Reckon it's a goin' 'roun us," observed Bertha with a note of disappointment. And it was not unusual in this flatland area for a storm to mount in all its fury then, unhindered by even the smallest of hills, to suddenly become overloaded and dump all its contents on one small patch depriving all the surrounding areas. Farms just three miles outside of Maylor could report two inches of rainfall while Maylor would bake under the broiling sun, or vice versa.

Disappointed, the women continued to work in reflective silence. It was Andy who first broke that silence when he came chugging toward the barn on his tractor revving it to its top speed and yelling, "Look over there!" He was waving and pointing hysterically.

The women ran around to the other side of the barn and trained their eyes in the direction of Andy's concern. A column of black smoke spiraled into the sky. The long flat acres gave the illusion that the smoke was a few hundred yards away. In fact it was nearly a half mile away.

"It's a barn goin' up," gasped Bertha.

By this time Sonny had brought his truck in with all the other boys hanging on to its sides. All were shouting and waving toward the black spiral that grew like a giant mushroom into the sky.

"Whose is it?" Kathy asked excitedly.

" 'Bout where Mr. Troy's barns would be," Bertha calculated.

"Oh, no!" Kathy groaned. It was one thing to feel the excitement of a fire in which you did not know the victims, but when it was someone you knew, a friend . . .

"Prob'ly got striked by lightning," Margie surmised with just a hint of concern in her voice. A faint wailing could be heard. It grew steadily louder and longer. The volunteer fire companies from Maylor, Gristown and Winterdale would be answering the call.

There was never much that could be done to save a barn once it began to burn. The timbers in the ancient flue barns were tinder dry from years of having the heaters burn day and night to dry the tobacco. The tobacco itself provided a dry, willing wick for the fire to pass from section to section. But the fire companies always responded. Their main objective was to keep the fire contained in the one barn so it did not spread to the adjacent barns or to the trees or the fields that were unwitting prey to the voracious appetite of the frenzied flames of barn fires.

The women and the boys stood some minutes just watching; a feeling of total inadequacy wrapped the heavy air around them. They were jostled to the urgency of the moment when Billy's truck came bouncing and jolting down the road toward the barn. Billy was honking his horn frantically and when he got close enough he began yelling out the window.

"You boys, get in, we've got to help the Troy's!" The boys ran to meet the truck. Hopping into the still moving vehicle, they clung to the sides as Billy made a U-turn in the barnyard and headed back down the road.

"Hey, wait for me!" Kathy yelled, running after the truck. Teresa ran after her and caught hold of her shirt.

"We don' go!" Teresa yelled breathlessly. "Why not?" Kathy demanded impatiently struggling to free herself.

" 'Cause we're womens."

"But I worked for Monroe; I want to help."

"Womens on'y get in the way."

"I won't. I'll help." Kathy pulled away from Teresa and ran down the road. Teresa stood helplessly behind and watched her fade into the dust trail left by Billy's truck.

"Mama, Kathy'll get hurt!" Margie wailed anxiously.

"No, chile, the mens won' let her get near."

Kathy sprinted on down the road in the wake of the truck, coughing and gasping in the dust cloud that separated her from the truck. Her bare feet slapped hard in the powdery sand sending out another smaller puff of dust behind her. The truck disappeared around a bend in the road. Kathy followed round the bend searching the dissipating cloud of dust in front of her for the familiar blue truck. She could no longer see it.

Looking over her shoulder, she could see the twisting billow of black smoke to her right. A long field of six-foot-high corn lay between her and the burning barn. Cutting sharply off the road she headed down a row between the hills of corn. The leaves, dried crisp by the hot August sun, cut across her face like razors. Folding her arms across her face she pushed on through. The plant roots, bared by the erosion of the early spring rains that were followed by raping winds, stabbed at her feet like barbed wire. Panting and choking she emerged from the corn onto another dirt road, Monroe's road. The burning barn was yet another five hundred yards to her right down the road. She could see the fire engines and Mr. Winston's blue truck among another dozen farm trucks. No one noticed as she burst into the crowd of men and boys who stood helplessly staring at the blazing barn. Sue was standing at the back edge of the crowd. Kathy ran to her.

"Why don't they do something?" she screamed.

"They're doing all they can," Sue answered numbly. Looking around Kathy saw that the pump trucks were directing a fine spray of water onto Monroe's other flue barn and also flooding the propane tank that was mounted on concrete blocks between the two barns. It was most important to keep the tank cool to avoid an explosion. The neighboring farmers including Billy Winston, helped Monroe pull all his equipment and tobacco trucks a safe distance away from the fire. There was little else now to be done except watch.

Suddenly a frantic cry went up from the crowd. "Did anybody turn off that gas line?"

The two men who had been hosing the gas tank dropped their hoses and ran to the unburned barn and gave the gas valve a twist, cutting off the fuel to that barn. But the fire was too hot and too widespread to do the same at the other end of the line at the burning barn. The men ran back into the crowd and began pushing the spectators back, yelling, "Get back! She's going to go!"

A few of the people panicked immediately and ran into the corn field on the other side of the road. The others had to be physically forced to give up their ringside positions.

Two other men, not firemen, had taken up the task of keeping the propane tank cool. But the heat from the burning barn was too hot and the men too slow to assume the task. A loud explosion lacerated the air. Flames shot into the sky. The crowd now ran back down the road covering their heads with their arms to shield themselves from the cascade of falling sparks.

Kathy blinked as the flashes from the exploding gas tank lit the storm-blackened sky. The clouds had completely covered the overhead sky now and the sun had disappeared. She stared in open-mouthed awe at the spectacle. An irrational thought came over her. It looked just like the fireworks display at Kings Island in Ohio. It was beautiful! The flames shot hither and thither like giant fireflies playing tag till one touched the other barn. Within seconds it too was a blazing inferno.

A loud cracking, like a hundred rifle shots, spiked the air as the tin roof of the first barn began to buckle in the heat. The spectators, who had begun again to creep forward toward the vicinity of the fire, moved quickly back into the corn field again. But Kathy was rooted to her spot. She was paralyzed at the majesty of the blaze. Never had she seen anything like it.

"Get back!" Someone tugged at her shirt. She stumbled backwards still gaping in utter disbelief as the roof crashed down through the smoke and flames. A new spray of flying sparks attacked the crowd of observers. A glowing ash fell on Kathy's cheek. Unconscious even to its cause, she slapped mechanically at the sting.

The second barn was burning in full flame now. The men stopped pumping water onto the conflagration. It was no use now. All of the firemen and spectators stood in silence and watched the flames devour the remainder of Monroe's flue barns. The hoses lay ready, just in case they would be needed, in case the fire spread further. With a groan, then a sickening crash, the second roof fell in on itself.

"It'll burn out now the roof is down," the chief observed without emotion.

"What about that corn yonder?" a fireman asked.

"Just watch it."

"Shouldn't we spray it a little?"

"Not yet, we don't have that much water. Save it in case these barns start acting up again.

"We need Winterdale's pumpers in a fire this size," another fireman noted.

"Would help," the Maylor chief agreed.

"Where are they anyway?"

"On a run."

" 'Nother barn?"

"A house trailer."

Monroe watched helplessly while his barns full of tobacco lay in two smoldering heaps. The air was permeated with acrid tobacco smoke. Kathy wiped the tears from her stinging eyes with the sleeve of her shirt. A drop splattered on her head; she looked up toward the laden clouds overhead.

"It's raining!" she shouted. A sigh of relief went up from the crowd as the drops continued to fall. The drops merged into large globs of water, a splash here then a splash there, quickly sucked up by the parched sand. A soft sizzling sound accompanied each drop. Suddenly, as if the heavens had split, the rain was dumped in a gush onto the burning piles of tobacco. Everyone cheered the groaning sky. A thin wail could be heard in the distance. The Winterdale pumper was on its way.

"Don't need 'em now," the fire chief said with a nervous laugh of relief.

The barns continued to burn, the roofs sparking and sizzling as the rain fell onto them. There was no chance of the corn field catching now. The firemen turned off their pumpers but did not roll up the hoses yet. These would remain ready just in case.

The barns were now just a smoldering heap of ashes with an occasional sparkle of flame dancing here and there. The people were coughing and gagging on the smoke as it rolled along the ground unable to flow upward through the rain. They began to disperse. A few stayed on to give Monroe moral support and to help him move his equipment down the road to his bulk barns.

The Maylor firemen would stay until the last ember had died. Gristown pumper and the unused Winterdale pumper returned to their towns.

Kathy stood in the drenching rain. The chilled water ran down the part in her tousled hair and dripped off the tip of her nose. It did not wash her sticky, tobacco-stained skin clean. Blessed rain; but why hadn't it come sooner, before Monroe's barns had burned down? She heard Monroe say to Sue, "Insurance'll cover some, but we're still going to take one hell of a loss. Just be glad we still got the bulk barns full."

"We haven't got all that much to lose," Sue answered softly.

"Hey, what are you doing here?" Rick asked, as he noticed Kathy for the first time in the thinning crowd.

Kathy didn't answer. Her first barn fire had left her empty and speechless. Such a waste, a terrible waste. Rick put his arm around her shoulder and guided her to Mr. Winston's truck. The others were already in the back. Kathy climbed numbly over the tailgate. The ride back to Mr. Winston's field was depressed in silence.

"He'll make it up," Margie soothed her friend. Kathy gazed into the brown eyes of the little girl. "How can you be so complacent? Monroe just lost two whole barns of tobacco!" she snapped.

It was Margie's turn now to teach the facts of life to Kathy. "Honey, it happens all the time," she said. "Farmin's a crazy business. Rains wash out the plants, the sun dries out the leaves, the win' knocks 'em over an' barns burn down. That's just life."

"But how do they survive?" Kathy asked in bewilderment.

"Don' know, but somehow they do. They just work harder nes' week, nes' year. Somehow they do," Margie answered solemnly. "Mr. Troy, he don' own his own fields, he's just a tenant. Tenants don' have much to start with in the firs' place so they don' lose much in the end."

"But how do they ever get ahead?" insisted Kathy.

"Then don'. Tenants don' mostly. On'y the big man like Mr. Winston. The tenant an' the workers don', mostly," But Margie added in her own private thoughts a final resolution for herself. "I ain' never goin' le' myself get stuck in the road rut what's got my Mama. I'm goin' make it out."

It was all beyond the comprehension of Kathy. She had never suffered a loss or a setback in her short life. Life had always been as secure as a Linus blanket for her. The thought of going on, even starting over, after a crisis was more than she could imagine. She knew she'd never make a farmer. She hadn't the stamina in her blood.

That night Kathy's sleep was smothered in the suffocating flames of the burning barns. She awoke several times sweating and tense. Looking around her room, she would sigh with relief as the shapes and shadows acknowledged themselves. She thought of Margie's devil, her puberty devil. She wished she could chalk up her own devil to the effects of puberty. But she could not. The ashes of Monroe's barns were too real to dismiss so casually.

Margie dreamed of barn fires too. She felt the suffocating smoke bundle around her thin body separating her from the large mound of her mother who lay next to her. But in her dreams she thrust at the binding acrid blanket of smoke to be free of its grasp. She knew she must somehow tear the imprisoning cocoon that held her in this road rut. She would not be like her mother, her Aunt Sissy, or Lenny. She did not know just yet who she would be; that would come with growing up, and she was growing very fast.

Chapter XI

Margie lay quietly awake next to the sweating bulk of her still, sleeping mother. The others in the room, too, gurgled with the deep breathing of sleep. The sun was already peeking over the row of pines that divided the fields near the house, but it was Sunday. They did not have to get up for several hours yet. Church did not start until eleven o'clock. Sunday school began at ten o'clock but they never went to Sunday school anymore. Mama didn't like the new Sunday school teacher, Rita Becker. Rita was too much "of the world" to be teaching the facts of the Lord. Once, Rita had even worn a pants suit to church. Pastor Brown had severely reprimanded her then and she had never worn pants to church again, but Mama would never forget that she had indeed worn them that once.

Margie liked to go to church. The family only went to church in the summer months when they could afford to buy church clothes. Mama would not think of approaching the Lord's house without the proper attire. Anyway, it was too far to walk when it was cold. The preacher once had offered to carry them in his car but Mama had refused his offer saying that it was too much to ask of him. He knew the real reason though and did not press her to attend. He thought of sending clothing from the mission society, but then Mama would never have accepted it. It was her pride, and he had respect for that pride; he didn't send the clothes.

Margie squirmed on the damp sheet. Her foot got tangled in one of its holes; she ripped it more in her efforts to extract herself. The night had been so warm that her pillow and sheet were soaked with perspiration and virtually stuck to her body. The room smelled sour with steaming flesh. She watched the sun rise slowly into the white and blue sky until it met the window pane and sent a golden blade of shimmering light across the pallet where her sisters lay. London stirred in discomfort, but continued to sleep.

It would be another hot day. In the past month the temperatures had hit 95° every day. And, aside from the brief storm on the day of the fire, there had been no rain. As usual, the insatiable Piedmont had gobbled up all the moisture before it could get to the flatlands. There was promise of rain from the Gulf but it was long in coming and would probably favor somewhere else along its route before it ever got as far north as Maylor. Meanwhile the farmers sweated and waited, mourning their scorched crops.

Margie knew that this morning's church service would be devoted to cajoling the Lord for His precious water. She tingled with excitement at the thought; such important matters always elicited an emotionally charged prayer service from the congregation. She didn't even mind that Preacher Brown would most certainly blame the drought on their sins. The raucous singing that would plead for deliverance would be well worth the beratement.

Unable to stay laying on the sticky sheets any longer, Margie quietly rose from the bed. Softly tiptoeing from the room she slipped out onto the porch. The morning air was heavy with hot sweet fumes that drifted in from the withered tobacco fields. She took a deep breath to wring a satisfying gulp of oxygen from the laden air.

The roadside in front of the house was rimmed with the bobbling heads of yellow wild flowers. Margie wondered how their heads could bobble so much when there wasn't a breath of breeze. They seemed so gay, so yellow, almost as if they were a part of the sun, completely oblivious to the torturing flames that leapt down from the parent solar disc to devour them. Margie wondered how the delicate wisps of yellow could withstand the endless heat while the thick leathery leaves of the tobacco withered and seared. But she was glad that the yellow flowers had survived. They made the stark sandy yard look almost pretty. Walking across the yard toward the ditch garden, Margie dug her toes into the wet cool sand. Later it would be too hot to walk on without taking hopping, dancing steps. She could hear the soft buzz of the bees that gathered their loads early before the sun's heat would drive them into their hives.

Standing on the edge of the ditch, she watched in fascination as the little stripped bombers dove unerringly into the center of each flower. She wondered how each bee knew which flowers he had already serviced, never doubling back on his own tracks. Someday, she thought, she would have a whole yard full of yellow flowers. Now, she carefully selected a large bouquet for their breakfast table. She sniffed at the yellow petals but found to her disappointment that they had very little perfume. But still she liked them; she liked their deep yellow; she held the golden bundle against her brown skin. It looked good. Someday she would have a dress just this same shade of yellow.

Bertha did not notice the bouquet in the Coke bottle on the table. She clomped, absentmindedly, about the kitchen. It was too hot to light the stove fire for coffee so she settled for a glass of iced tea. Iced tea did not do for her what hot coffee did, however, and she continued to bumble about the kitchen grumbling about the heat. She thought of the gas stove that Sissy always talked about getting—when Lenny got a job. The thought of the still-snoring Lenny filled her with angry repulsion. With what it took to feed him, she thought, she could have bought two gas stoves by now.

"Ain't the flowers purty, Mama?" Margie asked, in an attempt to distract her mother from her black mood.

"Humpf," Bertha grunted.

"Wouldn't a dress that color be purty?" Margie tried again.

"Humpf," Bertha echoed her first response. Margie sighed. She seemed to be the only one in this whole house who enjoyed pretty things. No one else even noticed the flowers by the road let alone enjoyed them.

Even Reggie didn't like her flowers. At first he ignored them but then he climbed onto the table and began pulling savagely at the lacy petals.

"Get your han's off those," Margie shrieked as she swept the baby from the table. Reggie set up an indignant squall.

"Will you let that chile be!" Bertha remonstrated.

"But he's pullin' the flowers apart."

"Them ain' flowers, them's weeds," Mama argued. "Poor peoples don' have no flowers. 'Sides, anythin' what would grow in this heat gots to be weeds." Margie left her and Reggie maligning her flowers and went out onto the porch to suffer in solitude. She would never understand why her mother simply refused to accept pretty things.

The dog, Spot, sidled up to her. Already his tongue lolled from his mouth panting in the early heat. His tail flip-flopped in languid response to Margie's pat on his head. He shivered as a flea dug into his flesh but it was too hot to expend the energy to scratch at the pest.

Reggie toddled out onto the porch. Gurgling delightedly at the sight of the dog he grabbed at its ear and gave it a twist. The dog stifled a yelp and wrenched away from the baby, skittering from the porch and wiggling under it in retreat.

"You're a nasty boy!" Margie slapped at Reggie's hand. Bertha stomped to the door in response to Reggie's wail.

"You sure is ugly today, young'un," she said to Margie as she hauled up Reggie into her arms to soothe him. Margie stared in amazement at her mother. Who was ugly!

"Do that chile always gots to be cryin'?" Lenny bellowed from the bedroom. "A body can't get no sleep 'round here."

"Time to get up fo' church anyways, honey," Sissy cajoled.

"Too hot to go to church," Lenny answered sullenly.

"We gots to go so we can pray fo' the rain," Teresa reminded him.

Lenny heaved his bulk off the side of the bed. He shuffled over to the corner and began to relieve his bulging bladder in an urgent stream that clanged resoundingly on the side of the bucket.

"Hey, that ain' the piss pot!" yelled London. "That's fo' the leak in the roof."

"Gawd can't make it rain so I will," giggled Lenny as he continued to fill the bucket with his hot acid urine. Sissy gasped at the blasphemy and rolled her eyes toward heaven in a repentant manner.

"That man's goin' burn in hell one of these days," warned Gayla. Lenny ignored the damning remark and waddled out to the kitchen.

"Where the hell's the coffee?" he yelled as he searched the empty stove top.

"Too hot to lay a fire fo' coffee," Bertha snapped. "Drink some iced tea."

"I can't go without my mornin' coffee," pouted Lenny.

"When we get our gas stove then we can have coffee anytime you wants it, honey," Sissy crooned.

"I can't un'erstan' why there ain' no gas stove in this house right now," Lenny said accusingly. "All civilized peoples has got gas stoves."

"All civilized peoples works too," Bertha shot back.

Lenny gave his sister-in-law a long dark look. He'd had about as much as he could take of that old woman's nagging and someday he aimed to set her straight. Now, he sullenly sipped at his iced tea.

"You think this dress is too tight lookin'?" London asked Teresa as she pulled and tugged to cover the ever-expanding hump of her belly.

"Yeah, it is, but I can't see what you can do 'bout it. It's the on'y one you gots what still fits at all."

"Shit, I wisht I had one of those maternity tops like Reetha Sands gots."

"That still won' he'p your skirt to button none."

"But, then I could tie it together with a string an' the maternity top would hide it."

"Well, nes' time you get youself a baby why don' you let a rich boy daddy it then he can buy you all them purty things like Reetha gots," Gayla suggested sarcastically.

"Randy'd buy me anythin' I want if I as' him to."

"I thought you said he wasn't the daddy," reminded Teresa.

"Well, mebbe he ain' an' mebbe he is. Ain' none of you business," London snapped to end the debate.

Margie had only half listened to her sisters argument as she jabbed vigorously at her hair with the pick until it was fluffed high into a mound. Her sisters' conversations were becoming very confusing to her of late and she was losing interest in them. Ever since she had met Kathy and had gotten into the reading habit the romance that her sisters spoke of seemed very mundane compared to those glamorous affairs she now read of in the books. She patted a sprig of hair into place then admired herself in the mirror.

Just then Bertha came into the room. Grabbing the pick from Margie's hand she stomped her foot and yelled, "You ain' goin' to church with your hair in that birds nest!"

"But, Mama, the other girls all have their hair like this," Margie protested.

"It's disgraceful!" Mama replied scornfully. "No chile of mine is goin' to go 'round lookin' like a Afr'can savage. Now plait it up like it 'posed to be."

"But, Mama, they do," she countered, pointing to her three older sisters.

"They're growed; you're a chile—anyways, don' sass me none!"

Margie knew it was useless to argue, it would only be misconstrued as sassing. She began obediently to separate the beautiful mound and twist it into thick braids. "Someday," she mumbled to herself," when I'm growed up. Nes' bithday, when I'm thirteen, I am goin' push my hair a mile high into the air, an' ain' nobody goin' stop me."

"An' don' sass me none under your breath, neither," Mama warned as she left the room.

Margie gave her braids a defiant yank to set them into position at the side of her head.

"We're goin' be late if ya'll don' hurry," Sissy called from the porch where she and Lenny waited already dressed and ready to go. She had coaxed Lenny into his suit. His suit coat no longer buttoned across his bulging belly but Sissy made him wear it anyway. Then she had pulled his tie into a neat knot at his throat to cover the gap left where the two ends of his shirt collar did not meet. He tugged impatiently at the juncture now as they waited for the others to join them.

No one in his right mind would be going to church in this heat, he thought. But he also knew that Sissy would pout all day if he didn't go; and though it was too hot for church, it was even worse to have to bear a pouting woman all day.

All together now, they began the mile long walk down the road toward the New Mission Baptist Church. Little blisters had already begun to swell on the baked asphalt. Their shoes popped the tiny bubbles of molten tar that made snapping little sounds as they walked down the road. Some of the tar stuck to the soles of their shoes. Margie could feel the heat seeping through the thin soles of her church shoes. Looking with envy at her sisters' high platform shoes she wiggled her toes to relieve the burning. Four one-inch-thick layers of cork were stacked together to form the teetering soles of their stylish shoes. The stilt-like height of the shoes made them clump stiff-legged and awkwardly down the road, but their feet were not burning.

An' I will get me some of them kind of purty shoes too, Margie vowed to herself, still feeling the ignominy of her braids. She now eyed the cool soft grass on the side of the road. She would have liked to walk on that for relief from the burning road. But Mama had said that ladies don't walk in the grass; this was Sunday and on Sunday they were all ladies, except Lenny, of course. But Mama wouldn't let him walk in the grass either. She didn't give a reason.

Arriving at the church just as Deacon Rawlins had begun tugging at the bell rope for the call to worship, they hastened up the church's steps and pushed through the doors, which had already been closed to hold out the heat. Their tar-stained shoes snapped and crackled as they stuck to the vinyl floor of the center aisle.

Bertha was embarrassed at the telltale sound. Margie didn't notice, however, as she smiled to her left and to her right at her friends. In summer, Sunday was the only time she saw her school friends.

"Uh-hum!" Deacon Whitely reminded that worship was about to begin. The Braxton family sidled into the third pew from the front, that was *her* pew when she was there and no one ever challenged Bertha the right. The choir entered the doors on the side of the church and, singing to the lilting rhythm of the slightly off-keyed, ancient organ, they clapped and marched to their seats.

"One step at a time—one step at a time . . . " Margie sang absently with the congregation as she let her eyes wonder among the worshippers to see the styles and colors of their outfits. Self-consciously, she smoothed the wrinkle in her skirt where it had hung over the hanger. A girl smiled in her direction, Belva Harris. Margie reckoned that Belva had noticed her wrinkle. She felt the flesh under her braids tingle with embarrassment. Belva Harris always dressed in the latest fashions and she never had a wrinkle anywhere. But then her father was a funeral director and owned the only black funeral parlor in a fifty mile radius. His business had to be good. Margie noticed that Belva also wore nylons. She glanced down at her own bare legs, the little nubs of black hair just beginning to prickle the smooth brown skin.

Bertha poked Margie with a daggerlike fingernail. Margie jerked her head toward the front of the church. Deacon Whitely had begun the prayer of supplication, begging the Lord to accept their humble worship. Margie concentrated on his words.

"An' Lawd, Father in heaven, 'member we are your weak little children. Father, 'member that we don' really wan' to aggrieve you," Deacon Whitely finished in a pleading voice.

"Amen," Margie echoed with the congregation.

The choir stood now and began singing a soul-stirring prayer to continue the mood of supplication. Everyone in the little church was acutely aware of his sinfulness and all felt the strong need to soften their nettles before really getting into this business of approaching God. Bertha swayed and hummed reverently to the gentle throb of the chorus. Softly patting her hands together she closed her eyes in prayer. Tilting her head back she basked in the cleansing power of repentance.

Margie shifted uncomfortably on the wooden bench of the pew. The heat had softened the years of layers of built up varnish and her skirt was sticking to its gooey surface. As the choir continued into chorus after chorus of self-chastisement, Preacher Brown swung down the aisle in a pompous, high stepping stride. His black, silk-lined cloak billowed behind him. Mounting the lectern he turned dramatically toward the congregation and bore into their hearts with his steely black eyes. He waited thus until the choir had wrung itself pure, then, bowing his head, he begged God for the necessary wisdom and fluency of tongue needed to reach these wayward children.

Then slowly, in a soft, droning voice, he began to preach. All eyes were riveted on his, all backs erect, all hands folded in tense, prayerful attitudes. Margie listened, hardly daring to breathe, as the droning voice gradually mounted in urgency. A large revolving fan swung lazily back and forth in accompaniment.

"An' the Lawd knows," he began to chant now to the slow measured rhythm of an inaudible beat. "An' the Lawd knows what lies in our hearts."

Margie tried desperately to keep her heart tight within her chest. She closed her eyes against the envious thoughts she was harboring of Belva Harris' nylons and chanted softly, "Amen."

Belva's mother chanted, "Yes, the Lawd knows."

Margie flushed. Did Sister Harris know?

"He knows what sins lay deep within us," Preacher Brown warned, the momentum picking up a beat faster. "He knows, even though we are as whited sepulchers on the outside, what ignominy sears our souls."

"Yes, Lawd—our souls," the people agreed.

"He sees our sins in cineramic dimensions. He sees the lies, the greed, the pride that sets a chasm between our souls an' paradise!" Margie was not sure of what he meant but knew it had to do with her own wickedness, the "lies," the "greed," and the "pride" that pricked at her soul.

"Yes, yes, Lawd. The lies, the greed, an' the pride!" she chanted humbly.

"He knows the wickedness that paves our lanes." The tempo mounted. "He knows of the rotted cores that hide inside the glistenin' fruits."

"Amen, amen, He knows!"

"Yes, yes, our Father knows. Our Father knows each idle moment that beckons Satan to our sides!"

"Yes, sir, yes; to our sides!" Margie remembered the devil that had accosted her that night in the corn field; she shuddered in humiliation.

"An' yes, He *knows*," a note of hysteria crept into Preacher Brown's voice. "He knows, He knows, He knows—sloth!" A long, bony finger punctuated the air. Lenny sucked his breath in a gasp of despair. The finger waggled directly under his own nose. Sweat pored forth from his pores.

The congregation echoed, "Yes, Lawd—*sloth!*"

"He knows when the body is idle that Satan reaps a plentiful harvest." The words boomed forth and echoed against the concrete block walls of the little church. The beads of perspiration poured into rivulets spreading through the cotton fibers of Lenny's shirt collar. All eyes were upon him now.

They prayed, "Yes, Lawd, the body is idle."

"Yes, yes, an' He knows that while the devil reaps in a man's heart a drought must sear the land 'round us, wreakin' ruin an' waste in our fields,

146

deprivin' our little children of food, turnin' our sweat into wasted salt." The voice bellowed in spastic jerks now. Spittle escaped the frenetic preacher's lips. He dabbed at the corners of his mouth with his handkerchief.

No "amens," no "Yes, Lawds," emanated from the guilt-ridden tongue-tied congregation now.

Preacher Brown had come down from his podium now and was standing in the center of the aisle, his legs spread stiffly apart, hands on hips in an attitude of judgment. He clutched the air in asthmatic gasps. His jugular veins swelled to near bursting in the heat of the realization of the wrath of the Lord. Then, suddenly dropping to his knees, he prayed, "He knows, He knows! O Lawd, Father, we beg you forgive those among us who dare to test the depth of you mercy."

Somewhere behind her Margie could hear the rat-a-tat of a woman's high heel clacking the floor in the paroxysm of a chastised soul. A voice cried out, "Mercy."

Her own pew groaned under the shifting of Lenny's slowly sinking body. She dared not to turn her head. She dared not to take her hands away from her chest where they pressed tightly over her heart in an attempt to keep it from bursting forth through her ribs. Her mother twitched in little flutters beside her; a low moan escaped her praying lips.

Margie sighed with relief as the choir rang out in the buoyant measures of a cleansed soul. Preacher Brown slumped exhausted into his chair, mopping his brow with one hand and sipping slowly from a glass of ice water he held in the other. It had been a good sermon, he could feel it.

Lenny stood on the steps of the church while the rest of the family moved among the crowd, exchanging notes about the weather and visiting friends whom they only saw on Sunday. When everyone had finally vacated the stifling tin-roofed church, Lenny reentered. Preacher Brown was expecting him. He waited patiently for this lost sheep to plod his way down the aisle toward him.

Arriving at a spot some three feet from the preacher, Lenny halted and stood staring at the floor. Moments passed. Then a strong hand, this time open and generous, not in a tightly clenched fist, reached out and touched Lenny's head. Lenny felt a surge of relief sweep through his gut. He looked up into the soulful eyes of this forgiving man of God.

"Here, take this." Preacher Brown pressed a piece of paper into Lenny's hand. "An' make good use of it."

"Yes, sir. Thank you, sir. Gawd bless you, sir," Lenny babbled in appreciation, even though he had no idea of what the paper might contain. He knew only that it had something to do with his salvation. That was enough for which to be grateful.

Later that afternoon, when he finally had a chance to examine the paper that Preacher Brown had given him, Lenny was confused as to its meaning.

"What the hell this mean, 'Willis Hardware and Repair, 310 East Street'?" It most certainly didn't sound like the address of a heavenly paradise, which is what Lenny was expecting, since he had been saved and all.

"That's the hardware store in Maylor," Bertha explained. She had seen it whenever she had gone into Maylor to clean the white ladies' houses. In fact, one day one of the ladies had stopped in there to make a purchase while on the way to take Bertha home. If you stayed on Gum Swamp Road all the way into town it became East Street at the town limits. At least, she thought that must be the place since there were no other hardware stores in Maylor that she could remember.

"Well, who the hell is Willis Hardward, anyways?" Lenny pursued the problem.

"Where at you get that piece of paper, honey?" asked Sissy.

"Preacher Brown, he give it to me," Lenny mumbled.

"Lemme see that," demanded Bertha, grabbing the paper from Lenny's hand even though she couldn't read. She studied it for a moment then advised, "This a job, I bet." She had seen the finger waggling directed at Lenny at the church service in the morning.

"You reckon it is, honey?" asked Sissy.

"Why me?" Lenny turned an accusing eye toward Bertha. "You been talkin' 'bout me to that preacher man?"

"Not me," Bertha denied innocently. "Reckon the Lawd done speak 'bout you to the preacher."

Sissy gasped at such a notion. Lenny simply uttered, "That's a lot of shit! Pro'bly this here Willis, he hear that I am a real good worker an' as't Preacher Brown to see mebbe he could get me to work fo' him."

"Mos' likely Preacher Brown ast Willis if he don' have no work fo' a lazy man like you," Bertha corrected.

"What you goin' do 'bout it, honey?" Sissy asked.

"Don' know. I gots to think 'bout it."

"Don' know! You're goin' go an' see 'bout it, that's what you're goin' do. You heard the preacher; he said that it's the likes a you what's givin us this here drought," Bertha admonished.

"What you goin' do, honey?" Sissy asked again.

148

"I reckon I can 'least see 'bout it," Lenny conceded.

"You just better see 'bout it!" warned Bertha. Lenny prickled with irritation.

"I *said* I'd see 'bout it!" he shouted, then stomped into the bedroom and flopped across the bed. The whole thing had given him an excruciating headache. He needed to sleep. Sissy put her finger to her lips and beckoned Bertha to go quietly with her out to the porch so Lenny would not be disturbed. Bertha was reluctant to be shoved from her own kitchen but was glad enough to have Lenny out of her sight for a little while, so she tip-toed quietly behind Sissy to the porch where they sat the afternoon together and fanned themselves while watching Reggie play with the dogs' empty food pans.

On Monday morning, after the others had all left in Billy Winston's blue truck for the fields and Sissy was busy setting up the tubs for the day's laundry, Lenny started down the road toward Maylor. It was a long walk into Maylor and Lenny's feet hurt even before he had started. He just knew that he'd be a cripple by the time he returned. There was very little traffic on the road this late in the morning. Now and then Lenny looked back over his shoulder to see if a car was coming, hoping someone would have the heart to pick him up. Finally he saw a shiny red car approaching. He stopped to watch as it grew nearer. He artfully lifted his hand, thumb extended in hitchhiking fashion. The white woman driving the car stared straight past him concentrating on the center of the road. He swore at her and spat onto the road to further indicate his derision of her status. Slowly he continued to plod toward Maylor.

About a half mile further down the road, a green and white Country Squire station wagon slowed to a stop beside him. The driver, a tall thin black man, called out to him. "Goin' to town?"

Lenny gazed at the stranger in the car. Sweat already had soaked his shirt and the waist of his trousers. Opening the door he gratefully accepted the offer.

"You're Bertha Braxton's brother-in-law, ain't you?"

Lenny looked at the man in surprise. He couldn't remember having ever met him.

"I'm Maury Sasser. I live right behind you on Hollow Pine Road. Where you goin' in this heat?"

Lenny unfolded the piece of paper he had clutched in his hand. Slowly he read, "Willis Hardware and Repair—310 East Street." The man studied Lenny for a moment.

"They lookin' for help? You fixin' to 'ply?" Lenny nodded. "Hell,

Willis is a real nice man. I knowed the feller what used to work for him; got hurt in a car wreck an' won' be out the hospital for a long time. You goin' 'ply, huh? Well, good luck."

Lenny felt a mixture of pity and gratitude pull at his stomach. He couldn't rightly be happy over another's misfortune—he had never been a religious man—but then, he had never met a preacher as convincing as Preacher Brown either. The remembrance of the sermon made him shiver in the intense heat that rose up from the road in the car.

The station wagon jerked to a stop in front of a low slung wood-sided building. The sign over the front door read, WILLIS HARDWARE AND REPAIR. Lenny thanked his benefactor for the lift and got out of the car. For a few moments he stood staring at the sign as if to make certain the lettering over the door matched those on the piece of paper he still clutched tightly in his hand. A train tooted in the distance and aroused him. The railroad tracks lay directly across from the hardware store, the line that cut the town in two, into East and West. Most of the town's business district was on the west side of the tracks. Willis Hardware was on the east side.

After having come in from the bright sunlight, the gloom inside the cluttered shop momentarily blinded Lenny. He stood still, near the entrance, until his eyes adjusted to the dimness. A voice from somewhere among the array of garden implements and racks of chain and screening material said, "Something I can do for you?"

Lenny, not being able to find the owner of the voice, answered timidly toward the rafters. "I'm lookin' 'bout that job."

A short, heavyset man emerged from behind a bench that was littered with sundry tools. "You the feller Preacher Brown was going to send around?"

"Yes, sir."

Willis thrust his hand forward in greeting and said, "Willis Manson— can you weld?"

"Weld? Weld? Preacher Brown sent me."

"I know, I know, you're Bertha Braxton's brother-in-law. But can you weld?" This was the second time today that he had been referred to as "Bertha Braxton's brother-in-law" and he was beginning to develop an identity problem.

"Yes, sir, I can weld," he replied, rationalizing his answer because once, about ten years ago, he had worked in an auto-body shop and had *watched* welding being done. He figured he could do it.

"Good. Two-ten an hour, five days a week, half day on Saturday, eight to six—when can you start?"

"When? I reckon—I reckon—now," Lenny stammered.

"Good. You can start hauling that stuff outside for display," Willis said, indicating a pile of bagged fertilizers and peat moss. Lenny started to explain about his back and how he couldn't do any hard work and especially no lifting, but Willis had disappeared into the jumbled stacks of merchandise.

"I ain' s'posed to lift none," he said weakly to the dusty shelves. They did not answer. Lenny sighed and began moving the sacks of fertilizer out of the building and stacking them in front for display.

Sissy watched the road from the porch. Lenny had been gone all day and she was worried. Reggie sifted sand through his toes while he sat on the step next to Sissy. She hadn't expected that he would start working right away and wondered if some disaster had befallen him. When the old black truck pulled to a stop in front of the house and her Lenny emerged from it, she ran bouncing and jiggling across the yard to meet him.

"Where you been, honey?" she asked, clasping her hand to her heart to indicate the stress she had suffered. Lenny smiled a toothy grin.

"Been workin."

"Lawd, have mercy, baby, that be wonderful!"

"Just hush the 'Lawd, have mercies' an' get me a beer; I *am* tired!" He plopped onto his box on the porch and opened his shirt all the way so the faint breeze that toyed with the heat shimmer of the tin roof would have full vent to his sweat-soaked body.

Sissy gleefully complied with his order and got him a can of beer from the refrigerator. Lenny pulled the ring tab off with a satisfied snap and tossed it to Reggie. Reggie snatched it up and poked his finger through the hole then waved his hand to set the ring to spinning around his finger. It was a small gift, but the baby was delighted. Lenny took a long swig of his cold beer. Sissy sat on the edge of the porch at his feet, hands folded on her lap, smiling in admiration at her man.

"We're either goin' to see a miracle or a 'tastrophy," Bertha said that night when she heard the news of Lenny's job.

"You're goin' to see the miracle of a gas stove, that's what," Lenny announced with prideful conviction. Sissy shivered with expectation.

"Humph," was all Bertha would admit.

Margie lay awake listening to the steady plink-plink of the water in the bucket. She was glad Billy Winston had never fixed the roof because the sound of the rain leaking into the bucket was beautiful to her. She reckoned that Mama would not agree with her on the beauty of a hole in the roof.

"That sure do sound nice, don' it," Bertha mumbled from beside Margie on the cot. Margie shivered with love for her big beautiful Mama. She reached over and took hold of her Mama's work roughed hand. Bertha gave a gentle squeeze to the small, still smooth hand in her grasp. Margie closed her eyes and drifted off to sleep dreaming of the miracle Lenny had wrought. The water plinked steadily into the bucket all the night long. By morning it was full to overflowing.

Lenny fingered the envelope in his pocket. It held his first week's pay. The sign on the windshield of the '65 Ford Falcon that sat in the front row of cars on Pete's Auto Sales lot read $240.

He knew that Sissy had her heart set on a gas stove, but he simply could not keep depending on someone to give him a lift into town every day. Besides, Pete said the car was in excellent condition and he would be willing to let it go for $200.

Once more Lenny lifted the hood and peered at the car's entrails. He wasn't sure just what he was looking for, but he knew that this procedure was vital in purchasing a used car. He heard the footsteps approaching from behind him. He nodded his head knowingly at the mysterious conglomeration that stared back at him from under the hood.

"Make up your mind yet?" the owner of the footsteps asked.

Lenny turned. He knew it would be Pete, but on seeing him he acted surprised anyway. "Well—just about. Givin' it one las' check," answered Lenny.

"Take your time," Pete invited.

Lenny went through a quick rehearsal of his explanation to Sissy and another calculation of expenses then said, "I reckon I'll take it."

"Good, good. I know you won't be sorry. She's a fine little buggy for the price."

"You said $200?" reminded Lenny quizzically.

"Did I say $200! Well, if I said it, I'll stick by it—but you're practically stealing it from me at that price!" Pete headed toward the little shack that acted as an office, nodding for Lenny to follow.

"Don't know how I'm expected to make a living," he mumbled for Lenny's benefit. "Selling a car for such a ridiculous price—there's absolutely no profit in used cars these days." The knowledge of his economic coup sent a pleasant tingle of victory up Lenny's spine. No one could best Leonard Caldwell when it came to finances; he smiled triumphantly at Pete's back.

"Now let's see here—how much are you putting down, again?"

"Fifty," Lenny answered, squeezing the money in his pocket a little tighter.

"Uh huh." Pete mumbled reflectively as he ran his fingers down the column of figures on the chart in front of him. "OK, now, do you want me to put your first year's insurance on this too?" (Pete also sold auto insurance.)

"I wasn't figurin' on insurance just yet, maybe later," Lenny explained.

Pete leaned back in his chair and shook his head. "Can't do that. It's the law in North Carolina. Can't drive a car without insurance."

"Oh? Well, I didn't know. Well, OK, then go ahead an' put it on," Lenny agreed. Pete ran his fingers down another column of figures and, after moistening the tip of his pencil with his tongue, transferred one of those figures onto the form on the desk in front of him.

"Now, about the license transfer." Pete knew who he was dealing with. He was familiar with the poor blacks who had just enough to put down on a cheap car but had not thought of the rest of the expenses of ownership. "You want me to add that in too?" Lenny nodded approval and squeezed the fifty dollars in his pocket until his fingers became numb. "Then, there's the Maylor sticker; that's only a dollar." Lenny nodded again.

Pete worked busily over the forms in front of him. Then, sliding the sheaf of papers across the desk toward Lenny, he indicated, with check marks, each place Lenny was to sign his name. Lenny carefully penned his name, Leonard Caldwell, Jr., on each line that Pete indicated.

"OK, now let's see—I'll give you a receipt for the fifty dollars and we're all set. You can pick your car up on Tuesday."

"But—but—I was figurin' on takin' it today," Lenny protested as he handed the fifty dollars to Pete.

"Well, I have to get all this stuff notarized and this is Saturday," Pete explained.

Lenny stood gaping in crestfallen silence, then stammering, he said, "But—I—but I was figurin' on not havin' to walk all the way back home again. It's five miles!"

"You haven't been walking all that way every day!"

"Yes, sir, I sure have," Lenny lied.

"Oh, jeez!" Pete whistled to himself. After a moment of reflection he looked up at Lenny and said, "Let me call around and see if I can find a notary at home."

He began dialing the phone on his desk. It took three tries before he found a notary who was at home on this Saturday afternoon, who also was willing to do business. "OK, thanks Bob. We'll be over in a few minutes," Pete said to the third try on the other end of the line. Hanging up the phone, he got up and started out the door toward his car beckoning Lenny to accompany him.

"You were lucky to catch me," the notary, Bob, said as he let the two men in the door to his living room. "Me and the Missus were just fixing to leave for the beach. The children are having us for the weekend."

"Much obliged to you, Bob," Pete acknowledged, presenting him with the title for Lenny's new automobile.

It didn't take but a moment to affix the notary seal to the paper. Lenny was grateful to Pete for having persevered in his hunt for a Saturday working notary.

Back at the lot Pete handed Lenny the keys to the beige-colored Falcon and said, "Good luck, Mr. Caldwell. I know you're going to enjoy your new car. You can use this dealer's plate, here, till your own plate comes in, a few days, maybe a week. I'll call you over at Willis's when it comes in." Pete affixed the dealer's license plate to the back of Lenny's car. Lenny thanked Pete effusively and began the struggle to slide his bulk into the driver's seat behind the steering wheel. Pete chuckled as Lenny's face contorted at the evident impasse.

"Here." Pete reached down to a lever beside the seat and gave it a push. Lenny plunged suddenly into the space behind the wheel. Grinning sheepishly he nodded a "thank-you" to Pete. Then after a couple of abortive attempts, he familiarized himself with the idiosyncrasies of the starting mechanism and successfully cranked the car and was on his way.

Sissy glanced at the new wall clock that Bertha had bought on sale at Pfeiffer's. Mr. Pfeiffer was selling the old stock clocks at $2.98 and she could hardly pass up a bargain like that, and besides being a necessity (they were finding it harder and harder to be on time for Mr. Winston), it was beautiful. The face of the clock was set into a huge round red apple, its hands were slender green leaves, and it did look proud on the wall over the refrigerator. Now those green leaves were moving toward three o'clock. Why was Lenny so late? A foreboding gnawing grew in Sissy's stomach.

"Oh, Lawd, please don' let—" She could not voice the fears she held in her heart.

"You reckon he'll have any of his pay left till he gets here?" Bertha asked sarcastically.

"Probably didn't get no lift an' had to walk all the way, poor baby," defended Sissy.

"Humph, an' probably got so thirsty from that hot sun he just had to stop at that cafe," Bertha accused. Sissy didn't answer. Lenny hadn't done that for years now. Still, there was a time—but, no, he wouldn't do that anymore, he had promised her.

Lenny bounced the Falcon over the ditch into the front yard in a flourish of triumph. Leaning on the horn he waited jubilantly for his audience of admirers to come out from the house. The dogs barked menacingly at the strange vehicle in their territory.

Sissy stared in disbelief at this anomaly that surrounded her husband's bulk.

"A automobile!" gasped Margie.

"Sure ain't goin' to make no coffee on that," Bertha grumbled. The group moved slowly toward Lenny's new throne. From the dim interior of the car, his teeth glistened through grinning lips. "Ain't it a beaut? Got it at a bargain too," he said proudly.

"You already got one car." London nodded toward the other car that lolled languidly in the sand of the side yard.

"But it don't run an' this does," replied Lenny.

"Ain't notthin' wrong with it 'cept the tires," observed Bertha.

"Seems that new tires would cost less than a new car," Teresa calculated.

"He ain't got a brain what can figure that high," sniffed Bertha.

"That other one was aimin' for to die soon," Lenny refuted. "An' if I'm goin' to work every day to feed these kids of yours, I sure as hell don' figure on walkin' ten miles every day."

Margie stepped back a little as her mother stiffened. She waited for the eruption. "Who are you feedin'?" Bertha sputtered. "That fat black mouth of yours is what gobbles up all the food in this house. An' who you think been workin' in them fields all summer?"

Lenny began to extricate himself from the car. "An' when the little bastard comes to bein' borned—who's goin' carry the girlie to the hospital?" he yelled self-righteously.

155

London spat at the dirt in front of Lenny. He shrugged his thick shoulders and walked toward the house.

Margie peered inside the car. She rubbed her hand over the smooth vinyl seat covers. She wondered if Lenny would let any of them ride in his car.

"Get 'way from that thing!" Mama grabbed Margie's arm and angrily jerked her away from the car.

Sissy moved numbly about the kitchen. She rearranged the salt and pepper shakers; she rubbed at a stain on the table oilcloth. She had so been counting on that gas cook stove.

Lenny pulled her to him and patted her soft round buttocks.

"Honey, come on an' smile," he crooned. "The car'll be nice. Just think, no more walkin' to church on Sundays. An' I can carry you in to Greensburg, an' you can shop in them big stores. An' 'sides, it won' be long 'fore the car will be paid for an' then I can get you that stove."

Lenny was right, of course. He needed the car for his job. She could manage a while longer with the old wood stove. Sissy bent over and kissed the sweat-shined forehead of her husband. Lenny smiled graciously.

Chapter XII

Margie was dressed and ready for church an hour before it was time to leave. She sat on the front porch staring in anticipation at Lenny's new car. Shivers went up her spine. To ride to church in a car; she had never had that pleasure. She hoped Belva Harris would notice.

Reggie tried to crawl up onto her lap. "Get down 'fore you muss my skirt." She shoved the baby away. Straightening the skirt with her hand, she stood up and walked away from the perplexed child. Reggie tried again. Running after Margie and grabbing the hem of her skirt, he tried to climb her leg as if it were a pole.

"You're goin' run my panty hosens!" she shrieked and bounced him onto the ground with a thud. Tears welled into his eyes. Margie carefully examined her nyloned legs for snags. Relieved, she grabbed Reggie's hand and pulled him to his feet. "Sorry, baby," she apologized, "but it took me all this week to get Mama to let me buy these hosens an' I sure don' want 'em to run 'fore I even get to church." Reggie smiled through his tears as if he understood and toddled beside her toward the Falcon.

"An' we won' get no tar on our shoes this week," Margie reminded the baby. He gurgled agreement.

"Help me zip this thing." London pleaded with Gayla. Gayla tugged at the zipper on the side of her sister's skirt.

"Suck your breath in."

"I *am!*" London gasped. Gayla tried the zipper again.

"Ain't no use' it ain't going to go. Let your blouse hang out over the top."

"Shit!" London grumbled as she pulled her blouse from under the waistband of her skirt and arranged it over her belly. "I sure wisht I had one of those maternity tops."

"Little bastard's gettin' big!" giggled Lenny, having watched the whole proceedings from the doorway.

"You hush your ugly mouth!" demanded London.

Lenny winked and giggled again. "Least I gots good reason for my big belly."

London sneered at Lenny as he headed for the kitchen. He turned back toward London and started to answer but then shrugged and continued on to the kitchen.

"How we all goin' fit in this thing?" Bertha grumbled as she wiggled into the back seat of the Falcon.

"You can fit if you squeeze together," Lenny assured as he pushed London through the door after her mother. Gayla and Teresa squeezed in beside London and Mama.

"You're squashin' my skirt!" shrieked Gayla as Teresa wiggled beside her.

"I can't help it. Where you 'spect me to sit?"

"Scrunch up to the edge of the seat."

"Why don' you scrunch up to the edge of the seat? You're the one what's worried 'bout you ol' skirt!"

"Hush, both of you. I can't hardly breathe," Mama demanded.

Teresa humbly scooted forward till she was just barely sitting on the edge of the seat. "I hope that satisfied you," she grumbled to Gayla. Lenny handed Reggie in and plopped him onto London's lap then slammed the door on his cargo.

"Margie, you set twix me an' your Aunt Sissy," Lenny said smiling at her. Margie scrambled in, forgetting all about her aversion to her uncle.

Bertha began a spasmodic panting in the backseat. "This is ridiculous, I feels like I'm havin' the life squeezed out of me," she complained. "Why can't *I* set up in the front?"

"You're too fat, that's why," snapped Lenny. "I gots to have room to drive." London pushed Reggie to the outer limits of her lap so he wouldn't press against her swollen belly.

"Look who's talkin' 'bout bein' fat," she snickered.

Lenny turned his head and gave her a vicious look. "You want to walk?" he threatened. Subdued, London settled back against the seat.

Margie watched expectantly out of the window as they pulled into the graveled parking lot beside the church. There were only a few people standing in front of the steps and none were friends of hers. Deacon Rawlings noticed the strange car and began walking toward them as Lenny maneuvered into a parking position. His face lit up into a smile when he recognized the occupants.

"Hey, man, that's cool," he greeted. "That sure 'nough you at the wheel, Brother Lenny?" Lenny beamed with pride. Sissy smiled lovingly at her husband.

One by one the members of the Braxton family pulled themselves free of the car. Margie walked very slowly toward the front of the church, glancing from side to side, hoping someone would notice her nylons. Arriving at the bottom step of the entrance, she reckoned she could stand just a few minutes, at least until the bell was rung for worship.

Another car pulled into the lot. Margie examined its passengers; she recognized Norma Suthers, a girl from her school class. Smiling broadly, she waved. Norma acknowledged the greeting with a friendly return wave. When Norma had caught up with Margie at the bottom of the steps, Margie said, "Sure is hot again!"

"Sure is," Norma agreed.

"That sun 'most burnin' the land!" Margie whistled and rolled her eyes to indicate the blazing sun above.

"Sure is," Norma agreed.

"I almost wasn't goin' even wear hosens," Margie admitted.

"Come on, get inside 'fore we're late," Mama said, as she pulled at Margie's arm and hauled her unceremoniously up the steps.

Margie stumbled behind her mother while Norma watched from below. When she had approached Margie, Norma hadn't noticed that she was wearing nylons. Now she stared at Margie's legs as Bertha dragged her up the steps. Margie's face burned with embarrassment.

After the glare of the sun the light inside the church was dim. Margie blinked a few times till her eyes adjusted then quickly scanned the interior to see if Belva Harris was there yet. Bertha located "her" pew and bumped Margie in ahead of her. The rest of the family had by now caught up and filed in behind them.

Margie continued to keep her eyes flitting about expectantly, awaiting Belva Harris's arrival. Joyce Manfred came in with her parents; Audrey Carter came in with hers. Margie noted that Audrey's hair was at least two inches higher since she had last seen her. She felt self-consciously at her braids. Audrey smiled her way. Margie closed her eyes in reverent prayer.

Margie thought they'd never start for home. She waited alone next to Lenny's car, impatient for her mother to give the "let's go" sign. It seemed hours before Bertha had made her way around all the little groups of Sunday gossips. Margie wondered why Belva Harris hadn't come to church today. She looked down at her nylons, now sagging for lack of a well-developed calf to hold them in place. She sighed a soft sob of disappointment.

"Mama," Margie asked, as she mixed the lard into flour for the dinner biscuits, "Mama, how old does a girl have to be 'fore she starts takin' shape?" Bertha looked at her daughter with a quizzical eye, her baby.

"Well," Bertha answered slowly, "it happens at different times with different girls. Take London, for example. She was built like a twenty-two-year-ol' woman by the time she was twelve."

Margie sighed. Bertha bit at her tongue—she realized too late that *that* wasn't the right comparison. "But then there's the ones what bud a little later, an' they usually ends up the pertiest blossom," she attempted to rectify her mistake.

"But what do the late ones do till they gets big 'nough to hold up their hosens?" Margie asked.

Bertha dropped her reserve for a moment to hug this worried baby of hers. She sincerely hoped that Margie would never grow up but knew that her wish was a selfish dream. "Baby, you'll get there," she assured the child.

After dinner Lenny went out into the yard and began polishing the dust from his car with a dry rag. Margie watched from the porch. When Lenny had finished and was returning to the shade of the porch mopping the sweat from his forehead with the rag, Margie queried, "Uncle Lenny, wouldn't it be nice to take a drive this afternoon? The wind blowin' in the windows sure'd feel good in this heat." Lenny smiled at Margie. It had been a long time since she had called him "Uncle."

"Maybe, maybe." He sat down on the step and gazed at her, wondering. "You'd like that a whole lot wouldn't you, baby?" She smiled demurely at him, just a twinge of guilt tweaked her conscience at her hypocrisy. For a long moment he sat staring at her, then, hauling himself up from the step, he went inside. A few moments later he returned to the porch. "Seems everybody's takin' a nap in there." He paused a moment then added, "Course I reckon I could take *you* for a little drive, just a little one if you wants to." Margie jumped up and ran to the car. Lenny lumbered, grinning, behind her.

She adjusted the vent window so the air would blow directly on her face. Oh, what a wonderful feeling! The hot air whipped and stung her cheeks. She closed her eyes so the dust wouldn't get into them. As they passed between woods on either side of the road the air suddenly became cool and fragrant with honeysuckle. She opened her eyes and watched the trees slip past the car. She gulped deep breaths of the sugar-laden air; she could taste the sweetness as it passed down her throat. At the end of the wooded stretch Lenny suddenly turned left onto a dirt road that followed the edge of the woods. Tobacco filled the field on the opposite side of the narrow road. The bitter sweet smell of the leaves ripening in the hot afternoon sun drifted into the car. Margie liked the tobacco perfume. The wind blowing in her face, the ambrosia of honeysuckle and tobacco, the swaying of the car down the dirt road, all had an intoxicating affect on her. She closed her eyes again and let herself sink deep into the upholstery of the car seat.

Suddenly the car stopped. Margie opened her eyes expectantly. Lenny had pulled the car up beside a deserted old farmhouse near the end of the woods. He turned the ignition off. Margie felt her stomach drop into her bowels. She stiffened and clutched the side of the seat. Lenny smiled at her through glittering white teeth.

Before Lenny could even grasp hold of her, Margie had thrown herself from the parked car and was racing through the adjacent tobacco field. The sun-limped leaves dragged heavily across her face and shoulders. She had no idea where she was going, just that she would not stay alongside of that hideous man. Her conscience burned with the guilty knowledge that she had coaxed Lenny into taking her for a drive. The wonderment of the automobile had taken over her senses. She knew that it was her own fault and that she had let herself into this dangerous situation.

Lenny waited for her to return. When an hour had passed and yet no sign of the girl, he backed the car around and headed slowly down the road toward the highway. He was perplexed by her behavior; he had thought her suggestion to take a drive was an invitation to intimacy.

Arriving onto the paved road without having seen Margie, he headed toward home. Maybe she was already there. But when he got back to the house, there was no sign of the girl. All the other members of the family were still napping to avoid the heat of the afternoon. Even the dogs did not venture out from under the house to investigate Lenny's proddings. Exhausted, Lenny sat down on his box on the porch. Where could she be? He knew Bertha would have his hide if her baby was hurt in any way. He should not have taken her! Where could she be?

"Margie!" Mama called from the kitchen. A chill went through Lenny. When she got no answer Bertha came to the door. "Where at's that chile?" she asked Lenny.

"Don't know," he shrugged innocently.

"Well, I needs somethin' from the store. If you see her, tell her to come in here." Lenny nodded in assent.

Later Bertha again appeared at the door. "She ain't here yet?"

"No," said Lenny, acting unconcerned.

"Well, I wonder where's she at. Probably off readin' somewheres."

"Probably," agreed Lenny.

"Gayla, you're goin' have to go up the road to Pfeiffer's an' get me some cinnamon."

"Why can't Margie go?"

"Cause she ain't 'round. Now get."

"She's always slippin' off to read those dumb books," Gayla grumbled as she started across the yard.

"Least she's gettin' some education from those 'dumb' books," Bertha reminded her. "Would do you good to read some."

"Shit!" Gayla mumbled to herself as she walked out to the road.

"Wait a minute, I'll drive you," Lenny called.

Gayla looked back in surprise. Lenny ambled out to the car and waited for Gayla to get in. "You reckon where your sister be?" asked Lenny casually.

"Off readin' somewheres, I reckon."

"Where at she usually go off to read?"

"Who knows?" shrugged Gayla.

Lenny thought a moment, then asked, "Reckon maybe she might of went visitin'?"

"Naw, she ain't knowin' no one to visit."

"Maybe she got a feller."

"Who, Margie?" Gayla laughed.

"Well, she growin' up."

"She gots a *lot* of growin' to do 'fore she goes huntin' fellers."

They drove the rest of the way to the grocery in silence.

Not having ever been anywhere away from her own house except to school and to church and to Pfeiffer's, it took only a few minutes of running directionless before Margie had become totally and irreversibly lost. Panic clutched at her gut as she continued to run and run in an effort to escape the jaws of lostness.

How long had she been running? Hours, perhaps days, she thought as she lay on the ditch bank gasping for breath. The hot air scratched at her dry throat as it wooshed past to fill her exhausted lungs. Tears welled into her

162

eyes; they quickly filled the dust-laden chambers and spilled out with the debris down her sweating cheeks.

How long had she been lying there? Hours, perhaps days, she thought, when she heard the rustling of the tobacco leaves near by. The man stared in wonder at the skinny child that lay limp and tear stained in his ditch. Margie stared back at him.

"What on earth you doing down there?" he finally asked. Margie did not answer.

"Are you hurt?" he asked. She shook her head. "Well, come on, get out of there. There's snakes in these ditches, you know." The flesh under her skin raised in prickly protest at the word snakes. She scrambled to her knees and crawled out of the ditch. When she tried to stand up, her knees buckled under her. The man caught her under her arms.

"Child, you look to be sick!" he said in a worried voice. "You sick?" Margie shook her head again but she could not prove herself to be not sick because, try as she might, she simply could not stand alone.

"Come on, child. I'll take you back to the house and my wife will know what to do for you." He scooped her light frame into his arms and carried her out of the field. She did not protest.

"What on earth have you got there?" the wife said, when the man deposited the child on a chair in her kitchen. "Don't know. Appears to be sick or something and don't talk none."

"Think maybe she's one of those deaf mutes?" the wife asked. At that Margie made a supreme effort to speak. . . . "I'm lost," she whispered.

"Lost! Well, how in the world did you get way back into that tobacco field to get lost in the first place?" the man asked in surprise. Margie observed him for a moment. Was he angry with her for trespassing?

"A varmint chased me."

"A varmint! What kind of a varmint?"

"Don' know what kind—big."

"There's been reports of a pack of wild dogs in the area; you think it was one of them?" the wife asked the man.

"Did it look like a big dog?" he asked Margie. Margie's eyes were popping with anxiety now as her lie began to grow. "Yeah, a big, big dog. An' it was goin' to eat me!"

"Poor child, how awful! She must be frightened to death," the wife crooned in sympathy.

"My Lord!" the man whistled softly.

The wife wrung a washcloth in warm water from her sink tap. She gently dabbed Margie's face that had become caked with dust, sweat, and tears.

"And I bet you're hungry," the wife added as she worked to clean the child. Margie watched her movements with tense curiosity. What would they do with her; call the police? Have her jailed for trespassing?

"Get those cookies out that I baked yesterday," the woman said to her husband. "And get a glass of milk—do you like milk, honey?" Margie nodded, relaxing a little now with the woman's gentle motions and soothing voice.

The man and his wife watched as Margie sipped her milk and nibbled daintily at the cookie. Margie watched the man and his wife.

"Reckon we'll have to find out where she lives so we can take her home," the man said.

"Have you any idea where you are in relation to your house, honey?" the wife quizzed Margie.

Margie stared at the wife—no, she had no idea. "No, ma'am," she finally whispered.

"We'll have to try to figure out from what direction she came," said the man.

"Did the dog chase you into the field from off the highway, honey?" asked the wife. Margie shook her head.

"Maybe she came in from the south side; there's a black government housing project, over there," said the man.

"Do you live in the projects, honey?" the wife asked. Margie shook her head.

"Well, I sure don't know how she got there, then," puzzled the man.

"Can you tell us what road you were on before you ran into the field, honey?" asked the woman. Margie tried to remember. "It were a dirt road," she finally answered softly.

"A dirt road? Reckon she was back by the old Salmon place?" the man wondered.

"Did you see an old house on the dirt road, honey?" asked the woman.

Margie remembered the abandoned old house that Lenny had parked next to. "Yes, ma'am," she answered timidly.

"I bet that's where she came in from. But I can't figure why she was back there in the first place," the man mused.

"The dogs probably chased her back that road first then she turned into the field. Did the dogs chase you down the dirt road, honey?" asked the woman. Wide-eyed now, the dog was growing into dogs, Margie nodded anxiously.

"Poor child!" the wife said again, wiping Margie's brow again with the damp cloth. Margie began to feel good. She had never had so much gentle attention. These people were so nice. She glanced shyly around the kitchen. It was beautiful! These folks must be rich. The woman watched her.

"Would you like more milk before we take you home, honey?" she asked. Margie nodded gratefully. She rarely had milk at home; the milk was reserved for Reggie. The man poured another glass of milk. Yes, they must be rich, she thought. This house was just beautiful!

"The only way she could have come on to that road would be from off Gum Swamp Road," the man said.

"Do you live on Gum Swamp Road, honey?" his wife asked. Margie nodded assent. "If we drive you down that road, will you be able to tell us where you live, honey?" the woman asked and Margie nodded again.

"That girl, she sure can set a body to worry," Bertha fretted after dinner when Margie still hadn't appeared.

"Reckon she's got a feller?" Lenny tried again.

"Margie, a feller!" London laughed. But Bertha reflected on this for a moment. She *had* asked those questions about growing up earlier that day.

"Reckon she has?"

"Mama, she's only a baby" London assured.

By nine o'clock even London was beginning to wonder if, indeed, her baby sister did have a fellow.

Lenny was sick with remorse by this time and suggested, "Reckon I ought to go out in the car to look for her?"

"Where at you goin' to look?" Bertha asked.

"Don' know, but I reckon someone ought to do something'."

They had only been driving down the road for a few minutes when Margie's house suddenly loomed into view. She cried, "There!" The man hit the brake pedal with a jerk.

"There?" he asked. Margie nodded.

How dismal it looked. How poor it looked. What must these fine people think of her living in such squalor? A picture of the beautiful farm house flashed through her mind.

"Do you want me to go in with you, honey?" the wife asked.

Margie quickly shook her head. She would never ever want anyone to come into her house again; she was suddenly overcome with shame at her poverty. She had known that not everyone lived as poorly as she did; Belva

165

Harris didn't, nor did Norma, but she had never seen it—having seen it made it so utterly real—her poverty. She slid out of the car onto the road in front of her house. The dogs were barking. Her skin prickled at the sound. Wild dogs . . . ? The man and his wife watched as she walked across the bare sand yard.

"That's a shame," the wife sighed.

"Yes, it is," agreed her husband.

Margie turned back toward her benefactors and shyly waved good-bye. They waved back from the car, then turned the car around on the road and headed back to their beautiful home.

"What's the dogs barkin' at?" Sissy asked, her voice tense with anxiety. The dogs never barked unless a stranger came into the yard.

"Go look," Bertha prodded Lenny's ribs with her elbow. But, by then, the barking had stopped. A sound of footsteps fell on the porch.

Margie walked through the door and headed directly to the bedroom without saying a word. The family watched in silent bewilderment as she disappeared into the darkened room. At last Bertha yelled, "Where at you been, girl?" Margie returned to the doorway. She stared straight into Lenny's eyes. The others looked questioningly at Lenny. He fiddled with a broken button on his shirt. He did not look at the girl.

"Well?" prodded Bertha. Margie sighed but still did not answer. Lenny glanced up at her from under his lowered eyelids. A feeling of revulsion filled her as their eyes met. Lenny quickly lowered his again and worked at the button.

"I as't you something' an' I expect a answer," snapped Bertha.

"She's been with a feller; I just bet she's been with a feller," gasped Teresa.

"You hush an' let her speak for herself," cautioned Bertha.

"Else why don' she want to tell?" whispered Teresa.

Bertha gave her a serious "Hush up" look. Teresa ducked her chin down and remained silent.

"You been with a feller?" Bertha asked accusingly.

Margie sighed another deep sigh and replied, "No, Mama, I ain' been with no feller."

Then she turned her back to them and disappeared into the darkness again.

Somewhat satisfied, but nevertheless still curious as to where her daughter had been, Bertha yelled after her, "Then, where at you been?"

"Just walkin'." The answer came from the recess of the bedroom.

Bertha pondered this a moment then, mumbling to herself, she said, "Just walkin', just walkin! I'll never understan' that chile. She'll drive me to a early grave."

Considering the issue closed with that proclamation, Bertha turned to the others and snapped, "You heard her. She just been walkin'. Now you all get on with what you was doin'." She did not understand and the confusion in her brain begged for a rest. She would think about the problem of Margie later.

Much relieved, Lenny could not quit twisting at the button and he leaned back in his chair with a grunt to relax the tension in his head. The others, not having been doing anything special before Margie came in, now coped with the problem of doing nothing again as Bertha had so ordered.

But Teresa could not restrain herself from whispering to London, "I just know she gots a feller. She gots that look in her eyes like when you been caught at doin' somethin' wrong."

Mama heard. "She said she don' an' she don'," she stated positively.

"No, she be too young. She be just a chile," reminded Gayla, siding with Mama.

"She be 'most thirteen," reminded Teresa.

The reminder pricked Bertha's soul. "Don' make no difference, she be still just a chile."

"Where you expect she been then if she ain' got no feller?" quizzed Teresa sarcastically.

"Just walkin'," Bertha reminded her.

"Yeah, just walkin'?" Teresa snickered.

And while they all sat about in the next room discussing the strange behavior of this "child," Margie lay on her bed and vowed that when she did grow up she would not be poor; she would not live in an ugly little shack; she would not sleep in a room with seven other people.

But she wondered just how she was ever going to make it to grown-up. For so long she had been setting her sights on thirteen as her goal for being a grown-up, and that time was drawing ever nearer; yet she was not herself responding to the call. Maybe it all happened just like that, on that very day. Her arms lay across her flat chest. Yes, that must be it, she reasoned. Anyway, she knew that something would happen. She felt it more and more every day. She just knew. She fell asleep . . . knowing.

Chapter XIII

Margie anxiously awaited the opening of school. Since Lenny was working now and adding to the family income, Mama had promised that she could start on the opening day this year. It was with great disappointment that she heard the news that the opening day of school would be delayed for one week, until after Labor Day, in order to give the farmers a week longer to get in their crops. Because of the long dry spell, followed by a week of heavy rains in late August, the tobacco crop was ripening just about a week behind time this year. Some farmers were behind even by two or three weeks.

Billy Winston was grateful for the delayed opening date. Most of his hands were school-aged children. But even with the extra week he would not be able to get his entire crop into barns. Knowing that the schools would make an exception if it was really necessary, he asked the Taylor kids if they would finish up with him before returning to school. Their father, however, was much more interested in their education than Billy's tobacco crop, so on the first day of school the Taylor children were found in their classrooms instead of the fields. All except Rick and Russ, that is, because they were in college and the colleges did not begin for another two weeks yet. Margie had pleaded with Bertha to keep her promise, but Bertha could not. Billy Winston, in a last-ditch effort to keep at least a skeleton of a crew, had threatened Bertha with the firing of her whole family if Margie did not work. What could she do? Margie knew that Mama would not break a promise except for good reasons, but she was still terribly disappointed.

On the last day of the week before school would open, Kathy called Margie aside at lunch time. "Don't go home with your folks for lunch today," she said. "Stay here at the barn with me. I packed me and you a special lunch for our last day together."

Margie looked to Mama for approval. Mama nodded assent. So when the others had gone off to their homes in Billy's truck, Kathy and Margie sought a shady spot under one of the big oak trees near the barns.

"This is like a picnic," Margie exclaimed excitedly.

"Yeah—well, I wanted to do something special for our last day together. We may never see each other again."

Margie looked at Kathy. Puzzled, she asked, "Las' time? Ain' you goin' work for Mr. Winston next year?"

"We might move back to Ohio. In fact, it's almost certain that we will."

"Then I won' never see you 'gain?"

"Maybe not."

The two girls sat in dejected silence for a moment. Then Kathy said, "Come on, let's not make this last day miserable. Let's enjoy it—forever."

Margie choked back her tears of another disappointment. It was getting harder and harder for her to accept disappointments, there had been so many lately. But finally she managed to smile and say, "OK, let's—forever."

Kathy tore open the brown paper bag she had brought from home. Margie watched as she pulled out numerous little plastic bags filled with sandwiches and carrot sticks and pickles. One little package was wrapped in aluminum foil. Kathy set it aside.

"That's a surprise for later," she explained. Margie tingled with excitement as she looked out of the corner of her eye at the silver-wrapped packet.

Kathy tore the big brown paper bag down the side and across the bottom, then spread it out flat on the ground between them for a tablecloth. Carefully, she placed a large thermos of iced tea in the center of the paper. Then she began dividing the plastic-wrapped sandwiches and tidbits between the two of them. She poured them each a paper cup of tea.

"OK, that's it," she said as she began unwrapping a pimento cheese sandwich.

Margie hesitated a moment, then said, "Ain't you goin' as't no blessin'?"

Kathy stopped in the middle of a bite. "Oh—yeah—I forgot," she mumbled, laying down her sandwich and folding her hands on her lap. "You do it, Margie."

Margie closed her eyes and bowed her head. "Lawd, our Father, we thank you for this food an' as'ts you to make it OK to eat an', an' . . . " Mama always asked the blessing at home and Margie was now stumped as to how to end it.

"And bless us who are sharing this meal," Kathy interjected.

Margie raised her eyes to Kathy and grinned. "Yeah—Amen!"

It was fun, sitting on the cool damp grass sharing with a friend. Margie savored every second of it. But always she watched the inert little foil-wrapped package. What was in it? What surprise?

"Your school starts day after Labor Day too, doesn't it?" Kathy broke into the spell.

"Yeah, it do, but Mama ain' lettin' me go," Margie answered, her mouth full of the sweet pimento spread.

"For gosh sakes, why not!"

"Mr. Winston, he said he needs me to work, an' if I don' he's goin' fire Mama an' the others."

"He can't do that. It's against the law." Kathy hit the ground with her fist indignantly.

Margie looked up in astonishment. "He can't?"

"No he can't. That's blackmail."

"But they say chir'uns is 'zempted from school if they has to work."

"OK, but that's only if they *have* to and *want* to. Mr. Winston can't threaten the rest of your family just to make you work."

"He can't?"

"No! And besides, he wouldn't fire your mama and sisters anyway, because then he wouldn't have anyone working for him. Then what would he do?"

"I ain' never thought of that."

The girls contemplated this problem as they finished their lunch. Margie swallowed the last of her sandwich. Folding her hands on her lap, she waited expectantly for Kathy to finish and bare the surprise. Kathy saw the excited and expectant look on Margie's face and deliberately dallied with her sandwich to prolong the expectancy. At last Kathy crumpled her sandwich bag and placed it on the pile with the other crumpled bags.

"Well, now, I wonder what we have here," she said with mock anticipation.

Margie beamed. Very slowly Kathy unfolded the aluminum foil to expose a miniature cake. From her pocket she pulled out thirteen birthday candles and proceeded to stick them into the top of the little cake. Margie's eyes widened. "It looks like a birthday cake," she gasped.

"Uh huh," Kathy agreed casually, as she sought for room on the top to put the last two candles. Jamming them in between the crowded mass, she began to light them.

"Is it your birthday?" Margie asked.

"Hu uh," Kathy shook her head then blew out the match.

"Whose birthday is it then?"

"Yours!"

"Mine? Ain' my birthday till March 18th."

"I know, but I might not be living here then, so—I thought we, just me and you, could celebrate it a little early."

"Two birthdays?" Margie asked, excited about having her birthday come sooner than she had expected, but yet reluctant to maybe have it cancel out her real birthday.

"Sure. One now and one on March 18th."

"But ain' that cheatin'?"

"No, of course not. It's done all the time. It's only the party that we're having; it's not really your birthday. You won't get older until your real birthday."

"Oh," Margie said, still puzzled but accepting Kathy's explanation.

"OK, now make a wish, then blow," Kathy said.

Margie looked at her questioningly. "Make a wish an' blow?" she asked.

"Yeah, you know, make a birthday wish, then blow out all the candles."

This was only the second time in her life Margie had had candles on her birthday cake. In fact, it was only the fifth time she had had a cake. Her birthday was in early spring, before tobacco really got started, and there was usually never any money in the house for things like birthday cakes and candles. Usually the day of a birthday was only important to the celebrant, who marked it as simply being one year older than the day before.

"What kind of a birthday wish should I make?" asked Margie.

"Oh, something very, very special. Something that you've really wanted for a long time; because if you blow out all the candles in one breath, your wish will come true."

"Sure, 'nough—it'll come true?"

Margie was wide-eyed with excitement now. She closed her eyes and thought very hard about her wish. There were so many things that she wanted, she didn't know which one to choose. Finally deciding, she began, "I wish . . . "

"No, no, don't tell me what your wish is," interrupted Kathy, with a twinkle in her eye. "You never ever tell anyone, or else then it won't come true."

Margie gasped; how close she had come to spoiling the whole thing. She closed her eyes again and wished real hard to herself. Then, opening her eyes, she asked, "Now—now, do I blow out the candles?" The candles had burned low on the cake by now, their wax spreading over the top of the chocolate frosting.

"Yeah, now, blow real hard," instructed Kathy. Margie sucked in all the air she could possible hold, then she let go with a gust of wind that very nearly blew the cake off the paper bag tablecloth.

"Your wish will come true!" Kathy clapped with glee. "You blew all the candles out." She was teasing, she knew, but it was a good kind of teasing.

"Yeah, I did!" Margie gasped with pride, unaware of the teasing note in Kathy's voice. "An' my wish will come true, sure 'nough?"

"You bet it will," answered Kathy as she began to cut the little cake in half. She wasn't sure just how Margie was taking this little bit of tomfoolery and suspected, maybe, she had gone too far, but it *was* only a game. Surely Margie realized *that*. She wondered, as they consumed the portent of the wish, just what Margie had wished for; a new dress, a pair of new shoes, what? She licked the frosting from her fingers and began to pick up the scraps from their picnic. Margie hugged her knees to her chest and watched her friend with reverent eyes.

"My wish will come true. I blowed out all the candles," she mused. Kathy winced with guilt at the little joke she had perpetrated. But it had gone too far now to correct without hurting Margie. Who would have thought that Margie would really believe the wish story?

"Here's your birthday present," Kathy abruptly interjected into Margie's reverie. Margie straightened herself. Another surprise!

"A birthday present?"

"Well, it isn't much, but I think you'll like it."

Kathy was embarrassed now. She wished she would not get all embarrassed every time she gave something to someone.

Margie tore open the pretty bow that held the package together. Suddenly she stopped. "A birthday present, an' it even ain' my birthday yet!" she exclaimed. "Wonder what it is—I ain' never had a . . . "

"Well, for gosh sakes, open it!" Kathy said impatiently.

"I ain' never had a wrapped-up birthday present 'fore. One time Mama give me a hair bow for my birthday, but it didn't have no purty paper on it. It was just a hair bow—plain." Somewhat subdued now, she carefully folded the flowered wrapping paper away a little at a time until she had exposed the entire gift. "A book!"

"Look what I wrote inside," Kathy urged. Margie numbly opened the book and looked on the inside of its cover.

"To my very dearest friend, Margie; from Kath." Margie's eyes filled with tears. She let them trickle on down her cheeks; she knew she'd never be able to hold them back.

"For gosh sakes, don't cry," Kathy said anxiously. "I thought you'd like it."

"I do, I do!" Margie sniveled, wiping her nose with the back of her hand. "It's just I ain' never had a wrapped-up birthday present 'fore, an' I ain' never had my own real book with a stiff cover 'fore, an' I'm so happy I can't help from cryin'."

"Oh," Kathy mumbled, even more embarrassed, as she continued to clean up the lunch scraps.

"*Little Women,* by Louisa May Alcott," Margie read. *"Little Women,* I like that name. What's it 'bout, Kathy?"

"I can't tell you. You read it. I read it when I was about your age. Every girl reads it sometime."

"Every girl? Reckon London an' Gayla an' Teresa read it?"

"Well, every girl *I* ever knew read it," affirmed Kathy.

"Reckon they did, then." Margie fondled the book, turning it over and over in her hands, then flipping it open to read, again and again, the message Kathy had written inside.

Both girls jumped up and hurriedly gathered their scraps together and tossed them into the corn field beside the tobacco barns. Billy Winston's truck was bouncing down the road bringing the crew back from lunch. An aura of dust engulfed the truck.

Margie ran to meet it holding her book up in the air for all to see. "Look Mama, I got a birthday present from Kathy."

"Ain't your birthday," Mama grumbled, as she stepped down from the cab of the truck.

"I know it ain'. But Kathy might be movin' 'fore my birthday so's she brung me a cake an' a present today. We had a birthday party."

Bertha gave Kathy a long dark look. "Shou'n't a done that," Bertha said.

"It was just a little token . . . ," Kathy explained.

"Shou'n't a done it," Bertha repeated. She stomped off to the shed. The others, who had stopped to examine Margie's birthday present, were shooed after her by Mr. Winston.

"Lunch time is over now; get on with your work." The boys hopped nimbly into the tobacco cart while Sonny started the tractor. They disappeared into the rows of tobacco.

"Come on," Mr. Winston urged again, giving Kathy a gentle poke, "I said, get on with the work."

The girls followed Mama to the shed. They began handing and looping, quickly establishing their rhythm. A pall of silence hung over them.

173

"You mad with me, Mama?" Margie finally asked.

"No, chile, ain' mad with you; y'all di'n't know . . . "

"Di'n't know what, Mama?"

"It be bad luck to have a birthday 'fore it's time," Bertha answered.

"Bad luck?" queried Kathy. Bertha gave Kathy a sympathetic look; Kathy just didn't know. She was a nice girl, but Bertha was beginning to wish that this city-bred white child had not messed into their life.

Margie looked up at the book that now lay nested for safe keeping on a rafter overhead. Panic began to well up in her stomach. There were so many things she did not know about. Why hadn't Mama ever told her about birthday regulations before?

"If I give the birthday present back," she asked anxiously. "Will the bad luck go 'way?"

"Reckon not, baby," Bertha answered sadly. "The damage done be done already."

Kathy stopped handing. How could people be so ignorant in this day and age! She was embarrassed by her position in the situation; but more than that, she was angry that her little friend should be a victim of such primitive superstition.

Billy's eagle eye noticed Kathy's pause that broke the rhythm for the whole crew. He broke into the middle of the group, "Come on. I told you, lunch is over. Let's get working and quit the talking. If we don't get this barn in on time, we're going to be caught in the rain." He indicated the southeastern horizon where storm clouds were gathering rapidly. Kathy resumed her beat in the cadence. The work progressed. Billy gave them a satisfied smile and headed for the field to check on the efforts of the boys.

"I'm sorry, Margie," Kathy said as they gathered the stem ends of the tobacco together to hand to their loopers.

"It be OK," Margie answered softly. "You di'n't know."

"But it isn't really true, Margie. That bad luck stuff—it's just dumb superstition."

Margie looked questioningly into Kathy's eyes. "I don' know—Mama says . . . "

"But, bad luck can't come about like that," Kathy snapped her fingers in the air for emphasis. "Bad luck comes from, well, comes from . . . " Margie waited expectantly for an answer. Kathy sighed. She didn't really know what did cause bad luck, she only knew it wasn't caused by early birthday parties, like Mrs. Braxton had said.

Margie lay awake in her bed long after all the others had gone to sleep. *Little Women* lay under her pillow. She hadn't been able to bring herself to begin reading it. It lay, an ominous lump, under her head. She might never ever read it, she thought.

The storm had broken over the fields just as dark had begun to settle. Its initial thrusts were now tempered to a steady drum on the tin roof over her head. Plink, plink, plink, echoed the bucket in the corner. Most of the time Margie liked to lie and listen to the rhythmic plink. The warmth of her mother's body next to her was evidence of a comfort that could buffer even the worst of storms. Tonight however, the steady pounding overhead served only to set her nerves on edge. She listened to the flip, flap of Lenny's nostrils as he breathed in and out. She shivered; she hated Lenny; she hated this house—this room; she hated being Margie.

Bertha grumbled as she poked at the fire in the stove. The wet kindling sputtered and sizzled. The rain fell steadily outside. They needed the rain, Bertha knew, but she dreaded wading through the lake that had already filled the yard. She wondered why God could not be more efficient with His precious water. There seemed to be no moderation. It was either drought or flood.

Margie woke stiff in the neck from laying all night on the book under her pillow. She twisted her head from side to side trying to relieve the kink.

"You up so soon," Mama remarked in surprise.

"Cou'n't sleep."

"I'll have some coffee ready d'rectly." Margie sat at the table and watched sleepy-eyed as her mother padded back and forth in the business of preparing the morning coffee.

"Get you a cup, baby, we'll sip together 'fore the whole house gets up."

It was a rare time for Margie to have her mother all to herself. She was grateful for the opportunity this morning. Bertha poured each a cup of strong, black chicory-laced coffee. Margie blew the steam from the surface and sipped at the hot bitter brew.

A mother knows when her child is struggling, and Bertha knew that Margie was struggling now.

"What's ailin' you, baby!" Margie winced at the term "baby." She knew it was just a term of endearment, but she was beginning to hate that too. She wished Mama would just call her Margie.

"Spill it out, baby," Mama coaxed. "It only gnaws you insides if you keep it there." Margie shivered. The dampness from the rain had permeated the little house. It was chill damp. She cupped her hands over the mug of hot coffee in front of her to capture the steam in her palms. She gazed reflectively at her mother.

"Mama, what makes bad luck?" she asked softly. Bertha sighed. Bad luck? It was one of those things you know about but can't rightly describe about. "Baby, it be hard to 'scribe it."

"But, yesterday you said . . . "

"I know. Yesterday I said havin' a birthday 'fore it be time was bad luck; but that ain' what it really is—it be the tamperin' with nature that's the bad luck. Birthdays is nature."

"Kathy says that it's all superstition."

"Kathy be a sweet girl, but she ain' knowin' nothin'." snapped Mama. "Oh, yeah, she be good with books an' that kind of smart, but she be too young to know 'bout nature yet; that takes 'sperience."

"But do it count if you don' even know it when you do somethin' that's bad luck?"

"Mebbe you don' know it, but the nature knows it."

"But, Mama . . . " Margie stopped; it was no use arguing. She'd never be able to understand it all, she'd just have to learn to live with nature. She squeezed her temples with her forefingers; her head throbbed in confusion.

"I'm glad that Kathy be movin'," Bertha reflected. "She be nice but she sure do stir up too much trouble." Margie tightened her jaw at the reminder that Kathy might be moving. She had been the only really real friend Margie had ever had.

It's funny, she thought now. *An' she be white.* Suddenly she remembered what Kathy had said about school.

"Mama, Kathy said it's against the law to not let me go to school."

Bertha nodded her head knowingly. "That's just what I mean," she responded. "Kathy's always messin' into 'fairs what don' concern her."

"But, Mama, she said it's blackmail for Mr. Winston to threaten you. She said he can't fire you an' the girls 'cause he won' have no way of gettin' his 'bacco in at all then." She did not know what blackmail was but used the term now to impress Mama.

"That be true, baby; but what Kathy don' know is that Mr. Winston can get ugly, ugly, ugly if he don' get his own way."

Yes, Margie knew. Mr. Winston had always been nice to her but she had often been a witness to his ugliness to the others. *Yes,* she thought now, *there is some things that Kathy don' know 'bout.*

"I sure do wisht I could start to school nes' week though," she sighed aloud to her mother.

176

"You'll get there in plenty time," Bertha assured as she pushed herself away from the table to get herself another cup of coffee.

The sounds coming from the next room indicated that the rest of the family was stirring to get up. Lenny emerged through the door buttoning his trousers as he approached the table. Margie observed to herself that he was even uglier than usual when he first got up in the morning. He squinted at her from under his sleep-puffed eyelids. She turned her head away. As he passed her chair, he laid his hand on her shoulder and gave a squeeze. Margie's whole body crawled with goose bumps at the feel of his flesh on her body.

"You sure gots it nice," he grumbled to no one in particular. "Layin' 'round all day Saturday whilst I gots to truck off to my job."

"It's only till noon," reminded Bertha.

"Still, it be workin' whilst y'all just set 'round."

"Humph, any day I gets to set 'round . . . " Bertha growled in response.

"This coffee is terr'ble!" he said, gagging on its bitter taste. Bertha ignored the complaint.

"Ain' it ever goin' stop rainin'?" he grumped again. Still Bertha ignored him.

Angered by the inattention, Lenny threw his cup onto the floor and stomped out of the house. He sloshed through the water-filled yard to his car. The wheels spun angrily in the soggy sand as he gunned the engine and took off down the road toward Maylor.

"If you as't me, he's what bad luck is," observed Margie, as she watched her mother mopping up Lenny's coffee from the floor.

"Yeah, you be right 'bout that, but then there's some bad luck a body can't void," Bertha agreed. Margie made another vow—the second one in a week—that she would do her utmost to avoid this omen of bad luck in her house.

"Ain' no way that Lenny is goin' to plague me no more," she mumbled to herself. She wrinkled her nose at the now out of sight Lenny. Then she continued to sip at the coffee, which had lost all its comforting heat and now was only bitter and black. She reflected on the problem of bad luck. Mama was right, of course; you must not tamper with nature. She shuddered a little wondering just what kind of bad luck was due her because of the birthday party yesterday; the anxiety was probably worse than the bad luck. She wondered just who had done what to nature to invite such a load of bad luck as Lenny into their house. She hoped hers would not be so bad or so long-lasting.

Chapter XIV

The first day of school is always a little scary. But when it is the first day for everyone, there is that support from your peers to ease the anxieties. For Margie, she had to endure these anxieties alone now as she sat in the school office waiting for Mrs. Biglow to finish all the "first thing in the morning" business.

There was a long line of students who were turning in their lunch money in exchange for lunch tickets. There was another line of students with the class absentee lists. And yet another line of students waiting for tardy slips.

Mrs. Biglow flitted back and forth from one line to another, vainly trying to keep all appeased. While she worked with the lunch ticket line, the students in the other two lines scuffled and bumped each other for diversion. When the tardy line got too noisy she shuffled over to attend to it, leaving the lunch ticket line to simmer in frustration.

Margie scrunched down in her corner chair trying to appear invisible. Still all the students in the lines stared, giggled, and pointed at her. Some she knew, others were strangers to her, but all had been going to school for two weeks now; she was a "new" student. She tried to not look so new; she concentrated on her sweaty hands that lay limply folded in her lap.

At last all the morning business had been attended to and Mrs. Biglow turned to Margie with a sigh. "Now, let's see, we have to get *you situated.*" She said the "you" as if Margie was just another onerous extension of that morning business. Margie rose from her seat expectantly. "Just remain seated." Mrs. Biglow ordered impatiently. "I have to find Mrs. Erland." Mrs. Erland was the school guidance counselor. Margie liked her a lot. She always seemed to really care about the individual child. Margie obediently reseated herself on the chair and waited.

It seemed like the whole morning would pass before Mrs. Biglow finally returned to the office with Mrs. Erland behind her. "Well, Margie Braxton, how good it is to see you. I was wondering if you would be coming back to us." Mrs. Erland cheerfully greeted. Margie knew her greeting was not just a rehearsal of kind words, she knew that Mrs. Erland probably was really happy to see her and that she probably really had thought about her return.

"Here's her folder from last year, Mrs. Erland." the secretary said, handing her a cream colored folder. Mrs. Erland flipped through its accumulation of pages.

"Hmm, you're special ed." She said, not to Margie exactly, but rather about her. "Lets see now, that's Mrs. Levine; but she's already got fifteen and that's about all she can handle right now. Then there's Mr. Wilson. But he's not really special ed., more remedial. Well, we'll just have to go with Mrs. Levine for now. Come along Margie, let's get you started." Margie rose from her chair to follow Mrs. Erland. She was sorely disappointed to be placed in Mrs. Levine's class again. She liked Mrs. Levine but she had hoped that she'd be advanced out of the special ed class this year. Mrs. Levine had a mixed class of fifth, sixth, seventh and eight graders in her class. Her students, though not legally classified as retarded, were most certainly borderline in their intelligence levels. The rest of the children in the school always poked fun at the special-ed students, calling them "dumb bunnies."

"Mrs. Erland," Margie stammered shyly as they walked out of the office together.

"Yes, dear?"

"Mrs. Erland, I kin read real good now." She waited for Mrs. Erland to respond. Mrs. Erland only smiled down at her and continued on down the hall toward Mrs. Levine's room. "Mrs. Erland, I mean, I can *really* read good now." Margie insisted.

"I'm sure you can, dear." Mrs. Erland answered accommodatingly and continued down the hall. Margie had to skip a little to keep up with her.

"Mrs. Erland, I don' want to be in Mrs. Levine's room no more." Margie flushed in surprise at her own bravado. Mrs. Erland halted suddenly and stared in wonder at the girl.

"Mrs. Erland," Margie said softly now, her eyes riveted to the floor in front of her feet. "A girl learned me how to read this summer." Mrs. Erland jiggled uncomfortably on her high-heeled shoes. She wasn't sure just what she was expected to do in such a situation.

Finally she said, "Well, in that case, maybe we ought to test you." Turning abruptly in her tracks she proceeded in the opposite direction toward the counseling office. Margie instinctively turned and trailed behind her.

Inside the counseling office Mrs. Erland nodded for Margie to sit at the table in the corner of the room. She then began to fumble through a stack of books on the long low shelf that bordered the one whole wall. She flipped through several, then finally settled on one, *Mary and Tom at the Circus,* and carried it over to Margie. Margie winced at the title, a baby book.

"Mrs. Erland, I kin read *real* books." Mrs. Erland stopped short of the table holding the book awkwardly in her hands, "What do you mean, *real* books?"

"Well, books like, like, *Little Women,"* she declared proudly.

"Little Women?" Mrs. Erland sucked in her breath with a little whistling sound. She seemed genuinely impressed. After a moment of reflection, she returned the book that she held to the shelf and chose another, *Teens and Their Parents,* and offered it to Margie for her to demonstrate her reading skills. Margie carefully opened the book and turned the pages directly to chapter one. She always skipped the preface and foreword because she was always so anxious to get on with the story. Mrs. Erland did not interrupt her procedure now.

Margie read the words on the page in front of her in a slow deliberate monotone. She was most anxious to pronounce them all correctly. Mrs. Erland listened in genuine amazement.

"Well, Margie, that's wonderful!" she exclaimed when Margie had finished reading. "I can certainly see why you don't want to remain in the special-ed class. Who did you say taught you how to read, dear?"

"Kathy Taylor." Margie answered. Mrs. Erland did not know Kathy personally, but was acquainted with the Taylor family. She nodded now in understanding. John Taylor, Kathy's brother in the eighth grade, was one of her best student tutors, so it made sense that the girl, Kathy, might well have taught Margie to read.

"Where did you meet Kathy, dear?" She asked, curious to know the circumstances of Margie's summer education.

"She worked wif me in 'bacco." As Margie answered, Mrs. Erland raised her eyebrows in a surprised expression.

"I see." She said. "Well, Margie, I think you are indeed ready for advancement. How about Mrs. Langhorn's class, how would you like that?" She smiled proudly at the progress Margie had made.

"That'd be nice." Margie said beaming in triumph.

All of the students in Mrs. Langhorn's class stopped working and stared at Margie with open curiosity. A new student was a legitimate reason for recess. Some of the students already knew Margie because they went to her church. She felt a wave of embarrassment sweep over her as Mrs. Langhorn introduced her to the class then showed her to a seat halfway down the second row from the door.

"Martin, will you please see to it that Margie gets all the books she needs?" Mrs. Langhorn said to the boy in the seat in front of Margie's.

Sitting down in her new seat Margie glanced shyly around the classroom, taking a quick survey of her new classmates. All but two of the students were black. Maylor Grammar School was an integrated school and it held integrated classes. However, in an effort to place the children in equitable intelligence levels a segregated learning program had emerged. Most of the black students of this predominantly rural area suffered from a kind of environmental retardation. They would have been totally lost in a normally advanced classroom. Many parents and educators were sincerely concerned with this anomaly of their system of desegregation; it was a problem, but just what did one do with children like Margie?

Margie smiled as her eyes met with Norma Suthers. Already the discomfort of the first day began to ebb and she anticipated a pleasant school year ahead. Someone poked her shoulder from behind; she turned to face the poker. It was Bernice Johnson, another friend from the New Mission Baptist Church. She smiled warmly at Bernice.

"Eat lunch wif us," Bernice whispered. Margie nodded in response, wondering who all was meant by "us." But at least she knew she would not eat alone, this first day of school. Yes, school was going to be okay this year.

Margie jumped off the bus as it was still braking. Waving over her shoulder to the remaining passengers she leapt across the ditch and bounded across the yard toward the house. The sand kicked up leaving a faint cloud of dust in her wake. The dog, Spot, crawled out from under the house and ran to greet her. She gave him an affectionate smack on his rump and the two continued toward the house together.

Mama had worked a few hours for Mr. Winston, cleaning up and bundling sticks for the winter but she was home now. Margie could see her through the open door of the house. She was sitting at the table snapping a pot full of green beans. Margie was glad to see her at her familiar duties in the kitchen. Mama hardly ever did any of the cooking now that Aunt Sissy lived with them.

"Mama, Mama!" she yelled as she neared the porch steps. Bertha, having let her thoughts drift in a nonsense of daydreaming, was aroused from her reveries now by Margie's excited fretting. She dumped the remaining beans onto the table and hurried to the door.

"What she screamin' 'bout?" London complained as she pulled herself from the big double bed. Her pregnancy seemed to have sapped her of all her strength lately. All she wanted to do was to sleep.

"Mama, Mama, I'm goin' be in level four. I ain' no special ed no more." Margie declared excitedly as she burst through the doorway right into her mother's firmly planted bulk. Bertha wasn't quite sure just what this all meant but deduced from the excited tone of Margie's voice that it must be good.

"That be good, honey," she congratulated appropriately. "That be real good."

"Lawd, I thought somepin happened to her?" London groaned as she lowered herself wearily onto a kitchen chair.

"Mama, Mrs. Erlan' listened to me read an' she say I be so good she jest *had* to move me to level four." Margie was fairly bursting with pride.
"Hell, that ain' nothin'. I was in level four all the time I was in school." London dashed at Margie's enthusiasm.

"Now, London, you hesh," scolded Bertha. "Margie gots a right to be prideful." Just then Sissy came into the house from the yard. Reggie tagged behind her holding firmly to the hem of her dress.

"Reggie used to holt onto my dress that same way." Margie thought when she saw them, just a tinge of jealousy pricking her heart.

"Sissy, you hear that? Margie's gettin' 'vanced." Mama announced for Margie.

"That what all the yellin' 'bout. Lawd, I would a thought she got kilt." Sissy answered, then turning her attention back to the baby she crooned, "Come on, baby, le's git a cookie." She pulled Reggie into her arms and proceeded to the sideboard where the box of vanilla wafers was kept.

Bertha watched sympathetically as Margie went quietly into the bedroom to change her dress. Margie folded her skirt and blouse neatly and laid them across the foot of the cot. Slipping on her everyday dress she reached under her pillow for *Little Women*. Bertha sighed as Margie walked softly past her and out the front door, her book in her hand, and headed toward the tire swing under the pecan tree. She was beginning to think that it wasn't good for this child of hers to escape reality in the pages of a book. Bertha knew that life was harsh and that only a stern upbringing could prepare one for the disaster of becoming an adult in this world. And, as an adult, she knew not to expect adulation from others, that this must be supplied from within one's own soul. But she felt sorry for Margie now, her spirits having been so rudely damped and she was glad, for the moment, that Margie

182

could escape into her book world, something she herself had never been able to do.

Margie wiggled her thin frame into the cradle of the tire swing. Giving it just one gentle push to set it to swaying in a slow relaxing arc, she opened her book and slid comfortably into that other world that beckoned from the pages. The late September afternoon was hot, humid and fragrant. The air over the area hung sweet with the aroma of golden ripe tobacco that still hung in many barns or lay sheeted in storage sheds. Priming of tobacco was a task of the past; harvesting of corn had taken its place. Priming machines had gone into hibernation for the winter season; combines, great hungry monsters, had emerged to devour the now crisp brown rows of corn, spewing their waste in helter-skelter fashion in their wake. It was a good day to rock in the arms of a pecan tree tire swing, and melt into another world, a world of undreamed of dimensions, to become a part of that world, leaving behind all the stench of the garbage dump that mingled with the attar of tobacco.

"Ah-a-a!" A long agonizing wail broke through the silken screen of dreamland pulling Margie abruptly back to the ugly present. She sat very still in her swing trying to orient herself to what had wrenched her forth from that other world.

"Ah-a-a!" the agonizing wail was repeated. Margie jumped from the swing and ran toward the house from where the sound had come. As she burst through the open door her ears were assaulted with another shriek of woe.

London sat on the floor doubled over, her head between her knees, fitfully rocking back and forth. Then she tipped her head back like a wolf baying at the moon and screamed for the fourth time.

"What be the matter!" gasped Margie. Bertha stood over London wringing her hands in despair.

"London, baby, what be the matter?" Bertha pleaded. London tilted her head back again, eyes rolling upward, she let forth with another ear-splitting scream. Reggie, frightened by the sight of her sitting on the floor screaming, set up an accompanying wail. Sissy pulled him into the warmth of her ample bosom and lolled back and forth to comfort him.

As London was about to turn on again, a yellow school bus stopped in front of the house. Gayla and Teresa jumped down from the bus to be greeted with, "Ah—h—h!" They ran to the house and burst in on the disturbing scene within.

"For Gawd's sake, what be the matter with her?" Teresa gasped.

Beads of perspiration had popped out on London's forehead and had begun to trickle down her face. Again, the, by now familiar, "Ah—h—h!"

"Oh, Lawd, I bet she's goin' have the baby now—an' Lenny be at work—Oh, Lawd, what we goin' do?"

Bertha was deeply perplexed. She had birthed five babies and none had begun in such obvious agony as London now displayed. She quickly calculated the months. "Oh, Lawd, it be too early! Oh, Lawd, Lawd!"

London screamed again.

"Gayla, run quick to Pfeiffer's an' ast to call the am'blance," Bertha ordered hysterically.

"She goin' have the baby *now*?" Gayla asked anxiously.

"Yeah—mebbe—don' know. Git!" Mama stammered.

Gayla took off running toward Pfeiffer's. Bertha bent over the stricken London and stroked her soggy hair in an effort to comfort her. Margie watched in terror-stricken awe as her sister groveled on the floor.

"Now pant, pant, you know, like a puppy," Dr. Watson coaxed. London sobbed and panted as instructed.

"No, push, push hard; it's almost here."

A loud, long, grunting groan emerged from London's parched cracked lips.

"It's coming, keep pushing." A moment later, London broke into hysterical sobs of relief. A hush followed. Dr. Watson laid the scrawny premature infant on London's subdued belly and deftly tied and snipped the cord that bound him to his mother. A nurse quickly lifted the detached fetus and, after first clearing the mucus from his mouth and throat, applied a tiny oxygen mask to its doll-like face. Another nurse urgently paged the resident pediatrician, while Dr. Watson attended to the welfare of his patient, the infant's mother, who was beginning to hemorrhage.

The wrenching pangs of birthing over, London slipped into a euphoric semiconscious state. The voices in the delivery room droned in her ears as if they were an old 78 record being played at 33. The bright overhead light seemed to move slowly toward her as a sun drifting down from the sky. Then the voices faded into the distance; the sun paled; her body floated in and out among the green-garbed phantoms.

Bertha rose to her feet when she saw Dr. Watson push through the swinging doors. He looked gray and drawn. The doors fluttered to a stop behind him.

"London's just fine, Mrs. Braxton," he said as he approached her. "You can see her in a few minutes; the nurses are cleaning her up now."

"An' the baby?" Bertha inquired softly.

"A boy—I'm sorry, Mrs. Braxton," the doctor stammered. "We did all we could; it was just too early." No matter how many times he would go through this sequence, he knew he'd never be able to do it gracefully. "A volunteer will be with you shortly to ask you some questions and make arrangements for, for—well—for whatever you wish to do about—about . . ."

"Thank you," Bertha said numbly, thus relieving the doctor of using that bitter word—"remains."

London was still spinning on her billowy cloud when Bertha walked into the room. "Hey, Gramma," she giggled as she looked at her mother through half-closed eyes.

Bertha took hold of her daughter's hand. She knew that the doctor would have told London; it was just that London was not yet cognizant of the world around her. "I'm goin' name him Martin Luther," London announced in slurred speech.

Bertha's big shoulders quivered. "Yes, baby," she whispered, patting London's hand.

Breathing a satisfied sigh, London slipped back into her nether world. Bertha sat down on the chair next to the bed, to wait; to wait for the moment when London would remember what the doctor had told her. In the beginning, London had not wanted another child. And when that child was not yet a recognizable human baby to her, it had seemed appropriate to abort it. The abortion attempt having failed, however, London had settled quickly into the maternal role of expectancy. A birthed baby was a gift from God—London's baby was a gift—but it was dead.

Sissy hustled and bustled busily about the chilled kitchen. "I best lay a fire in the stove," she fretted. "It sure is a cold day for this early in the year."

"Well, lay it then, woman, an' quit dancin' 'round this room. You the one what's makin' it so airish in here," Lenny grumped.

The others sat around the table in silence. London had gone into the bedroom and had stretched out across the big bed. The twenty-mile ride home from the hospital had drained all energy from her. Reggie watched her from the foot of the bed. He did not disturb her. When her eyes closed in sleep, he left the room. In the kitchen he looked from one to the other. No one noticed him. Slowly the tears welled up into his eyes; his tiny frame began to shake under his silent sobs. Sissy turned toward him just as his sobbing began to merge into a low, humming wail.

"Baby, baby, baby." She reached her arms toward him. Warily, the little boy moved into them. "It'll be OK, baby," Sissy crooned, as she swayed back and forth with him in her arms. She thought of the little sweater she had knitted. There was no one to wear such a small garment now. She sighed. Well, at least she still had Reggie. She squeezed him tight to her and kissed him effusively on his face. He grunted in delight as the embrace left him breathless.

"For Christ's sake!" Lenny boomed, as he pushed his chair from the table sending it toppling to the floor with a crash. "You'd think the worl' was comin' to a end." He looked from one to the other; no one acknowledged him. "Christ's sake, she'll get 'nother baby in her belly by the year's over." He stomped out of the house. No one took note of his leave, except Mama, who righted his felled chair.

London, being young, quickly regained her strength. Bored with just sitting at home with nothing to do, she became restless and irritable. Sissy, deprived of the expected infant in her life, now poured all her maternal affection into the care of Reggie. Mama was back to working two days a week for the town ladies, helping them get their houses ready for their extravagant Christmas season. London's sisters were at school and Lenny at work.

Soon her irritability merged into the depression of fruitless days. Her nights became mere extensions of those days with still more sleepless boredom. Even Saturday night at the Paradise Inn did not revive her spirits. Randy, who had grown bored with Mary and had returned to London, was now perplexed with her attitude and again sought greener pastures. London became bogged in an endless procession of lonely hours.

"I can't stan' this little bitty shack!" she screamed one day. Reggie cowered behind Sissy.

Miss Virginia was just letting Bertha out of her car when London ran out the door, letting it slam behind her. Bertha watched as London ran across the yard and out onto the road. Miss Virginia pulled away; Bertha still stood gaping as London ran on down the road.

"London, London," she finally called. London kept right on running.

Margie stared out the bus window at the figure coming down the road toward them. "Hey, isn't that your sister?" the driver asked over his shoulder to her.

"It looks like it," Margie agreed, puzzled.

"Where is she going in such a hurry?"

"Don' know." Margie watched out the window at the retreating figure. The bus jerked to a stop in front of her house. Still looking down the road, she got off.

"Bye, Margie," Norma called.

"Bye," Margie answered vaguely, her thoughts on the figure fading into the distance.

"Where at's London goin, streakin' down the road like that?" Margie asked Mama, who was still standing where she had gotten out of Miss Virginia's car.

Bertha shrugged in answer. Margie thought a moment, then she too shrugged and headed for the house. Bertha followed slowly behind. She knew inside herself that her first born had left the nest and would not be back; she just knew. It had been difficult for her, so young, to be thrust into a seemingly permanent position of sitting—waiting—alone—for something—whatever. Yes, the time had come; she would not come back, Bertha knew. There had been urgency in her flight; Bertha remembered another day, another one, who had had such an urgency. That was a long time ago; life repeats itself. Yes, London was gone. She knew.

Margie changed her clothes and began working on her homework. She had an unusually large amount of it this day and wanted to be sure she gave herself enough time to get it all finished. She was just finishing her math when Gayla called from the window. "Now, what's he got?"

"What's *who* got? Margie asked.

"Lenny," Gayla answered. "He's fretting' with somethin' out there."

"Lemme see." Margie pushed Gayla aside at the window. "It looks like a valise."

"It do, don' it," agreed Gayla. "Reckon he's fixin' to leave?"

"Mebbe," Margie whispered, a tinge of hope in her voice.

"Open the door!" Lenny yelled as he stepped up onto the porch. Margie pulled the door open wide and peered from behind it. She stared at the large object that Lenny was huffing and puffing over as he struggled toward the table. Her eyes widened. "It be a TV!"

"That be right, a TV." Lenny grinned as he set the portable TV on the kitchen table. Bertha and Sissy stared at the set. Teresa ran in from the bedroom.

"A TV!" Gayla announced to her. The three girls clapped their hands with glee. Lenny beamed from one to the other.

"Where at you get that, Lenny?" Sissy asked suspiciously.

"Bought it," he proclaimed proudly.

"Bought it!" Bertha queried.

"That's right. Got the car all paid for, so I bought this here TV so's we can watch the 'lections nes' year."

" 'Lections?" asked Sissy, puzzled.

"Yeah, 'lections is nes' year," explained Lenny. While watching the TV set that Willis had at the hardware store, which ran constantly, he had been exposed to the pre-campaigns that had already permeated the media. "An' they're startin' already to have it all on the TV. You gots to know 'bout who's runnin' for the president so's you can vote proper." Sissy sighed and dropped her bulk onto a chair. She and Lenny had never voted in their lives and she expected that Bertha had never either.

Why? she thought. *Why?* Lenny noted the despair in her eyes.

"Oh, that's OK, honey. We goin' get your stove. We'll get it just as soon's the TV paid for," Lenny promised. Sissy nodded numbly. Yes, she knew—when the TV was paid for.

"You knows he be lyin; you ain' never goin' get no gas stove. When he gets the TV paid for, then he'll fin' somethin' else to buy; but you can bet it ain' goin' be no gas stove," Bertha advised Sissy.

"What you talkin' 'bout, woman?" Lenny said in his most authoritative voice. "Where at's your patriotic spirit? The whole country's goin' on 'bout the 'lections. We gots to keep up, tsk, tsk."

"Well, I for sure certain will vote for the man what can make you disappear from off the earth!" snapped Bertha. The girls all laughed at their mother's rare joke. Sissy blushed in embarrassment for her husband. Lenny dusted at an invisible speck on his TV.

Until now they had all been standing at a respectable distance from the new TV that sat on the kitchen table. Lenny alone hovered over it. Suddenly, Bertha took a step forward to examine it for herself. Lenny, not sure of her intentions and remembering the fate of his radio, flung his arms around the TV and shouted, "Oh no, you ain'. You ain' goin' bus' this up!" Bertha stopped in her tracks. "It's my money this time an' I gots a right to spend it the way I wants. An' I judges I wants a TV for the 'lections." Bertha didn't answer. She just shook her head in bewilderment at this lunatic of a brother-in-law of hers and went over to the stove to poke up the embers. Lenny sighed with relief; standing up straight he beamed triumphantly at his audience. Then, slowly, he unrolled the cord.

188

The little house had only one wall receptacle. It had two outlets in it, one for Bertha's wall clock and the other for the refrigerator. However, Bertha had screwed an adapter into the light fixture that hung over the table, which would accommodate a light bulb and the plug for her iron. It was very convenient, because she used the kitchen table for an ironing board. Now, Lenny reached over his head and plugged his TV into the empty receptacle that was meant for Bertha's iron. Gently, now, he twisted the on-off knob then stepped back to where the girls were standing to join them in expectation. A light flashed onto the screen, faded, then reappeared, finally focusing into a fuzzy picture. From a brown paper bag he pulled a "rabbit-ear" antenna and connected it to the back of the TV. He fiddled with the ears until the picture cleared.

"Ain' that somethin'!" gasped Margie. She could not get over the fact that this was a TV, a real TV, just like the one they had at school, and it was working in her own house.

"Sure is," the others echoed, just as bewitched as she. Bertha kept her head turned away. But Sissy joined the others in the little circle around the set. It was here to stay. She might as well enjoy it.

"Ain' it purty, Sugah Babe?" Lenny cooed in Sissy's ear. Sissy smiled lovingly at her husband.

No one seemed to remember that London was absent, except Bertha. She would miss her daughter, her first born, but she could not pine for her—it was the way—when the fledgling feathered, it left the nest.

Suddenly Margie remembered the figure of her sister running down the road. "London ought to be here now," she said wistfully.

Lenny looked away from the TV questioningly. It was the first he had been aware of her absence. "Where she at?"

"Don' know," Margie answered vaguely, still watching the movement on the screen in front of her.

Lenny did not prod for an answer. But Gayla did. "Where she at, Mama?"

"She's growed." Mama replied as vaguely as Margie had.

Gayla shrugged, her interest in her sister was short lived. Teresa, if she had noticed the absence, said nothing. It was the way . . .

Bertha sighed a deep, torn sigh as she poured herself a cup of coffee. The dinner was all ready, the biscuits browned and now cooling hard. The thick slabs of ham continued to simmer in their own juices desperately trying to recapture their life's blood. Yes, dinner was ready, but—well, the TV now held occupation of the table in the house. And no one seemed to be hungry anyway. Bertha wondered that Lenny, at least, did not bellow for his meal, but he was like a child with his new toy.

Sipping at the thick black coffee, Bertha watched the benumbed faces of the others as they became one with the blaring TV set. No one took notice when she rose from her chair and walked out into the chilled night. She squinted her eyes and peered into the direction of London's flight. The heavy night did not part in her search.

A mama gots to suffer a whole lot for her chi'runs. Bertha thought. She knew it was the way—but still there was an ache where her oldest child had been wrenched from her.

"Mama!" a voice from the door said. "Mama, come in an' watch the pitcher with us."

Bertha turned to contemplate the pleading eyes of her youngest. "Please, Mama, it's real nice," Margie pleaded. Bertha didn't answer. "You ain' mad with me are you, Mama?" Margie now hovered beside her mother, her brown eyes fretfully begging forgiveness—for what?

"Will you watch with us then?"

"Mebbe." Bertha knew that she too would eventually succumb to the magic of the box, just as she had succumbed to being packed into Lenny's car every Sunday. But just now, she needed to stand firm under her burdens. A large lump welled up in her chest as she watched Margie return to her place in front of the new TV. Would that she could keep this one for herself forever. But she knew that that was not the way—someday Margie too would run down that road. Bertha squinted one more time into the darkness. She thought she saw—no, it was just the shadow of an old pine stump. She turned her back on the stump. Leaving her burden in its shadow she slipped, unnoticed, into the kitchen. She stood for a moment on the outer edge of the audience. The meal was now being eaten, finger fashion, right from the pots; Lenny had gotten hungry after all. She shook her head in disgust, then slowly, she allowed her eyes to come to rest on the flickering picture in front of her. The others were laughing heartily at the dialogue between Tony Orlando and Ruth Buzzi. Bertha felt a twitter rise up from her belly. In a moment the twitter burst forth in a loud guffaw. The others stopped laughing and turned and stared in amazement at her. Bertha blushed, then said, "That's dumb," then hurriedly turned her back on the set.

For a moment the others just sat there, then Margie squealed, "Mama looked at the TV!"

"An' she laughed, too!" added Teresa.

"That's dumb," reiterated Bertha as she poured herself another cup of coffee.

"Here, Mama, sit here in the rockin' chair," Margie said, relinquishing her seat to her mother.

Bertha hesitatingly sat down in the proffered chair. Margie plopped down on the floor at her feet and continued to watch the capers of the actors in front of her. Suddenly Bertha giggled softly. "That's good, that's good!" she said almost inaudibly and clapped her hands in excitement. No one paid any attention this time; Bertha had melted into the body of the audience. They were all one now.

Wisht London be here . . . Mama thought with a wince, then returned her attention to the magic of the TV and allowed it to soothe away the maternal amputation.

Chapter XV

The weather was gray. The last of the leaves had deserted the trees. Pecans lay scattered among the leaves under the old tire swing. December was usually a mild month as far as temperatures go, the bitter weather not coming until after Christmas. But the cold winds had born down from the Great Lakes early this year.

Margie could not help the feeling of satisfaction and gratitude that swept over her now as she sat with the others in front of the TV. The glowing red belly of the stove radiated snugly around the family. The air in the room still hung heavy with the strong smell of collards and the pungent aroma of pepper vinegar from dinner. Lenny wasn't all that bad, Margie thought, as she observed his enormous stomach heaving gently in the rhythm of sleep. She wondered, again, how he managed to stay erect on his chair, never faltering one way or the other, though he seemed well relaxed.

A gunshot, emanating from the TV, brought her jerking back to the *Rookies.* Margie liked the comedy shows and looked forward to watching the reruns of all the old shows, *Beverly Hillbillies, Hogan's Heroes,* etc. during the dinner hour, but those handsome young cops on the *Rookies*—they provided dream material for a girl who was almost grown up. This being their first full exposure to the TV media, of course, nothing was a rerun to the Braxtons. Bertha had even bought an extension cord from Pfeiffer's so the TV could be plugged in over the table but sit on the sideboard, giving her table back to its proper use, but also making the set visible to all those at the table. She had neatly tied the drooping cord up along the ceiling then let it run down the wall behind the sideboard to accommodate the TV.

Sometimes Margie missed the old dinner banter that used to occupy her sisters at the table. No one ever talked at all now. Even so, it probably wouldn't have been much of a conversation, what with London gone. Gayla and Teresa, who used to fill London in on their days at school, now discussed all these things while riding home on the bus because Mama was not really interested in such goings-on. There were times when Margie would have liked to interject a bit of news into the family forum, but since the

TV—well, no one would have found interest in her petty grammar school news anyway.

Sissy no longer mourned the absence of her coveted gas stove. The TV provided her and Reggie a happy interlude on the days when it was just the two of them, on the days when Bertha went out for day work. And even when Bertha didn't go out, which was more often than not, the three of them enjoyed it together. Since the staggering economy had pulled at the nation's purse strings many of the ladies in town were doing their own cleaning. The first of November, Miss Virginia had told Bertha that she wouldn't need her anymore, just now, but maybe in the spring. That left only Miss Francis and she had even cut down to one afternoon a week. Thank God Lenny was working, Bertha had thought at the time, then had quickly squelched the feeling of gratitude that had attempted to surface.

But even Lenny's job was always teetering on the brink of jeopardy. Ingy Rowe, Willis's former employee, was out of the hospital now and it was being rumored around town that, once he got his strength back, he intended to hold Willis to his promise of giving him his old job back. Lenny tried hard to make himself indispensable to Willis in an effort to keep in his favor. As much as he hated working he had grown accustomed to the luxury of the car and the TV and meat on the table every day. Even though he usually slept in front of the TV all the time he knew that without it he would fast lose his regency in Bertha's house. And without a steady income in the house, it would not be long before Bertha had the electricity turned off to make ends meet so the TV would be useless as a bargaining tool with Bertha. And Lenny couldn't help but notice that Bertha no longer rode his back about his bad habits, well, at least not very often, since he had been working. Yes, it was well worth his onerous days at the hardware store to deserve such a seat of honor in his sister-in-law's house.

"You do your lessons?" Bertha now interrupted Margie's attention with a vagueness of inquiry that did not put upon Margie the need for an entirely truthful answer.

"Yes, ma'am," Margie responded just as vaguely. She hadn't really, but thought she might have enough time in homeroom in the morning. Yes, the TV had made a difference in her attentiveness to her schoolwork. She no longer read anymore either. *Little Women* still lay under her pillow, only its first four pages having been creased, now just a vague memory of the summer.

Just the other day Mrs. Erland had called Margie into the counseling center and warned her that if her grades continued to slip downward she would be put back into the special ed class. Margie had promised then, to do better, but tonight the *Rookies* was on and that was one of her favorite shows. But then, every night seemed to have one of her favorites on. Well, she promised herself, as she watched the two cars on the screen careen around the corner, narrowly missing a parked car, she would begin again next week to study.

When Margie received her report card on the next Wednesday she was truly shocked at the marks she found on it. She knew she hadn't been working very hard, but she hadn't realized that she had fallen so badly. The only passing grade she had made was a D in reading. All the rest were Es. There also was a note inside requesting a conference between her mother and Mrs. Erland.

Bertha stared at the report card. She could not understand all the intricate coding on it, but she knew that the letters her daughter had received for marks were very poor indeed. Instinctively, she felt anger at the system that was apparently not educating her child. This poor report card was clearly an indication of poor teaching, she ought to tell those people a thing or two—but the idea of a conference intimidated her. In all the years her daughters had been in school, she had never put her feet inside one of those schools.

"This Mrs. Erland—she nice?" Bertha now asked in trepidation.

"Yeah, Mama, she's nice," answered Margie. "But I wisht you wouldn't go to see her. Can't you say you're too busy to be traipsin' off to no school?"

"I sure don' relish no conf'rence with nobody," admitted Mama. "But the note say I gots to have one, don' it?"

Margie flushed, she should have read something else from the piece of paper that was inserted in the report card; Mama would have never known the difference.

"They can't make you do nothin' you don' want to do, Mama," she now advised.

"Well, now, just le' me steady the sit'ation a spell," Mama requested.

Bertha mulled the question of the conference over and over in her mind. As much as she feared the confrontation with the school, she still felt strongly that it was her duty by her child to admonish a system that had caused that child to receive such poor marks. Finally, that night, she announced to Margie, "I'm goin' have that conf'rence."

Margie's heart sank several inches within her chest, "Yes, ma'am." she conceded.

The next time she worked for Miss Francis, Bertha arranged for her to pick her up at the school on her next cleaning day in the following week. That way she could ride into town with Lenny; then Miss Francis would be taking her home after work.

She felt uncomfortable now, and very out of place as she sat in the corner of the school office, just as Margie had done a few months before. All the children who came and stood in the lines waiting to be taken care of for the morning business stared at her with unreserved curiosity. As she rarely came into the town, few of the children knew her. There was Joyce Manning from church, but she had acted so surprised at seeing Bertha in the office that even knowing the child now was embarrassing.

At first she smiled benignly at the children who stared, but gradually she felt the warm flush of embarrassment overtake her and began to examine her fingernails with the greatest of care. This did not stop the stares, but it made them less obvious to Bertha if she concentrated hard enough.

At last Mrs. Biglow said, "Now, Mrs. Braxton, I believe it was Mrs. Erland you wished to see?"

"Yes, ma'am," Bertha answered, grateful that the morning business was over, which left her to cope with only Mrs. Biglow.

"Well, you know, Mrs. Erland has a counseling group first thing in the morning." Mrs. Biglow explained. No, Bertha had not known that Mrs. Erland had a counseling group first thing in the morning. "You should have called first and made an appointment; now Mrs. Erland won't be able to see you until at least 9:30."

Bertha did not explain to Mrs. Biglow that she had no phone; and even with the phone at Pfeiffers, she always asked Mr. Pfeiffer to carry out her communications over it for her. Telephones scared Bertha.

"Would you like a magazine or something to pass the time?" Bertha shook her head. She would content herself with picking a little more at her nails.

The time passed slowly. Bertha glanced anxiously at the large clock on the office wall. It gave a definitive click every time the big hand moved forward a notch. She frowned at the face of the clock. She knew her numbers and could tell time well but, with this clock, she was not sure. There were no numbers on the great staring face, just a series of Xs, Vs and Is. She had no idea what these meant so concluded the clock must be of foreign origin. She tried to guess at the time by the position of the hands. But, without the familiar numbers to guide her, she just couldn't be sure.

Mrs. Biglow seemed oblivious to her presence and flitted about behind the office counter in a busy abstract fashion. Several times the phone rang; the loud clanging bell startling Bertha so that, each time, she jumped spasmodically. She sure wouldn't want one of those noisy things in her house!

Suddenly, an earsplitting clang emanated from the direction of the foreign clock. The noise brought Bertha abruptly to her feet. Mrs. Biglow looked up and smiled reassuringly.

"Change of class," she explained. Bertha smiled and returned to her seat. But she would remain sitting forward on its edge from now on.

It seemed like a long time since she had arrived at the school. She looked inquiringly up at the clock again—it was no use, she could not decipher the time code. Then she heard Mrs. Biglow talking into the phone again. This, time however, she mentioned Bertha's name. Bertha listened expectantly.

"Margie Braxton's mother is here to see you, Mrs. Erland. Should I send her in now?" There was a long pause, then Mrs. Biglow said, "Yes, Mrs. Erland, I'll explain to her." Hanging up the receiver she turned to Bertha. "Mrs. Erland is very sorry for keeping you waiting so long, Mrs. Braxton, but she didn't know you were coming today. You should have called. Mrs. Erland has a previous appointment for nine-thirty. She'll be able to see you at ten o'clock, if you wish to wait."

"I'll wait," Bertha answered, resuming the mutilation of her finger tips. There wasn't much else she could do but wait; Miss Francis wasn't due to pick her up until 10:30, so she had time yet, she reckoned as she looked up at the clock once more—it was no use.

Her thumb was raw and bleeding where she had scraped away all the cuticle flesh. She sucked at it in an attempt to soothe the stinging pain of the open wound. Mrs. Biglow continued her busy ritual behind the desk. After what seemed an eternity to Bertha, the loud clanging split the air again. Again it brought her to her feet with a start. She looked expectantly again at Mrs. Biglow. She wondered if the bell meant a change of class again—perhaps it meant ten o'clock, she thought hopefully. But Mrs. Biglow only smiled this time without offering an explanation and went back to her work. Bertha sat down again to wait.

Various people, both children and adults, came into the office as the morning wore on. Mrs. Biglow attended to their various needs and requests then returned to her mysterious work behind the counter. Bertha stretched her neck to see just what it was that kept Mrs. Biglow so busy. Mrs. Biglow looked up and smiled: Bertha ducked her head in embarrassment and worked frantically at her nails again.

Bertha was just about to assume that it must be well past 10:30 by now and maybe she had better not wait any longer; Miss Francis would surely be waiting for her in front of the school. Mrs. Biglow spoke into the phone again.

"Yes, Janet, is Mrs. Erland free yet?" Again there was that expectant pause. "Oh, she is. Well, all right, let me know as soon as she gets back." At the mention of Mrs. Erland's name Bertha had risen from her chair and was standing now in front of the counter with an air of expectancy.

Mrs. Biglow smiled and said, "I'm really very sorry, Mrs. Braxton. It seems that Mrs. Erland has been called to attend to an emergency in one of the classrooms. I'm sure she won't be long, however, so if you'll just wait a few minutes longer . . . " Well, she reckoned she could wait—just a few minutes—yet. But for the first time, Bertha began to wonder just where she did fit into this vast complex of the business of education, parent, and teacher. Why couldn't Margie just move along like her others girls had done? Except for London, the others had never given her any problems. Even with London, she had never had to concern herself about her schooling. Margie was certainly giving her a lot of unnecessary trouble, she thought, becoming angry at her for having put her in such an awkward position.

The door opened and a smiling, round-faced middle-aged woman came into the office. "I'm so sorry to have kept you waiting, Mrs. Braxton," the woman said, as she extended both her hands warmly toward Bertha. Bertha was uncomfortable with the familiarity. She shrank back. The woman seemed about to embrace her. Confusion flooded Bertha's brain.

"I'm Mrs. Erland, the guidance counselor," the woman introduced herself.

"Oh—oh—yes, ma'am. I'm Margie's mother," Bertha blurted, a little relieved by the introductions.

"Please, let us go into my office where we won't be disturbed," Mrs. Erland invited and turned to leave the room. Bertha followed obediently.

"Make yourself comfortable, Mrs. Braxton," Mrs. Erland said when they had arrived in her office. She closed the door behind them and began to busily straighten her desk. Bertha watched her, thinking how she, too, always hurriedly tidied up on the few occasions she had had an unexpected guest. The familiar motions put her at ease. She felt a kindred spirit with the women who had just a moment ago been a phantom attending to emergencies within the school.

197

"There now, let's talk about Margie," Mrs. Erland said as she finished with her little chore and seated herself behind her desk. Bertha looked at her blankly. She was not sure just what they were supposed to say about Margie.

"You've noticed the severe drop in Margie's grades?" Mrs. Erland prodded. Bertha nodded. She had seen the report card, yes, but she didn't know what she was expected to do about it; it was the school who was supposed to make the children learn.

"Well—can you explain her sudden disinterest in school?" Mrs. Erland asked patiently. Bertha thought for a moment. She did not know how she was expected to know the answer to this when she herself was not in the school with Margie.

"No, ma'am," Bertha finally answered. Mrs. Erland sighed.

"There must be some reason. She was doing so well—we were all so pleased with her progress in reading." Mrs. Erland paused; Bertha stared at her blankly.

"You know, Mrs. Braxton, Margie really came a long way in her reading skills, which are so important; you must be very grateful to the young lady who tutored her last summer." Bertha winced at the mention of the young lady and Margie's reading. At first she had been proud that Margie could decode those mysterious books with their tantalizing cover pictures. But she could not help but feel that the young lady who Mrs. Erland said she should be grateful to had somehow stirred a storm in her otherwise placid little girl. She couldn't help but feel that it was because of that white busybody that she was now sitting in this office.

"Mrs. Braxton," Mrs. Erland said pleadingly, "isn't there any explanation you can give for Margie's behavior?" Bertha wanted to tell this woman, who insisted upon an answer, that it was the school's problem, not hers, to answer these questions. But she could not. She shook her head slowly. Mrs. Erland sighed in exasperation.

Bertha could feel her dissatisfaction with her but was at a loss as to what she could do to make her daughter learn any better. Finally she said, weakly, "When Margie be in school, then she's the school's 'sponsibility." She held herself stiffly to ward off any forthcoming attack. She had never accosted a public official before, which is what she considered Mrs. Erland and the teachers. She was not exactly sure just what might happen.

If Mrs. Erland was surprised at Bertha's accusation, she did not register it. For a moment the two women just stared at each other in benign noncommunication. Then Mrs. Erland sighed and said, "Mrs. Braxton, I'm afraid we're just going to have to drop Margie back into the special ed class. She's just simply not able to keep up where she is." Bertha nodded assent. She agreed with whatever it was that the school felt was needed to do whatever it was they felt they must do for Margie. She felt satisfied now that the school was finally accepting its responsibility toward her child and she was glad she had been brave enough to have pointed this out to Mrs. Erland.

"I'm sorry, Mrs. Braxton," Mrs. Erland said as she rose from her chair to dismiss Bertha.

Bertha got up accordingly. "It sure's been a pleasure to meet you," she said, graciously offering her hand to this fine lady who had so much interest in her daughter.

Mrs. Erland watched her retreat down the hall. She wondered just how one could reach these people. She had tried so often and had failed so often.

Margie walked slowly from the bus to the house. Her spirit was deeply depressed. She watched the hard dirt in front of her feet, barren hard dirt that would never know life. She stopped a moment to stare at the piece of black plastic with its still shiny knobs sticking brazenly out of the packed earth. Part of a fragment of the doomed radio had worked its way into the ground during the rains. Suddenly, Margie felt an irrational giggle dribble up into her throat to momentarily lighten her mood. She thought it would really be neat if a new radio could grow from this little slip planted in the earth. Rationality returning quickly, she gave the plastic intrusion a kick with her toe, dislodging it and sending it to rest in another barren spot for transplantation a few feet away. She continued on to the house, her mood restored to its black depths.

"What's your chin so draggin' 'bout?" Sissy asked as Margie came in the door and headed directly for the bedroom without so much as a "hey."

Reggie looked up from his place in front of the TV and echoed, "Chin draggin'?" then returned his gaze to the flickering picture before him.

"Humph, she sure do have a draggin' chin," Sissy repeated and rejoined Reggie in viewing the TV.

Having changed her dress, Margie came out to the kitchen and, sitting down on the floor next to Reggie, she asked in an absent tone, "Mama home yet?"

"No, she be home d'rectly, though; it's 'most four o'clock," Sissy answered as she rocked back and forth in the rocking chair snapping beans with an automation that came from years of experience, her eyes never leaving the action on the TV.

By the time Bertha arrived home after a day of dusting and polishing Miss Francis's myriads of knickknacks, she had forgotten all about her visit at the school that morning. She was just glad to be back in her own home where she could kick off the shoes that squeezed unrelentingly against her throbbing bunions.

"Lawd, that woman, she gots a doodad from ever' place in the worl'," she sighed as she dropped her tired body onto a chair and rubbed at the enflamed bulge behind the big toe of her right foot.

"Get me a cup of coffee, Margie." Margie, startled to attention at the sound of her name, jumped up from the floor. It was the first time she had realized her mother had come home. The depression flooded back into her as the TV dam was removed.

"Mama, they put me back," she said dismally, as she filled a cup with hot coffee and set it on the table in front of her mother.

Bertha was puzzled for a moment. Yes, that's right, Mrs. Erland had said she would put Margie back, she had almost forgotten. "I know. Mrs. Erland said you can't do good where you was," Mama now answered indifferently.

"But, Mama, it's terr'ble!" Margie wailed. "All the kids is makin' fun of me."

Bertha looked at Margie with a confused inquiring look. "Why they makin' fun of you?" she asked, genuinely puzzled.

"Mama!" Margie wailed again in despair.

Lenny pushed through the door. "I can hear you all the way out on the po'ch," he grumbled in greeting. "What's all the howlin' 'bout?"

"Margie says the kids'er makin' fun of her at the school," Sissy explained looking momentarily away from the TV.

"Course they do, she ain' got no class," he agreed, as he pulled a chair away from the table and positioned it in front of his TV.

"Well, we *are* poor," Bertha said. "But we can't help it, so it ain' Margie's fault we don' have no class."

"Mama!" Margie wailed at the irrational turn the conversation had taken. "It ain' that at all."

"Well, what the hell is it, then?" snorted Lenny, impatient at all the noise that interfered with the TV audio.

"It's 'cause I'm dumb," Margie blurted.

"Yeah," Lenny agreed and turned his attention to the *Beverly Hillbillies* on the TV.

"You ain' dumb," Mama defended.

"Sh! Sh! *Sh!*" Sissy warned, knowing that Lenny had just so much patience and would be upset if the noise in the room continued.

"She ain' dumb, is she?" Mama whispered to Sissy.

"Not so much," Sissy agreed.

"They say you're dumb?" Mama asked Margie.

"Yeah, Mama, they say I'm dumb an' I *am* dumb else I wou'n't be put back."

"Well—I—don' know," Mama reflected. "Mrs. Erland says . . . "

"Mama, you don' know nothin'!" Margie screamed and ran from the kitchen into the bedroom and threw herself across the cot in a fit of despair.

"She sure gots a sassy mouth," observed Sissy.

"Sure glad she 'cided to take it out of *here*. Oughta have her ass whipped though," Lenny said, who had been becoming more and more irritated with the disturbance. He could watch his TV in the peace he deserved, now, after his long day at work. Bertha glared at him. She knew when her child was sassy and she needed no advice from him. Anyway, she was too tired right now to attend to the problem; she would settle it later. Now, she sipped at her coffee, chuckling softly as Jethro of the *Beverly Hillbillies* slid down the long banister rail of the elegant Beverly Hills mansion.

Margie lay sobbing in despair across her bed. Nobody understood. They were all so ignorant they could not understand. She thought about London. One of the kids at school had said they had seen London with Freddy Prince; she wondered where Randy was. *London did the right thing,* she thought, *got out of this old house with its crazy people, its beds on the floor, its broken-down furniture, its old wood stove. Got out and made a whole new life.*

The great wide world suddenly loomed large before her. She shivered at its cold expanse. What if she did as London had done? Where would she go? What could she do? London was grown—yet, she was *almost* grown.

"Margie, *Hogan's Heroes* is on," Bertha called from the kitchen, forgetting all about the sassing. Margie lay there for a moment. Maybe she ought to wait a while yet. Soon she would be thirteen and *grown*—then she would leave. She would get herself a grand house like the one she had seen when she had gotten lost because of Lenny. She would get herself beautiful clothes. She would have grand furniture in her house and a long sleek automobile in her yard. *Then*, the kids at school would have some respect for her. *Then*, the teachers would not put her in the special ed class. She was *not* dumb, it was just like Lenny had said, she just didn't have any class—and she would *get* class when she was old enough to shed this awful hovel that

201

imprisoned her—probably next year, when she was thirteen.

"Margie . . ."

"I'm comin', Mama." Margie sniffed the flood of tears back into the reservoir of misery she held in her heart and joined the little audience in front of the TV. Sitting on the floor next to Reggie she let herself become one with them and melted into the drama unfolding before her. Sweet salve—the blare of the audio drowned her fears, the glare of the video glossed the ugliness of her home. She could wait till next year . . .

Chapter XVI

Sissy prodded the faint-hearted embers. They danced upward, catching onto the new wood. In minutes the old black stove growled with satisfied burps of approval. Lenny swayed out from the dark bedroom, squinting his sleep-swollen eyes against the light in the kitchen.

"A body could freeze his ass in here."

"It'll be warm in a minute, honey," Sissy crooned as she bumped about the kitchen making elaborate gestures of preparation for Lenny's morning coffee.

"It's goin' be a cold one 'gain," Lenny grumbled.

"Uh huh," mused Sissy.

"It's sure too cold to go out on that road," Lenny continued his complaining. "An' that workin' shop ain' got no heat neither." He looked at Sissy to see if his whining was getting the proper amount of sympathy.

"Don' they have no stove?" Sissy asked in surprise.

"Sure; but they opens that big door all the day; ain' no stove big 'nough to heat all the town." The hardware store was divided into two sections, one for sales and one for repairs. The repair side, where Lenny worked, had formerly been a blacksmith shop, open on one end to admit the horses. A big overhead door now covered the open end but was kept open during work hours to accommodate the large farm machines that were repaired there.

"Poor baby!" Sissy soothed, with just the right amount of sympathy, as she set the steaming coffee on the table in front of Lenny. "The grits an' ham'll be ready d'rectly."

"Don' want none," Lenny grumped keeping in character, as he poured the hot coffee into his saucer to cool it. Sissy continued to stir the grits, ignoring Lenny's refusals; Lenny always ate what was put in front of him, regardless. It was just his way of greeting the day to be irritable at everyone and everything. Sissy placed the plate of grits and ham before him. Without another word he began methodically shoveling the hot food into his mouth.

Sissy had forgotten all about her desire for a gas stove by now. With the coming of the cold weather, the old wood stove burned continuously anyway. There really was no need for a gas stove now. It would just take up extra space in the already crowded room and would cost extra money. They had gotten a big load of green wood from Mr. Winston when he had cleared a half acre of land behind his barns. They weren't sure just what he planned for the acreage but it was rumored that he might have succumbed to the new way and was installing bulk barns. Whatever, the green wood burned long once it was tindered with fast-burning, seasoned kindling and it cost them nothing except a little effort to split it. Sissy now stood with her backside to the stove, enjoying its cozy warmth, as she devotedly watched her husband consume his morning repast.

Bertha emerged from the bedroom, her slippered feet patting and sliding in a peculiar rhythm across the wood floor. Bertha always wore slippers at home. She had cut convenient slits here and there to allow the many bunions and corns to poke through. The old slippers were a latticework of felt-backed plastic. It was a wonder they stayed on her feet at all, which was the reason for the pat-slide rhythm they produced as she shuffled about in them. She flicked on the TV. It hummed, buzzed, rolled, flickered brightly, faded, then suddenly popped forth with the glaring continence of Mort Holister of the *Carolina in the Morning* show.

"I can't stan' that man," she said with disgust, then settled back in her chair to watch the show. Lenny mumbled something through the mouthful of grits he was masticating, about dumb people who "watches any ol' thing." Bertha ignored whatever it was he said. She got up and poured herself a cup of coffee and sat down again to watch the man whom she hated. Sipping slowly she stared at the set shaking her head occasionally in disapproval of some "ignorant" thing Mort Hollister had done or said. Sissy watched from her place beside the stove.

"He sure is a disgustin' man," she agreed with Bertha.

Lenny threw his fork onto the table and yelled, "Why the hell y'all look at the man if he be so 'gustin'?"

Bertha just gave him a long exasperated look.

Lenny, finished now with his breakfast, pushed his chair roughly away from the table. Struggling his bulk into a standing position, he swayed momentarily till his feet accustomed themselves to his weight. "Sure mus' be nice to just set all day an' watch that TV *I bought*—whilst I goes out to work my ass off to pay for it."

Bertha did not even honor him with a look this time. Sissy busily cleared away Lenny's plate, nervously brushing the table clean, hoping he would leave it at that and not pursue the issue. She hated beginning the day in ill temper with Bertha. Lenny glared a moment at his sister-in-law, then, without further words, pushed off from the table toward the door. As he passed the rocking chair that sat between the table and the door he grabbed up his coat that had hung there all night. Lenny never used the pegs on the wall for his coat. The rocker was more convenient to him, and anyway, he didn't like the little puckered bump that the pegs left on the back of his coat.

As he slammed the door behind him, he hollered sarcastically, "Hope y'all enjoys yourselfs."

The old car was loath to crank up in the icy chill of the morning. Lenny prodded and pleaded with the stubborn engine then, in a stream of profanity, he gave it one last chance. As if heeding its master's threats, the motor gave a wheezing churn, sputtered, coughed then caught hold and chugged in spasmodic throbs. Lenny let it run a moment to warm up before pulling out onto the lonely dark road. His teeth chattered rapidly as he swung the wheel into the lane and headed for town. The car's heater had stopped working the day before and the wind now cut bitterly through the invisible cracks in the floor, biting at his toes as they tromped numbly from clutch to break then onto the gas pedal. Oh, how he hated this drive into town! He envied the others left behind in the little house, the girls still snuggled under their warm blankets.

"Damn lazy-ass womenfolk. A man spends his whole life feedin' them an' buyin' for them an' do they 'preciate it?" he grumbled to himself.

Willis had just arrived at the hardware store as Lenny pulled up. "Morning, Lenny," he called cheerfully as he fumbled his key in the lock of the front door.

"Mornin'," Lenny grumped in response.

While waiting for Willis to manipulate the intricacies of the old timey lock, Lenny noticed a large-framed figure limping toward them from across the railroad tracks. He did not recognize the figure in the early morning gloom. Willis now had the door opened and the two men entered the store together. Willis reached for the light switch beside the door and flicked on the overhead fluorescent lights. The cold lights sputtered on and off a few times then one by one loomed on permanently for the day. The inside of the store was almost as cold as outside except that the wind did not blow as strongly inside. The fire in the big woodburning stove had gone out early in the night and its sides were now a chill gray. Willis rubbed his hands briskly together to generate heat. Then he firmly grabbed hold of the shaker handle that extended out the bottom of the stove and thrust it back and forth vigorously to drop yesterday's ashes out of the grate.

The door of the store opened, setting the little bell over it to jingling. Lenny turned to observe the man, who had come into the store. By the limp he recognized that it was the man that he had seen coming across the tracks. Still, even in the light of the store, he did not know him. He wondered what would bring a man out so early on this frosty morning. No one ever came to the store before daylight in winter. And on cold days, like this one, no one usually showed up before noon, though Lenny always had work to do because most of the farmers brought their equipment into the shop during the winter months for repair. The whole side yard was filled with farm machinery and tools waiting for repair. He had had problems at first with the welding because, though he had told Willis that he could weld, he really had done very little of it, only once, for two months when he worked at a body shop and that was years ago. But, under Willis's tutelage, he was now quite good at it and Willis had turned over all the welding jobs to him.

Willis now turned to see who had caused the bell to jingle. "Well, how the hell are you, Ingy?" he greeted enthusiastically.

"Doin' real good, Mr. Willis, doin' real good," Ingy replied.

"Good to see you up and around."

"Yeah, an' it's good to be up," Ingy agreed. Lenny observed and listened in confused silence. "Mr. Willis, I think I'm fittin' to be workin' 'gain," Ingy continued. Suddenly, Lenny knew who the man was; a cold chill, one not generated by the weather, crept up Lenny's spine.

Willis hesitated a moment. He looked from Lenny to Ingy—he would, in a moment, make one of these men very unhappy.

"Good-good," Willis answered slowly. "I told you your job would be here when you were well again." Then looking at Ingy's lame leg he asked, "Are you sure you'll be able to handle it?"

"Oh yes, sir. Yes, sir, Mr. Willis," Ingy assured.

Willis turned to Lenny. "Lenny, this here is Ingy Weatherington. Remember the fellow I told you was working for me before he had his accident?"

"Please to meet you," Lenny mumbled as he politely extended his hand toward his competitor.

"Yeah," the man acknowledged. Then, to Willis, he said, "Mr. Willis, I need the work right now. My chi'runs is hungry an' my wife, she's down with her nerves an' can't work days no more. I need my job *now.*" Willis scuffed at the floor for a moment in embarrassed silence. He could feel the beseeching eyes of Lenny awaiting his response.

Finally, he said softly. "Yes, Ingy, I did promise you."

Then, turning again to Lenny, he said apologetically, "I did promise him . . ."

For a moment the three men stood in silence, Lenny looking at Willis imploringly, Willis staring at the floor in front of Lenny, and Ingy's eyes flitting anxiously from Willis to Lenny and back to Willis.

"Lenny, I'm sorry. You know when I hired you I told you it was probably only temporary." Lenny nodded. "I'm really sorry, Lenny. You've worked real good for me. But, you know Ingy has been with me for five years now and I did promise I'd hold his job for him." He paused for a moment, searching for something to say that would ease the severance. "I'll give you recommendation wherever you go," he finally offered lamely. Lenny nodded. Yes, he had been told that the job was probably temporary but in the months that had passed he had forgotten that contingency. He really didn't like to work and hated getting out of bed each morning to come here but, at this moment, he suddenly found disappointment in being jobless again; he had grown accustomed to the status his pay envelope had given him at home.

Willis opened his cash drawer and extracted two twenty-dollar bills. After pausing for a moment he reached in and took a ten-dollar bill also. Handing them to Lenny he completed their contract. Lenny thanked him for the generosity of the extra ten dollars, nodded to Ingy, and left the hardware store.

As he went out the door Ingy called, "Good luck, buddy." Lenny did not acknowledge the gratuity.

It was daylight now as he drove back toward home. The sun was coming up brightly. Lenny quickly lifted his depression by noting that he had been working for several months now without a vacation and really, a body shouldn't work all that steady, anyway. It was going to be good to lay snuggled under those blankets every morning until Sissy's fire had warmed the kitchen to a comfortable temperature. It would be nice to sit and watch *his* TV for a change. He thought of the generosity that Willis had shown him with the extra ten dollars. He made a mental note not to mention that part to Sissy; spending money would be rare to come upon now that he wasn't the working master again. Of course, he would file for unemployment, but it was usually weeks before the first payment came in. And maybe after he had rested up a bit he would look for another job—maybe.

Bertha was carrying an armload of green wood into the house when Lenny pulled into the driveway. She looked up, surprised at his early return, and asked suspiciously, "What you doin' home so early in the day for?"

"Got laid off," Lenny answered curtly.

Bertha almost dropped the load of wood from her arms. "You what!"

"You deaf, woman? I tol' you I got laid off."

"Lawd, help us!" Bertha prayed, fervently scanning the clear blue sky.

On entering the house, Lenny was again greeted with, "What you doin' home so early for?" This time it came from Sissy.

"Got laid off," he answered for the third time.

Sissy didn't respond with words immediately. She just sat firmly on her chair and stared at him in disbelief. Lenny flung his coat onto the back of the rocker and plopped onto a chair near the table. "Get me some coffee," he demanded testingly.

Sissy got up and obediently got the cup of coffee.

As she set it before him, she asked, somewhat timorously, "Was it somethin' you done?

Lenny glared at her, then pounded the table with his fist. "What you mean, 'was it somethin' I done'? Don' you have no respect for me? 'Course it ain' somethin' I done. I be the bestest damn welder Willis ever had. But Willis, he be a gen'leman, an' he done already promise that son-of-a-bitch Ingy feller that when he got well he'd hire him back. An' Ingy did an' Willis did—an' that don' leave no place for me. 'Sides, I needs the res' anyway." He closed the issue.

Ashamed for having doubted her husband, Sissy put her arm around his neck and patted it tenderly, saying, " 'Course you does, honey, 'course you does." Lenny settled the flesh of his rumps cozily onto the chair and prepared for his long winter vacation. Bertha "humphed" in disgust.

"Mama, Mama!" Margie burst through the door, panting breathlessly from her run across the yard through the crisp December air. "We're goin' do a play; I'm in it! I gots to have a long dress—a fancy one—like an' ol'-timey lady."

"Humph," grunted Bertha.

"Hush, girl—I can't hear the TV," Lenny complained.

In her excitement Margie hadn't noticed that Lenny was at home when he shouldn't have been, but her news now blurred his figure and she went on. "Mama, it's goin' be a purty play—all 'bout the ol'-timey days—for the Bicenten'l—an' ever'body in the seventh grade is in the play—an' me too."

"That be nice," Bertha responded absently, staring into the eye of the TV without seeing it or hearing it or even Margie. Her thoughts were troubled—everything had been going so well; she hated Lenny, but since he had been working her life was so much sweeter. She just knew he wouldn't go out to find another job—and she just knew that *she could not* find enough day work to support the family. Why, oh why, did Lenny have to go an' mess things up again! She thought of throwing Lenny out. That would make her feel better even though it would not solve her new financial problem. But, well, she couldn't. As much as she hated the fat black hunk, he was her sister's husband and she loved her baby sister and—oh, why must love and hate be so closely related?

"Mama," Margie pleaded for her mother's attention, "Mama, the play is for Chris'mas." The word "Christmas" jolted Bertha from her chasm of contemplation. Christmas, just three weeks off!

"We ain' goin' have no Chris'mas," she said firmly, giving the back of Lenny's head a pouting and "so there, too" look. Margie, at a loss for a response for such devastating news, just stared in bewilderment at her mother.

Finally she recovered enough to ask timidly, "Why, Mama?"

" 'Cause your Uncle Lenny done got hisself fired, an' we ain' goin' have no money to have Chris'mas," she explained, still staring accusingly at Lenny.

At the mention of his name, Lenny's attention was pulled from the program he was watching. "What Uncle Lenny do?" he asked testily.

"Mama said you got fired. That true?"

"I din't get fired. I got laid off," he yelled.

"Same thing. Don' neither bring no money," Bertha calculated.

"Woman, that all you can think 'bout is money, money, money, money?"

"*You* sure likes to have the stuff what money, money, money buys," Bertha mocked.

"I can do without . . . " Lenny answered, righteously thrusting his chin in the air.

"Then you can do without eatin'; then we'll have 'nough money from the welfare people's for the res' of us," dared Bertha.

Margie's head was swimming in the confusion of the argument. What did any of it have to do with her play? What did any of it have to do with Christmas? Christmas came—no one could stop it—whether there was money or not. In fact, she could not ever remember having had money in the house ever at Christmas, and they had always had Christmas. And her play—for Christmas . . .

"Mama, the play . . . "

"You ain' goin' be in no play for Chris'mas. We ain' goin' have no Chris'mas," Bertha reiterated.

"Mama!" Margie cried.

"I wisht y'all would hush up so's a body could hear what's goin' on," Lenny thundered impatiently.

Margie sighed and choked a frustrated sob back into her throat. She went into the bedroom, closing the door behind her, and began pulling off her school dress. Catching a glimpse of her pigtailed hair in the mirror, she shivered in disgust at herself. "Oh, just wait!" she hissed through clenched teeth to herself. "Some day I'm goin' be growed an' I can wear my hair up an' I can do anything else I want, an' I can be in a Chris'mas play."

She turned toward the closed door of the bedroom and stuck her tongue out with a sizzling hiss at those who were sitting on the other side. Immediately she felt a sweep of guilt rise up within her. If Mama ever caught her—she rubbed her backside gently in memory of her last whipping. Any impulsive thoughts of further irrational action were quickly curbed. "Oh, well . . . " she mused, and joined the others in the kitchen in front of the TV to watch the reruns of *The Brady Bunch.*

"Has everyone gotten his costume ready for the play?" Mrs. Levine asked the class. Margie had forgotten all about the costume—the play. She had a way of doing that, blocking out the things that caused confusion or pain in her. All she had to do was to store her desires in that little corner of her brain that was marked "When I grow up, when I am thirteen." Right now, however, Mrs. Levine had rudely plucked open the door of her private little hatch. The class was buzzing as the students passed information among themselves and the teacher with details of their costumes.

Margie slid down in her seat a little, hoping that no one would notice that she was in the classroom. No one did, then . . .

At lunchtime, Norma caught up with Margie. The girls still ate lunch together even though, since Margie had been put back, they were not in the same class.

"Wait till you see the dress I'm wearin' in the play," she boasted. "It's really my Mama's. She weared it to convocation las' year. They had this real big meetin', with a real fancy dinner in a real fancy place. And anyway, it fits me an' she's goin' let me wear it for the play."

"I thought we was s'posed to dress ol'-timey," Margie said.

"Well, it's sort of ol'-timey. It gots all this lace on it an' it's long, all the way to the floor, just like an ol'-timey dress. What you wearin'?"

"Oh, I ain' 'cided yet," Margie answered. She had really forgotten all about the play since that first night. She wondered if it would be worth opening the issue again with Mama, maybe.

"What you mean, you ain' 'cided yet? I bet you ain' even got nothin'," Belva Harris butted in.

"I do so," Margie insisted. "I gots *two* dresses an' I can' 'cide which one is the most ol'-timey."

"What they look like?" Norma pumped.

"Well, the one's red with all these purty laces an' ribbons all over it," Margie said. "An' the other one's black with buttons all the way down to the floor an' a big white collar on it."

"I'd wear the red one," Norma suggested.

"Hell, she ain' got neither," Belva said. "I can tell in her eyes she be lyin'. They be white." Margie instinctively squinted her eyes to hide the whites.

"I do so!" she insisted, this time a little louder than before. "You just wait an' see, Miss Smarty Ass."

"Here, here, what's goin' on?" Mrs. Levine approached their lunch table tch-tching. "We are supposed to have silence. You can be heard all over the lunchroom."

"Margie ain' got no ol'-timey dress for the play," blurted Belva.

"I do so," Margie shouted, tears of frustration welling up into her eyes.

"Well, now, if Margie says she has a dress, I'm sure she has. Margie wouldn't lie, would you, Margie?" Mrs. Levine said, attempting to cut the argument short and restore order to the lunchroom. Margie felt the burning in her scalp; the shame of lying tingled and made her want to scratch her head. But she inhibited such action for fear the others would notice. She hated Belva.

After lunch, out on the playground, Norma pulled Margie aside.

"Le's get 'way from Belva, she's a snot." Margie went willingly with Norma. The two girls ducked behind the Occupations Building. There they sat on the trash cans and contemplated Margie's problem, for by this time, somehow, Norma felt responsible for Margie's embarrassment and somehow, she knew that Margie did not have a dress.

Norma's nice, thought Margie as she sat close to her friend leaning just enough so their arms would touch. *She brags a lot but she don' try to get peoples in no trouble.*

"Margie," Norma said softly, interrupting Margie's silent admiration of her. "Mebbe those two dresses you gots won' look so good on the stage in

211

all those lights, you know; black don' never look good on the stage, an' red—well, it might look—well, a li'l *too* bright." She paused a moment. Margie carefully scrutinized her feet that she swung in a careless attitude against the side of the trash can. She wondered just what Norma was getting at. "Now," Norma babbled on. "I gots a real purty blue dress, well, it really is my Mama's too; the one I'm wearin' is green, but she gots this blue one too, you know, she gots to have lots of purty dresses for the convocations, an' mebbe you could wear the blue dress, I know yours is prob'ly purtier, but the blue might look better in all them lights." Norma observed Margie's reaction to the offer from the corner of her eye while she too pretended to examine the arc that her own swinging feet made against the trash can. A loud bell clanged. It was time to go back to class.

"Well?" Norma prodded as she held Margie's arm to keep her from leaving without answering.

"Mebbe," Margie conceded. "I have to think on it . . . " She knew very well that Norma knew the truth but added, anyway, "Them two what I gots awful purty." Then she jumped down from the trash can and began sprinting toward the school. "Race you," she called back to Norma. Norma shook her head to herself and sighed, then took off running to catch up with Margie.

Margie's thoughts drifted far away from the study of the systems of the human body that the class was studying in health that afternoon. She only vaguely heard Mrs. Levine's voice drone on and on about the marvels of the human lung. Her own perplexity of plight superseded anything else. Now that she did in fact have a dress, or at least the hope of one (she wasn't at all sure that Norma's mother was going to be as generous with her clothing as Norma appeared to be), would Mama let her be in the play? In fact, she wasn't at all sure just why Mama had said she couldn't be in the play in the first place. She assumed that it had to do with Lenny losing his job and there not being enough money now to buy her the required old-timey dress. But then—Mama was like that; when she was ill-tempered with one person, the whole world suffered the consequences. It might be that Mama was punishing Margie to get back at Lenny, a phenomenon that only made sense to Mama. And, of course, the only one who suffered was Margie, Lenny being totally unaware if his involvement in the punishment. It seemed to Margie that life had been much simpler before Sissy and Lenny had come to live with them. Even when Lenny wasn't personally molesting her he was messing things up some way else. Would Mama let her be in the play?

Margie jumped from her seat at the sound of her name. "Yes ma'am?" she sputtered.

"Answer the question, Margie," Mrs. Levine said impatiently.

Little drops of sweat began to pop out on Margie's forehead. She looked down at the floor, wishing she could somehow slip through one of the cracks between the boards. "I don' know," she whispered.

"Speak up, I can't hear you." Mrs. Levine's voice seemed to crack at the walls of the room.

"I don' know the answer," Margie said a little louder.

The class burst into uproarious laughter. The boys stomped their feet and slapped at their thighs. Margie burned with confusion and shame.

"You mean to say you don't know if your lungs are working right now?" Mrs. Levine asked sarcastically. The children renewed their laughter as Margie stood numbly rooted to the floor under her feet.

"She's dead!" a boy shouted gleefully from somewhere behind her. The laughter around her surged uncontrollably, engulfing her until she thought she would suffocate. Finally she pulled her feet free of the oiled floor and made a hysterical dash for the door.

Mrs. Levine caught her by the arm as she passed her desk. "I think Mr. Gaston would be interested in observing our 'dead' student," she mocked amid the laughter and hoots from the class as she propelled Margie into the hall.

Finding her voice Margie squeaked, "Please, please, Mrs. Levine. Please don' take me to the office."

Mrs. Levine stopped momentarily. Somewhat subdued, she said, "But, Margie, I don't know what else to do with you. You're not the same young lady who came to this school in the fall. You've become a dreamer—and—and, even at lunch today, look how you had the whole lunchroom in an uproar."

"Please, Mrs. Levine," Margie pleaded in choked sobs. "Please, I'll try, I won' dream no more. Please don' take me to the office."

Mrs. Levine melted under the pitiful sobs of the skinny little girl before her. She sighed. "Well—all right; but I think we'll have to do *something* to impress upon you the seriousness of school."

"Yes, ma'am," Margie agreed humbly, just grateful that she would not have to face Mr. Gaston, the principal.

Mrs. Levine observed the child and pondered the problem for a moment, then said, "Perhaps if you weren't allowed to be in the play—perhaps that would impress you." She paused to see what effect her words were having. "Well, would it?"

Margie's heart was pounding so hard in her ears that she could barely hear Mrs. Levine and when she tried to answer her voice cracked like a frog's. "Yes, ma'am," she agreed.

"All right, then," Mrs. Levine said as she gently guided Margie back into the classroom.

"Children, children . . . " She banged her hand on her desk to gain their attention. "That will be enough!" Gradually the giggles, twitters, stomping, and banging subsided and within a few minutes the classroom was restored to order. Margie didn't know why she felt so relieved. She had wanted so badly to be in the play. All the class was going to be in it, but she felt like a giant weight had been lifted from her shoulders. She wondered just what she would tell Mama though, about her not being in the play. Mama was like that, even if she didn't want Margie to be in the play she would be angry if she was not *allowed* to be in it. She decided that she would say nothing, unless, of course, Mama mentioned it.

Mama never mentioned the play. She didn't mention much of anything anymore, except, maybe, that Lenny was a "lazy good for nothing . . . " She never ever finished the derisive description but everyone always knew what the rest of it was. Yes, most of the time Mama could be found sitting in depressed silence at the kitchen table, a cup of stale cold coffee sitting in front of her, her eyes fixed listlessly on the TV.

Margie contented herself with the reruns, new to her, of the cartoons, situation comedies and detective shows that blared forth from the TV that Mama had made the final payment on with Reggie's aid for dependent children check. And the winter days grew short and the cold winter nights grew long and they all, the whole Braxton family, except London, who they had all but forgotten, grew to accept the marvelous panacea of the flickering pictures that flew through the air to provide balm for their bitter existence.

Chapter XVII

Bertha absently stirred the hot coffee. The TV was grossly out of focus but she did not seem to let it interfere with her intently critical observation of Mort Hollister. "That man's pure sick," she mumbled.

"Why you watch him ever' day, then, Mama?" Gayla asked.

"Ain' nothin' to watch this early 'cept that."

"Yeah there is—try channel seven, why don' you."

"Uh uh," Mama answered, still engrossed with what Mort was saying. Teresa reached out and switched channels.

"What you go and do that for?" Bertha jumped up and gave the channel selector a savage twist back to its original position, channel 9. Teresa shrugged to Gayla. Bertha settled back on her chair with a satisfied sigh. "He's a lunatic, that's what he is," she observed. The girls shook their heads. Who could figure Mama?

Nor did Bertha notice when Margie came into the kitchen. Margie stood timidly contemplating her mother, hoping she would look up at her, but yet, fearing that she would see her standing there. She stood there for several seconds before Bertha finally did look up. When she did it was with unobservant eyes. Margie sighed with relief that she had passed this moment of confrontation. Bertha had not noticed her carefully coifed and frizzled hair.

Without disturbing Bertha's apparent hypnosis by Mort Hollister, Margie slipped her coat on and quietly left the house. It was bitterly cold outside. The wind bit into her bare legs and scuttled up under her dress to send chills through her entire body. It would be another fifteen minutes before the bus came, if it came on time, which it rarely did. She was hungry, having come out without taking breakfast. But having gotten past her mother's scrutiny she did not want to take a chance on lingering inside long enough for Mama to catch up with the moment. It was important for Margie to look and feel pretty—mature, this day.

"What the hell you doin' standin' out in the cold like that for?" Teresa called from the door of the house.

"I don' want to miss the bus," Margie explained lamely.

Teresa shrugged and closed the door against the icy wind that swept past her. *Crazy kid,* she thought.

Margie's feet were numb beyond feeling by the time Wade Linsey pulled the long yellow school bus up to the side of the road in front of her. As soon as Wade had swung open the door she hopped up the steps. Shivering, she quickly surveyed the double row of seats; he was there—Cleveland Whiting. Margie stood, swaying in jerks, as the bus pulled out onto the road to continue on its route. Cleveland did not look her way. Norma called out to her.

"I saved you a seat, Margie, here," Norma slapped the seat next to her, enthusiastically inviting Margie to share it with her. Margie waited a moment longer and when it became apparent that Cleveland was not going to look her way, she fumbled and jerked down the aisle of the bouncing bus to sit next to Norma.

"Your hair looks real cool, Margie," Norma said with genuine admiration as Margie slid into the seat.

"Thanks," Margie answered nonchalantly.

"What your Mama say when she seen it?"

"Nothin'."

"Nothin'! You mean she don' care; she's lettin' you?" Norma asked in surprise.

"Reckon," Margie answered noncommittingly as she stared intently at the back of Cleveland's head.

Almost at the edge of town now, the bus stopped in front of Belva's house. Belva was not waiting outside as Margie had been; no one waited outside when the weather was cold, they always waited for Wade to pull up and toot before they came out, running, to keep the time of exposure to a minimum.

Belva's mother waved to her as she ran across their immaculate lawn that was green even in the middle of winter. Belva stopped running when she got to the door of the bus and mounted the steps in subdued dignity. Wade started the bus forward as soon as she was at the top step. She moved quickly to get to a seat before Wade would jerk the bus to a stop at the stop sign at the next corner and send her sprawling unceremoniously to the floor It was a game he played, "Splatter the boogie."

When she caught sight of Margie's elegantly picked Afro, she hooted, "Well, if Miss Pigtails ain' somethin' today with her hair so stylish done up."

All the other passengers in the bus turned to observe the object of

Belva's comments. Margie shrank into the cracked vinyl seat. No one had noticed her hair, except Norma, when she had gotten on the bus. She had hoped Cleveland would notice but he hadn't then, and now, as she saw him staring at her, she wished she could disappear.

Belva sat down in the seat across the aisle from Margie and Norma. "Your Mama finally lettin' you out without you dickie?" she taunted.

The other passengers began to hoot and holler in delight at this bit of wit from Belva. Enjoying the center stage, she continued, "I bet she 'bout even growed up 'nough to get a good screw." The resulting laughter was deafening. "I bet . . .

But Belva was cut short by a deep male voice. "Why don' you suck eggs."

Everyone stopped laughing and turned to observe the speaker, Cleveland Whiting.

Belva sat helpless in droop-mouthed stupidity. Margie shyly allowed her eyes to turn toward Cleveland. Her heart was racing a mile a minute; she began to breathe rapidly in short, shallow gasps. Things began to blur. Belva hastily pulled a book from her simulated leather bookbag and began to pore intently at its contents, allowing herself to melt inconspicuously into the seat. A low hum swept through the bus as the others began to discuss the matter among themselves. Cleveland went back to gazing out his window at the frosted, flat landscape that slipped past the bus.

The Queen of Hearts fundraising dance was just three days off. The proceeds of the dance were slated for the National Heart Fund. Margie knew that Freda Simpson, one of the black contenders for queen, had asked Cleveland to be her escort but that he had declined. There were six candidates in all for the Queen of Hearts, three white girls and three black girls; two queens would ultimately be chosen, a white queen and a black queen. (All school offices and honors were thus chosen, one of each, in order to make "desegregation" work.) The winners of the coveted crown would be the girls who received the most "votes." Votes were cast by the other students at a penny a vote, the winner being crowned at the Queen of Hearts Ball to be held in the school gym on Friday afternoon. It was an advantage for a candidate to have a handsome and popular escort to help her secure a winning number of votes. But—Margie smiled inside herself—Cleveland had not accepted Freda's invitation—he was still available.

Margie had never gone to one of the school dances before. First of all, they were usually held at night. Her mother would never allow her to go out

217

at night even after Lenny had bought the car and could have driven her to and from the event, though he probably would not have consented to that arrangement anyway. Secondly, there was the religious taboo against dancing. But this dance was being held in the afternoon during school hours. It really was a part of the school day, so Margie absolved her conscience about attending it.

Admission to the dance was fifty cents, which was also designated for the Heart Fund. As was always the case, many of the children did not have the price of admission to these school functions. However, when the event was part of the school day, as this one was, whichever child who could not afford the admission could go to the counseling office and plead his poverty and receive a free ticket as reward for his humility. Most of the children who were without funds chose not to expose themselves to such humiliation, however, and did not attend the events. One teacher always volunteered to monitor those children in a classroom during the time of the scheduled programs. Margie had always stayed in the classroom before; and though she would never dream of asking for a free ticket, she wanted very much to attend this dance. She solved the problem of the admission by selling to another child one of the free lunch program tickets that her mother erroneously thought was paid for out of money taken out of her pay along with the welfare and aid-for-dependent-children money. Margie had done without lunch on Monday and now carried the fifty cents in her shoe for safe keeping.

Cleveland had spoken to Margie on two occasions the week before. Once, when she had dropped her pencil in the hall, he had picked it up and handed it to her, saying "You dropped this." The other time he had accidentally bumped into her when he had turned around in the lunch line; then he had said " 'Scuse me." Small tokens, nevertheless, admissions of recognition. Margie's heart had been set on fire by these two encounters and now, this morning, he had stuck up for her under Belva's attack. She could hardly endure the flames this new sign had enkindled. She was sure, after such brazen overtures, Cleveland would ask her to dance with him at the Queen of Hearts Ball. The thought of such a possibility made her dizzy.

When Margie came into the house after school, her mother was sitting at the table sipping coffee. Margie wondered if she had moved at all since she had left her in the morning. The TV still blared loudly, but Mort Hollister was no longer visible; Porky Pig of Looney Tunes cartoons had usurped him. Sissy sat in the rocker with Reggie asleep on her lap. The scene was the same everyday when she got home. Today, however, Lenny was not in his usual viewing place. His absence, though welcomed, disturbed the balance of the room.

"Where at's Lenny?" she asked the room in general.

Without disturbing her viewing posture Bertha answered, "Went to collect unemployment pay." Margie had not noticed that the car was gone from the side yard when she had come across from the bus. She looked out the little front window of the house—the car wasn't gone—it still sat placidly alongside its companion, the defunct '68 Oldsmobile.

"His car's still here," Margie pointed out.

"Don' run," Bertha answered, still without looking up.

"What's the matter with it?"

"Don' know."

"Radiator busted," informed Sissy vaguely.

Margie waited a moment to see if the subject might be further pursued. When it became apparent that there would be no further eulogy for the demise of the Falcon, she went into the bedroom to change her clothes.

So far, so good, she thought. *Mama ain' said nothin' yet.* She took the pick in her hand and jabbed the huge ball of frizz here and there to enliven it. She smiled at herself in the mirror. She did look much more mature with her hair fixed like this. If only she wasn't so flat chested. She cupped her hands under her breast buds and pushed upward in an attempt to give them sustenance. Nothing much happened in her efforts. Her smile faded. When was she going to mature? She was still just a skinny baby, flat-chested, no calves, not even any pimples! She grabbed the pair of rolled panty hose from the drawer and stuffed them into the one side of her petticoat. Examining the results, she glowed with satisfaction and rooted around in the drawer for another appropriate prosthesis. She found a ragged silk scarf and judged it to be the right bulk. Stuffing it into the opposite side she stepped back from the mirror a little way to get a complete picture of her handiwork. One side was a little lower than the other. She patted and adjusted a bit until the two sides conformed with each other. Perfect! Oh, what a little bulge on the chest could do for a woman! Now, she would have to decide between wearing her one pair of panty hose on her chest or on her legs to the dance. She decided that bare legs were more acceptable than a flat chest.

Just then Gayla burst into the room, Teresa right behind her. "That son's a bitch, Miss Rivers; I'm goin' split her ass one of these days," Teresa shrieked.

"I'll help you when you ready," Gayla offered. She flung her purse onto the bed and kicked the door shut with her heel. "That woman's crazy if she thinks I'm goin' write no com'sition on how to be a lady."

"The whole class—jest 'cause one—well, I ain' goin' do it neither," agreed Teresa.

"They been playin' cards in that study hall ever since the 'ginning of the year—an' there always was *some* girls what been playin', it ain' always been jest the boys. Why she all the sudden gots to get so uppity an' think it ain' ladylike to play cards, anyway?" reasoned Gayla.

"Well, I don' see what it gots to do with bein' a lady an' I ain' goin' do it." Teresa yanked her sweater off over her head and stuffed it into a drawer. Looking up, she noticed, for the first time, that Margie had been standing gaping at them. Still angry at Miss Rivers, she yelled accusingly at her, "Well—who you gawkin' at, nigger." Margie, having no retort simply shrugged.

"Hey, what you doin' with your hair all frizzed out like that?" Gayla now also noticed Margie.

"You gots yours all frizzed out," Margie snapped, her hands placed firmly on her hips, chest thrust forward in defiance.

Teresa examined the new hairdo, plucking at it with inquisitive fingers, saying, "Mama goin' beat your ass if she sees you like that."

"I went to school with it like this today an' she didn' say one word when I lef'."

"That's why you was standin' out there in the cold so early—you was askin' to pull a fas' one on Mama!" Gayla laughed at Margie's finesse.

"I jest want to be sure to be on time, that's all," Margie defended.

Teresa's scrutinizing eyes swept over Margie. "Hey, what's this?" she squealed, poking a bony finger into Margie's chest, leaving an indentation in the soft ball of her new bosom.

"You hush!" Margie shrieked, throwing her arms across her chest for protection.

"Lemme see, lemme see," Gayla tugged at Margie's crossed arms. Margie pulled free and ran from the room, slamming the door behind her in their faces.

"What the hell's goin' on?" boomed Lenny, who had just come in the front door.

Margie ran right into his bulging belly, staggered a moment from the impact, then ducked under his arms, that were ready to ensconce her, and headed for the door.

Bertha reached an arm out and firmly halted her forward movement. "Where you think you're goin'?"

Panic welled up in Margie's heart. Her mind froze for a brief second, then, "I gots to piss," she shrieked as she tugged at her tether. Bertha let go and Margie ran outside, the door banging back against the wall then bouncing shut behind her.

"That chile be crazy," Lenny observed, shaking his head as he pulled up a chair to join the family in front of the TV.

After sitting in the outhouse for an hour, her olfactory nerves had fatigued and she could no longer notice the stench that drifted up through the hole in the bench. But she was miserably cold and was considering on taking her chances and going back into the house when Gayla's head popped around the corner of the door frame. The door had long ago fallen off the little box and someone had propped a large sheet of warped plywood against the front of it to somewhat cover the full exposure the gaping doorway offered of the occupants.

"We're goin' eat. Mama want to know if you fell in," Gayla jibed.

Margie glared at her and said, "I was jest comin' in."

"You better put a bucket over your head 'fore you do; Mama's mighty s'picious." Gayla advised.

"She say anythin'?" Margie asked anxiously.

"Not yet—but she will—then watch out, baby!"

Margie felt at her hair. "You reckon mebbe she might not?"

"If she be int'rested in the TV, she won'; but I wou'n't want to be you when she lose int'res'," Gayla continued to tease her.

Margie fretted within herself. Well, she couldn't stay out here all night; she'd just have to take the chance. She pulled herself up from the floor of the outhouse.

"Wait for me. I might's well piss whilst I'm in here." Gayla sat down over the hole in the bench. "Christ! It stinks in here; how you stan' it!"

When they came into the house, no one really noted their return. The TV—King TV—had its audience mesmerized as usual. The pot of collards on the stove was boiling so hard that the water splashed out onto the hot stove top and sizzled a merry tune, but Sissy didn't bother to move the pot to a cooler spot on the stove. Margie sighed with relief. If Bertha just kept a close eye on the TV; she would never notice the radical changes in her daughter; and if Margie managed to get by just one day at a time she figured, after a while, the whole thing would become commonplace and Bertha would not even realize there had been a change.

And everything probably would have gone along in this expected vein except that Teresa couldn't leave well enough alone and later, right in the middle of dinner, during a TV commercial, when everyone, for a moment, lost some of their intense concentration on the set, she said, "Cleveland sure's goin' be pleased with them new boobs you gots there, Margie."

"What you know 'bout Cleveland?" Margie snapped, instinctively covering her chest with her arms. All eyes immediately came to focus on her suspiciously placed arms.

"They sure is somethin' all right," Lenny grinned as he reached out toward Margie to examine the phenomenon. Margie averted his approaching hand by throwing one arm out to block it, thus baring one side for Mama to view.

"Lemme see them things," Bertha demanded. Margie dropped her arms and sighed in defeat. Bertha gently probed the two round bumps that had so suddenly sprouted on her daughter's chest.

"What you got in there?" she exclaimed, when her probing finger sank deep into the soft mounds.

"Nothin'," Margie whispered in humiliation.

"There is so somethin' in there," Bertha accused as she reached into the front of Margie's dress and began slowly extracting, inch by inch, the long legs of the panty hose.

Tears flooded Margie's eyes as the panty hose kept coming and coming and the others burst into hysterical laughter. Bertha did not think the incident a moment for merriment however; she was genuinely shocked at her daughter's sinful pride.

"Oh, Lawd, what have I done to deserve such a shameless chile!" she lamented.

The laughter around the table was tempered by the fervent prayer. Margie felt the room begin to spin under her; faces blurred, Mama's voice retreated into the distance.

"You get yourself 'way from this table!" Bertha ordered sternly but quietly. "An' go to the bedroom." Somehow Margie managed to rise from her chair without falling on her face. Swaying sickly, she walked slowly to the other room. Once inside, with the door closed between herself and her persecutors, she let the world slip from under her and fainted across the big double bed.

When her merry-go-round spun to a stop and Margie was able to bring her eyes to focus, she saw her mother standing over her, arms akimbo, face grim.

"What I'm goin' do with you chile?" she lamented.

Margie didn't offer a solution; she knew none was really expected of her.

"What you 'spect to get with them things stuffed in your petticoat like that?" Bertha continued. Again, Margie knew no answer was expected.

"Can't you jest wait till nature takes care of those things?"

There was a long uncomfortable pause, then, "Who's this Cleveland?"

Margie waited a moment to see if an answer was expected here. She watched her mother's toes as they thumped nervously up and down through the holes in her slippers; yes, Mama wanted an answer to this one.

"He's a boy what goes to my school," Margie relayed timidly.

"He gots somethin' on you?" Bertha asked suspiciously.

"No, no," Margie said hastily. "He's jest a boy what I see in the halls an' on the bus."

"He ever touch you—*there?*" Bertha asked, glancing furtively at Margie's lopsided chest.

"No, no, he ain' never touched me," Margie assured hastily.

"He better not, neither," Bertha warned her with relief. "You hear that? He better never!"

"Yes, ma'am," Margie whispered.

"Now you get yourself straightened up an' get out there an' help with those dishes."

Bertha turned to leave the room but stopped and, with one more prick of the sword, completely dashed Margie's whole day. "An get that frizz braided up like it s'posed to be."

The door banged shut on Margie. She sat on the edge of the bed staring unseeingly at her reflection in the mirror. She hated Teresa.

"The dance's this ev'nin'," Norma whispered excitedly to Margie as they waited together in the lunch line. Margie's heart began to beat in an erratic tempo. She had been contemplating that problem all morning. The fifty cents was still nested in her shoe. She wanted to go so badly. But what would happen if Mama found out—she'd kill her, that's what. And, anyway, Cleveland hadn't even looked at her since the incident on the bus with Belva, and she was sure he wouldn't ever look at her again—not with those dumb pigtails sticking out of the side of her head.

Finally she said, "I ain' goin'."

"You ain'!" Norma echoed in surprise. "But, why not?"

"Changed my mind," Margie answered as casually as she could.

"But why?" Norma gasped.

"Ain' got no money," Margie lied.

"But you sold your lunch ticket the other day," Norma reminded.

"Los' the money," Margie said as she nonchalantly reached for the plate of barbecue the cafeteria aide held out to her.

"Los' it! How could you do that? You put it in your shoe, din' you?"

"Musta fell out."

Norma shook her head in bewilderment at her friend. She'd never understand Margie. Margie always went to such extremes to get what she wanted; then, at the last minute, she always changed her mind. It had been the same way with the play.

The girls moved silently on through the lunch line. Carrying their trays over to the only table that still had room at it, they saw that Belva was there, like a vulture, waiting for them. "Can't you jest wait till the dance?" Belva bubbled, as the girls prepared their places at the table.

"Yeah," Norma agreed as she popped a sizzling hush puppy into her mouth then whistled. "Man, that's hot!"

"Can't you, Margie?" Belva prodded.

"Can't I what?" Margie asked innocently, as she sipped her milk through a plastic straw.

"Wait for the dance!" Belva repeated impatiently.

"Oh, I ain' goin'," Margie answered, unconcernedly testing one of her hush puppies to see if it was as hot as Norma's had been.

"Ain' goin'!" Belva exclaimed. "Why not?"

"Changed my mind." Margie popped the hush puppy into her mouth then made blowing gestures to indicate that hers was also too hot.

"Changed you mind!" blurted Belva. "I thought you was goin' try to 'make' Cleveland." Her voice rang out through the lunch room. Heads turned their way and stared, then the giggling began to trickle around the tables. Margie hastily stuffed her mouth with another hush puppy.

"You hear that, Cleveland," someone yelled across the room. The students roared with mirth.

Miss Biglow clanged a bell and called for order, "That will be enough!" The laughter subsided, leaving only a giggle here and there. Margie hated Belva.

224

Arriving home after having spent the afternoon in a classroom watching slides on dental health while most of the rest of the school was attending the dance, Margie sat on the edge of her cot. She didn't want to go out to the kitchen and watch TV with the others; she wanted to be alone with her misery. She examined the calendar with its red Xs indicating the number of menstrual periods she'd already had. Sixteen—and she was still a baby. At least her mother thought so. She'd probably be a baby all of her life! She began to count the days left until her birthday. Ordinarily it would have been thirty-two days, but this was a leap year and there being twenty-nine days in February made it thirty-three days until her birthday. Even the calendar seemed set on keeping her from growing up.

A notion popped into her head. Just what was so special about becoming thirteen? What would she do if nothing happened? Could she really be sure that it was *the* day when all that she had been waiting for, all these years, really happened? Where had she gotten that idea in the first place? She began to doubt the one thing that had, till now, offered sustenance to her life. Shaking her head vigorously, she rattled the doubts out of her head. She had been thinking and believing it for so long now that it just had to be so.

Yes, only thirty-three more days and the magic would begin. Mama would recognize her as a real grown-up woman; she would not call her "baby" anymore. Her body would suddenly respond to nature and there would be no need for stuffings and such. And surely, Cleveland would notice all of these changes when they were the real thing and be completely overcome. She'd "make" him, whatever that was. She wasn't really sure, but she was certain that she wanted to do it and that when she was finally thirteen and grown up, she *could* do it.

Chapter XVIII

As soon as the school bus rounded the bend, Margie saw the blue pickup truck parked in the yard. Through the long winter she had all but forgotten about Mr. Winston. She took her time now walking across the yard to the house. In spite of the chilly season the daffodils already bloomed on the ditch bank. She stopped to pick one.

Mr. Winston was sitting on the edge of the porch talking with Mama. Mama leaned lazily against the open door jamb, her arms crossed across her bosom to ward off the brisk March wind.

As Margie neared the porch she heard Mama saying, "Don' reckon I can do it no more."

"But I was counting on you, Mrs. Braxton. Yeah, I know you're getting on and don't want to work so hard anymore, but you could still work as a— as a—*foreman.*" Billy Winston pleaded, hoping the title foreman would prick her interest.

"I don' know . . . " Bertha drawled, as she stared out across the bare, newly plowed fields. A stray gull that had ventured in from the coast swooped across the field to break the quiet panorama.

"Well, hello there, Miss Margie," Mr. Winston greeted, momentarily changing his attitude as Margie hopped onto the porch.

"Hey, Mr. Winston," Margie replied, grinning in response to his cheer.

"Good gracious, haven't you grown up!" he exclaimed in genuine surprise.

Margie beamed. "I'll be thirteen years old on Thursday," she announced proudly.

"Thirteen! Lord, have mercy, how the time does fly. Why, seems like just last week you were a tiny little tot hanging on to your Mama's petticoat." Margie grinned and rubbed the toe of her left shoe with the heel of her right shoe.

"Your Mama, here, says she isn't able to work any more," Mr. Winston continued, dropping his cheery tone now and reverting to the seriousness of the moment. "I sure hope you will work for me. Now that you're such a grown up young lady you ought to be a real fine worker." Then, turning to Bertha, he asked, "Can I depend on your other three girls?"

"Gayla an' Teresa, mebbe. Can't speak for London; she done lef'."

"Really? She finally get married?"

Bertha glared at the insinuation then answered evasively, "Mebbe."

Billy Winston did not pursue the topic of London's marital status, but he turned to Margie and asked, "Those Taylor kids, reckon they'll work for me again this year, Margie?"

Margie winced at the memory of the Taylor kids, of Kathy. "They moved back to the city, Mr. Winston."

"The hell! I'm not going to have crew one before you know it!"

"You got yourself those new bulk barns, ain' you, Mr. Winston?" Bertha asked.

"Yes, I've got four bulk barns."

"Well, then you don' need so many hands this year."

"The hell I don't! I'm still going to have to use my flue barns; and besides, it takes just as many hands to fill a bulk barn as it does to fill a flue barn. Oh yeah, I know they say they save on labor, but I can't believe that you can do the job right if you skimp." Bertha didn't agree or disagree; she just yawned and scratched at a spot under her sagging breast.

Mr. Winston sat staring at the ground for a moment then, with a sigh of despair, rose, saying, "Well, I best get on if I expect to find enough hands by the end of the week. You sure you won't at least pull some plants, Mrs. Braxton?"

Bertha shook her head saying, "The arthritis too bad."

He strolled slowly across the yard to his truck. Just as he was about to open the door, he remembered Margie and turned and called back, "Margie, you have a good birthday, now. I'm going to bring you something—something real nice for such a pretty young lady." Margie shivered with pleasure, not so much at the promise of a present but at the words "for a pretty young lady."

But Bertha didn't like the attention that Mr. Winston offered to Margie. She just didn't trust him.

"That sweet talkin' white devil," she mumbled as she shuffled back into the house.

Gayla and Teresa's bus pulled to a stop in front of the house. The two girls jumped off and raced each other across the yard. They were in a fine mood; the warm spring sun that cut through the chilled air had seemed to thaw their ever-pending problems with their teachers. As they approached the porch, Margie called excitedly, "Hey, Mr. Winston just was here an' we're goin' start workin' soon."

The two girls slowed to a trot and a glum cloud swept the smiles from their faces. "Oh, shit. I know'd it coun't last," Teresa grumbled.

"We can use the money," Gayla reflected.

"But I hate to think of sloshing 'round those wet fields 'gain."

"They ain' wet; we ain' had no rain for weeks."

Teresa glared at her sister's contrary observation, then mumbled, "Shit!"

"Mr. Winston said he's goin' bring me a birthday present," Margie said gleefully.

"Sure 'nough?" Gayla asked.

"Yeah, he's goin' bring you a present, OK—twelve hours in a 'bacco patch," grumbled Teresa sourly.

Lenny appeared at the door. "Hey, baby," he said coaxingly. "How 'bout runnin' to the store an' gettin' your Uncle Lenny a can of soda."

The three girls looked from one to the other. "Which one's us his *baby?*" Teresa asked sarcastically.

"I know *I* ain'," said Gayla.

"An' I know I ain' neither," said Teresa. "Mus' be Margie."

Margie sighed, she knew there was no point in arguing; she'd never win and would just use time that she could be on her way and back sooner. Besides, it was such a pretty day that she really didn't mind the walk to Pfeiffer's.

"OK," she said, holding out her hand for the money. Lenny dropped a quarter and a dime into it.

"Get me a Mountain Dew an' you can use the change for somethin' for yourself—somethin' for your birthday." Teresa and Gayla laughed.

"Soda's thirty cents—what she goin' buy with a nickel?" But Margie didn't mind. At least Lenny did remember that her birthday was coming. But then, she *had* made a point of giving a daily countdown as the ever-awaited day approached.

Wednesday was a glorious day! The whole countryside was abloom with daffodils. More gulls had wandered in from the sea and circled the fields in majestic sweeps. The fields lay plowed smooth waiting for the first tiny plants to be set, like open, welcoming wombs awaiting conception.

Margie absently fingered her pigtails as Mrs. Levine talked on and on about the need for good study habits to be formed when one is young.

Tomorrow—tomorrow, she would fluff those braids into a regal crown of carefully picked frizz. Mama had finally relented after much constant persuasive yammering by Margie, that she could, in fact, shuck her braids when she did become thirteen. Margie had wanted to be allowed to buy a bra too, but here Mama had drawn the line—No, no, not until she had *something* for a bra to hold, something real, not just panty hose. But Mama had also assured her that once she was thirteen, she probably would blossom rapidly and there would be no need for stuffing.

She was now acutely aware of the slow, jerking click that the minute hand on the big clock made. She thought the minute hand would never get all the way around to the twelve to set its clapper clanging the three o'clock dismissal. Just a few more hours now and the marvelous, magic thirteenth anniversary of her birth would commence. When the bell rang, she jumped from her seat and headed for the door.

"Where are you going in such a hurry, Miss Braxton?" Mrs. Levine asked.

"I goin' to the bus."

"Really?" The other students giggled. "Since when does the bus come at two o'clock?" Mrs. Levine asked. Margie turned toward the big wall clock. How could she have been so stupid? Her eyes must be going bad! The hands on the clock stood brazenly at two. She could have sworn it was three. Amid twitters and whispers from the others, she sheepishly returned to her seat.

When the snickering had stopped, Mrs. Levine said, "Since it's such a beautiful day and it is Saint Patrick's Day, I thought we would all go out to the playground and celebrate." Though she herself was not Irish and, though this section of the country did not recognize Saint Patrick's Day as an occasion for unusual celebration, Mrs. Levine had begun a policy in her class, in celebration of the bicentennial year, of having a small party for all the little ethnic occasions that cropped up during the year. It was a way for her to teach the developmental history of the United States and still have fun. Now she paused for the class reaction.

"What we celebratin'?" a boy asked.

"Saint Patrick's Day," Mrs. Levine repeated.

"Who be Saint Patrick?" another student asked.

Milly Malone shouted out, "You dumb ass, he's the patron saint of Ireland."

Mrs. Levine sighed and gave Milly a long look of disapproval. Milly slid down in her seat in appropriate repentive attitude.

"Yes, children, Saint Patrick was the patron saint of Ireland. Many of our forefathers came to settle in the United States from Ireland. Has anyone here got ancestors from Ireland—besides Milly, that is?"

The children looked back and forth among each other. One girl giggled and said, "Looks like most of the people in here came from Africa."

"Hey, honky, what's so bad 'bout that?" a very big black youth asked, as he raised himself slowly from his seat.

"N-n-nothing," the girl stuttered. "J-j-just that we ain't got too many dumb Irish in here."

"That's what I thought you meant."

"Please, children," Mrs. Levine pleaded. "This is our country's birthday year; can't we, just for a little while, act civil toward each other? Now let's get ready for our party—we're going to have refreshments . . ." She waited to see if this new promise might have the desired effect on the class and give them a unified goal.

"What kind of 'freshments?" someone asked, to see if it was worth a brotherly attitude.

"Aha, now that's a surprise," Mrs. Levine teased.

"We goin' have *eat?*" another boy quizzed.

" 'Freshments is *eat,*" chided a girl in the back of the room.

"You just wait and see," Mrs. Levine said, her own eyes now twinkling with excitement. "Everyone line up at the door and very quietly we will walk out to the playground—ssshh, now very quietly—the rest of the school is still working.

The children did as they were told with a minimum of pushing and chatter. When they were far enough away from the school so as not to disturb anyone, they began to hoop and holler, dancing crazily around Mrs. Levine to express their appreciation for the free time.

"George, will you come with me to my car, please?" Mrs. Levine asked. "The rest of you stay here and behave yourselves for a moment."

Mrs. Levine and the boy, George, disappeared around the corner of the building.

"What you think she goin' do?" a girl named Betty asked Margie.

"She be gettin' the 'freshments," another girl interjected before Margie could answer.

"Le's 'tend it be Margie's birthday today," suggested Betty.

"Who's birthday be it today?" a boy asked.

"Margie's," Betty answered.

"No, it's not till tomorrow," Margie protested.

"That be OK. We can 'tend it be today 'cause *today* we gots 'freshments," Betty reasoned.

Margie had a vague feeling of discomfort. At first she couldn't put her finger on it, but then the picture began to come into focus. There had been another precelebration of her birthday last summer, when Kathy had brought the little cake. Mama had warned her then of the pending evil that accompanies premature celebrations.

Mrs. Levine and George were coming toward the group now, both carrying something. Mrs. Levine held a large flat box across her outstretched arms; George carried a two-gallon thermos, swinging at his side.

Squealing with delight, the children all began running to meet them.

"Nothin' no badder than usual ever did happen," Margie muttered to herself.

"What you say?" asked Betty.

"Oh, nothin'," answered Margie.

"Come on, le's see what the 'freshments is." The two girls ran to catch up with the others.

"Don't crowd, don't crowd!" Mrs. Levine remonstrated cheerfully. "There's enough for everyone."

"Mrs. Levine, it be Margie's birthday," someone announced.

"Really? Saint Patrick's Day? How nice!"

"It be really tomorrow, but we be celebratin' today 'cause of the 'freshments," Margie felt obliged to explain.

"Oh, I see," Mrs. Levine said, with a little laugh of understanding. "Well, that is nice—we'll just pretend it's today—should we all sing 'Happy Birthday'?" The group burst into discordant harmony.

"Happy birthday to you-u-u-u . . . " Margie blushed with embarrassed pride. She'd never had a birthday party before this year and now she was having her second one for the same birthday. When they had finished the song and Mrs. Levine had obliged the class by giving Margie her thirteen birthday spankings, plus one to grow on, she opened the box that she had carried from her car. The children oh'd with pleasure when they caught sight of the beautifully decorated sheet cake. It had creamy white frosting with green squiggles all around its edge.

"You made that bee-uu-tiful cake, Mrs. Levine?" Betty gushed.

"No, Betty, I bought it at a bakery shop."

George had begun pouring limeade from the thermos jug as Mrs. Levine cut the cake into generous squares. The children watched in awe as the knife slid through the snowy icing of the bakery shop cake. Each child received a square of cake and a paper cup full of limeade. Margie relished every bite of her cake. She couldn't remember ever having tasted anything so sweet and delicious before; she had never had a bakery shop cake before. She licked her finger tips to capture any stray flavor that might have stuck to them.

"Hey, Mrs. Levine, you gots one piece of cake lef' over," George noted.

"So I have. I'll tell you what—let's give the extra piece to our birthday girl." There were a few disgruntled murmurs, but on the whole the class generously agreed that Margie should have the extra piece. Margie accepted the prize graciously and enjoyed every crumb.

On the way home on the bus Margie felt just a little twinge of guilt from having done it again—jumped the gun on her birthday. Not because of the bad luck that threatened—after all, nothing all that bad had happened from the last time—but rather, well, it was just a little scary to be so brashly tempting nature.

As the bus pulled up in front of her house, Margie could see Mama on the front porch talking with someone. The other person had her back to the road so Margie couldn't see who it was. As she walked across the yard, the figure turned toward Margie. Margie's heart gave a little flutter and she let out a loud war-hoop and burst into a run.

"London, London, you be back!" London caught her little sister into her arms and gave her a crushing hug.

"You be back forever, London?"

"No, baby, just passin'."

"You mean you ain' stayin'?" Margie cried in anguish.

"Can't, honey, gots to get. S'posed to be in Durham by tonight."

"Durham! Where at's Durham?"

"That be where my husband is. He be goin' to work there."

"Husband! When you gots married?"

"Las' week."

"Randy?"

"Yeah, Randy."

"But can't you stay till just my birthday. It be tomorrow?"

"Tomorrow! You mean your birthday tomorrow! How ol' you goin' be, baby?"

"London! You know I'm goin' be *thirteen!*"

"That's right! Lawd, have mercy! How this chile have growed up!" London exclaimed with mock surprise.

"Please, please, say you'll stay."

"No, honey, I just stopped to pick up Reggie, an' I gots to get the bus at a quarter to six—an' I gots to walk all the way into town. I was countin' on a ride from Lenny." She glanced wistfully out at the cadaver of the Falcon. "We'll make it, though, won' we, baby." She optimistically poked Reggie under his double chin. He drew back at her gesture.

"You don' want to have my birthday with me," sulked Margie.

"Now, baby, I do, but I just can't. Anyways, it don' matter whether I be here or not for your birthday. What matters is you're goin' be some growed up tomorrow!"

"Yeah." Margie turned away so London would not see the great tears welling up into her eyes. Then suddenly it dawned on Margie what London had said earlier.

"You ain' takin' Reggie?"

"Course I am. He be my baby ain' he?"

"But he lives here with us!"

"He belong to London," Mama reaffirmed.

"Don' seem right he should be took off though," Margie whimpered.

Sissy was holding Reggie in her arms. She had dressed him in his Sunday best and had put the remainder of his clothing in a small brown paper bag. The baby clung tightly to her neck, eyeing London suspiciously.

"Now, baby, you just go with your mama," Sissy crooned. Reggie began to sob in great gulps. His little fingers dug into the soft flesh of Sissy's neck. London was a stranger to him; she had been away so long.

"Come on, baby," London said softly as she reached out for him. Reggie buried his face in Sissy's bosom and screamed hysterically. Margie felt the lump tighten in her throat.

"If you 'spect to catch the bus, you best get," Mama urged, in an attempt to shorten the agonies of farewell.

London caught hold of Reggie as Sissy thrust him forth. The baby screamed unrelentingly as London ran toward the road.

"Write us a letter," Bertha called.

"I will," London answered, without looking back so they would not see her tears merging with Reggie's.

"He don' wanna go," Margie lamented.

"He'll get used to it—she be his mama," Bertha answered coolly. Sissy dabbed at her eyes with the sleeve of her dress.

"Ain' right," Margie murmured as she went into the house.

Bertha stayed on the porch until the two figures, her daughter's and her grandson's, had gone around the bend toward town. Then she too went in.

"Tell you what," she said cheerfully. "You can go up to the store an' get the candles for your cake."

"You make it already?" Margie squealed.

"No, no, but you won' be here tomorrow when I do make it, so's you can get the candles this evenin'," Bertha explained.

"Oh," Margie replied, somewhat disappointed.

"An' wait till you see what your mama gots you for your birthday," said Sissy excitedly.

"Sissy! You ain' s'posed to tell. Now it won' be no s'prise," Bertha scolded.

"Oh, I'm sorry," Sissy apologized.

"Don' matter none now; you already done spoilt it," Bertha pouted.

"No, she di'n't, Mama," Margie said, attempting to comfort her mother. "I don' know what it is."

"Humph," Bertha said as she handed Margie a quarter from a jar on the sideboard. "Go on, get, 'fore it gets dark."

Margie skipped off across the yard. The sun was settling low in the sky; Mama was right; she would have to hurry. She skipped awhile then walked awhile in order to catch her breath. She wondered about the present Mama had for her. She remembered the hairbow. She wondered if this would be another. She wondered how a girl could be so lucky as she. Thirteen was for sure the best birthday of all. Tomorrow would be the *third* time she would celebrate this most important of all birthdays. And—she was going to have a cake with candles on it and—she was going to get a present from her Mama and—Mr. Winston had promised her one.

She thought about the present Kathy had given her during the summer. She must get back to reading that book. She had never gotten beyond the first chapter; there was always a favorite program on TV. She would finish it though, she promised.

"I need some birthday can'les," Margie announced to Mr. Pfeiffer as she plunked her quarter on the counter.

"Well, now whose birthday is it?" Mr. Pfeiffer asked cheerfully as he reached behind him on the shelf for the little box of candles.

"Mine," Margie whispered shyly, looking intently at a spot on the counter.

"What do you know!" Mr. Pfeiffer exclaimed. "And just how old are you?"

"Goin' be *thirteen* tomorrow." Margie found her voice booming in a loud staccato. Mr. Pfeiffer jumped back in surprise. Margie blushed. She too was surprised at the loudness of her voice.

Mr. Pfeiffer gave Margie the candles and her change then he reached into the little box of three-penny chocolate mints that sat on the counter next to the cash register and took one out and handed it to Margie.

"Happy birthday—young lady," he said with a grin.

"Thank you," she answered, beaming—there was that "young lady" again.

Dusk was falling quickly now as Margie walked back down the road toward the house. The birds were still singing, though, so Margie was not lonely. She was happy. The whole world suddenly loomed lovely before her. And she knew that it was all because, tomorrow, she would be thirteen.

Even in the gathering dusk Margie could see the yellow trumpets of the daffodils waving in the evening breeze. Just before the bend near her house she spied a long solid bed of the golden heads in the ditch bank on the opposite side of the road. Such a huge bouquet was meant to be picked.

The driver of the sleek new Grand Prix did not see the black shadow dart across the road. The bend—the dusk . . . He hit the brake with both feet and pulled the wheel sharply to the right when the dull thud jolted the car.

He sat for a moment after the car stopped. Was it a deer? He knew it wasn't. When the blur had receded from his eyes he opened the car door and stepped out onto the road. As soon as his feet touched the still warm asphalt a wave of nausea overcame him and he went limp against the front fender of the car. A thin stream broke away from the glistening red splatter on the polished chrome strip and trickled down the fender until it dripped in a splash of finality on the road. He retched violently.

A truck carrying propane gas slowed to a stop next to the figure draped over the fender of the Grand Prix.

"You OK?" the driver called down from his cab. The man did not look up. The truck driver pulled his rig to the side of the road in front of the car. Getting out he walked back to where the man still leaned over the fender.

"You OK?" the trucker asked again. The man shook his head and gagged.

"I didn't see nothing." As the trucker bent over the man he caught sight of the red glob that had now settled into a shimmering jelly on the fender. He gasped and looked around him over the surface of the road.

"You hit a deer?" he asked hopefully. Was it a deer? The man knew that it wasn't.

235

The trucker walked back across the road to where the Grand Prix skid marks began. A movement in the ditch bank caught his eye. Looking down among the daffodils he gasped again. It was not a deer. Scrambling down the steep sides of the bank, the daffodils crushing under his heavy boots, he slid into the small brown bundle. The bundle shuddered ever so slightly; a soft gurgle seeped from its edges then it was still. The trucker sat in the daffodils, sat staring at the quiet heap. His heart throbbed in double time; it was not a deer.

It was only a moment until he could pull himself up and climb back out of the ditch. He staggered giddily across the road to the man who still could not support himself but had to brace against that red-speckled fender.

"It's a little kid," he said softly. The man knew it was not a deer. They stood there, both staring, unseeing, at nothing. "A little kid."

Adrenaline began gathering in the trucker's legs. They began to jerk spasmodically. "I got to get the Life Squad!" He ran to his truck, jumped in, and sped down the road leaving the man still hanging over his fender, his retching resuming.

Bertha paused momentarily, then slid down the bank, bumping into the man in white coveralls who was wrapping her baby in a length of sheeting.

"Leave her be! Leave her be!" she screamed at the man. Another man, a blue uniformed man, caught hold of her from behind and began dragging her up the bank. She flailed violently at him. "Leave her be! Leave her be!"

Up on the road again she saw, for the first time, the man by the Grand Prix. With a blood-curdling scream, she tore herself from the policeman and lunged toward the man. He turned away as she hurtled toward him. Arriving at where he stood, his back toward her, his head resting on the fender, she began to pound the man on his back with her fists, all the while screaming. "You devil! You devil!"

The policeman finally managed to subdue her and while he held her sobbing body in his arms another policeman went to the aid of the driver.

Suddenly Bertha looked at the other members of her family, who stood off to the side of the road wailing a soft mournful dirge.

"Oh, Lawd," she groaned. "Tomorrow's her birthday! Now it ain' no more tomorrow for her—Oh, Lawd!"

The policeman continued to hold the grief-stricken woman; he swayed gently back and forth in an attempt to comfort her—what else could he do?

They all watched as the squad men solemnly pulled the sheet tight over the thin, broken bundle. Though momentarily physically subdued, Bertha sobbed in long deep gulps as the men gently lifted their package into the waiting ambulance. Then Bertha tore herself away from her would-be comforter and ran to the back of the van. At the sight of the mummy-wrapped figure of her daughter, she let out a long banshee wail and began pounding the attendant's chest with her fists. The big policeman recaptured her flailing arms and sang, murmured soothing words into her ear; she would not be comforted. She continued to wail as the antiseptic white van pulled away, its bubble light spinning slowly to set a red blinking warning signal in action.

The women of the family joined her in the ghoulish dirge. Suddenly Lenny felt his position as man of the family surge into his veins. He tightened his hands into fists and set a firm jaw. Slowly, deliberately, he walked toward the villain of the tragedy. His eyes glowed in righteous anger. The young man shrank behind the policeman who had been interrogating him.

"Please, please, I didn't see her; please don't let him near me!"

The policeman turned to face Lenny. He held his arms out to the side of him in a protecting gesture. Lenny continued forward. The policeman flinched, then called out a warning.

"Stop right there!" Lenny disregarded the order.

"I said, you better stop!" the policeman repeated, this time bringing his right hand down to rest on the handle of his billy club.

Lenny observed the motion. He stopped. Everyone just stood firmly in position. No one said a word. The only sound was that of the pitiful wailing from the women. After a moment, Lenny relinquished his post and walked back toward his womenfolk, calling over his shoulder. "You're goin' fry for this, white boy."

The man in custody cringed, a new wave of nausea swept over him. Lenny reiterated, "Yeah, white boy, you're goin' fry."

Little delay was necessary for the funeral. There were no out-of-town relatives to await and only a handful of church friends to expect at the visitation. Sister Elvira, Preacher Brown's wife, had collected $115 for the bereaved family. Knowing the circumstance, Norwood Harris had offered to make the final arrangements for no more than the cost, for "one of his own." Another offered an extra plot in the black cemetery for the final resting place. Bertha was proud—but sometimes it was necessary—to accept—she agreed.

She was prepared for viewing by the next evening—March 18, 1976.

Bertha was grief-worn now and stood next to the casket in silence viewing her baby—no, her *grown daughter*—she would have been thirteen, and grown, today. The reminder brought one last tear struggling to the surface of her eye, where it lingered momentarily before sliding slowly down her leathered brown cheek.

Margie looked like a sleeping angel in her satin-lined bed. She wore a white dress with a pink satin sash. She held a single pink rose bud in her folded hands, the hands that had held daffodils the day before. Bertha looked at the neatly frizzed coif. She had instructed Mr. Harris to do it that way because she had promised Margie that today she could begin wearing her hair in that long-coveted style.

There were, perhaps, seven or eight church members in the parlor with the family. Norma Suthers was there and Belva. Some of the mourners provided the necessary background of soft wailing; others stood silently staring at the back of the big woman who lingered next to the coffin. But no one saw the woman take a paperback book from her purse; a thin book, but a pretty book, with a glossy red and white cover that had garish blue letters that spelled *How to Make It on Wall St.* Bertha couldn't read. She didn't know what the book was about, but it was pretty, pretty enough for a present, a birthday present. Margie would have been proud to have received such a beautiful book, no matter what the title or contents, as a present from her Mama.

Bertha gently laid the book inside the coffin next to her baby—no, grown daughter. She carefully pulled a corner of the white dress over the book to hide it from view. She had bought the book for Margie; it belonged to Margie.